Rafael Sabatini, creator of so was born in Italy in 1875 a Switzerland. He eventually sett___ ___ ___giand in 1892, by which time he was fluent in a total of five languages. He chose to write in English, claiming that 'all the best stories are written in English'.

His writing career was launched in the 1890s with a collection of short stories, and it was not until 1902 that his first novel was published. His fame, however, came with *Scaramouche*, the much-loved story of the French Revolution, which became an international bestseller. *Captain Blood* followed soon after, which resulted in a renewed enthusiasm for his earlier work.

For many years a prolific writer, he was forced to abandon writing in the 1940s through illness and he eventually died in 1950.

Sabatini is best-remembered for his heroic characters and high-spirited novels, many of which have been adapted into classic films, including *Scaramouche, Captain Blood* and *The Sea Hawk* starring Errol Flynn.

TITLES BY THE SAME AUTHOR
ALL PUBLISHED BY HOUSE OF STRATUS

The Minion

Rafael Sabatini

HOUSE OF
STRATUS

This edition published in 2001 by House of Stratus, an imprint of Stratus Books Ltd., 21 Beeching Park, Kelly Bray, Cornwall, PL17 8QS, UK.

www.houseofstratus.com

Typeset, printed and bound by House of Stratus.

A catalogue record for this book is available from the British Library and the Library of Congress.

ISBN 07551-154-7-3

Being The Rise and Fall of Robert Carr of Ferniehurst, Earl of Somerset, Viscount Rochester, Baron Winwick, Baron Brance-peth, Knight of the Most Noble Order of The Garter, a Member of His Majesty's Most Honourable Privy Council, etc., etc.

Contents

Contents (contd)

Chapter 1

In the Tilt-Yard

King James, fully recovered from the terrible fright occasioned him by the Gunpowder Plot, had returned to his norm of pusillanimity. Guy Fawkes, unbroken in spirit, however broken in body by torture, had expiated on the gallows in Paul's Yard the attempt – in his own bold words – to blow the Scots beggars back to their mountains.

The beggars remained and profited by the distribution amongst them of the acres and possessions of the conspirators, most of whom were gentlemen of substance.

For the King, too, the matter had not been without ultimate profit of a more spiritual kind. It had enabled him by an exercise of the arts of kingcraft – a term signifying little more than the shameless use of falsehood and dissimulation – to parade before the world the divine inspiration vouchsafed to monarchs. It was, he pretended, the acuteness with which kings are supernaturally endowed which had enabled him to enucleate from obscurest utterances the true aim and nature of the plot, and thus, almost miraculously, to avert a national catastrophe.

Some material profit, too, was to be extracted from it, in the course of a further display of the spiritual graces and accomplishments of this astounding prince. He was enabled to argue, cogently enough, that people themselves so intolerant as the Papists, on whose behalf it had been sought to blow him and his parliament into a better world, deserved no toleration; that the Scarlet Woman on her seven hills propounded indeed the mystery of iniquity. Hence he was justified in proceeding against Papists and at the same time against Puritans – so as to be perfectly consistent in his exclusive upholding of the Established Church – by means of heavy fines and confiscations. Thus he replenished his sadly depleted treasury and was enabled further to relieve the necessities of those Scots beggars – and some English ones, too – who clustered about him.

It did not trouble his elastic royal conscience that the plot of a few desperate men, for which he now punished an entire community, was directly sprung from his own bad faith in an earlier exercise of his art of kingcraft. Readily enough had he promised toleration alike to the co-religionaries of his mother, and to the Puritans when they had approached him on the subject in Scotland in the days of his own anxieties touching his succession to the throne of England. They were foolish to have trusted him. They should have perceived that a man who would not raise a finger to save his own mother from the block, lest by doing so he should jeopardise his inheritance of the English Crown, would never scruple about a false promise or two that would help to ensure the unanimity of all classes of Englishmen in his favour. By breaking faith when he discovered that the Episcopalian religion, which made him head of the Church as well as of the State, was the only religion fit for kings, he provoked not only the Gunpowder Plot, but that earlier conspiracy in which Catholics and Puritans were united, the strangest bedfellows adversity ever made.

All this, however, was now happily overpast. The heel of authority was firmly planted on the neck of Papist and Puritan, and their recusancy was being sweated out of them in the gold that was so urgently required to maintain the prodigal splendours of the court of this new kingdom of Great Britain. For now, in the year 1607 of the coming of Our Lord and fourth of the coming of King James, his majesty was in dire straits for ready money.

Never before in the history of the country had there been, and never since has there been, such reckless extravagance as that which distinguished the descent of the Scots from their northern fastnesses in the train of a king who was a veritable beggar on horseback.

Out of the stern and arid North he had come into the promised land of plenty, a land that flowed, and flowed richly, with milk and honey at his command. His commands, however, had been so free and frequent that at last the springs were showing signs of exhaustion. Fortunes lavished upon favourites by a prince who had never learnt and never did learn the value of money were draining the resources of the nation. Finding his hands, which hitherto had been ever empty, to be suddenly filled with gold, he had scattered it in almost childish recklessness, spending for the mere love of spending, who in thirty-seven years of life had never had anything to spend. Similarly, finding himself a free and uncontrolled fount of honour who hitherto had been overborne and browbeaten by rude nobles and ruler clerics, he spouted honours so freely that in the first three months of his reign, apart from the new Earls and Barons he created, he distributed no less than seven hundred knighthoods, so that to be a knight became so common as to be almost disreputable. There was no lack of point in the announcement nailed by a satirist on the door of St Paul's offering to train weak memories in the titles of nobility.

When at last he began to feel himself hard-pressed for money he had summoned Parliament so that it might provide, only to make the discovery, next in horror to the discovery of the Gunpowder Plot, that the Commons, far from acknowledging his divinity, would scarcely acknowledge his majesty. His own views and Parliament's on the function of the Commons were found to be widely divergent. The session resolved itself into a battle between absolutism and constitutionalism; and it was in vain that, with the polemical skill in which he took such pride, he argued that kings are in the word of God called gods as being His lieutenants and vicegerents on earth, and therefore adorned and furnished with some sparks of Divinity. The Commons, perceiving no spark of divinity in his majesty's very human if excessive need of money, were so impudent as to treat him as a man, and to vote him certain subsidies which would not even pay the monstrous debts he had piled up.

If this annoyed him, it nowise served to curtail his extravagance or the munificence in which he delighted, largely no doubt because in its indulgence he gratified his desire to feel a god. So he went his ways, junketing and banqueting in this land of milk and honey, with revels and maskings, tournaments and mummeries. He discovered that the exercise of hunting was not merely pleasant in itself but an absolute necessity to the preservation of his health, whilst cock-fighting was so important a relaxation to his mind, so that its vigour might subsequently be renewed, that he paid the Master of the Cocks as much as any two Secretaries of State. And for the rest, as Sir John Harrington wrote from court: *Now that the gunpowder fright is got out of our heads, we are going on hereabouts as if the devil was contriving that every man should blow himself up by wild riot, excess and devastation of time and temperance.*

Being at heart a woman, his majesty loved to look upon fine men, and he saw to it that those immediately about him were fine not only in person but also in apparel and equipment, and he showered upon them honours and riches at the expense of his new kingdom. There was Philip Herbert whom he had made Earl of Montgomery, the handsome, oafish, rowdy and unworthy brother of the splendid Pembroke; there was Sir John Ramsay, whom he had created Viscount Haddington, between whom and himself lay perhaps the truth of the dark Gowrie business; there was the magnificent Sir James Hay, who eventually became Earl of Carlisle, a courtier trained in France, where he had served in the Scots Guards; and there was a host of lesser handsome satellites, mostly Scots, who sunned themselves in the royal favour, had their will of the weak prodigal king, and preyed upon him much as light wanton women will prey upon a man who delights in feminine companionship. His want of dignity in his relations with his minions was as ludicrous as his excess of it in his relations with the Commons.

Surrounded by a cloud of these lively, gorgeous fritillaries, you behold him on a fair September morning in his pavilion in the tilt-yard at Whitehall. There was to be riding at the ring, and there were to be other joustings of a mild order, in the nature of pageants rather than of tourneys, so as to display fine horsemanship and athletic beauty without danger to life or limb, for his majesty did not relish shows that were too warlike.

Dazzling as Phoebus himself rode forth the magnificent James Hay in a doublet of cloth of gold, a short cloak of white beaver trailing from his shoulders, a white-plumed white beaver hat above his golden curls. He was attended, as became so magnificent a paladin, by close upon a score of esquires, who again were followed by as many pages in his cerulean livery, with his arms embroidered on each breast. To be his shield-bearer Sir James had chosen the handsomest of his esquires, a youth of twenty, who for beauty of face and straight shapeliness of limb must draw the eye in any assembly. He drew now the eyes of all in the ladies' gallery, as he rode forward alone, in advance of the others, mounted on a mettlesome white horse, to do his appointed office and present his lord's escutcheon to the King.

The King rolled his big liquid eyes, and under the veil of his thin sandy beard the heavy lips of his loose mouth smiled approval. His majesty loved good horses and admired good horsemanship, an art he was never to master for himself, although more than half his days were spent in the saddle. He was lost now in admiring wonder of the superb mastery of the advancing rider.

"Like a centaur. Ay, and a bonnie," he muttered thickly in his sing-song Scots voice.

A final curvet at the very steps of the royal gallery, and the horse was pulled up, so sharply that it almost sat down on its haunches like a cat. Yet all would have been well with the horseman if he had not already disengaged one foot from the stirrup intending to complete his display by a leap to the ground which should bring horse and man to a simultaneous standstill. The result was that he lost his balance at the very moment of gathering himself for his leap, and cumbered as he was by the shield, he came heavily to the ground.

Philip Herbert at the King's elbow advertised his inherent boorishness by a loud guffaw.

"Your centaur's come in pieces, sire."

But the King never heard him, which was perhaps as well for him. The royal eyes were upon the young man, who sprawled in a curiously helpless attitude upon the dusty ground after an instant's aborted effort to rise.

"God's sake!" the King muttered. "The lad's hurt." And he heaved himself out of his crimson chair and stood forth, a man a little above the middle height whose thick ungainly body was carried upon thin rachitic shanks. He had been suckled by a drunkard; and to this it was attributed that he had not been able to stand until his seventh year; nor did his legs thereafter ever grow to normal strength.

Already esquires and pages were on foot and hastening to the fallen young man's assistance, Sir James Hay, on horseback, close at hand, directing them. There was silence in the assembly of spectators, all of whom had risen. In the ladies' gallery, the Countess of Essex, a fair-headed child of fifteen, of an extraordinary loveliness, leaning forward, clutching the wooden rail before her with a slim gloved hand, drew attention to herself by the anxious note of her outcry and the insistence with which she demanded to know the extent of the young man's hurt, which none yet could tell her. Her mother, the Countess of Suffolk, that ample-bosomed, sneering-mouthed, pock-marked woman, restrained her, whilst smiling upon the tenderness of her solicitude for an unknown youth.

Then the King became the centre of interest. Leaning heavily upon Herbert's shoulder, he shambled down the steps. He bent over the young man who lay supine and helpless, his right leg at an odd angle. This leg, they informed his majesty, was broken. A page had already gone to summon bearers and a hand-litter.

"Poor lad! Poor lad!" mumbled the King on an almost maudlin note. Small ills observed could singularly move this man to tenderness, who yet could perpetrate great and bloody cruelties which he was not called upon to witness.

The youth shifted his head upon the pillow it had found on the knee of another esquire, and his fine eyes looked up in awe at compassionate majesty. Though livid and drawn by pain, the beauty of his face remained singularly arresting. Not more than twenty years of age, he was still beardless, and only a little auburn moustache shaded the shapely mouth, at once firm and sensuous. He pushed back the tumbled red-gold hair from his moist brow and made as if to speak, then checked, not knowing what might be required of him by etiquette in such a case.

But the King had little thought for etiquette. Goggle-eyed he considered this long slim lad, and he was so overcome at the thought of so much physical perfection being perhaps permanently marred that a tear rolled down his prematurely furrowed yet florid cheek.

"Who is he? How's he called?" be gruffly questioned.

Sir James, who had dismounted, pushed forward, hat in hand, to answer him.

"His name is Carr, may it please your majesty; Robert Carr of Ferniehurst."

"Carr o' Ferniehurst!" The King seemed taken aback. "The son of Tom Carr! God's sake!"

He bent lower to scan more closely the handsome man grown out of one who some years ago had served him as a page in Edinburgh, but who had been dismissed for his persistent bad Latin at grace, which to the King had smacked of irreverence.

Young Carr's white mask of pain was irradiated by a smile to behold himself remembered.

"God save your majesty," he said in an accent even more broadly Scots than the King's own.

"It's thyself needs saving now, lad," the King mumbled. He stood upright again and became brisk in the issuing of orders and more indistinct in speech than usual in this briskness.

Mr Carr was to be conveyed no farther than Mr Rider's house in King Street, near at hand. Let word be sent ahead at once that a room be prepared for him. At the royal nod one of his gentlemen sped upon the errand, whilst another departed in quest of his majesty's own physician. The repairs to the lad's leg were to be carried out by the most skilful hands available, so as to ensure that so lovely a body should suffer no permanent impairment.

Philip Herbert, Earl of Montgomery, holding premier place among the favourites, looked down his handsome nose in disdain. Why did his old dad and gossip, as he familiarly called his sovereign, make all this bother about a raw Scots esquire of no account?

Dull fellow that Herbert was, he lacked the wit to perceive that another of Guy Fawkes' beggars was come to court.

Chapter 2

The Rising Sun

Very soon it became apparent that the fall in which Mr Robert Carr had broken his leg had flung him headlong into the lap of fortune.

The King had outstayed the show in the tilt-yard. So much he owed to the gentlemen who were providing this entertainment. At its conclusion, however, he had postponed his return to the palace, to turn aside and visit Mr Rider's house in King Street, so that he might personally ascertain the exact extent of Mr Carr's injuries. He went attended by a group of gentlemen, among whom was Herbert, very sulky now at what he accounted a fresh and excessive manifestation of royal caprice.

At Mr Rider's they found his majesty's physician, who relieved anxieties which could hardly have been greater had the patient been an old and valued friend.

Mr Carr, his leg set, and now out of pain and moderately comfortable, lay in a pleasant room whose latticed windows stood open to the September sunshine and Mr Rider's pleasant garden behind the house. As the door opened he turned his head with its tumbled mane of red-gold hair, and from his pillow looked to see who came.

It startled him to behold under the lintel the figure of the King, loutish and ungainly despite rich saffron-coloured velvet and gleam of jewels. The corpulence to which his majesty's body already tended was aggravated in appearance by thickly bombasted breeches and a doublet stuffed and quilted so as to render it dagger-proof, and thus quiet his congenital timorousness and abiding dread of cold steel. This affliction of physical fear under which he was to labour all his days was perhaps to be traced back to that night in Holyrood, two months before his birth, when Rizzio was brutally stabbed to death at his mother's feet.

He stood now upon that threshold, rolling his big wistful eyes in a face whose lines bore the imprint of an age considerably beyond his forty years. In repose his countenance ever wore that vacant quality of melancholy that is to be seen in the brute creation. And it reflected, no doubt accurately, a soul which was not to be beguiled from its fundamental sadness and loneliness either by the free indulgence of the man's egregious vanity or the liberal pursuit of sensuous satisfactions.

Closely followed by the physician, who had met him in the outer room, he shambled forward to the trundle-bed, leaving his gentlemen on the threshold. He came, he announced, no more than to inquire of Mr Carr, himself, how he did.

Mr Carr, flushing deeply, between awe and gratification of an honour so far in excess of his poor deserts, answered in his broad Northern accent that he did very well, which immediately opened the door to the King's ever-ready and usually trivial facetiousness.

"Ud's death!" He spoke thickly and indistinctly, his tongue being too thick for his mouth. In theory he condemned all blasphemy, and, indeed, had written a treatise upon the evils of it; in practice he seldom sought vehemence of expression without having recourse to its emphatic aid. "If you account yourself very well with a broken leg what'll ye deem yourself when it's whole again?"

The courtiers in the background offered the murmur of laughter that was expected. But Mr Carr did not even smile.

"Your majesty's gracious concern had been cheaply bought at the price of both legs broken."

10

If his accent was uncouth to English ears, his manner at least left little to be desired in courtliness. The King pulled at his thin tuft of sandy beard and smiled, nodding his head in approval.

"Say you so? Faith, it's a graceful enough answer. Ye'll have been in France I doubt, with Sir James?"

Mr Carr confessed it. He had spent two years at court there.

"And ye'll have learnt among those leeching loons to cast French capriolles of speech. Nay, never look downcast. I bear no rancour for civilities even when they're but clavering."

The handsome young face flushed again, and the bright eyes slid away abashed under the benevolent gaze of royalty.

Not until the King had left him, which followed presently, did the possible significance of that visit begin to break upon the dazzled wits of Mr Carr. Not until the visit was repeated on the following morning and again on the morning after that did Mr Carr permit himself to believe that which until then appeared almost too daring a suspicion. When three mornings later he was waited upon by a Gentleman of the Household accompanied by a page bearing a basket of such rare exotic fruits as peaches and musk melons, sent by the King from the royal table, certainty was piled on certainty. Moreover, the bearer of these gifts, a very splendid Scots gentleman who named himself to Mr Carr as Sir Alan Ochiltree, was very civil, very solicitous on the score of Mr Carr's hurt and health, and very ready to profess himself at Mr Carr's orders and eager to serve him.

The sudden change of fortune which all this seemed to presage for the penniless young Scot bewildered him a little. It had happened so abruptly, had been so utterly the fruit of chance, and was so far beyond any calculation he would have dared embark upon, that despite the abundance of the confirmation, and whilst already believing, he yet hesitated to believe. It lent truth to the courtly speech he had used to the King, for it was true enough that to penetrate so far into the royal esteem he would willingly have suffered both his legs to have been broken.

The King's visits continued daily, and daily became more protracted. Soon there was scarcely an hour of the day but some great gentleman or other, eager to follow his majesty's example, came to wait upon Mr Carr to inquire into his state of health. By the end of the week the outer room of the house in King Street might have been mistaken from the quality of its tenants for one of the antechambers of the Palace of Whitehall.

Sir James Hay, who whilst Mr Carr was in his service had paid but indifferent attention to him, was now a daily visitor, and of such assiduity that the erstwhile patron seemed almost to have become the suitor. Even my Lord of Montgomery did not disdain to court the favour of the young Scot, and then one day, as if to set a climax upon all, the Lord Chamberlain, the great Earl of Suffolk, came in person to wait upon Mr Carr and to overwhelm him with civilities.

He had heard of Mr Carr, he announced, and of Mr Carr's unfortunate accident, from his daughter Lady Essex, who had been a distressed witness of the event and had spoken of it daily since. Mr Carr, although he had never heard of the lady, was deeply flattered to have drawn upon himself the eyes and thoughts of such exalted nobility. Her ladyship, my lord continued, had, in common with his own countess, been moved to deep concern on Mr Carr's behalf, and it was in the hope of being able to allay their anxieties that his lordship now sought news of the invalid in person.

Mr Carr thanked him becomingly. After all, the young Scot was well-bred, he had profited by his courtly experience in France, and gathering now confidence and self-assurance rapidly from the consequence with which he found himself treated, he put forth an easy charm of manner of the kind that rarely fails to win friends for a man.

My Lord of Suffolk was relieved. At least this youth, of whom men spoke already as the new favourite, was no rowdy, overbearing oaf like so many of the royal pets; like, for instance, Montgomery, with whom his lordship almost collided as he issued from Mr Carr's chamber.

Montgomery came in boisterously. "What brings the old sea-fox to your bedside?" For all that his lordship was not yet out of the house, young Herbert made no attempt to subdue his vibrant voice. That was the rude way of him: reckless ever of what offence he gave.

The demureness of Mr Carr's reply seemed almost a reproof. "No more than the desire to be civil."

"Which is when most he is to be mistrusted, like all the Howards: a greedy, self-seeking pack made up of wolves and foxes; and he the worst of them. Beware of Howards! Avoid their embraces as ye would the devil's. There's as much profit to a man in the one as in the other."

Mr Carr made no answer beyond a pensive smile. A book was closed upon his forefinger to mark the place where he had been reading before the coming of the Lord Chamberlain had interrupted him. He smiled to think how fully he was already accounted of the court that his choice of a party was being guided for him, if, indeed, his suffrages were not being sought.

Anon came the King in a blue velvet doublet which he had buttoned awry, thereby increasing the ungainliness of his appearance. It was stained too with gravy, like all his suits, for, clumsy and untidy in all things, he was in nothing more so than in his eating, unless it was in his drinking. To behold him at table was to understand why the impudent Buckingham at a much later date entitled him his sowship.

The King drove out Montgomery and took the chair at the head of the bed, as was now his daily custom. He mumbled inquiries as to how his dear lad fared and what the physician had to report upon his progress, then asked him what he read. Mr Carr held up the book, and smiled. The King smiled too; he put back his head a little with a certain jauntiness and his eyes gleamed pride. For the volume was a copy of the *Basilicon Doron*, that monument of pedantry which his majesty, like a new Machiavel, bad produced some years ago for the instruction of the Prince his son. Mr Rider, an experienced courtier, had, in Mr Carr's own interest, procured him the copy.

The King grunted approvingly. "So, so! Ye take the trouble to become acquainted with the best parts of me."

13

He desired to have Mr Carr's opinion of the book. Mr Carr considered that it would be a presumption for one so rudely tutored as himself to utter an opinion of a work so scholarly and profound.

"Ye're none so rudely tutored after all since ye perceive the scholarliness and profundity." Squirming with satisfaction, he pressed Mr Carr to tell him what part he had liked best.

Mr Carr, who had found the work of an intolerable, soporific tedium, and could remember of it only that which he had last read, spoke of necessity to this. In all this monument of erudition, said he, written it was clear, by one who was at once a philosopher and a theologian, he would venture to select for his preference the part that dealt with marriage.

The King's satisfaction seemed diminished. He knew how far in this matter his own performance had fallen short of his precepts. In public he could be almost uxorious. But in private there was little in common nowadays between himself and Danish Anne, for all that she had borne him seven children. At Denmark House in the Strand she kept not only her own establishment apart from him, but was assembling a court of her own: and it began to look as if she would make of that court the foundations of a party in the State that might yet come into conflict with the King's desires and policies. Yet since this troubled him less than the Queen's constant company might have done, he was well content.

His majesty changed the subject. He talked of horses and horsemanship, of dogs and hunting and falconry, matters these of a gentleman's education in which Mr Carr showed intelligent knowledge. Then the talk shifted to Scotland and to the days when young Robert Carr, by favour of Esmé Duke of Lennox, who had been his father's close friend, had entered the royal household as a page. Laughing now, the King alluded to his annoyance at the lad's incurable blundering over the Latin grace when it was his duty to say it before meat, which had ultimately led to his dismissal.

"No doubt ye'll have mended that lack of learning since?"

Mr Carr in confusion confessed that he had neglected to do so. His majesty was shocked into sudden incredulous gravity.

"A gentleman without Latin! Ud's death! It's worse than a woman without chastity. For whereas to the latter Nature herself may at times oppose obstacles, as it becomes us to remember lest we judge too harshly of their frailty, to the former there is no natural obstacle at all."

Taking that for his text, he descanted at great length, with a wealth of recondite verbiage and classical allusion, in one of those vain displays of erudition in which this royal pedant delighted. The end of it all was a declaration that he could not have Mr Carr about his person as he intended unless the shortcomings of the young man's education were repaired. He loved to have about him, he vowed, gentlemen of taste and learning, which did not explain the favour he showed to Philip Herbert and some others whose taste and learning did not go beyond the matter of dogs and horses.

Mr Carr abased himself in regrets for the neglect he had practised. It should be repaired without delay.

"I mean it so to be," the King assured him. Himself, he would be the lad's preceptor. "I care not," he vowed, "if I fling away as much time as shall teach you. It might be less profitably wasted, Robin." He stroked the young man's cheek with a finger which, if thick, soft and jewelled, was none too scrupulously clean.

Thereafter, daily, during the mending of his limb, Mr Carr struggled bravely with a Latin grammar whose intricacies were expounded to him by the royal pedagogue. It was a form of torture to which he submitted with great fortitude, for the sake of all that he now supposed to hang upon it. If he was conscious of his own dullness, at least he was relieved from anxiety by the patience of this King who was born to play the schoolmaster, a patience founded upon the satisfaction which his vanity derived from the free display of his own learning.

Mr Carr was still at declensions and conjugations, when towards the end of October the doctors at last permitted him to set foot to the ground again, his leg now mended, and so soundly that its shapely symmetry was nowise impaired.

King James was there to witness those first steps in convalescence as gleefully as a fond father observing the first steps of his own offspring, and he sharply commanded Philip Herbert to lend the lad an arm for his support. My Lord of Montgomery complied, however deeply it may have galled him to play the valet to this young upstart. If he was rancorous he did not suffer it to be perceived, and this not even when, from being courted by those who sought the royal favour, he found it prudent to do some courting in his turn and join the ever-growing stream of those who wooed Mr Robert Carr.

The throng of gentlemen of birth and quality to be met in the outer room of Mr Rider's house in King Street during the last two or three weeks of Mr Carr's confinement there was but an earnest of the crowds that were to assemble in Mr Carr's own antechamber at Whitehall when presently be was translated thither by the infatuated monarch. Had the young Scot been acquainted with the Arabian Nights he must have conceived that he lived in one of them, befriended by some benevolent djin whose fiat had transmogrified his world. Sumptuous quarters were allotted to him, indeed the best that Whitehall, now fallen into a ramshackle state, could provide. His lodging overlooked the privy gardens. It was a lodging that for some years had been tenanted by Sir James Elphinstone, a gentleman of great lineage and greater pride, who had enjoyed the esteem of the late Queen. Sir James, when ordered to vacate the premises, went vehemently protesting to the Lord Chamberlain, who conveyed the protest in more temperate terms to his majesty. His majesty would listen to no pleas, enter into no discussions.

"I maun ha' it for Carr," was all he said, and this with such grim finality that my Lord of Suffolk went out backwards at once, to inform Sir James that he must pack and quit.

By the King's orders these new quarters were extravagantly refurnished to receive their new tenant. Rich hangings and rare carpets were procured to adorn them, and when installed there Mr Carr found a regiment of grooms and pages to minister to him, who hitherto had been his own body-servant and whose highest consequence had been reached as another man's esquire. There were tailors to provide a sumptuous wardrobe to replace the few threadbare garments that he owned, pronounced by the King as fit only for a peasebogle, and there were tiremen to array him in these glories under the supervision of the King himself, who did not disdain to display himself as much an arbiter of elegancies as he was proud to boast himself a theologian and a poet. Jewellers from Goldsmith's Row spread gaudy, glittering toys before young Robin, of which the paternal monarch commanded him to make choice. Barbers and hairdressers combed and curled and scented his red-gold locks and trimmed to a dagger-point the little auburn beard which he had allowed to grow since his accident.

If the lad was allotted no preceptors, this was because the King himself desired to continue in that office. He could trust no tutor in England to give the boy's Latin that genuine Roman pronunciation practised in Scotland, and upon which his majesty prided himself not a little. The wits accounted it a pity that His Majesty was not attracted by the same purity of diction where English was concerned, both in his own case and that of his pupil.

In those wintry days, if Mr Carr was not closeted with the King at his studies, he was at table with him, or riding with him, or lending him his arm when he went to give audience, for such a hold had the young Scot's beauty of person and charm of manner taken upon King James that he could no longer bear him out of his sight.

By Christmas the name of the new favourite, who had outstripped all rivals and perched himself on a pinnacle of eminence such as none had ever yet scaled, was on the lips of every man and woman in London. At Denmark House, where the Queen held her court under the virtual leadership of the elegant accomplished Pembroke, much frequented by the austere young Prince Henry, and where it was the fashion to contemn the minions by whom King James surrounded himself, lampoons were being freely written with Mr Robert Carr for their butt. Whilst naturally enough there were many to sneer at the sudden exaltation of this penniless Scots nobody, and many envious ones at court who hopefully predicted that the upstart's fall would follow soon and prove sharper even than his rise, yet all who came in contact with him succumbed to the charm of his engaging personality. Even amongst those who came jaundiced by jealousy, there were some whom he converted at the first meeting by his frank boyishness and the modesty with which he bore himself in circumstances which must soon have begotten arrogance in a nature less finely tempered. His breeding saved him there. For let men sneer at him as they would for an upstart, the fact remained that, if poor, he was gently born and of courtly rearing, to which his graceful easy carriage bore constant witness, despite the uncouthness of his northern speech. His good looks, youthful eagerness and the bright joyousness that flowed from him, making him a creature of warmth and sunshine, brought men easily to understand and even to approve the royal infatuation.

His success remained still in his own eyes an unreal dream-business from which he might at any moment awaken to his former precarious estate. It continued so even when one day he found Sir James Hay, his former patron, actually inviting his suffrages. Sir James, whose ambitions were pre-eminently ambassadorial, desired to be appointed envoy to the Court of France. He had taken advantage of the fact that the King used him intimately to solicit the office, and he now begged of Carr that he would endorse the request for him. Mr Carr almost gasped. If anything could make him realise to the full the change in his fortunes which a few months had wrought, this should do it.

He bowed very gravely, almost pale as he answered: "Sir James, it is not for you to beg anything of me; but to command me. You may count upon me in this. I will speak to his majesty today since you require it; though if you are granted the office you will owe it rather to your own deserts and influence than to any poor word of mine."

Sir James had stared a moment; indeed, he had looked hard to see if he was not perhaps being mocked, so unusual was such a tone as this in a favourite. But perceiving the lad's earnest sincerity, he had bowed in his turn.

"Sir," he said, smiling, "you make me proud to have been your friend."

As in this, so in all. Mr Carr's purse, which the doting monarch kept well supplied, was ever in those days at the disposal of the needy whom he could not succour otherwise, and that he was free from the venality which others in his place have seldom failed to manifest he gave early proof. Wooed by a placeseeker for a post in the Customs, who came to him recommended by no less a person than the Attorney General, he lent the usual ready ear to the man's representations of his worth and fitness for the office. He promised readily to lay the petition before his majesty. Thereupon the man, instructed perhaps by Mr Attorney himself in the place-seeker's sure way to a favourable patronage, made it plain that he did not ask to be served for worth alone, and that upon his receiving the appointment there would be three hundred pounds for Mr Carr.

The young man stiffened and changed colour. A moment he paused, his clear eyes hard as they measured this presumptuous trafficker.

"Wait upon me again tomorrow, and you shall ken his majesty's pleasure in the matter." Coldly he inclined his head, and passed on to the next suitor.

But there was no coldness in his manner when anon he came to tell the King of this insult. The King's cackling laugh cropped his indignation in full flow.

"God's sake! If my faithful Commons would but insult me in such like manner I'ld greet for joy."

Mr Carr looked askance at him, which increased his mirth.

"Did ye discern," quoth the King, "if the carle had qualities to fit him for the office?"

"He boasted of them; and there was a letter from Mr Attorney to assert it. But… "

"Why, then, he'll serve as well as another, and it's not every suitor for the place will be as ready to part with so much silver. A God's name, take his three hundred, give him the office and bid him go to the devil. Customs, is it? Tell him his own customs commend him finely."

His majesty laughed over the matter at the moment. But anon when once more alone, he became serious on a belated thought that suddenly assailed him. Robert Carr was honest! It was a startling quality to discover in a courtier. The fellow was a prodigy. To have singled him out for trust and favour was an instance of the acuteness of his royal wits in selecting servants. It confirmed him in the belief that he could read a man's worth at a glance. King James was pleased with himself, and therefore the more pleased with Carr who had made him so. At last amongst all these self-seeking flatterers, these leeching carles, who fawned upon him for their own profit and who were ready to sell him whenever occasion offered, he had found an honest man; one who had desired nothing of him and was so little disposed to take advantage of his favour that he denounced the first suitor who had sought to bribe him.

This was a man to grapple to him with hoops of steel, to lean upon and to trust.

Decidedly Robin must make better progress in Latinity.

The highest destinies awaited him.

Chapter 3

Thomas Overbury

Mr Thomas Overbury, gentleman, scholar and poet, sometime gentleman-commoner of Queen's College, Oxford, where he had taken a degree in arts, and law student of the Middle Temple, was homing from foreign wanderings. Enriched in worldly experience, but in no other gear, he was lured back to England by the hope of finding employment worthy of his undoubted talents and exceptional accomplishments.

Whilst not himself a Scot – he was the son of a Gloucestershire squire and bencher of the Middle Temple, who in the old days had enjoyed the patronage of Sir Robert Cecil – he counted several high-placed Scottish friends, made during a visit to Edinburgh, three years before the old Queen's death. On his return from that visit, Mr Overbury had been charged with a delicate mission from the King of Scots to Elizabeth's Secretary of State, which he had fulfilled zealously, discreetly and intelligently. Sir Robert Cecil thereafter had employed him for a while, hoping much from a man of his attainments. But Overbury's restlessness and desire to widen his knowledge of the world had sent him upon those foreign wanderings.

Mr Overbury's ambitions were not immodest, and he hoped by the aid of some of his possible patrons to gratify them in securing some appointment about the court, in which he might stay his own necessities with anything that the Scottish locusts might have spared.

He put up at the "Angel" in Cheapside, a house of indifferent comfort but modest charges, attuned to the modest means at his command, and thence reconnoitred the position he intended to attack. In this his patience was not greatly taxed. The landlord of the "Angel" was garrulous as all his kind, and perceiving in certain details of gear and manner that this guest was newly-landed from foreign parts, accounted him a suitable victim. Again after the fashion of his kind, his talk was chiefly of the doings of the great world, the events at court and the minutiae of courtly life. True, he began his discourse with a lament on the subject of the plague, the ravages it had wrought in the city in the year of his gracious majesty's accession, and the wise measures by which the City Fathers had at last stamped it out. Thence at a stride he reached Whitehall and its gay doings, and drew a parallel, which he intended should be flattering to King James, between the present court and that of the old Queen, which in the later years of her reign had been what the Scots would have called dour. But there was no dourness he vowed about King James. That was a man after the heart of any honest vintner, a great trencherman and a prodigious drinker of strong wine.

Mr Overbury rose from his breakfast of salt herrings and Scottish ale, a tall, wiry gentleman of a deceptive slenderness that lent him an appearance almost of delicacy. His pale saturnine face was long and narrow with a good nose and chin, a lofty brow about which the brown hair clustered crisply, and full eyes, wide-set and observant, whose keenness he had a trick of dissembling by a sleepy droop of the lids. The comely whole was saved from asceticism by the red fullness of his lips. By the discerning he was to be read at a glance as a man strong in all things: strong in his passions and desires, and as strong in his power to curb them. In his carriage there was an indefinable aloofness, a stateliness that offered barriers to presumption; in his movements and gestures, in the way he turned his head and used his hands, there was a grace that was inherent. He was in his twenty-eighth year, but he looked older, having lived hard, and worked hard in lucubrations from his Oxford days. He had immolated his youth on the altar of ambition, and ignoring the lures which life offers to the young, he had laboured at equipping mind and spirit with the scholarly knowledge which he regarded as the necessary weapons of one who looks to prevail by his wits alone.

He rose, then, from his salt herrings and Scottish ale, and looked down his aquiline nose at the vintner.

"You tell me, sirrah, that King James is a drunkard and a glutton."

The landlord's fat body quivered like a jelly, being shaken by a sudden gust of terrified indignation.

"Sir, sir! Here's wanton twisting of my words!"

"Your words? I heard no words from you touching the King save in commendation of his vast appetite and unquenchable thirst. These may be goodly virtues in a vintner's eyes, but in plain terms they are no better than I've named them. Nay, never sweat, man. I am no spy of Cecil's as you may be supposing now; neither am I in the pay of Spain as you may have supposed before."

The man quailed before that lofty, almost contemptuous manner.

"Your worship," he faltered, "the very words I used were scarcely my own. They were the talk of almost every man in the city since the banquet at the Guildhall, offered by the Lord Mayor to his gracious majesty."

Mr Overbury sneered. "Faith! It may be worthy of yon city hucksters to ask a gentleman to dinner, and then weigh the food he eats, measure the wine he drinks." Abruptly he dropped the subject. "When was this banquet?"

"A week ago, worshipful sir. You might have seen the procession from these windows: as brave a show as the city's seen for many a day; the velvets and satins and the jewels and the housings of the horses. There was the king's grace on a white palfrey, and there was Sir James Hay in cloth of gold, and my Lord of Montgomery, and my Lord Chamberlain, and – bravest of them all – there was Sir Robert

Carr riding at the King's right hand, with a smile for everybody, and… "

"Whom did you name?" So sharp was the tone of Mr Overbury's interjection, so taut on a sudden was his tall, slim figure, that the vintner checked at the very beginning of the catalogue he was proposing to rehearse.

"Sir Robert Carr I said, worshipful sir: the new favourite on whom they say his majesty dotes as on a son. And faith, no man who sees the gentleman could grudge him his good fortune. A frank-faced, winsome, golden-headed lad, with as honest a blue eye and as merry a laugh as ever you saw."

The vintner rambled on in eulogies. But Mr Overbury was not listening. His breath had quickened a little; there was even a stir of colour in his pale cheeks. Presently he interrupted again, to ejaculate the single word: "Impossible!"

The vintner checked to stare at him.

"Impossible does your worship say? But I assure you, sir, that I tell you no more than… "

Mr Overbury waved him contemptuously into silence. "I answered my own thoughts, master landlord, not any words of yours. This Robert Carr, whence is he, do you know?"

"Why, from Scotland, to be sure."

"From Scotland, ay. Whence else with such a name? But from where in Scotland? Do you happen to have heard?"

"Why, yes. I've heard tell." He scratched his bald pate to stimulate recollection. "They do name him Sir Robert Carr of Fernieside, or Ferniebank, or Fernie-something."

"Would it be Ferniehurst?" There was a faint excitement now in the calm gentleman's tone.

The vintner smacked fist into palm. "Ferniehurst it is. That's it. You have it, sir. Ferniehurst it is."

Mr Overbury startled him by such a burst of laughter as you would never have expected from a man of his countenance.

"Robin Carr o' Ferniehurst! And the King's favourite? Come, landlord, tell me more of this." He sat down again. "Tell me all you know."

Readily enough the vintner rehearsed for him the town talk on the subject. The sum of it was that whoever had a suit to prefer at court should prefer it nowadays, not to my Lord Chamberlain as heretofore, nor to my Lord Treasurer, or my Lord Montgomery, powerful though they both were, but to Sir Robert Carr, whose influence with the King was the weightiest of all.

To Mr Overbury this news was fantastic. Robin Carr, the stripling with whom he had been acquainted in Edinburgh, had in those days sat at his feet and offered a brotherly love to the older man, who although then but two and twenty had seemed of a full maturity to the boy of fifteen. And mature Overbury had been even then; a scholar, a lawyer, and with the airs already of an accomplished man of the world, or at least so they appeared to the raw Scots lad. That he should have taken notice of this boy, and treated him in every sense as an equal, had transmuted into worship the awe and wonder with which Robin had at first regarded him. This Robin had been a sweet lovable lad, as Mr Overbury remembered him. What changes, he wondered, had been wrought by the six years that were sped. How would Robin regard now the man whom once he had esteemed so highly? In those days he had been constrained to look up at Mr Overbury; now, from the eminence to which a turn of Fortune's wheel had hoisted him, he would of course look down, and his perspective would of necessity be different.

Speculation Mr Overbury realised was idle. His course lay in ascertaining.

He spread out the meagre contents of his saddle-bags, and selected, without difficulty where the choice was so restricted, a suit of dark purple velvet which had already seen much service. He brushed it carefully, and arrayed himself. Jewels he had none wherewith to set it off; not so much as a gold chain. But the collar of fine Mechlin, which in France was already superseding the starched ruff, lent him a certain modishness, and his fine figure, graceful carriage and air of assurance must do the rest.

He sallied forth into the noisy street and the gusty airs of that March morning, and made his way to Paul's. Here he found a place in one of the new hackney coaches that drove to Westminster, carrying four for a shilling. His companions were a merchant bound for the court and two gentlemen from the country on a sightseeing visit to the capital, all of whom he chilled by his aloofness.

Set down at Charing Cross, he proceeded on foot along Whitehall, past the bourne posts and into the broader space set off by gilt railings and dominated by the imposing tessellated gateway which Holbein had built for Henry VIII.

After that he was for some time tossed like a tennis ball, as it seemed to him, from Yeomen of the Guard to lackeys, and from lackeys to ushers; and had he not in one of the galleries, by great good fortune, come upon the new Earl of Salisbury, it is odds that he would have had all his pains for nothing.

A gentleman usher armed with a wand had ordered him none too courteously to make way, and as he stepped obediently aside and half-turned to face the little limping gentleman who, with two attendants following him, was bustling to audience, he found himself confronting the First Secretary of State.

The little gentleman's keen eyes returned his glance. The little gentleman checked in his stride, and named him in accents of surprise.

Mr Overbury was justified of his faith in Sir Robert Cecil's memory.

In answer to my lord's swift probing questions, Mr Overbury rendered a brief account of himself. He had arrived but yesterday, and was intending to wait upon his lordship tomorrow.

"And why not today?"

Mr Overbury offered a truthful explanation. The handsome sensitive face of the deformed, splay-footed little earl was lighted by a smile of bitter-sweet understanding. Mr Overbury, answering this, explained further that he was urged rather by his memory of his old friendship for Robert Carr than by any news of the position that young Scot now held in the King's favour. Yet his lordship's smile persisted.

"The latter would quicken the former, not a doubt," said he. Then abruptly, he added: "Come you now with me. I am on my way to the King; and where the King is, there shall you find Carr."

It was as he promised. His majesty was moving down the Privy Gallery when they entered it, and Robin Carr – a full-grown resplendent Robin Carr in whom Mr Overbury barely perceived traces of the Scots lad who had been his friend – stepped beside him. As he moved or stood, the King leaned heavily upon him, his left arm flung about the favourite's shoulders. This was not merely, and as it may have seemed to many, in token of his maudlin affection, but actually as a measure of support rendered necessary by the weakness of his royal legs. Yet maudlin only was his habit of permitting his gross fingers to toy with the lad's red-gold ringlets, or pinch his cheeks, what time he stood to hear one suitor or another.

They were pausing thus before the vulture-headed old Earl of Northampton, when Sir Robert's wandering and rather vacant gaze alighted on Mr Overbury, straight and tall beside the little secretary.

Instantly that gaze quickened into life, and in a flash the handsome young face was aflush and irradiated by delighted surprise. If the old affection had lain dormant now for years, so strong was its call in the moment of undergoing this abrupt awakening that Sir Robert unceremoniously disengaged the royal arm from about his neck, and flung forward with both hands out-held to greet his friend.

The King broke off his speech in amazement to look after him, and a frown rumpled his brow. Instantly Haddington, one of those who followed in attendance, stepped into the place at his majesty's side which Sir Robert had so abruptly vacated. The King took his arm in silence, what time his big eyes continued to stare after Sir Robert and to con the man who had drawn him as a magnet draws a sliver of steel.

Northampton's crafty face was slewed round on his scraggy neck, and he too followed the course of the young Scot with dark old eyes that seemed to smoulder in his parchment face.

Meanwhile Sir Robert, ever in boyish oblivion of all but this old friend, this paragon about whom his earliest illusions had been woven, was wringing his hands and asking him a dozen questions in a breath.

Mr Overbury laughed at so much and such generous impetuosity. Then, observing the King's aggrievedly indignant stare, he realised the breach of manners into which Sir Robert's eagerness had betrayed him. He observed also, for his eyes missed nothing, the evil leer of Northampton and the tight-lipped satisfied smile of my Lord Haddington. It imported at once to repair this situation. Therefore he laughed as he replied:

"My answers shall be full in season, Robin. Presently his majesty claims your attendance."

Sir Robert looked over his shoulder, met the royal glance and grew conscious of his fault. Lord Salisbury saved the situation by advancing with him and drawing Mr Overbury after him to be presented.

The King's curiosity, being awakened, required no less. His reception of this stranger, however, was cold; and upon hearing his name, he punned upon the name as execrably and cruelly as once he had punned upon Raleigh's.

"Overbury? Ah! And a thought overburying in his port, I think."

That said he turned his shoulder upon the bowing gentleman. But Salisbury would not leave it there.

"May it please your majesty, Mr Overbury is no newcomer to your service or to mine."

The King's brows went up in chill inquiry.

"Once he was your majesty's trusted messenger to me, and diligently he discharged his trust." And his lordship added a mention of the occasion.

Now it was an amiable trait in the character of King James that he never forgot – unless there were strong reasons why he should – the debt to any who had served him in those hungry anxious days of waiting for the English crown, or to any who had contributed in however slight a measure to his ultimate translation from the wilderness into this Land of Plenty. Fortunate was it for Mr Overbury that my lord could name him for one of those, else it is certain that his first appearance at court would have been his last.

The King turned and scanned again the pale saturnine face more closely and less coldly.

"I don't recall him, which is odd, for my remembrance is the kingliest part of me. But since it's as you say, little beagle, we shall look to see him here again." He took his arm from Haddington's. "Come, Robin," he commanded, and with Robin once more to lean upon, he passed on.

But Sir Robert had whispered a word to Lord Salisbury, and this word was a message which his lordship now delivered.

As a consequence, some hours later, when the audience was over, and when his majesty, having dined, had retired to sleep as was his wont in the afternoon, the friends met again in Sir Robert's lodging, whither Mr Overbury had gone to await him.

No mean suspicion – such as might have beset another in his place – touched young Carr's frank generous nature that he was being sought from motives of worldly advancement. Warmly he embraced his friend and demanded to know why his Tom had not sought him earlier. Mr Overbury, more self-contained as his nature was, quietly explained that he had only just arrived in England. His saturnine eye conned the young man closely and commented at once upon his fine vigorous growth and dazzling appearance. The full-skirted doublet of dull red velvet with its waspish waist was in the height of fashion; his silk stockings, each gartered with a bunch of ribbons, were drawn over the knees of his cannioned breeches; a starched ruff made his golden head, in the words of Mr Overbury, look like that of John the Baptist on a charger. There were jewels in his ears and a rich gold chain upon his breast.

He called for cake and wine to regale his visitor, who had fasted whilst awaiting him, and Mr Overbury was again enabled to admire the rich blue and silver liveries of Sir Robert's lackeys, the costly service of gold plate which was set before him, the wrought gold cup and the golden jug containing the choicest of sweet Frontignac. Here indeed was a change from the Northern fare of small beer served in pewter and oatcakes presented on a wooden platter.

They sat and talked far into the afternoon until the March daylight was fading, and the spacious, richly-hung chamber was aglow in the light of the great sea-coal fire that blazed under the wide chimney-cowl. At first there had been reminiscences of Scotland in the days of their first meeting. Then Mr Overbury talked of his travels and of foreign ways with a dry-witted liveliness that made sharp pictures leap to the eye. At last they came to consider the fortunes of Robin Carr; and Mr Overbury learnt the stages by which his friend had climbed to the vertiginous heights on which he found him perched.

But oddly enough this narrative of achievement, which should have glowed in the telling, grew more and more sombre as it approached its end. There was, Mr Overbury discerned, a shadow over the sun of this romantic emprise. Bluntly he said as much, and desired to know its nature.

Sir Robert fetched a sigh. He passed a hand over his brow in a gesture of weariness. He stared into the fire as he answered haltingly.

"I am enviable only in appearance and to the vulgar. To be as I am is to be a toy, a minion; and that's unworthy, unmanly. I am well enough to walk with the King, to hunt with him, to carouse with him. He'll lean upon my shoulder, pull my hair as if I were a lapdog, or pinch my cheek as if I were a woman. He loads me with gifts. I am finely lodged, as you see. I may command what moneys I require. Were I a king's son I could not lie more soft. For all this the unthinking maybe envy me, the charitable pity me perhaps; but certain it is that the worthy despise me. I never meet Pembroke's eye, or Salisbury's, but I meet frank and undisguised contempt. In Suffolk's and Northampton's I meet the same, but thinly veiled, because they are men whose stomachs are above their hearts. Mean tool though they account me, they know that I may serve them, and the knowledge keeps them striving to be civil. The Queen never looks on me but she sneers openly, and Prince Henry who is accounted – ay, and rightly – the noblest lad in England, follows the example of his mother. So that no friend of the Prince – and his friends are many and of worth – can be anything but enemy of mine.

"At times I am tempted to strip myself of all and go my ways. I am weary of it, too, on other grounds. The King is exacting. My presence is too constantly required, my attention must all be at his command. I can have no friends, no associates of my own choosing. He's sulky as a jealous woman now, because I was overfree with my joy at seeing you. God help me, Tom, the burden of it grows at times intolerable."

Moved by passion he had risen, and now he leaned his arm upon the chimney-cowl, his brow upon his arm.

Mr Overbury sat silently aghast at these revelations.

"What I've said to you, Tom, I've never yet said to any but myself; indeed, scarcely to myself. It's as frank a confession as ever papist made to priest. And it was a necessary confession; necessary to my sanity, letting out some of the humours that fester in me. I think God must have sent you, so opportunely you are come."

"Opportune to what? "wondered Mr Overbury.

"To advise me, Tom."

Mr Overbury sighed. "From what you've said I opine your heart advises you already."

Sir Robert groaned. "Ay!" He swung round to face his companion, who sat grimly thoughtful, elbow on knee, chin on clenched hand. The interview was taking a turn very different from all that Mr Overbury could have supposed, and, for his own sake, hoped. "If the King needed me for aught that matters all would be so different.'

"Aught that matters?" quoth Mr Overbury. To a sensitive ear his tone might have implied a doubt of the real consequence of anything in this curious business of living.

Sir Robert explained himself. "If I could be of use in affairs; do honest work; fulfil some position of service, real service; discharge some office."

"What hinders? You are a recognised fountain of patronage, they tell me. You can obtain such things as these for others. Why not for yourself?"

"Because I lack the ability, so the King supposes. I am not scholarly. I haven't much Latin." He spoke bitterly.

"Latin?" Mr Overbury laughed. "What Latin has Tom Howard, whom I find Chancellor of the University of Cambridge, in addition to being Lord Chamberlain and Earl of Suffolk? You may become a man of affairs without Latin."

"It is objected that I have no knowledge of affairs."

"Yet of all knowledge that is the most easily acquired. Why, Robin, I vow you're needlessly dejected. If you've the will, a way were easily found."

"Not as easily as it is for you to assert it. You have advantages. You were at Oxford and ye're learned in law."

"What I know, I learnt from books; and those are free to all."

"Books, ay! I ken. I've been at books. The King himself has been my Latin tutor. But progress is slow. And meanwhile, I am what I am. Admitted to the King's council, I have to recognise that every man who fawns upon me for my patronage and favour with his majesty is my better. I sit silent, like a silly bairn or feckless woman, when affairs are being discussed. But yesterday it was this Dutch business to which I had to listen shamed by my own ignorance."

Mr Overbury smiled tolerantly. "Whilst others talked who knew perhaps as little. The first art ye've to learn, Robin, which it needs no books to teach you, is the art of dissembling this same ignorance that afflicts you. Ignorance is more common than you think."

"Pretence would not have served me then."

"Why not? What was the business?"

Sir Robert shrugged almost impatiently. The nature of the business seemed an irrelevancy to his grievance. Briefly, nevertheless, he stated it.

"The King's in sore distress for money. His debts are something over a million pounds, and the new taxes devised by Salisbury since he became Lord Treasurer are but a drop in the ocean."

"Come now! This alone shows some knowledge of affairs."

"I but rehearse what yesterday I heard. The King, it seems, has a claim on the Netherlands for some eight hundred thousand pounds, for services rendered by the old Queen in the war with Spain. He holds as security the towns of Flushing, Brell and…another."

"Rammekens," said Mr Overbury.

"Rammekens; that's it. I see ye ken."

Mr Overbury smiled to himself. Sir Robert continued: "Since the Dutch cannot pay and the King must have the money, it is his notion that he should sell the towns to Philip of Spain."

Mr Overbury laughed outright. "And how did that crackbrained notion fare at the hands of his majesty's advisers?"

Sir Robert was startled by the promptitude with which Mr Overbury had qualified the business. But he answered his question.

"They talked from dinner until supper, some for and others against it; but they reached no conclusion."

Mr Overbury's face wore a curious look as seen in the firelight. "What reasons did those urge who opposed it?"

"That the sale would be regarded as a betrayal of the Protestant cause, and would give rise to bitter discontent in England." Then dismissing the matter, he reverted to his own personal grievance. "I could but sit there mute, a useless fribble without opinion to offer."

"Why should you not have had an opinion?"

"Because I have had no means of forming one."

"Neither had they. But it skilled not with them. Ha! You rail at others for faults that are your own. It's human enough, but it leads a man nowhere. The matter, you say, is to be discussed again. Now mark me closely. I am newly out of Holland, and I lack no warrant for what I am to tell you. Make your own use of it. Convert it into your own. By which I mean, do not recite it merely as a lesson learnt."

33

Thereafter at length, in detail and deliberately, Mr Overbury expounded the state of things Spanish in the Netherlands, whilst the young man listened avidly. "With that knowledge," he concluded, "advise boldly. As a last resource, you may cite me as your authority. But if you do, remember to make it plain that you drew the information from me because you accounted that thus you might serve the King's interests. All information of affairs must be derived from some source or other. He is fittest for the control of affairs who knows how to discern the sources and how to reach them."

He rose and held out his hand. Night was closing in by now, and still there was no light in the room save the glow of the fire.

Sir Robert clasped that hand eagerly and firmly. His voice was anxious.

"You'll come again?"

"Whenever you require me. I am your servant, Robin. I am lodged at the 'Angel' in Cheapside where at need you'll find me."

Sir Robin passed an arm through Mr Overbury's, and went with him from the room along the gallery leading to the stairhead. Here at last he surrendered him to an usher who was to reconduct him.

Thus Mr Overbury might appear to take his leave without having discharged any part of the business which had brought him. He had made no mention of employment for himself. That was because his methods were more subtle. The man who can discover himself to be required is in no need to offer himself. He can better serve his ends by waiting to be sued.

Chapter 4

The Bond

His majesty sat in council with his Lord Treasurer, his Lord Chamberlain, his Lord Privy Seal the slender, supple Sir Thomas Lake, who had been so valuable a servant to the old Queen, the ponderous swarthy Sir Ralph Winwood, and some others who matter less.

On a stool beside the great gilded chair in which the King lolled and fidgeted at the head of the Council Board sat Sir Robert Carr, not yet a privy councillor, and therefore feeling that his presence here was just such a tolerated intrusion as might have been that of Archie Armstrong the King's fool.

The greybeards were talking. The Dutch towns were again the subject, and divergent views were being freely expressed. The two Howards, being Catholics in sympathy even if they did not in secret attend Mass as was commonly supposed, were stout advocates of the proposed sale to Spain, which might have the effect of tightening the friendly relations between James I and Philip III. Salisbury, who carried no interest but those of England in the stout heart contained in his frail body, as vigorously opposed the sale, on the ground of the well-founded discontent it would engender throughout the land.

The King listened to both sides, interjecting now to answer one and now the other, and enjoying himself vastly in the part of

Solomon, a role so dear to his vanity that it was with difficulty he was restrained from sitting as a judge in the court of King's Bench.

He answered Cecil now.

"You urge a matter of sentiment against a matter of necessity, and I cannot call to mind that the history of the world, of which my knowledge is considerable, shows any single case in which sentiment is able to triumph over necessity in the end. Necessity must be served. If, so that the sentiments of the nation may be honoured, Parliament can be induced to remove the necessity, by granting adequate subsidies, Parliament may be convened for the purpose. But I am none so very hopeful there. Because if Parliament had shown a proper sense of its duty and obligations to the anointed sovereign, and a seemly obedience to his wishes, we should not now be considering these other measures for furnishing supplies."

The Howards applauded him. Northampton, the greatest sycophant of his time, pronounced the discourse an unanswerable marvel of lucidity and logic. Suffolk bluntly declared that it was idle to respect the sentiments of a nation which did not respect the necessities of its King, and that if the towns were sold to King Philip and the nation were presented with an accomplished fact it must be made to see that the blame for anything distasteful to it in the bargain must fall on Parliament which had left the King no other course.

Northampton, returning to the assault, and carrying matters further, his vulturine head and smouldering glance challenging Salisbury at every word, asserted that too much was being assumed on the subject of so definite a measure of alliance with Spain. Such an alliance made for peace; the peace of the world; and thus for general prosperity. This required only to be understood by the general to be applauded, and the old rancour fostered by men such as Raleigh and other sea-robbers would soon die down.

This carried the debate into byways in which it was in danger of being lost, when Sir Robert Carr, taking his courage in both hands, made bold at last to intervene.

"Have I your majesty's leave to say a word on this?"

It startled them. Scornfully it amused them. So much their countenances showed. The King, who had been toying with the lad's shoulder-knot, paused in the act, and turned to regard him, rolling his eyes fearfully in his alarm.

"Ye'ld intervene in the Council!" he muttered, scandalised. Then he recovered, and laughed his thick laugh. "Ecod! Is it not writ: 'out of the mouths of sucklings'...? To it, lad. Let's hear this word of yours."

Sir Robert cleared his throat. "Since this matter was last discussed two days ago, I've had an opportunity to look into Dutch affairs. Let that, sire, excuse my presumption now."

"Ye've been looking into Dutch affairs!" The King laughed and the Council laughed with him, all but Cecil, who suddenly remembered Overbury, and already blamed himself for having neglected to ascertain what that man, whom he knew for a shrewd observer, might have discovered on his foreign travels. Young Carr, he instantly perceived, either by accident or design, had forestalled him there. Therefore he alone preserved a solemn countenance; he alone was not surprised by what ensued.

Sir Robert's opening was blunt.

"Your discussion here is so much waste of time and labour. For it rests upon the assumption of a state of things which does not, in fact, exist." He paid no heed to the snortings of contemptuous impatience, but ploughed steadily ahead. "You assume upon inadequate information – information which, if it was once correct is so no longer – that King Philip will buy these towns, which it certainly would be within your majesty's rights to sell."

Men shrugged and turned their shoulders to him. This upstart presumed too far upon his favour. Only the King troubled to question him.

"And for why would he not buy?"

"Because he cares, I take it, as little as another, to waste money. As long as Spain's intention was to continue the war, so long was it possible to do what you now deliberate. But the chance is gone! The Archduke Albert is still in the Netherlands, it is true. But he is already taking measures for their evacuation. Spain recognises herself, at last, at the end of her resources. Within three months, maybe less, she will be negotiating peace with the United Provinces. Therefore Spain no longer wants these towns. It follows, then, that to offer them for sale to her would merely be to provoke discontent at home to no purpose, and to rouse in the Dutch a resentment which must render the ultimate recovery of the debt more difficult than it now is."

It was a bombshell to scatter dismay among those supercilious gentlemen.

Cecil and those who thought with him were not displeased by news which rendered impossible an act whose effect on public opinion must be disastrous. The others mingled with annoyance at the news, annoyance at the source from whence it came. Each one of them would have challenged it had not the King forestalled them.

"Ud's death!" he ejaculated. "How came you by all this knowledge of Spain's intentions!"

If to magnify himself Sir Robert was disingenuous, he but practised the disingenuousness which Mr Overbury had counselled. He represented that having been sought yesterday by a gentleman of his acquaintance who had but lately landed from the Netherlands, Sir Robert had seized the opportunity to gather information which should perhaps be of assistance to their lordships in deciding this matter which be knew to be vexing them.

"This gentleman of your acquaintance," quoth the King, "would be that long-legged carle my Lord Treasurer presented to us."

"The same, sire. Mr Overbury."

"Overbury. Ay! I mind me. But what do we ken about him that we should heed his words?"

"My Lord Treasurer can speak to the worth of his opinion."

My Lord Treasurer did so. He was impressive. "In the past I have found him shrewd and cautious. If he says that Spain is on the eve of making peace, he will have good grounds for it in what he has observed. That being so, Sir Robert's reasoning from the facts is not to be assailed."

"Ay, ay! But if this man were mistaken in his speerings? Humanum est errare, you know, my lord; and human inferences are to be taken cannily."

Young Carr, eager to follow up his advantage and to impress himself upon them whilst the occasion served as something more than the fribble they had hitherto regarded him, was swift to supply the answer.

"A very little time will show whether Overbury's report agrees with the fact. Meanwhile prudence suggests no action whatsoever. If in two or three months' time it be found that, instead of withdrawing from the Netherlands, the Archduke is renewing or increasing measures against them, then will be the time to consider this sale, and then the time to make the sale to best advantage. If the war drags on there can be nothing lost by waiting."

"It's a Daniel come to judgment!" crowed the King, and his delight to discover such qualities of mind hitherto unsuspected in this handsome lad of his affection was freely displayed then and thereafter.

Later, when alone with Sir Robert, the King having further considered, expressed a desire to test for himself the extent of Mr Overbury's knowledge of Netherlands affairs. As a consequence a messenger from Sir Robert waited next morning upon Mr Overbury to bid him to Whitehall. Sir Robert's own barge, which had come down on the last of the ebb, awaited him amid the press of boats at Queenhithe.

The King, having need of him, received him kindly, and played the well-rehearsed part of a genial good-humoured fellow. In reply to the royal questions, Mr Overbury expressed himself crisply, lucidly and wittily upon the state of affairs which he had lately found in the Netherlands.

His majesty quoted Lucian, and Mr Overbury capped the quotation with such scholarly fullness that the King congratulated him upon his Latinity whilst censuring his Oxford pronunciation.

Mr Overbury accepted both criticisms with a bow, making no attempt to defend his accent.

"Ye don't take my corrections amiss," said his majesty.

Mr Overbury bowed again with the utmost gravity. "He that hates to be reproved by the master sits in his own light."

The King's eyes quickened at the phrase. Its modesty, subtle flattery and neatness, all pleased him. "Ye're a wit, I perceive."

A pale smile illumined that narrow melancholy face. "My wit, sire, is but as the marigold. It opens to the sun."

Thereafter, the King's dinner-time being at hand, Mr Overbury was given leave to depart, having done something to remove the bad impression his first appearance at court had created upon the royal mind.

He stayed to dine with Sir Robert, and, a lover of good food and good wine, he had occasion to admire the sumptuousness in which he found his friend in these respects. When the cloth was raised, and they were come to the comfits, Mr Overbury opened the matter that was in his mind.

"Yours, Robin, was not the only messenger that sought me this morning at the 'Angel.' There was a note from my Lord Treasurer, bidding me to wait upon him at the earliest."

Sir Robert nodded, but said nothing. Mr Overbury resumed.

"His lordship and I have already some acquaintance. I served him once in the old Queen's time, and his message means that I may serve him again if I wish, or so I conjecture. Why else should he send for me?"

"Why else, indeed?" Sir Robert smiled. "I am glad, so glad, a door is to be opened for you."

Mr Overbury displayed surprise. "You're glad?" A little smile that was tinged with regret flickered upon his lips. "In that case there is no more to say."

"No more to say of what? And what for would I not be glad? Do I not wish you well, Tom?"

"Of course you wish me well: as I wish you well." And he repeated: "There's no more to say. I shall wait upon my Lord Treasurer tomorrow."

"Have you been hesitating?"

"Not hesitating. Waiting. Waiting to know your will with me."

"My will with you?" Sir Robert understood less and less. Inwardly Mr Overbury damned the sluggishness of his wits.

"Cecil sends for me because what happened yesterday shows that I may be of use to him. But before going, I bethought me that perhaps the same notion might have occurred to you. And I should be loath to serve another, Robin, if you had need of me."

"Need of you!" Sir Robert rose in the excitement that accompanied understanding. "Why, so I have: great and urgent need, as you have seen. And ye could serve me as could no other man; for in learning and knowledge of affairs you supply all that I lack."

"Why then… " Mr Overbury was beginning; but the other swept warmly on.

"But what have I to offer you compared with the employment you could find with Cecil?"

"No matter for that."

"Ay, but there is matter to it. It were to abuse your friendship, to trade upon your love."

"The trading would be mutual." Mr Overbury adopted complete frankness. "You have the graces of person and of manner that have already conquered the King's affection. I have the knowledge and resource which would enable you to win a real position at court, to rise from being a mere minion – the word is yours, Robin – to become a powerful influence in the State. Thus you and I united compose a whole that should be irresistible. Each of us in this is the complement of the other. Apart each of us counts for little. United we could rule, if not the world, at least this England.

"Yesterday, in this matter of the Netherlands, you increased your credit with the King and no doubt with every member of the Council. Already they discover in you an unsuspected force. Let that be maintained a while – and I could teach you to maintain it – and you will be the power behind the throne; you will be consulted and your views respected on every matter of weight that's to be decided. Cecil grows old and sickly, riddled with ills; and he, poor cripple, is the only man amongst them. When he relinquishes the helm of this ship of State, it should be yours to grasp it."

Standing, Sir Robert had heard him out. As he ceased the younger man sank back into his chair, his face flushed, his eyes aglow. He was trembling in his excitement at the dream prospect spread before him. Had Overbury the power to convert it into reality? It was possible. If his own favour with the King were backed by such knowledge as Overbury could supply, it was probable. Already he beheld the fruits of it: saw his position at court justified by something more than a comely face and a shapely figure, and a King's capricious fancy for such externals. He saw the sneers converted into looks of deference; saw his self-respect restored by the respect he inspired in others.

"Well, Robin?" quoth the watchful Mr Overbury at length, to rouse him from his daydream. "What is your will in the matter? It lies with you."

Sir Robert raised his glowing eyes to look at his companion.

"You offer much, Tom," he said.

"No more than I'll perform."

"I doubt not that." He held out a hand across the board, a hand that trembled. "Do as you propose. Stand by me, Tom, to make common fortune with me as I with you."

Mr Overbury took the hand in his own grip, which was as steady and cool as the resolute brain controlling it. "It is a bond," he said.

"A bond in which I'll never fail of my part," said Sir Robert fervently.

Chapter 5

Lady Essex

As in the person, so in all the actions and transactions of Mr Overbury there was the neat tidiness which proceeds from methodical habits. With him thought and plan were ever the precursors of speech and act. Thought revealed to him that the success of his alliance with Sir Robert Carr must depend upon the world's assumption that Sir Robert moved upon his own unsupported inspiration. Therefore Mr Overbury took good care completely to efface himself for the present.

He waited on the morrow upon the Lord Treasurer. But the offer of an under-secretaryship which Cecil made him he declined with a polite show of gratitude and reluctance. The reason he advanced was, truthfully, that he had made other plans: less truthfully, that these plans might entail his going abroad again shortly, in obedience also to a restless, roving disposition.

They parted with mutual expressions of good will, sincere on both sides, and of regret which can have been sincere only on the part of my Lord Treasurer.

Mr Overbury removed himself in the course of the next few days from the "Angel" in Cheapside to a more commodious lodging of his own near Paul's Wharf. Here for the next few months he remained comfortably established, with a single servant to wait upon him, a sleek, discreet, intelligent Welsh lad named Lawrence Davies, who

43

quickly became devoted to him. Here he was visited at least twice a week by Sir Robert, who came by water, and with hired sculls, his identity unsuspected. He would commonly dine or sup with Overbury and remain for some hours, to be primed with such information as he sought, and tutored in the uses of it.

From this lodging Mr Overbury would sally forth, sometimes to the Inns of Court to renew old acquaintances and to seek fresh ones among the men of law; sometimes to Paul's, in the Middle Aisle of which between the hours of three and six all manner of folk were to be met and all manner of news was to be canvassed. Often he was to be seen dining in ordinaries, and occasionally he would visit the Royal Exchange and the taverns thereabouts, the "Three Morrice Dancers," or the "White Horse" in Friday Street, where the fishmongers drove their trade. Wherever he could set his finger upon the pulse of the town, which again was to be accounted the pulse of England, he was assiduous. As much with this intent as to indulge a poet's natural taste for the drama, he was often at the Globe Theatre on Bankside, where Mr Skakespeare was still at work, and because he was in a sense kin with such men, he frequented the suppers at the "Mermaid," introduced there by Mr Ben Jonson, whom we know esteemed him highly. Easy and affable in manner, he ingratiated himself into all companies, engaged all and sundry in conversation, assuring in some assemblies the character of a lawyer, in others that of a poet and man of letters.

Often he would, himself, be the bearer of tidings in his various haunts, announcing new measures which as yet were in the egg – matters which Sir Robert informed him were under contemplation – so as to put them to the touchstone of public opinion and study the various comments they provoked. In this manner he was able to advise with confidence that the enactments touching the fines upon recusants, which of late had been relaxed, should be fully enforced so as to replenish the ever-empty purse of royal prodigality. Similarly he dictated leniency in dealing with certain lingering activities of the levellers, perceiving that public opinion was strongly on their side and that indignation was all against the usurpations which had provoked those outbreaks.

In short, had he been a spy in Cecil's pay he could not have acted other than he did throughout that year (when he was generally supposed to be abroad) save that no spy of any Secretary of State was ever half so diligent, alert, accomplished and insinuating as was he.

Invisible and unsuspected he dictated policy to the Privy Council through the lips of Sir Robert Carr, who garnered all the glory and increased in credit at a rate that to some appeared alarming.

Towards the consolidation of Carr's position nothing contributed more than the fulfilment of his timely prognostication touching Spain and the Netherlands. Early in the new year came an invitation to England to co-operate in the peace settlement, as France was already disposed to do.

The King slobbered and dribbled in sheer rapture to discover in his beloved Robin the gifts of statecraft not only in this but in almost every subjects. The lad's penetration and insight into the heart of the nation seemed almost uncanny. With so little experience of the world and so few opportunities of observing national life at first-hand, his shrewd comments, trenchant criticisms, lucid inferences and daring forecasts argued a power of deductive reasoning amounting to genius.

The Howards – and old Northampton in particular – began to perceive in him a person to be respected, one who, if provoked to enmity, might presently be able to crush them without effort. Therefore with gifts and flatteries they studied all ways of making him their friend.

Forewarned against them by Overbury, and obeying implicitly the dictates of this shrewd famulus, Sir Robert held aloof, received their advances with a distant frigid condescension oddly at variance with his ordinarily friendly nature, and thereby drove them to almost frantic lengths of sycophancy.

Because the King favoured him, and because he now revealed himself in all senses worthy of that favour, these men courted him assiduously. And the more assiduously did they court him, the more did the King favour him, taking ever increasing pride in a creature whose merit flattered the discernment of his creator. Thus his popularity and influence spread in ever-widening circles as that year advanced.

As a result of all this he found himself ultimately with so much business on his hands on the King's behalf, that it became necessary – as he represented to his majesty – to seek a secretary who should assist him more closely and to whom he could give his confidence more freely than to any of the three or four amanuenses whom already he employed.

When his need became known there was no lack of candidates for the office. Scarcely a gentleman about the court but had some nephew or cousin or even son who would be proud to serve under Sir Robert Carr. Sir Robert looked into the qualifications of those submitted, but could not be satisfied. And then one day he announced to the King a piece of great good fortune. Mr Thomas Overbury was returned to town and had been to wait upon him. Mr Overbury was in need of employment, and his reappearance at such a moment seemed to Sir Robert singularly opportune. For he fulfilled the requirements of Sir Robert more than any man alive, and subject to his majesty's approval Sir Robert proposed to take him into his service.

Thus had it been concerted between them.

By now Sir Robert's reputation for ability in affairs was so completely established that none could attribute the continued display of it to any wits but his own. Mr Overbury, therefore, might now without damage to Sir Robert step into the open from behind the arras which had hitherto concealed him.

The King demurred. He thrust out a sulky nether lip. "I mind me of him, ay. The horse-faced carle that was here nigh upon a year since." He remembered with a pang the flash of intimacy which he had seen pass between the two. "Is he not maybe an over-important gentleman for your needs, Robin? A dour fellow I deemed him. Overburying I named him, and rightly I think."

But Sir Robert insisted, employing craft, and reluctantly the King yielded his consent.

However unobtrusive Mr Overbury might be in his character of secretary, the moment was one in which it was impossible for him to be unobtrusive in his own. His famous "Characters," those inimitable sketches of contemporary life, penned to beguile the loneliness of idle hours in his lodging at Paul's Wharf, had lately been published by Lisle, the bookseller at the Tiger's Head, in Paul's Yard. The little work had attracted the attention of the wits. They were loudly acclaiming it, and purchasing it widely to use it as a whetstone for their own small talk. A copy of it reached the hands of the King, who read it with reluctant admiration mingled with envy. His jealousy of any man who might rival him in scholarship was irrepressible, which may have contributed to his scandalous treatment of Sir Walter Raleigh, and to his affection for Philip Herbert, who made butts of all scholars below the royal rank, and indulged at their expense his ignorant buffooneries. His majesty, however, dissembled his envy, swallowed the spite which is the inevitable fruit of it, and condescendingly, from his own Olympian heights of learning, bestowed a benediction upon an author so generally acclaimed. As a result Mr Overbury began to be seen about the court much earlier than would otherwise have been the case.

If on the score of his own merits he was the recipient of courtesies from those who could appreciate them, as the favourite's favourite he shared the open contempt in which Sir Robert was still held by the few – those of the Queen's party and of Prince Henry's – and the secret animosity of which Sir Robert was the object at the hands of those who had learned to fear his influence and to perceive in it an obstacle to their own advancement.

The perspicuous Mr Overbury missed none of this. But he was not perturbed. He met the contempt that was rooted in envy with the deeper and deadlier contempt that springs from the consciousness of intellectual superiority, and he knew how to wound whilst preserving an inscrutable sardonic urbanity of surface towards the victim of his pitiless wit.

The improved relations between Spain and England resulting from their co-operation in the peace settlement of the Netherlands led the King in the course of that year 1610 to turn his thoughts to the promotion of a Spanish marriage for his son. Despite his stout Protestantism, King James was anxious to prove himself a King who ruled by love, and who by the loving arts of peace could achieve more than had ever been achieved by force of arms.

As a preliminary to any definite proposals, his majesty offered a great banquet at Whitehall to the Spanish Ambassador, the Count of Villamediana and the Constable of Castile, Don Pedro of Aragon. It was the most lavish of the many lavish junketings that had piled up King James's enormous load of debt.

About himself, his Queen, and their son Prince Henry, his majesty assembled the nobility and beauty of the court, to welcome the two illustrious representatives of King Philip and their train of Spanish grandees.

They dined in public state in the great audience chamber, and after many toasts, in the course of which his majesty became mildly intoxicated and very maudlin, the tables were removed and the floor was cleared for dancing.

First came a coranto, in which the stout, flaxen-haired, freckled Queen, deep-bosomed, broad-shouldered and almost masculine of countenance, was led forth by Don Pedro of Aragon.

After this the King, sleepily benign and slightly lachrymose, lolling in his great brocaded chair under a canopy of cloth of gold with the blazonry of united England and Scotland behind his head, desired to show off his son's paces to the Spaniards. He commanded him to dance a galliard, and gave him leave to choose a partner, subject to his majesty's confirmation of the choice.

The handsome boy who was the hope of England and the ornament of his not very decorative house assented willingly enough. He delighted almost as much in dancing as in the sterner exercises for which he was already renowned. Although still in his seventeenth year, he was of a good height and excellently shaped, as graceful in body as in mind, and in all things the very antithesis of his sire.

High-spirited, valiant, gracious, and even at this young age a patron of all deserving arts, he was fast becoming the idol of the people, whilst the very flower of the nobility was to be found surrounding him at St James's Palace, where he held his court. Athletic in his pursuits and austere in manners, God-fearing and studious by inclination, he contrived to be dignified and princely beyond his years. Inevitably a gulf was widening daily between himself and his father, opened by jealousy on the one hand and disdain on the other. Each, however, masked his feelings. Prince Henry studiously preserved the appearances of filial piety, and King James displayed a fatherliness which was as much a pretence as his uxoriousness.

The young Prince, standing now beside his father's chair, swept the brilliant assembly with his glance upon no random quest. It travelled purposefully until it reached the young Countess of Essex, and was there arrested. Then he leaned towards the King, and announced his choice in a murmur audible to his majesty alone. The King smiled, and nodded his great head covered by the heavily plumed and diamond-buckled hat. The Prince, thus authorised, stepped forward to claim the Countess.

Blushing a little, but displaying no more agitation than was proper in a child as yet unfamiliar with the court, she suffered herself to be led forth, full conscious of the great honour done her, but unconscious of the envy it provoked in other feminine breasts. But a few months older than the Prince, this daughter of the Earl of Suffolk was already acknowledged to be the loveliest ornament of King James's court, where as yet she had been all too rarely seen. Delicately featured and very fair, the fire of life glowed brightly in eyes whose colour shifted with the light from blue to violet. As in the case of Prince Henry, it was universally agreed that her outward graces were but a reflection of inward spiritual worth. We have it on the word of one who knew her well and had no cause to judge her generously, that her goodness of heart, her gentleness and her sweetness of disposition, outshone the ravishing beauty of her person. And with all this she was sprightly, lively and gay, and utterly adorable. She stood a little above the middle height, and at this stage was almost sylph-like in her virginal slimness. For although she had been four years now a wedded wife, she still remained a maid. Her husband, the Earl of Essex, a year or so younger than herself, had been parted from her at the altar and sent upon his travels to complete his education and to grow to manhood before claiming the custody of his wife. The marriage had been one of policy in which the wishes of neither child had been consulted.

One of the early acts of King James's reign had been the reinstatement of the son of that Earl of Essex whom Elizabeth had loved and beheaded in the titles and confiscated estates of his unfortunate father. The Howards, too, had found favour in his royal eyes for the sake of that Duke of Norfolk who had suffered similarly under Elizabeth for his devotion to King James's mother. And the marriage of Robert Devereux and Frances Howard, because desired by her family, had been promoted by the King as being to the advantage of both houses.

Until lately the young Countess had been kept more or less in retirement at Audley End. Accounted until now too young to take her proper place at court, she had pursued in the quiet of the country, and saving for occasional visits to Whitehall, the studies that should enable her to adorn the station which was hers by birth and marriage.

That she had profited by them she now evinced as she moved through the sprightly measure of the galliard with the Prince for partner, displaying a grace and liveliness as well as an assurance in her steps which captivated the entire court, and made the stately Spanish gentlemen about his majesty almost as eloquent in their praise of her beauty and art as they were in the praise which etiquette prescribed of the person and deportment of the Prince.

Having reconducted her to the care of her mother, and constrained her to resume her chair, the Prince, instead of returning to his father and the Spanish guests as would have been more fitting, lingered in talk with her, bending over her where she sat. The court looked on, and with covert amusement was blended open surprise at conduct so very unusual in this austere young man. If embarrassed at being made the object of these open attentions, Lady Essex was nevertheless flattered by them, considering from whom they proceeded, particularly when remembering his reputation for reserve where women were concerned.

But even whilst she listened to the Prince and spoke to him in her turn, Lady Essex scarcely looked at him, and this not from any shyness, but because her eyes were busy elsewhere. Covertly their glances were directed towards the royal dais, drawn thither by one who stood near the King, one whom the King used familiarly, patting his shoulder or pinching his arm as he addressed him. A tall, straight-limbed young man this, in blue velvet that glittered with jewels, broad of shoulder but tapering thence to a graceful slimness; his handsome head, framed in a cloud of red-gold hair, proudly carried and radiant with youth and health and ready laughter.

Once before she had seen him, on a day nearly three years ago, in the tilt-yard at Whitehall, when be had been flung from his horse, and she had cried out in fear and pain for him, and had long thereafter been haunted by the memory of his white face, as he lay helpless and swooning in the dust. If he had looked radiant and splendid as he rode that day on his big white horse, infinitely more radiant and splendid he looked now, standing so self-assured beside the royal chair.

Meanwhile the Prince, bending his auburn head, continued to utter amiabilities, and she knew without looking at him that his eyes were devouring her the while. Thus until the King, grown impatient, put an end to the matter. Court usage required that either he or his deputy should tread a measure with the Countess of Villamediana. Since James' own rachitic legs did not permit him to dance, it was necessary that his son should represent him. He despatched Sir Robert Carr to summon the Prince to his duty.

My Lady Essex, covertly watching them, caught the flash of jewels on the royal hand as it was raised to point in her direction, and then saw Sir Robert detach himself from the group about the dais and come straight towards her and the Prince.

If she had flushed when his highness had approached her, she paled now at the approach of Sir Robert, which she could not even suppose to be in any way concerned with her. By the time he came to halt before her at the Prince's side she was conscious of quickened heart-beats, of a sense of embarrassment amounting almost to panic. She dissembled it by making play with her fan of peacock's feathers, and masking with the edges of it the lower part of her face.

Sir Robert bowed to her formally, as if to crave her indulgence, and she admired again at close quarters his grace and his air of noble self-command. Then he addressed himself to the Prince, and his broad Scots accent startled her. Yet she reflected instantly that it was no worse than the King's, and scarcely out of place in a court presided over by a Scottish monarch. It was indeed almost a maxim that a king, even in his shortcomings and infirmities, would be the model of his courtiers.

"His majesty is asking for your highness."

The Prince nodded almost imperceptibly, as he might have nodded to a lackey.

Sir Robert stood his ground a moment, with the feeling that his face had been slapped in public but his lips retained their deferential smile. Retaliation was out of the question. Humiliation might be avoided only by ignoring that contemptuous dismissal; but to remain some pretext was necessary. He found it instantly in the person of Lady Suffolk, and he turned to address her where she sat beside her daughter, a stout woman in whose crafty, pock-marked face it was difficult to discover the source of any of the grace and beauty that earlier had distinguished her. Ordinarily he might have feared from her an imitation of the Prince's manner such as sycophancy prescribed. But Lady Suffolk was a Howard, and the Howards were too actively wooing his friendship in those days to leave him under any apprehension here. If her ladyship was uncomfortable in this situation, she dissembled it. After all, the Prince's discourtesy to Sir Robert had been no more than a lightning flash which she might easily have failed to perceive. She spoke to him civilly, even pleasantly.

His highness stared haughtily at Sir Robert's shoulder, which was quite deliberately turned to him. Then, with a low bow to Lady Essex, he swung round and walked stiffly away to obey his father's summons.

Malice whispered in Sir Robert's ear, showed him how he might gall the Prince, who had so deliberately slighted him. Acting upon it, he reminded Lady Suffolk that he had not yet been honoured by presentation to her lovely daughter, thereby increasing the unsuspected tumult in that lovely daughter's virginal breast.

The fiddlers in the gallery were tuning up for the last coranto, as Sir Robert, bowing low before the youthful lady who was to shape his destiny, murmured conventional amiabilities. No embarrassment had tied her inexperienced tongue when a prince had similarly addressed her under the watchful eyes of a whole court. Yet now she was dumb. She could do no more than smile, and look up at him, to look away again as quickly, as if dazzled by the radiance of his lovely countenance, the effulgence of his steady glance which yet had none of that devouring, wooing quality which had marked Prince Henry's.

The Prince, as his father's deputy, was leading forth the handsome Spanish Countess; the Queen had partnered with the stately Earl of Pembroke; the Princess Elizabeth had given her hand to the Count of Villamediana; and other noble couples were making haste to take the floor. Sir Robert surrendered completely to the impulse of his playful malice. Humbly he craved the honour of Lady Essex's hand for the coranto. It was so instantly surrendered that he was almost startled. Indeed, a pretext for refusing him the honour would have surprised him less.

The musicians struck up, and the dance began. Sir Robert displayed himself fully as graceful in the more sedate coranto as the Prince had done in the sprightlier galliard. He carried his head high, and there was a gleam of mockery in his eyes with which to meet the occasional frosty glances of his highness. Lady Essex moved with less certainty and self-possession through this measure than she had shown in the more intricate paces of the earlier dance. She was vexed with herself for this; yet so far as her partner was concerned she need not have troubled. His mind was so intent upon levelling the score with Prince Henry that he scarce gave a thought to the ravishing lady who was affording him the means to do so.

As he was leading her back to her mother's charge, he thanked her becomingly.

"Your ladyship has honoured me beyond my poor deserts."

She had herself in hand by now and flashed him a quick answer: "Your deserts are small then, Sir Robert."

"Compared with the honour, madam, they are naught. All things are relative."

She looked up at him, and quickly away again. "You rally me, I think," she said, and he caught a note of odd complaint in her voice. Was this bewitching child, he asked himself, already a graduate in the arts of dalliance, and did she affect this tone to challenge him? Or was she honest? He would meet sincerity, real or simulated, with sincerity which was both at once.

"Judge for yourself, my lady, upon the truth; which is that when I begged the honour I feared it would be denied me."

"It would tax you, sir, to show reason for the fear."

"I accept the challenge. The reason lay in that you had last condescended to a prince."

"Now that is almost treason. Condescension is for princes."

"Saving only where Lady Essex is concerned."

She grew so daring as frankly to laugh at him. They had reached her mother now. "You take advantage of my youth, Sir Robert."

He bowed as she resumed her seat. "No advantage, madam, but to serve you, and that were an advantage I must always covet."

He commended himself to Lady Suffolk, and took his leave.

As he was retracing his steps to the royal dais, the Prince swept past him, moving with a stride better suited to Blackheath when playing there the game of golf which the Scots had newly brought with them to England. Straight for Lady Essex he steered his course, as if determined to complete the work of giving her name to the gossips which his choice of her for the galliard had already started.

And there was more to follow. The courtiers were crowding now to the windows, to witness the baitings in the yard which the King had ordered for the entertainment of his Spanish guests. The Prince offered his hand to Lady Essex, and conducted her to a little balcony in which there was room for not more than three, and into which no third intruded since her mother did not see fit to do so. The Countess of Suffolk, greedy of royal favour and the perquisites accompanying it, saw no disadvantage in leaving her daughter alone thus with the Prince. After all, my Lady Essex had a husband of her own (if one who was absent and not yet of age) and on that score was entitled to be her own guardian.

Lady Essex, still a little bemused, as Sir Robert had left her, suffered his highness almost listlessly to have his way.

She leaned beside him on the parapet of the little balcony and looked down into the wide quadrangle, where a crowd of townsfolk surged behind the barriers about the ring. In this a great shaggy bear, chained to a post, now shambled to and fro as far as the length of his chain permitted, now stood still with rocking body and plaintive grunts expressive of his apprehension.

His highness was speaking, but no longer with any of the sprightliness with which he had erstwhile addressed her. There was a touch of sulkiness in his manner, of resentment even, as if his having danced a galliard with her gave him certain rights.

"That fellow Carr," said he. "You danced with him. Why?"

The audacity of it took her breath away. Only on the recollection that he was Prince of Wales and her future King did she restrain her indignant mirth.

"For the same reason that I danced with your highness. Because he did me the honour to invite me."

"Honour! Faugh! The word is hollow. Your ladyship is not so easily honoured."

"Your highness mistakes me. I am but a simple child."

"Which is why I would not have your simplicity deluded."

"Would he delude it, sir, do you suppose?" There was mischief in her eyes, which but increased their witchery upon him.

"Ay, by making you suppose him something, who is nothing, an upstart nobody from Teviotdale."

"Your highness does not like him. Is being Scottish the worst with which you can reproach him?"

He bit his lip and glared at her, to be distracted by the archness of her smile.

"The fellow is not fit to approach you; an upstart, scarcely gentle."

"Nay, now there you wrong him. For I found him all gentleness."

"I mean in birth, not in manners."

"Surely manners are of more account than birth. And his manners were faultless. He spoke no ill of any."

His highness was out of patience at the implied rebuke. "You defend him?"

"I have not yet perceived the need. And why does your highness speak of him?"

"Why?" He checked and laughed. "Why, indeed, when there is so much that is better worth our while."

Came a babble of voices and a baying of dogs to draw their attention to the scene below.

The bearward and his men were entering the enclosure.

The grooms retained by their leashes four pairs of straining eager mastiffs, furiously barking now at sight of their uncouth prey. The great bear reared himself upon his haunches to receive the charge of which his instincts warned him. Two dogs were loosed and bounded forward with a last short yelp to leap gallantly at the beast's throat. One he cuffed aside with a blow of his great paw which rent its flank. The other he received in a hug which crushed its ribs, then hurled it from him dead.

The crowd, in which city prentices ever eager for such a show as this were conspicuous, howled its delight in Bruin's prowess. The King and his nobles from the windows and balconies above looked down almost as eagerly.

Lady Essex, seated upon a stool which a gentleman usher had placed for her, used her fan of peacock's feathers to screen the view from her piteous eyes. She was white and nauseated by that first glimpse of bear-baiting.

"Oh cruelty!" she murmured.

The Prince faced her, leaning his elbow on the parapet, his shoulder to the show, as if to proclaim that his interest in it was far less than in his companion. With the arguments of a boy and a sportsman he set about combating her aversion. The cruelty was more apparent than real. Dogs and bear obeyed their respective natures, which were combative. Each yielded to the lust of battle, which the sight of the other aroused, and therefore relished it.

If his discourse carried no conviction to that gentle lady, at least she preferred it to the brutality of the spectacle itself, and so was content to listen to expositions until the show was ended and she could lower her fan without being sickened by what confronted her.

The bear-baiting was followed by a performance of tumblers and rope-dancers in which the displays of skill and agility delighted her as highly as the previous displays had disgusted her.

The Prince, watching her eager face and parted lips, delighted in her delight and was growing oblivious of his surroundings, when suddenly a step sounded behind them. His highness swung round irritably, to be confronted by a splendid figure in blue velvet. It was Sir Robert Carr again, who now came to make a third upon that balcony.

"Sir," the Prince informed him curtly, "we are private here."

The lady's breath seemed suspended at that rudeness. There was distress in her eyes.

Sir Robert, very calm, a man well-schooled by now in courtly deportment and secure in his sense of consequence, smiled easily into the boy's angry face.

"Your highness should not suppose that I intrude here without orders."

The lady's distress increased. Perhaps she feared that he might suppose that she too regarded his advent as an intrusion.

The Prince's glance lost nothing of its hardness, nor Sir Robert's anything of its suavity.

"His Excellency the Count of Villamediana is taking his leave, and his majesty desires the attendance of your highness." He paused to add with a touch of peremptoriness. "They wait, your highness." He stood aside to give passage to the Prince, as if inviting him to depart. Prince Henry hesitated, looking at the lady. Sir Robert, as if answering that look, added further: "I will be her ladyship's escort if she will suffer it."

The Prince looked beyond him, into the room. Espying Sir Arthur Mainwaring, he suddenly beckoned him. "Her ladyship shall have a gentleman of my own for escort," said he, to put the favourite down. And added rashly: "I am master here."

Sir Robert commanded himself with a difficulty none would have suspected from his maintained urbanity. He bowed formally as Sir Arthur approached. To his amazement, however, the lady was suddenly on her feet, a bright red spot in either cheek.

"No master of mine, your highness," she hardily informed the young Prince, and hardily met the instant discomfiture of his glance. The child had suddenly become a woman. "I own no master, other than my husband, and in his absence I am mistress of myself." Her glance shifted to the favourite. "I thank you, Sir Robert, for the escort you have offered."

Prince Henry had the sense to perceive that his boyish arrogance had carried him too far and that her ladyship was justified of her self-assertion. The perception, however, did not suffice to soothe his ruffled spirit.

He bowed abruptly. He was determined to have the last word in the matter and to cast a final insult at Sir Robert. "I do not felicitate your ladyship."

On that he stalked angrily from the balcony into the room, and went to attend his sire.

Lady Essex quitted the balcony a moment later with Sir Robert in attendance. The favourite shouldered Sir Arthur aside as if he had been so much rubbish and all but trod on that gentleman's toes in his concern to clear a way for her ladyship. Once past him, Lady Essex spoke.

"I am no party, sir, to the ill manners of his highness."

"You are gracious, madam, to give me in words an assurance with which your acts had already provided me. But the ill manners are naught. I shall forget them."

"You are charitable, Sir Robert."

"Just understanding. Ill manner springs from ill temper, and perhaps in his highness' place an interruption might similarly have distempered me."

Her mother advanced to meet them. He resigned his charge and took his leave, unconscious that the eyes that followed him as he went to rejoin the King were questioning and a little wistful.

Chapter 6

Venery and Tennis

King James observed signs which led him to suspect that he was not as deeply loved as he deserved to be for his great gifts of character and intellect. This from infancy had ever been his secret grievance. Loneliness had ever overwhelmed him, and in his desperate efforts to escape from it he had gone to odd lengths and strange shifts, himself lavishing affection and gifts with an utter lack of discrimination, in almost hysterical endeavours to purchase that which he could not inspire. He might at times delude himself that from this person or from that he was the recipient of the great blessing he sought so ardently. But he could not now blind himself to the fact that with the nation as a whole – noble and simple alike – he was being regarded without reverence.

There were various sound reasons for this which his majesty overlooked, persuaded as he was that all that he did must be right, since in absolutism it was an article of faith that a king can do no wrong.

His cousin the Lady Arabella Stuart was languishing in the Tower – where soon, as a result of this unjust confinement and her broken heart, she was to go mad and die – consigned thither by this superficially genial and good-humoured king, whose royal bowels were not to be touched by compassion in the case of any man or woman whom his pusillanimity could construe into a possible agent of danger to himself. All her offence lay in that with royal blood in her veins she had made a runagate marriage with William Seymour, whose blood, remotely, was also royal. King James, yielding to fantastic fears that his throne might be menaced by this unfortunate couple or by their offspring, practised upon them the dreadful pitilessness of the coward. The world of gentle and simple alike, being ever tender of lovers, looked on and muttered against the inhumanity of the King.

The project of a Spanish marriage for Prince Henry, upon which his majesty was said to have set his heart, was being censured openly or tacitly by the worthier part of the nobility, headed by the Prince of Wales himself, and by sound Protestants of all classes, who agreed with the Prince's assertion that two religions could not lie in one bed.

The King's desperate straits for money – the very servants of the household and officers of the Crown were clamouring now for wages which must somehow be paid – had constrained him to such measures as the sale of monopolies, which rendered him unpopular in the city; the levying of forced loans – so-called benevolences – which had offended the gentry who were concerned to provide them; whilst Puritans and Catholics were being ground down under the fines for recusancy, now remorselessly enforced.

And now as a last and most desperate expedient came the sale of honours. King James had invented and instituted the order of baronets, membership of which was to be purchased for a trifle over a thousand pounds. This did little harm. The purchasers of the title were stamped by the very title itself. But when presently other patents of nobility were offered at prices on a rising scale, culminating in ten thousand pounds for an earldom, it was perceived that the hallmark of worth was to be acquired by the worthless, and the stamp of nobility to be set upon the ignoble – the huckster, the haggler, the truckler – with ten thousand pounds to spend on spurious honours. This fired the indignation of that small section of the nobility which was not already out of conceit with his majesty upon other grounds.

Few indeed now were those who remained loyal, and these few were loyal to the office rather than to the man.

The contemplation of such a state of things reduced his majesty to tears. He wept easily, especially when swept by gusts of self-pity, and never so easily as over lack of response to the affection which flowed so generously from his loving nature.

Tearfully he unburdened himself to Sir Robert Carr. He inveighed, in terms which characteristically mingled piety with lewdness, against human ingratitude and the hardness of the heart of man, pointing out how fatherly had been his conduct towards the nation, how unfilial the nation's conduct towards himself. Working up from tears to anger, he finally announced in a passion that all of them "maun gang to the Deil!" and gave his attention entirely to the pursuit of venery.

But even here new sorrows awaited him.

He hunted at Richmond. The weather was fine and warm, the country air invigorating, and he was at the pastime dearest to his heart. Finding himself attended by a vast concourse of members of his lately disgruntled court, his spirits rose. Things could not be so bad as in his depressions he had imagined. He did not perceive that it was not himself who had attracted so noble an assembly, but Prince Henry, whose attendance he had commanded.

Booted and spurred, in the suit of Lincoln green which he affected on these occasions, a little feather in his hat and a hunting-horn slung at his side in place of the detested sword, his majesty followed the hounds on a horse of which it might be said that it carried him rather than that he rode it. Sir Robert Carr, Montgomery and Haddington kept close to him as a bodyguard; the huntsmen hung on the flanks; the court trailed after them.

At the end of a hard chase, on the edge of the forest, near the river, a stag was pulled down by hounds as it was making for the water, and the jubilant monarch, who felt the achievement to be entirely his own, blew a mort over the carcase.

Followed, under the shade of the oaks, a generous collation, with abundance of wine and much gaiety, in which the easy-going King, having completely recovered his usual spirits, set the example. He was almost gallant towards the few ladies who had shared the chase, and gave particular attention to the Countess of Essex, all in green like himself, who had accompanied her cousin, the Earl of Arundel. The King made merry upon the absence abroad of her ladyship's husband and on the subject of the reception awaiting him on his return. His majesty's pleasantries, which were a little questionable, brought a frown to the brows of Prince Henry. With difficulty his highness curbed the annoyance aroused in him, and no sooner was the collation ended than he rose and begged his father's leave to depart with those who had accompanied him. He explained that as he was returning to St James's, he was at the mercy of the tide. He would ride to Kew, where the wherries waited, and there leave the horses in the charge of the grooms.

His majesty, who by now was coming to regard the heir to the throne as the most troublesome of his subjects, gave leave readily enough to him and his company. Not until they were actually departing did he realise what this meant to him and why the concourse that day had been so numerous and brilliant. Only a small group of courtiers, apart from the huntsmen and servants, remained with the King. The main body trailed off in the wake of the Prince.

King James observed this departure in goggle-eyed dismay, all the joviality gone out of him. Seated on a cushion, his back propped against an oak, he seemed to sag together like an empty bag. A tear ran down his cheek.

"God's sake!" he muttered. "Will he bury me alive?" He fetched a ponderous sigh. "The Lord's Will be done!"

Sir Robert offered him wine. He thrust the offer aside. "No, no. I've drunk deep enough this day; and of a bitter cup, God knows. Help me up, Robin; and let's be going."

As they came by an avenue in the forest, in the neighbourhood of Sheen, Sir Robert thrust forward to the side of Lady Essex, who, with her cousin Arundel, was of those who rode back with the King to the palace at Richmond where Elizabeth had breathed her last. He chose a moment when she was alone, riding two or three lengths in advance of her cousin, who was deep in talk with the sprightly Lady Hay.

She looked round to see who came, and went first white then red upon perceiving the identity of the green-clad gallant drawing level with her. She contrived to smile a greeting to him, and even to utter one, with a boldness that almost surprised herself.

"You compassionate my solitude, sir."

"No need for that since it is of your own seeking; besides which I find you in the best of company: your own. My fear was to intrude."

"Then we are both at fault in our surmises, Sir Robert."

"I am honoured, madam, that you should have borne my name in your remembrance."

"You were supposing my memory infirm."

"Rather myself scarce worth remembering by one for a place in whose recollection there are many suitors."

"Here's gallantry in the garb of modesty, I think." There was a hint of wistfulness in her playful tone, as if she could have desired the gallantry to be sincere.

"Am I different in that from others?"

"Alas! no."

"Is it matter for a sigh?"

"That you should be cast in the common mould of courtiers? Is it not?"

"Madam, I'll cast myself in any mould you favour if you will designate it."

"You might find that of sincerity becoming."

"So I might if I knew the precise fashion of it. I was bred up in courts, my lady."

"Were you so?" She turned her head to look at him. The surprise in tone and glance provoked a smile in him, a radiant smile displaying strong white teeth behind the auburn beard.

"What else had you supposed?" he wondered. "Am I so loutish a gouk as to make the thing incredible?"

"It is that Prince Henry said..." She checked, realising her indiscretion.

"Ah! Prince Henry!" He sighed in his turn, but with mock solemnity. "He'll have represented me as a swineherd, so as to commend me to your regard. You may have observed that he does not love me. But is it matter for wonder? Here you behold a house divided against itself; and to serve the King is to offend his highness. I am conscious of no other offence."

She made him no answer. Child though she might be in years, yet she was woman enough to know that another cause of offence existed, provided, however unwillingly, by herself.

They rode some little way in silence. The head of the cavalcade had spurred ahead. Keeping pace with it at first, they presently slackened rein when they perceived that the remainder of the company advanced more leisurely. Thus they came to find themselves almost alone among the sunshine-dappled shadows of the forest. It lent a sense of intimacy to their companionship, of which the Countess was intensely conscious. At last Sir Robert spoke.

"Your ladyship came, I think, in the Prince's train?"

Her answer supplied a slight amendment. "At the bidding of my cousin Tom, to behold a stag-hunt for the first time."

"Yet you did not choose to return with his highness."

"Why, no; since Tom remains."

"That need not have hindered your ladyship from following your inclinations."

"You assume too much, Sir Robert." She was a little on her dignity all at once. "I am following them. I am a Howard, and loyalty is our tradition."

Sir Robert smiled as he thought of one or two Howards who had lost their heads through departing from that same tradition. That, however, was irrelevant.

"Loyalty, madam, is a duty. I spoke of inclinations."

"Inclinations?" The spirit of mischief smiled in bright eyes. "A woman's duty when performed must be taken to display her inclinations."

Thus she evaded him, and left unanswered the question that was in his mind.

Soon it was to arise again; for the Prince's hostility to him, which had been covert hitherto, seemed now to seek occasions for open expression.

The next one came a week later in the tennis court at Whitehall. Sir Robert and Mr Overbury had matched themselves against my Lord Montgomery and Sir Henry Trenchard, a gentleman of the Prince's household.

The Lord Chamberlain's quarters overlooked the court, and at one of its open windows appeared now, attracted by the game, a group of ladies which included the Lord Chamberlain's wife and her daughter.

Victory fell easily to Sir Robert's side. As it was being achieved Prince Henry sauntered into the little gallery above the court, attended by some gentlemen of his following. Perceiving Lady Essex at the window, his highness was prompted to seize the opportunity which the tennis court afforded him of serving two purposes at once: to display his prowess to her ladyship, and to put down this upstart who seemed to have found some favour in her eyes.

It is distressing to present a youth of such fine parts, normally so amiable, gifted and accomplished, in these scenes of pettiness into which an unrequited passion thrust him. His very inexperience in dalliance but served further to betray him.

He came forward now with all the assurance of his athletic skill, for in all bodily exercises he was of an unusual address. He had trained his muscles against fatigue by long and arduous walking. He was an expert with the long bow, the art of which he strove to keep alive; and he was always ready to match himself against any man at tennis, at tossing the caber, at riding at the ring or any other feat of horsemanship.

"Sir Robert, they tell me you are accounted a doughty opponent at tennis. Will you make a match with me?"

If the invitation surprised Sir Robert, the haughty unfriendly tone of it left him no doubt that it was not from love of the game that he was challenged. Since it was not to be shirked, he bowed submissively.

"Your Highness' servant."

The Prince threw off jerkin and doublet, bound his auburn hair in a white kerchief, and, being lightly shod, was ready.

He derived an advantage from his freshness in opposing one who was scarcely rested from the game. But the advantage was not sufficient for his needs. Sir Robert, sound in wind and limb, more mature of body, and of a natural strength which was more than a match for the Prince's cultivated vigour, combined with the endowments of nature an expertness at the game which was probably unrivalled. Tardily the Prince learned the lesson that it is prudent first to ascertain the strength of him you propose to challenge. Not that he was yet suffering defeat. But – and this was even more galling – he was being made gradually to perceive that whether he suffered it or not would be entirely as his adversary elected. Point by point Sir Robert kept level with him, playing easily, without exertion, and making it clear to the onlookers that he found here no need to call out his reserves.

As the Prince's suspicion grew that Sir Robert toyed with him, he put it to the test by deliberate slackness, and found Sir Robert still avoiding the advantage. Finally the Prince took the point which gave him the lead, and in a moment, without effort Sir Robert was level with him again. His highness, deeply mortified, lost control of himself. He walked furiously forward, without attempting to take the last ball his opponent had driven. His face was white.

"I'll play no more, sir."

Sir Robert looked at him a moment with raised brows. Then he bowed. "As your highness pleases."

The Prince confronted him, his glance so menacing that instinctively the gentlemen who were present drew nearer.

"You do not ask, sir, why I break off."

"I am not so presumptuous as to probe the reasons of a Prince."

"Then you may have them without probing. You are too much the courtier even when you play at tennis."

Sir Robert smiled a little as he bowed again. "No less at least, I trust, than I am now."

The Prince blinked and frowned a moment over his meaning; then, perceiving it, he loosed the full tide of his anger.

"You insolent dog!" He swung aloft his racket to strike.

With a cry of, "Sir! Sir!" Mr Overbury slipped in and caught his wrist. He gripped it as firmly as he dared, but not so firmly as to prevent his highness from instantly wrenching it free. The intervention, however, gave him time to recover from his momentary fury.

"Why do you hinder, sir? I desired to test the extent of Sir Robert's courtiership."

"A blow, your highness, is no test from one whose rank makes him secure from its return."

The Prince stared wide-eyed amazement at the long, pale, masterful countenance. Slowly the colour came to suffuse his young face from chin to brow.

"What do you mean, sirrah?"

"To serve your highness." And he explained: "The racket would have hurt Sir Robert's head less than your own honour."

The Prince looked round at his gentlemen, all of whom were grave as mutes. He laughed on a hard, short note. "I am at school again, it seems. I am being tutored in tennis and in honour." Abruptly be flung down his racket. "Come, sirs," he commanded shortly, and stalked off to the little gallery to resume his garments. Thence be presently departed, all following him save only Sir Robert and Mr Overbury.

"We remain upon the field, it seems," said Sir Robert, smiling grimly.

"With all the honours, saving perhaps the honour of war," said Mr Overbury. "If we survive I'll add a chapter to my 'Characters' and entitle it 'The Prince.'"

"If we survive?"

Mr Overbury shrugged. "This was the skirmish. The battle is to follow. And unless I've little skill at guessing it will be fought in his majesty's closet."

"Bah!" Sir Robert was contemptuous. "Let the boy bear his tales. The King's none so fond at present."

"It depends upon how he presents his story. Between us we've singed the divine quality of royalty."

Sir Robert shrugged, and turned away to get his doublet. As he went he raised his eyes to the window occupied by the ladies. A kerchief fluttered a greeting to him; bright eyes smiled mischievous commendation upon him. He bowed, his hand upon his heart.

"Poetic!" said Mr Overbury. "Most poetic! You receive the tribute which was all the prize his highness sought. Have you observed, Robin, that in this world things never happen as the foolish and presumptuous plan them?"

The ladies were withdrawing from the window. Perhaps my Lady Suffolk accounted her daughter excessively imprudent.

Mr Overbury sighed pensively. "A sweet child, that daughter of the House of Howard. I could write sonnets to her if I thought his highness would buy them against his need: something in the manner of Mr Shakespeare, who is a master of the Italian measure."

"Why, thou venal rogue, is not the lady a sufficient inspiration?"

Mr Overbury was helping him into his doublet. "Inspiration, yes: but there's the translation of it in labour. With a golden rod I could strike Castalian springs from any rock. But soft! Here comes an ambassador of wrath, or I'm mistaken."

It was Sir James Elphinstone, one of the Prince's gentlemen, that same knight who once had been dispossessed of his lodging in the palace to make room for the favourite, a matter which he had never forgotten or forgiven. He bore down upon them truculently, his right hand twirling his moustache, his left on the pummel of his sword, thrusting it horizontally behind him.

He came to a halt before the Scot. "Sir Robert," quoth he, "certain words fell here a moment since."

Mr Overbury slipped neatly between them. "You're right, Sir James. And the best of them fell from me, as commonly happens when I'm of the company. I've an uncommon gift of words in prose or verse, and it's a gift entirely at your service. Peace, Robin! The gentleman's concern is with words and me; and I'm here to give him both – or as much of them as he can stomach."

Tall Sir James, his eyes level with Mr Overbury's, scowled darkly. "Sir, I have no affair with you."

"If I thought that were true I could soon mend it." Thus Mr Overbury on a light note of badinage. "But I'll demonstrate your error. You are come, I take it, as the deputy of his highness?"

"You are correct so far."

"I am correct however far. I make a habit of it."

Here Sir Robert sought again to elbow him aside. But he would not budge. "Let be, Robin. D'ye not perceive this is an affair between deputies? I as your deputy will meet his highness' deputy, or jackal, or bully swordsman, or roaring boy, or gutter-blood, or whatever else be accounts himself."

"Sir!" roared Sir James, "you are insufferably offensive."

"I told you I have an uncommon gift of words."

Sir James was out of countenance before this frigid mockery. He could but storm.

"By God, sir, d'ye rally me?"

"What then, Sir James? What then? Will you skewer my vitals and devour me whole? I exist to do your pleasure whatever it may be."

Sir James's furious eye measured him from head to foot. Sir James recovered some of his wits and employed them.

"I have said that my affair is not with you, but with the fellow who skulks behind you."

After that Sir Robert was not to be restrained. "Skulks?" he roared, and "Fellow!" He put forth his strength and thrust Mr Overbury aside. The next moment Sir James was rolling in the dust, knocked over by a blow from the infuriated Scot.

He gathered himself up, dissembling his hurt, grinning his rage and satisfaction. Though at some cost to his person, dignity and apparel, he had, he considered, accomplished the mission on which be came. "By God, you shall meet me for this!"

"Meet you? Meet you?" Sir Robert, tense and athletic, snorted scornfully. "I'll beat your bones to a jelly when you please; and that's the only way I'll meet you. I do not fight with jackals."

Mr Overbury laughed. "Did I not tell you so? Lord! Sir James, had you listened to me you might have saved your pains; ay, and your breeches."

Sir James, white-faced and glowering upon Sir Robert, had no ears for the taunt.

"This ends not here," he said. "Nor thus. Be sure of that." He paused. Then, very minatory, he repeated: "Be sure of that." Since he could think of nothing else to add, he departed abruptly.

Sir Robert watched him go. Then he took up his hat. He looked at Mr Overbury, who was solemn.

"Again we remain upon the field, Tom," he laughed.

Mr Overbury shook his head bodefully. "It's but another skirmish. The battle is still to come. Let your Te Deum wait until it's over."

Chapter 7

Preferment

King James, in bedgown and slippers, his head swathed in a multi-coloured kerchief, sat on the edge of his great canopied bed, looking like Pantaloon in the Comedy. His fingers tugged fretfully at his thin sandy beard. There was humidity about the corners of his bovine eyes, and a melancholy beyond the usual in their depths.

The Prince of Wales, tense with choler, strode restlessly to and fro in the royal bedchamber talking briskly and vehemently. He was inveighing against Sir Robert Carr and Sir Robert's henchman, Mr Thomas Overbury. Sir Robert, he complained, had ever been wanting in respect to him; but today his insolence had transcended all pardonable bounds. Mr Overbury had been his accomplice in this, and thereafter Sir Robert had gone to unutterable lengths of audacity. He had grossly manhandled a gentleman of the Prince's following, and this within the very precincts of the palace. His highness seemed to imply by his tone that the locality magnified the offence into a sacrilege.

So long as the complaint had been concerned with Sir Robert's conduct, the King had sought to stem the vigour of his son's invective and to belittle the whole matter.

"Tush! Tush! here's a garboil all about naught. The truth is ye can't abide Robin, which is but a sign of the lack of discernment I've remarked in you. That not liking him ye should have put yourself in his way, as ye seem to have done, is a sign of the lack of prudence which I've similarly remarked in you. Being my son, I cannot refrain from marvelling at the general want of judgment in you, for which you have my profound commiseration."

Whereafter he added with a touch of peremptoriness: "Be off home to bed with you, a God's name, and sleep yourself into better sense."

Anger, however, had rendered the young man insubordinate. "My tale is but half-told," he answered, and thereupon resumed his pacing and his stormy narrative.

The King groaned, and aloud inquired from his soul of his God what he had ever done to be plagued with such a son as this, who came demanding of him the impossible. For to punish Robin for a matter in which his majesty's heart told him Robin was not to blame was as unthinkable as it would be unkingly.

Then came the mention of Mr Overbury and the gross insults to Sir James Elphinstone by which he had fanned the flames of discord. The King grew less disconsolate. A scapegoat might be found for Robin, and thus would his obstreperous son be satisfied. And than Mr Overbury no scapegoat could have been preferable to his majesty, who had no love for the horse-faced carle.

King James assumed the mantle of Solomon, and the canopied bed became the judgment throne.

"On my soul, ye clutter my wits wi' your clatter and clavering. If you want justice of me, let me have a plain tale, so that I may pronounce upon it. How came Robin to lay hands upon Sir James?"

The Prince's tale – which we may suppose to represent his gentleman's report to him of what had passed – was that Sir James had been grossly insulted by Mr Overbury with the object of provoking him to a duel.

"A duel?" The King was genuinely horror-stricken. "A duel, did you say? I'll deal with Mr Overbury. As God's my life he shall learn to respect the laws I make. Get you gone and leave this in my hands. I'll deal with it before I sleep."

The Prince, however, was far from satisfied. Mr Overbury, he protested, was by no means the chief offender.

"Ye'll leave me to be the judge of that when I've sifted the matter, as sift it I will. God save us all! Are we to have duelling again? And here in my very court? Away! Away!"

He summoned his gentlemen-in-waiting and constrained his highness, still unsatisfied, to take his leave. Then he dispatched Lord Haddington in quest of Sir Robert Carr.

The messenger found Sir Robert with Mr Overbury in the severely-furnished chamber which served them as a workroom. Here, despite the lateness of hour, Mr Overbury was still at those labours which were increasing almost daily in arduousness.

In a high-backed padded chair, at a vast oak table which served him for a writing pulpit, sat the favourite's secretary. He was entrenched on three sides, as it seemed, by a parapet of piled up documents, and lighted in his labours by two clusters of candles in great silver branches.

Here were papers concerned with petitions of all kinds, with monopolies, benevolences, matters of poundage and tunnage, and foreign dispatches, all awaiting the immediate attention of one who virtually discharged the duties of a Secretary of State.

Mr Overbury, in a wine-coloured bedgown worn over shirt and breeches, sat, quill in hand, making marginal notes upon an imposing document.

To receive his visitor Sir Robert rose from the window-seat where he had been lounging at the open casement, for the night was hot as with the threat of thunder. A faint odour hung upon the air, vague to the nostrils of Lord Haddington, who was only slightly acquainted with tobacco.

Sir Robert, who had been on the point of going to bed, dissembled his reluctance at the summons. This reluctance was increased when his lordship told him significantly that the Prince had been with his father. By now the afternoon's scene in the tennis court was the talk of all the court. Here, then, it seemed, was the battle which Mr

Overbury had predicted. Metaphorically, as he went, Sir Robert girded up his loins.

He found the King alone, awaiting him. His majesty no more desired witnesses for the scene with Carr than for that which had taken place with the Prince.

Enthroned once more upon the canopied bed, the skirts of his gown swathing his lean shanks, the King received the favourite with a countenance of unusual gravity. He laid before him the complaints of the Prince, alluded severely to the manhandling of Sir James Elphinstone, and was very hot upon the subject of Mr Overbury and his endeavours to put a duel upon Sir James.

He would have, he announced, no brawlers about his court, and no duellists within his kingdom, and not a day longer would he tolerate the presence of a man who set his known wishes at defiance. He was King, and he would be obeyed. He would so, by God's death! Breathing noisily, from rage and adenoids, he paused and gave Sir Robert at last a chance to answer him.

"Your majesty is not correctly informed of what took place."

"How?" The King scowled upon him. "Have you not heard that I had Prince Henry's word for all?"

"Prince Henry was not himself a witness of all. This matter of Tom Overbury, now, is at once true and false; but more false than true. Sir James was the brawler. He came to brawl with me. He was the duellist in this. He came to force a duel upon me – came back to do so after his highness had left us."

"On you! He came to force a duel upon you, Robin?" Majesty was appalled. The current of the royal wrath was instantly diverted. "Body o' me! What are you saying?"

"It was so as to forestall him, so as to shield me from this fire-eater, that Tom got between us and offered himself as my deputy."

The King's goggle eyes were glaring at him. This mention of Overbury, this warm defence of him, once again changed the direction of the King's anger. His mounting tenderness was suddenly converted into suspicion.

"How came ye, then, to lay hands upon Sir James?"

Sir Robert told him. The King rolled his eyes as he listened. His answer, when it came, was indirect.

"Among ye, ye make a bear-pit of my palace. Ye provoke his highness into derogation from his royal dignity, and ye so anger him that he comes storming here to me, forgetting that if I am his father, I am also his King. Say what ye will in defence of that rogue Overbury, if he had not used the words he used to Sir James Elphinstone, the affair might have been kept within the bounds of decency."

"I have already informed your majesty... "

"I ken well what ye've informed me. But my eyes are keen enough to see through words into the very heart of the matter, and to form opinions for myself. There's no way but one to end this, to restore peace and provide against repetitions of anything so unseemly. This fellow Overbury must go."

Sir Robert stiffened, and the colour deepened in his face. He would have spoken, but the King stayed him, raising his hand and assuming a masterfulness of air and tone such as he had never yet employed to his favourite.

"Not a word of protest, Robin. It's not a request ye've heard, but a command. A royal command. See it executed."

Sir Robert used his wits briskly. He bowed, utter submission in every line of his stalwart graceful figure, utter submission in his voice.

"I am your majesty's most loyal subject and most obedient servant. Mr Overbury will have left Whitehall and your majesty's service by this time tomorrow."

The King's face lighted with triumph, and remained so until Sir Robert added: "Have I your majesty's leave to accompany him?"

"Accompany him? Accompany him? For God's sake, tell me what you mean?"

"What I have said, sire. My wish is to go with Mr Overbury."

"By God, you don't!"

"Your majesty may send me to the Tower for disobedience. But short of that I go with Mr Overbury."

The King stared his gloomy dismay and vexation into that resolute countenance. The royal lip began to tremble. The royal eyes grew lachrymose. Then rage exploded from him.

"Ye maun baith gang to the Deil!" he roared in broadest Scots, and slipped off the bed to stand shaking with passion.

Sir Robert bowed, and moved backwards towards the door.

The King's bellow arrested him. "Where are ye going?"

"I understood your majesty to dismiss me."

"You understood nothing of the kind. I vow ye desire to exasperate me. I warn you, Robin: I'll not be trifled with." He shambled forward a little, and grew maudlin. "I've been good to you, Robin: and this is an ill requital. Are you as ungrateful as the rest?"

"Sire, naught that you can do – not if you send me to the Tower, or even to the block – will quench my gratitude and love..."

The King interrupted him, taking up the word. "Love? You have no love for me. You're like the rest. All is make-believe, play-acting to gain your ends. Love joys in giving. You, like the others, seek only to take."

"Sire, I have not deserved this. You are unjust."

"Unjust am I? In what am I unjust? Have you not proved yourself when you announced that you'll desert me for this rogue Overbury?"

"If I did less I should be a party to the cruel wrong that is being done this man, for having shown himself ready to risk his life for mine. That is all his offence, sire. What a contemptible rogue should not I be if I did not insist upon sharing a punishment which I have brought upon him?"

"It remains that I count for naught."

Sir Robert looked him straightly between the eyes. "Could your majesty ever again trust or esteem me if I were so dead to honour and to obligations as to abandon that loyal man at such a moment?"

Again the King evaded the question. "Obligations? And what of your obligations to me?"

"I have never been unmindful of them. To the best of my poor ability and strength I have served your majesty loyally and faithfully, ay and unsparingly. My life, sire, is yours. I would yield it up willingly in your service, as God's my witness."

The appeal to tenderness, fervently uttered, played havoc with the royal emotions, ever vulnerable to such assaults.

"Robin! Robin!" He advanced upon the young man, holding out his hands, and brought them finally to rest on Sir Robert's shoulders. "You mean that? For God's sake say that you mean it! For God's sake say that ye'll not forsake me; that ye'll not break my lonely old heart!"

Sir Robert smiled with the irradiating irresistible tenderness of which he had the gift.

"In forsaking you, sire, I should be breaking my own heart together with my fortunes. Yet... "

"Say no more, Robin. Say no more, man." The King's grip tightened on his shoulders. "I believe you. You're true steel in a world of painted laths."

He loosed his hold and went shambling away again, wiping his eyes. "Henry'll be angry if I do naught. He'll no doubt come raging to me again with his hectorings and his insolences. But I'll bear it. For your sake, Robin lad, I'll bear it all."

It was a capitulation which might have satisfied Sir Robert. But he did not yet choose to be satisfied. He knew the vacillations of the royal mind; knew that this might change again.

He did not desire, he announced, that the King should suffer griefs on his account. He did not deserve it and, all things considered, he thought it would be better if the King dismissed him together with Mr Overbury. As it was, he had too many enemies at court; there were so many great lords who treated him cavalierly, whose eminence placed them beyond the reach of his resentment.

He drove the King to frenzy by his determination. He was bidden to hold his clavering tongue. He was assured by a fond monarch, now utterly terrified of losing him, that he should be made as great a lord as any in the land, so that he should take precedence of any insolent gentleman who in the past might have presumed upon superior rank.

Then, finding that Sir Robert still wavered, the King had recourse to cajoleries and pettings, and finally made an abject surrender. Not only should Mr Overbury remain, but he should receive the honour of knighthood and be raised to the dignity of a gentleman of the household. As for Sir Robert himself, he should have the Castle of Rochester with the title of Viscount, besides the vacant Barony of Winwick in Northamptonshire; he should be invested with the Order of the Garter, become a Member of the Privy Council and Keeper of Westminster Palace for life. Thus should men know the love and esteem in which he was held by his King, and they should honour him or it would be the worse for them.

On that, long after midnight, the King embraced and dismissed him, and went at last to bed exhausted by the emotion of the evening. Robin's determined championship of Mr Overbury, reviewed in retrospect, fanned the King's singular and abnormal jealousy. The circumstance that he had been compelled to yield at all where Overbury was concerned rendered that detestable fellow more detestable than ever in the royal eyes.

It is characteristic of weak, unstable natures to give generously under pressure, and thereafter, hating their own weakness, to hate the recipient of the gifts.

Chapter 8

Importunate Wooers

Prince Henry's pursuit of my Lady Essex showed little sign of prospering. There were few opportunities of meeting the lady, and none of being private with her. To create or increase them his highness was driven to odd shifts, of which the oddest was his tightening relations with the Earl of Northampton.

He knew his lordship to be, like all the Howards, a crypto-Catholic, which in itself was a thing detestable to the fervently Protestant Prince. He knew him for a friend of Spain and suspected him of being secretly in the pay of King Philip, which was still more detestable. He knew him also for one of the most ardent advocates of the Spanish marriage, which was most detestable of all. But just as the pangs of hunger will make a thief out of an honest man, so will the pangs of love compel the most scrupulous to discard his scruples.

The Lady Essex, beloved of her great uncle, was often to be found at Northampton House, the magnificent palace which he had built himself in the Strand. Prince Henry, informed of this, came nowadays to be found there scarcely less often.

Surprised at first by this sudden friendliness of a prince who hitherto had hardly acknowledged his existence, the crafty old nobleman looked about him for the reason. His keen vulturine eyes were not long in discovering that his little golden-headed niece was the lure that drew this royal tiercel. Now, despite his affection for her, which was probably as deep as any affection his lordship was capable of feeling, he saw here only matter for self-congratulation. It signified little that his niece's honour should run the risk of being tarnished so that his own insatiable ambitions should be served. And with the Prince on his side, the head of a party hitherto hostile to himself, there appeared to be no bounds to the achievements that might yet be his. Robert Cecil was growing old and infirm – his lordship took no account of the fact that he was himself over seventy, and the older man – and soon now would have to make room for a new Lord Treasurer and chief Secretary of State. It would not be the fault of my Lord Northampton's planning if he did not succeed to that coveted office. But not in his most sanguine moments had he ventured to hope that the friendship of the Prince of Wales would come to strengthen the ladder by which he meant to climb. Therefore he blessed the little niece who made this possible, and was careful, by the courtier arts of which he was a master, to remove all obstacles from Prince Henry's path.

The Earl became all at once of an extreme sociability, and for a season Northampton House was rendered the scene of extravagant gaieties. There were banquetings and dancings and masques, to which all the court was bidden, and there were more discreet and private affairs, little water parties and little intimate dinners for not more than a half-dozen, whereafter his highness would be free to wander with the lady in the cool garden by the river.

But be it that the young Countess was the victim of an excessive prudery, be it that she feared the tongue of gossip, be it that other causes were at work, whilst the Prince's opportunities of being in her company were abundant, his opportunities of being private with her were scarce and fugitive.

Nor was this all that went to stir vexation in his highness. A certain Sir David Wood was much about Northampton House in those days, and he contrived, consciously or unconsciously, to put himself damnably in the Prince's way. This Sir David was a gentleman newly out of Spain and deep in the Earl's confidence. A boldly handsome man, something under thirty, gay of temperament and engaging of manners, he fell an instant victim to the beauty and witchery of the Lady Essex. Being a masterful fellow, accustomed to take what he lacked, and to practise an utter directness of aim, he made no secret of the matter. He laid siege to her ladyship, was ever at her elbow, and either did not or else refused to perceive that in doing so he put himself in the Prince's way.

Northampton looked on aggrieved. Sir David knew too much about his lordship and his Spanish dealings to be incontinently dismissed. Therefore the Earl took at last the course of speaking to his niece in mild reproof of the apparent lightness of her conduct.

The suggestion offended her.

"In what am I light? I do not beckon Sir David, or detain him at my side. Indeed, I find him almost as importunate as his highness. I desire the attentions of neither. Yet I am glad to have both, since each serves to protect me against the other."

This was more than his lordship cared to hear.

"His highness is one, and Sir David quite another. The attentions of a prince are not lightly to be repulsed. Loyalty forbids it, unless those attentions should become unwelcomely insistent. But a plain gentleman such as Sir David is easily whipped to heel by a lady who values her good name. She needs but to show him plainly that she values it."

Her ladyship acted that very day upon this advice; although her uncle's words were not by any means the spur that drove her.

Sir David dined alone with the Earl, and as dinner was ending, espying her ladyship in the garden, announced his intention to take the air.

Scarcely was Sir David gone forth than the new Lord Rochester was announced.

Robert Carr came accompanied by the lately knighted Thomas Overbury to discuss with the Lord Privy Seal certain matters arising out of letters newly received from Spain.

The Earl gave him the cordial welcome he reserved for all men who might be useful to him, and conducted the twain to his handsome well-stocked library above stairs.

Their business was soon done, and then, the day being warm and his lordship's terrace pleasantly cool, Lord Rochester proposed that they should remove themselves thither to discuss what yet remained.

In the gardens below my Lady Essex wandered with the assiduous and enterprising Sir David. The gallant knight was making the most of his opportunity, and her ladyship was listening without any positive annoyance, for Sir David, after all, was no clumsy-footed wooer. Chancing, however, to raise her eyes to the terrace, and finding herself suddenly surveyed by one of the two gentlemen who sauntered there with her uncle, she abruptly checked, and the half-smile with which she had been listening perished on her lips.

My Lord Rochester paused to doff his plumed hat and to bow low in salutation. Then he passed on with his companions.

Sir David looked hard at her ladyship. "And who may be that fine fellow?" said he in his easy way, for he was no respecter of persons.

"That is my Lord Rochester," she answered him.

"Robin Carr!" he ejaculated, and he looked again, interest quickening in his eyes as they took stock of one so famous. Then he transferred his gaze once more to his companion.

"Your ladyship feels the heat!" he exclaimed in sudden solicitude. "You are pale."

She looked up at him with her deep-blue, candid eyes, and smiled a little wistfully.

"You look at me too closely, Sir David."

He took the mild reproof for challenge. "Who would not that were blessed with the occasion? I gaze on you as I've seen them gaze in Spain on images of worship, save that I never saw one gaze with the half of the devotion that I feel."

She lowered her eyes before his ardent glance. "Their piety, then, is small," said she.

"On the contrary, it is great. But my adoration is still greater."

Her brows were puckered in a frown. Her tone became severe. "Sir David, I am no object for your adoration."

"If I find you so, can I help myself? It is something none can deny me."

"My husband might. I have a husband somewhere. You are forgetting it, Sir David."

"Not fifty husbands could deny me the freedom of worshipping you."

"Yet if you respect me, the existence of one will make you deny yourself the freedom of uttering it."

"Unless you give me leave."

"How could I?" Her tone became impatient. "You are mad, Sir David."

He fetched a sigh. His face was oddly white. He spoke in tones of utmost humility.

"What do I ask, when all is said, that you should so harshly refuse me? I offer. I do not beg. I am ready to give without guerdon. I demand nothing in return."

"Sir David, I do not understand you. It is as well perhaps."

"Yet what I say is plain and simple. I simply announce myself your servant now and always. Since you can give me nothing, that is little matter. I give myself to you against your need of me. That's all, my lady – my dear lady. Rest in the knowledge that there lives one man at least who will adventure all to serve you. To you it may seem a little thing… "

"Surely no little thing, Sir David." She sighed. "Yet something that I wish you had not said; for I can say nothing in return."

He grew vehement. "Have I asked you to say aught? All I hope is that you will bear my words in your memory. The knowledge of that will bring me happiness."

It is difficult to credit Sir David with such abstract chivalry as he professed. It was skilful in that on the one hand it opened a line by which he could retreat in good order from a position upon which his assault had been too precipitate, and on the other he left the way prepared for a renewal of the assault should the occasion ever offer. For that his words must touch her and linger pleasantly in her memory he knew as surely as that she was a woman.

Whilst he stood waiting, hoping for some answer, the Earl's voice summoned him to the terrace. His opinion was required on some question of fact or policy connected with King Philip. He gave it, and a discussion followed provoked by Sir Thomas Overbury. The discussion dragged on, and Lord Rochester grew evidently impatient, for presently, leaving the group of three to talk the matter out, he sauntered down the steps to pay his respects to Lady Essex.

His willingness to leave the business to Sir Thomas was no more than his normal habit, just as nowadays it was increasingly becoming his majesty's habit to leave affairs in the hands of his lordship. The King adopted this course because at heart he was indolent, hating all labours, apart from politico-literary ones, such as his present *Counterblast to Tobacco*, which flattered his vanity, and detesting all business that was not directly concerned with the raising of money. Lord Rochester, following the King's example, entrusted affairs to a deputy, because – unlike the King – he knew the deputy to be more competent than himself.

Had Sir David been aware of this, he would have watched Lord Rochester less closely as he joined her ladyship where she wandered in the green alleys of the garden.

She wore a rose-pink gown with a short Dutch waist above the Catherine wheel of her farthingale, and hanging sleeves that showed a lining of paler pink. Her golden head was covered by a cap with side wings coming to a little peak in the middle of her brow, which like her tall pickadell was of snowy linen and flimsiest lace. Her dark blue eyes smiled a greeting into the paler eyes of the approaching gentleman. It was a smile which might have increased Sir David's anxieties could he have beheld it at close quarters.

The new Viscount received with becoming modesty her felicitations upon his recent preferment. Then he spoke of Sir David Wood, his

Spanish travels, his accomplishments, his knowledge of affairs. Thus until her ladyship interrupted him, laughing.

"Is it ever to be your lordship's habit to entertain me with talk of other men?"

He remembered their last words, a month ago in Richmond Park, and again their words on the occasion of the banquet to the Spanish Ambassador, and he joined in her laughter.

"Not my habit, I trust. But, indeed, it seems hitherto to have been my misfortune."

"And mine, I think," said she.

"Why yours?"

She paused a moment, hesitating; then took courage. "I might prefer that you should tell me of yourself."

"Of myself? " He looked at her, a faint surprise upon his face. But her eyes were averted, and the lovely tranquil mask of her countenance told him nothing.

"It is a topic on which you should be able to speak with much authority," said she, by way of explanation.

"Perhaps," he said. "But would I?" He laughed. "Is his own self a topic upon which any man dare be truthful?"

"Yet if he dare not, who can be? Not his enemies, for they traduce him out of hate; nor his friends, for they magnify him out of love. How, then, does one learn the truth of any man?"

"None ever does," said he. "Truth is an over-elusive thing. Sir Francis Bacon is asking through the lips of Pilate what it is. And Sir Francis is the last man in England to supply the answer to his own question."

"You are bitter, sir," she told him. "I wonder why?"

"Neither sweet nor bitter, madam. I but study to be honest."

"Honesty is another word for truth. Why trouble after that which you say is over-elusive?"

He laughed again. "You are too shrewd for me. You batter me with my own weapons. I cry you mercy."

"You shall have that from me and more," said she on a betraying note of gentleness.

His lordship looked at her, faintly wondering; and became perhaps for the first time conscious of the bewitching appeal of her fresh young loveliness. "More?" he echoed. "What more could I presume to ask of you?"

"Can I tell until you ask? I have no gift of divination."

"Have you not?" He was still looking at her, and a new light was quickening in his eyes. Very softly and slowly he added: "I wonder is there any gift you lack."

"Oh, a many. I can assure you."

"But not such, I'll swear, as any man would miss or desire to find."

Her manner remained light, but her pulse beat faster. "Now speaks the courtier to whom truth is elusive because he so renders it."

Thus she spurred him on with natural feminine guile, which requires no tutoring. But his lordship's eyes wandering in that moment from her gentle face were caught by a metallic sheen, and looking through a gap in the laurel bush by which he stood he discovered a great gilded barge of twelve oars with the royal standard trailing in the water astern, coming alongside the steps of Lord Northampton's garden. Out of the canopied stern stepped a glittering group, aptly described by Lord Rochester's next words.

"What dragonflies are these that come rising from the water?"

Ahead of some four attendant gentlemen the lithe stripling figure of the Prince of Wales stepped briskly towards her ladyship, until presently, beside the laurel bush which had screened him hitherto, his highness beheld her tall companion.

He continued to advance, but the eagerness had departed from his young face, the elasticity from his stride.

He stood bowing before her. She, wishing him at the bottom of the river, dropped him a curtsey. My lord, bareheaded, and inwardly almost as vexed by the interruption, offered an obeisance. Peace, superficially, had been restored between Prince and favourite, as a preliminary to their receiving the Order of the Garter at the same investiture.

Possibly the Prince perceived that if his complaints were in their sequel to accomplish no more than the favourite's preferment, he had better in future hold his peace.

Compliments being exchanged, his highness stared coldly into his lordship's face.

"You have leave to go, my lord," he said in curt dismissal.

Tone and glance combined to sting his lordship. But disobedience was out of all question. He bowed.

"Your highness is gracious," he murmured, not without sarcasm, and would have turned to depart but that he found his loose sleeve caught in her ladyship's grip. She had been stung with him and for him, and far more deeply than he. So far as in her power it lay, she would salve the wound.

"We will seek his lordship together," she said demurely, in allusion to her uncle. "He is on the terrace there, and he will be honoured by your highness' visit."

"Nay, nay," said the Prince. "We'll not disturb his lordship yet awhile."

She smiled brightly in answer. "He would never forgive me if I did not." And turning on her heel, she led the way.

Her assumption that the Prince came to visit her uncle was usual and fully justified. Since she, herself, was no more than a casual visitor there, it was not to be supposed that he came on her account.

His highness, blaming his own hesitancy in making the point clear to her, promised himself that he would amend it at the earliest moment. Meanwhile, sulkily he followed but a half-step behind her, Lord Rochester keeping pace with him, and the Prince's gentlemen bringing up the rear.

Having delivered him up to her uncle, my lady took her leave upon a pretext that she was awaited by her mother, and so departed in some vexation at the course of things.

Her departure rendered Prince Henry conscious that his visit to the Earl was really without purpose, and very soon thereafter he re-embarked with his gentlemen in his stately barge. He made little attempt to dissemble his ill humour or the source of it.

"Carr! Carr! Always Carr! Is there no place in the world where I can be safe from that fellow's intrusion?"

He uttered the question aloud; addressing it to no one in particular, but rather to the Universe in general. Nevertheless, among his immediate following there was one who understood that this was less a question than a prayer, and addressed himself to contriving that it should be answered.

Chapter 9

Mrs Turner

The understanding gentleman who undertook to play Providence to his highness was Sir Arthur Mainwaring, a slight, elegant fellow of an almost Spanish complexion and with all a Spaniard's traditional heat of blood. He was alert, swift, ingenious, alive in every fibre of him, expert to his fingertips in every kind of intrigue, and without scruples of any kind to hamper him.

Sir Arthur plied his nimble wits to serve his prince with a courtier's usual hope of being served himself on the rebound. And he went to work with all an artist's reticence, disclosing nothing of his aims, so as not to blunt the dazzling surprise of the accomplishment when he should present it.

Sir Arthur had a mistress, chosen with great discrimination, the beautiful, clever and equally unscrupulous Anne Turner, who affluently maintained herself in the early widowhood to which Fate had doomed her by the exercise of her abundant talents, enterprise and industry. She conducted in Paternoster Row, at the sign of the Golden Distaff, a considerable establishment for the purveyance of modish luxuries to the wealthy and the noble. Already she was well known at court, and almost it might be said that she held a court of her own wherein she was sought by great ladies who desired the secrets of beauty and elegance which she – in her own young person a mirror of elegance and of beauty – was induced to dispense. She drove a brisk trade in perfumes, cosmetics, unguents and mysterious powders, liniments and lotions asserted to preserve beauty where it existed, and even to summon it where it was lacking. The widow of a physician of some skill, she had turned to good account certain notebooks which he had left, containing a serviceable collection of prescriptions of an infinitely varied character. Among them was the recipe for yellow starch, which she dispensed as her own invention. This had become so widely fashionable for ruffs and pickadells that of itself it had rendered her famous.

No less brisk was the trade she drove in fashionable appliances, many of her own devising, and in articles of apparel, chiefly of her own confection; whilst her services had been more than once engaged by Ben Jonson and others to design and provide the costumes for the masques so frequently held at Whitehall.

It was also rumoured that she amassed gold in another and less licit manner: that she dabbled in fortune-telling and the arts of divination. But such matters were only whispered, for none wished any harm to Mrs Turner, and it would have been dangerous to utter these things aloud during the reign of a King who was the author of a monument of pedantic nonsense on the subject of demonology and who employed witchfinders to harry unfortunate old women throughout the land.

A pretty, fluffy, fair little woman, sleek and luxury-loving as a cat, Mrs Turner provided abundantly not only for her own expensive tastes, but also for those of her lover, Sir Thomas, whose unaided resources would scarcely have sufficed to maintain him at court.

She owned a very pleasant country house at Hammersmith, with a fair garden on the river, and it was the thought of this garden which set the ingenuities of Sir Arthur's mind in movement. To convey the Prince thither, and so earn his gratitude – and all that this implied – should be easy when the time came. The difficulty lay in procuring the presence there of Lady Essex. It was a problem worthy of our gentleman's ingenuity. To its solution he applied himself at once with diligence and confidence.

Circumstances opened a way for him at the outset. The Queen's brother, King Christian of Denmark, was about to visit the English court. Preparations of lavish entertainment were afoot, to include a masque – the Masque of Solomon – which Ben Jonson was writing and for which Inigo Jones was designing and constructing the mechanical and architectural parts. Mrs Turner was entrusted with the confection of the dresses for the Queen of Sheba and some other characters in the masque.

Sir Arthur took an early opportunity of enlarging to Lady Essex upon the tiring talents of Mrs Turner so eloquently that he moved her ladyship to desire to be dressed by her for the ball that was to follow the performance. Thus was the elegant little widow – duly informed of the ultimate purpose to be served – introduced to the lodging of the Lord Chamberlain's lady.

She was well received, and she exerted all her talents on behalf of Lady Essex, and delighted her ladyship by the gown of cloth of silver which she fashioned for her. She showed herself of an extraordinary assiduity, sparing no pains to achieve perfection, and in the course of these the acquaintance ripened and widened, enabling Mrs Turner to display other than tiring talents which were equally at the service of the Countess. She praised, and very justly, the pearly beauty of my lady's skin. It was, she admitted, beyond human power to improve it, but she had a creamy perfumed pomade that would preserve its glorious perfection. She possessed also the secret of a special glove to be worn of nights, which would enhance the white beauty of my lady's hands. And she had other beauty secrets, whose mention excited my lady's desire to possess them, and moved my lady to use her with more than ordinary friendliness considering their different estates.

Out of all this it followed that on a day of the week following the Masque of Solomon a coach drew up at the sign of the Golden Distaff in Paternoster Row. Out of it stepped a dainty female figure, wimpled in grey and hooded to screen her features from the gaze of inquisitive city folk.

She was admitted by a lean, knock-kneed man of perhaps fifty, whose dress of rusty black was relieved only by a broad unstarched collar of lawn. His face was long and bony and sallow; all the blood in it seemed to have fled to the thin pointed nose. There was a slight cast in one of his beady black eyes, and his expression was one of sinister melancholy.

The young Countess shivered at sight of this unlovely usher to a beauty parlour.

Within, however, her ladyship found an air of comfort and refinement. A portrait in oils of the late Dr Turner, imposing as a privy councillor, looked down austerely from the tall overmantel upon his widow's pleasant, dimly-lighted parlour. The floor was strewn with aromatic herbs, which combined with the freshly cut roses in a bowl of Italian ware to render the room agreeably fragrant. An eastern carpet, bright-hued, covered the long table; chairs upholstered in red velvet stood beside it, and some delicate pieces of Venetian glass sparkled on a tall buffet that was richly carved with little images of nymphs and satyrs.

Here, to her waiting ladyship, came the bright little widow, all eagerness to give welcome and service. My lady suffered herself to be conducted above-stairs to a more spacious room, lined with coffers and presses, whose varied contents were displayed to her admiring and interested eyes. Thus, the Countess, who in reality sought no more than the widow's beautifying gloves, spent a full two hours surveying brocades for gowns, embroideries from the Levant, laces from Flanders, comfit boxes and scent phials from Italy, knitted stockings of spun silk from Spain, besides ribbons, garters, shoulder-knots and a dozen other fripperies of home manufacture. And in the end she departed without the gloves, because the widow assured her that she kept no stock of them, since to be effective they must be freshly prepared. A pair of them should be ready for her ladyship in two days' time.

Thus it came to pass that two days later my lady was again in Paternoster Row.

Mrs Turner received her with the announcement that she had stayed in town especially in order to serve her. Now that the hot weather was upon them, it was her custom to spend most of her time at her country house on the river, leaving the conduct of affairs in Paternoster Row to her woman Foster and the girls under her charge, as well as to her man Weston. This Weston, the unprepossessing fellow who admitted Mrs Turner's patrons was, she said, a trained and able apothecary, who had been in her late husband's service. He was skilled in making up the various pomades and unguents to her recipes.

She summoned him now to bring the gloves which had been specially prepared. Together with these she supplied a little pot of pomatum that was fragrant with some hyacinthine distillations, of which Mrs Turner asserted that the secret was hers alone. To demonstrate exactly how it should be used, she took the Countess' right hand in her own left, and proceeded to stroke it from the finger-tips to wrist as if applying the unguent.

And now there came a sudden oddness in the widow's conduct.

Midway through this operation she abruptly checked, and the Countess felt her hand gripped with almost hurtful firmness. Mildly surprised she looked up to find Mrs Turner's face enigmatically set. The dark eyes were dilated under the arched brows, now slightly raised; the red lips were tightly compressed.

"What is it?" quoth her puzzled ladyship.

"Sh! Wait! Don't speak! Don't move, or it will escape me. Wait, wait!"

The tone, so mysteriously impressive, wrought upon the younger woman's imagination. This and the tightened grip upon her hand, the altered countenance and the quick, excited breathing of the widow gave her the impression of being in the presence of something abnormal and uncanny.

"Yes," said Mrs Turner, her voice hushed almost to a whisper. "Yes! I feel it plainly. It is all about you, like… like a mist. It saturates you, yet you yourself are scarcely aware of it."

"What?" begged the Countess. An odd indefinable fear began to stir in her. "What?"

"The longing, the yearning, the love that is being poured out for you, offered up to you like an incense. It is all about you in billowing clouds. I feel it so plainly. Oh, so plainly."

"You feel it?" The Countess began to be afraid. She sought to release her hand; but the effort was too feeble to defeat the other woman's firmness. "What do you mean? What do you feel? How do you feel it?"

"Do not ask me how." Mrs Turner's tone was vehement, for all that it remained low and awed. "There are mysteries none can explain: forces known to some only because they have experienced them. I gather it all from the touch of your hand. Almost I see the man whose longing wraps you about. He is noble and great, comely, gallant, young; he is high-placed. High-placed. He stands near the King himself. And you... And you... "

She broke off abruptly, and let fall the hand. Abruptly her voice returned to its normal pitch. "I can tell you no more. At least, not now."

The girl was staring, wide-eyed, amazed, even troubled. Her face had lost some of its colour; there was an agitation in her breathing. She was in the presence of something she did not understand, something that perplexed, disturbed and awed her.

She said so frankly, and begged for explanations, a request that seemed to shake the widow with sudden fear.

"Oh! I should not have told you. I should not! I could never make you understand these forces which I do not understand myself. They govern me; they compelled me to speak. I had no more will than the leaf that is swept up by the breeze. Of your pity, sweet lady, forget what I've said. Forget it."

The Countess was moved by her distress. Compassionately she set a hand upon the widow's shoulder. "Why, so I will, since you ask me. Say no more."

"And you'll tell no one? You promise me that? It was my affection for you betrayed me. Promise! Promise!"

"I promise it." The Countess was emphatic in her desire to allay the little woman's alarm. "I've forgotten it already."

Mrs Turner knew too much of womankind to suppose that the affirmation was exact, and my lady discovered it on her way home. Far from having forgotten the little incident, she could turn her thoughts to nothing else.

Those words so oddly spoken in that hushed voice, subtly conveying almost a suggestion that the speaker uttered them despite herself, continued to ring in her ears.

" ...the man whose longing wraps you about. He is noble, great, comely, gallant, young. He is high-placed. He stands near the King himself."

To whom could these words allude but to Robin Carr: that noble, comely, gallant young man whom her thoughts never quitted, and than whom no man stood nearer to the King?

There was something as supernormal and uncanny about the matter of the disclosure as about its manner. Lady Essex had heard, of course, of seers and diviners, who had power to perceive distant, past and future things, and she believed in the reality of their powers as implicitly as did most people in her day. It must be that gifts of this nature were in the endowment of Anne Turner. They were accounted unholy of origin by the general, from the King himself who condemned them in his essay on demonology. But did it follow that they were really so? And, unholy or not, they touched upon the one matter on which her ladyship passionately desired more knowledge.

It is not surprising, therefore, that early on the following morning she was to be found again at the sign of the Golden Distaff driving the widow hard with questions which appeared to terrify her, and which she struggled fearfully to elude. Driven mercilessly to the last ditch by the Countess' importunities, she made a distracted appeal ad misericordiam.

"Oh! I was mad, mad, to have told you what I felt. I should have been on my guard against it. If I had esteemed you less it would have been easy to have found strength."

"But why? Why? Where is the harm?"

"The harm?" Mrs Turner's fair winsome face was distorted by fear; the plump body, so warm and shapely, was shivering. "There is no harm. There is no wrong in what I did. But there is the danger of how others might regard it."

"If that is all you fear, Anne, be at peace. No living soul shall know of it from me."

"Dare I trust you?" The widow clung to her. "Will you promise that?"

"I will swear it," said the Countess solemnly.

Profusely Mrs Turner thanked and blessed her, pronouncing her an angel of goodness as of beauty.

Her ladyship, standing slim and straight, smiled gently down upon her, chiding her for her foolishness in so unnecessarily alarming herself.

"Perhaps I have been foolish," Mrs Turner agreed, now entirely soothed. "After all, it is not as if I had read the future for you."

"The future?" Her ladyship was quick to fasten upon this. She set a hand, a fine jewelled hand, upon Mrs Turner's shoulder. "Would that be possible? Would it?" Eagerness and apprehension were blended in her young face and parted her red lips.

Mrs Turner recoiled, and back came the panic to her countenance.

"Why do you ask? Why do you seek to probe?"

"Why don't you answer?"

"Do you seek the ruin of a poor woman who desires only your good, my lady?"

Lady Essex accounted that her question, after a fashion, had been answered.

"Why will you suppose that of me? How could I have any such intentions? I need your help, dear Turner. I need knowledge of what is to come; knowledge of…of… " She broke off in maidenly hesitation, and her cheeks grew red. "Oh, Anne! If you have this power and you will use it for me, I will pay you well."

"My God! My God!" The widow was in obvious distress. She wrung her hands. She sped on tiptoe to the door, opened it and looked out into the passage. They were in the little ground-floor parlour with its Venetian glasses and cut flowers and the stern portrait of the late Doctor Turner.

Having reconnoitred, the widow seemed to breathe more easily. "My God! If Foster or one of the women should have overheard you! It is not safe even to mention such things here. They are too dangerous. So dangerous that I would not venture on them for all the gold in the world."

Lady Essex sighed. She was pale now, and full of hesitation. "You give me no hope, then?"

"Hope?" The widow stared at her out of a face that was now expressionless. "What do you want of me? That I take the risk of being burnt for a witch?"

"Where is the risk in serving me? I can be silent. For my own sake I should have to be. You are forgetting that. And I would pay you well, Anne," she repeated.

At this the widow flared up. "Have I not said that not all the gold in the world would tempt me? I do not do such things for gold. I drive no such trade. God be thanked, I am in no need to do so. But... if your need is urgent, I would do it for love of you!"

"Why then... When, Anne? When?" cried the eager child.

The widow smiled wryly. "You are quick to take me up. Well, well, you shall have your way; and I pray God I may not suffer for it. I know no other living soul for whom I'ld do so much. Nor can I promise a deal, for my skill is not so great as that of some. Still, what I can I'll do since I've promised."

"God bless you! Oh, God bless you, Turner."

"But not here. It is too dangerous here. And I need things which are not here at hand. Also in the peace and quiet of the country results are better. I go to Hammersmith this afternoon. Come to me there. Not tomorrow. Not on the Lord's Day. Come Monday. I'll give you full directions. There we shall be quiet, and you shall have your wish, or as much of it as I can afford you. But on your life, my lady, no word of this to anyone, whoever it may be."

The Countess, eager and grateful, pledged herself solemnly to secrecy, and so at last departed content.

Content the widow watched her go. She should deserve, she thought, the warm commendations of Sir Arthur.

Chapter 10

Metheglin

If Mrs Turner's black-and-white timbered house at Hammersmith was not imposing, at least its creeper-clad exterior was attractive, and its interior snug almost to the point of luxury; whilst the garden, which ended in a flagged terrace above the water, extended to some two acres, well planted with trees and shrubs and parterres of flowers. Privet hedges enclosed a kitchen garden, a section of which was devoted to the growth of special herbs, spurges, euphorbiae and plants of a saponaceous nature, employed by the widow in some of her wonder-working preparations. All was well-tended, trim and neat, like Mrs Turner's own person. As a parapet to the terrace on the river's brink there was a low brick wall, in which at intervals little bays had been practised, equipped with seats.

On this terrace on a languid afternoon in July sauntered Mrs Turner with my Lady Essex.

This was the third visit paid the widow by her ladyship in the course of a week, and so far the results had been meagre. The Fates had given but a poor response to the sybil's endeavours to propitiate them.

On each occasion she had retired alone with the Countess to a cool, partially darkened room, opening directly upon the garden, and there, having locked the door, she had taken from a sandalwood box a sphere of solid crystal of the size of an apricot, swathed in black velvet. Her elbows resting on the small table before her, her neat golden head in her white hands, she had sat gazing intently into this lucent sphere, wherein she hoped to see mirrored some of that immediate future into which the young Countess desired so ardently to pry. In the aggregate however, the results had been vexatiously scanty, and they added little to what Mrs Turner without any crystal to assist her had already been able to descry.

Greater success might have attended her endeavours had they not received a check from the Countess on the occasion of the first visit.

In the heart of the crystal, Mrs Turner announced, the comely, gallant, noble youth of whom she had formerly spoken resolved himself out of a mist.

"His blue eyes gaze out at me with a longing that is akin to pain. His lips part. He speaks a name. It is Frances. He bows his auburn head in thought."

But here the Countess had interrupted. "Auburn? Nay! His hair is bright gold."

Instantly, in confusion, she sucked in her breath, as if she would have sucked back the betraying words. The widow, however, sitting as one entranced, gave no sign beyond a momentary dilatation of her narrow eyes that she had so much as heard the interruption. But it clearly conveyed to her two facts. That however much Prince Henry might be enamoured of the Countess, it was not upon him that her ladyship's thoughts were dwelling, and that the eagerness with which the Countess desired more knowledge concerned some other than himself. Like the Prince, this other person must also be young, gallant, comely and noble, and so high-placed that he, too, stood very near the King, since so far, it was clear, these details had described him. The matter required reflection and information. Mrs Turner, therefore, was carefully vague in her disclosures, postponing any definite revelation until she should have had an opportunity of conferring with Sir Arthur.

The ingenious knight had little difficulty in naming the gentleman so inadvertently described by her ladyship.

"Hair of bright gold and stands very near the King?" He frowned a moment in thought. "Who should it be but Carr? Plague take him! Do you say he occupies her thoughts?"

"Should not you conclude as much from what I've told you?"

Sir Arthur considered. "Perdition swallow both him and his trick of commanding fortune. He finds all that he seeks; and all that he doesn't seek, seeks him. Look, Anne; she must be turned aside. Wound her pride. Persuade her that he is indifferent. Tell her… "

"Teach hawks to stoop," said the widow. "You may show me what to do, but never how to do it."

So when next closeted with her ladyship in the seclusion of her cosy bower, she peered into the gleaming orb, she beheld there a figure which she described in greatest detail: tall, handsome, broad-shouldered, magnificent of mien and apparel; the George upon his breast; a jewel in his ear, gleaming through a cloud of hair of the colour of spun gold; a little peaked beard and upturned moustachios about a comely mouth; eyes of clearest blue that were full of laughter; a careless attitude towards all the world.

The Countess listened intently, greedily, unblinking, her bosom stirring under her bodice of green taffeta, which rose to the throat and was there closed by a ruff, encircling her upright collar.

The dreamy, monotonous voice continued: "He stands so high, deems himself so secure in the King's regard that he can be careless of the regard of others. He has lately been preferred. The George upon his breast is newly come there. I see great nobles bowing before him. They address him…by name… 'Lord Rochester.' "

The Countess clasped her hands, leaning farther forward.

"But he recks little of them, or of any. Carelessness is the greatest attribute of his nature. Love has never touched him, cannot touch him, unless it be love of himself; for beautiful as Narcissus, like Narcissus he is in love with his own image. Yet there is one who, misguided, bestows her thoughts on him. Let her poor soul beware the fate of Echo, and put this Narcissus from her mind. He fades. A mist is forming."

The widow paused. Lady Essex had sunk back in her tall chair. Her eyes, a moment since so bright and eager, were veiled now behind lowered lids; her hands, still clasped, had fallen listless to her lap; the colour had perished from her cheeks.

Soon Mrs Turner, still peering intently into the crystal, announced a fresh vision.

"Another comes. This is he who was here before; one who, younger than the other, yet stands even higher, and stands there by right of birth and noble blood. His nobility is stamped upon his face. It comes from the very soul of him. He is the Prince of Wales. He is very earnest. Sh! He speaks. 'I love you, Frances; I love you so that I shall find you wherever you may hide yourself. Soon, very soon we shall meet. I am coming to you now." She paused, to add a moment later: "He's gone; the crystal clears. I can see no more."

She lowered her hands from her face, and sank back in her chair with a sigh. Then with one of her brisk movements she turned her head to glance, smiling, at her companion. At sight of her ladyship's white face, drooping glance, and the lines of pain about her lips, the little widow cried out in sudden concern.

"Why, what has happened, child, to distress you? Is't what I've told you?"

A wan smile lighted momentarily the sweet pale face. "It is nothing." Her voice faltered a little, as if tears were not far off. "You did not tell me quite what I had hoped to hear. Perhaps we are not meant to pry beyond the reach of our natural senses."

"Oh, dear, my lady!" Mrs Turner was on her feet. "Let us out into the air. It is cool in the garden."

And so they came to seek the terrace. Awhile they paced there, then rested, and then paced again, and my lady spoke of going. But Mrs Turner, whose eyes ever and anon raked the bend of the river towards Chelsea, beguiled her to linger, with talk in the course of which she skilfully drew from the Countess a deal more of her mind than her ladyship intended to reveal.

An hour or so was spent in confidences, when at last a gilded red barge of six oars came into view rounding the bend. It kept close to the Middlesex shore, and as it approached two gentlemen in plumed hats were to be seen in the stern-sheets, one sitting and the other standing. He who stood suddenly doffed his hat and bowed, and the widow cried out in delighted surprise.

"Why, it is Sir Arthur, as I live!"

She waved a hand in almost rapturous acknowledgment of the greeting.

Sir Arthur stooped to speak to his sitting companion, who nodded. Then he issued a command to the watermen in their beefeater liveries, and the barge came gliding towards the little jetty at the wall's foot.

Sir Arthur stepped from the vessel, and turned to proffer his arm to the other gentleman, who, disregarding it, leapt nimbly ashore with the easy grace of the athlete. Sir Arthur preceded him up the steps to announce him.

"My dear Anne, I have so praised your metheglin to his highness, that he must stay to taste it."

Mrs Turner gave evidence of being flustered, of being taken by surprise. "His highness! " she gasped, and dropped a low curtsey as the Prince stepped up beside his gentleman.

Into the surprise and even vexation of Lady Essex was woven a suspicion that here was being played a concerted scene, until she saw the blank amazement that overspread the boy's handsome high-bred face, with its finely-arched nose and full glowing eyes. That he was not acting she was instantly assured. He frowned as he turned impulsively to question Sir Arthur.

"You knew of this?"

"Of what, your highness?" The slim dark gentleman seemed taken aback. "On my life," he protested, "I had no thought for anything but the metheglin."

The Prince uncovered, and bowed low to Lady Essex. "This, madam, is a happiness I had no thought to find here."

Her ladyship curtsied in silence, a little trouble showing in her eyes.

Almost before she realised it she was alone with him. He had declined the widow's invitation to go within. He would taste her preparation of metheglin, of which Sir Arthur boasted, out here in the cool; and she had gone off to fetch it, accompanied by Sir Arthur.

Lady Essex remained despite herself in some embarrassment, born of a desire to withdraw, which she knew not how to fulfil. The Prince observed her as she stood leaning on the parapet, straight and slim in her gown of pale green taffeta, her face half averted, her eyes upon the water and the wooded shore beyond. He addressed her without assurance.

"Madam, I have said this is a happiness I had no thought of finding here. Yet I must bless the chance." He drew nearer, and standing close beside her, uncovered, leaving the breeze from the water to ruffle the thick auburn locks about his smooth white brow. "I hope, madam, that you do not altogether contemn it."

"That were discourteous and undutiful, and I trust that I am neither."

"I am not concerned, madam, with either courtesy or duty in you."

She gave him a fleeting glance that was cool and discouraging, as was the half-smile that flickered across her lips. "That is a pity, highness. For I offer both."

"And nothing besides?" He was very eager.

"Nothing besides, I think. Your highness has no claim to more; nor has any man unless it be my husband." Her lips came together firmly.

The Prince's face displayed his boyish annoyance. "Your husband? Pshaw! That's what my father would call a peasebogle. What do you know of a husband, or he of you? Were you ever lovers ere you entered your child-marriage? You use his name deliberately to deter me."

"If your highness perceives so much, why is it your pleasure to ignore it?"

"That is a clear question, Frances." He used her name for the first time.

"But one that your highness need not be at the pains of answering."

He smiled with the least shade of bitterness. "It were a discourtesy not to do. I ignore your coldness because I account it to spring from a mistaken sense of duty."

"Your highness is modest." She turned to face the house, and leaning against the parapet wondered would the others never return.

Prince Henry bit his lip, and as he looked at her, pain was blent with ardour in his eyes.

"Why so cruel, Frances?" Abandoning all subtleties he cried out frankly: "I love you so deeply; so sincerely!"

She allowed her agitation to display itself. She spoke sharply. "Your highness must not say these things to me... "

"Why not, since they are true? Why not? Is your absurd marriage – a marriage that is yet no marriage – to make the obstacle?"

She looked at him steadily. "I have understood that my Lord Essex was your friend from boyhood, your playmate before he became my husband."

He flushed. "What's that to the matter? Does it make his marriage with you less than a crime of your elders? You'll not pretend that you love him, who was scarcely thirteen, a gloomy, awkward boy, when you saw him last?"

"I need no pretences of any kind. I am a wife. That should make me safe from other men's wooings."

"A wife in name only," he insisted. "That is not to be a wife. Such marriages as yours are easily annulled."

"Annulled?" Almost she laughed, but without suspicion of mirth. "And to what purpose the annulment? Or does your highness offer marriage to follow thereafter?"

She looked him straightly between the eyes as she asked the question, and she saw his glance momentarily falter, saw the flush deepen in his face and spread to his brow. An instant he hesitated, brought thus face to face with his own hitherto scarce-considered intentions. Then his boyish ardour and impetuosity supplied the answer.

"By my faith, I will do even that, Frances."

"Even that!" said she, and smiled now with very definite scorn. "I thank your highness for the 'even.' There's a whole world of revelation in that 'even.' It tells of sacrifice, as a last resource."

Her irony stirred his anger. "Am I to be denied the dearest thing in life because I am what I am?" He was passionately sincere. "Am I to go loveless because I was born heir to the throne of England? If so…"

She interrupted him without ceremony. "I have for you, Prince Henry, no such love as you desire of me. Of your pity, then, do not torment me further."

From red that he had been he now went pale. Long he looked at her with hurt, brooding eyes, eyes in which there was something of that bodeful look that haunted the eyes of all the Stuarts. Then he bowed in token of absolute submission to her will, and, like Sir David Wood, before a similar dismissal at her hands, he offered service where love was unacceptable.

"I thank you for your plainness; and I honour you for it. I but beg you to remember that my love for you remains; that I am your servant, Frances, a friend and servant to count on in your need."

"Ah! Now you are good and generous and princely indeed." Impulsively she held out her hand. He took it and bore it to his lips. "For this I honour you so that you almost make me regret that I have not more to give."

"I am content," he said. "Content to be your friend."

But that was not quite all his thought. To have been entirely frank he must have said that he was content to be her friend until he could be more. Lacking though he might be in worldly experience, yet his mother wit revealed to him that between man and woman friendship is to be regarded as the antechamber of love, and in that antechamber he was – since perforce he must be – content for the present to wait with such patience as he could command.

107

At the stage to which things had come, the return of the others was almost as welcome to his highness as it was to her ladyship.

Mrs Turner led the way, followed closely by Sir Arthur, bearing a tall jug. After them came Weston in a white jerkin, carrying a silver tray on which were four Venetian glasses, fashioned to look like agate cups.

The widow's metheglin, cunningly flavoured with ginger, rosemary, betony, borage and thyme, proved to the Prince's palate as rare and pleasant, he protested, as Sir Arthur had predicted. Whilst they quaffed it, Weston was despatched for ale, which he dispensed to the watermen.

Then, to the infinite surprise of Sir Arthur, who had supposed that some hours would be spent here in pleasant dalliance, even at the cost of abandoning the journey to Richmond, the Prince announced that he must push on while the tide served. They re-embarked and departed, leaving Mrs Turner intrigued and Lady Essex very thoughtful.

"You had no knowledge, Anne, that his highness would be coming?"

"I had," said Mrs Turner shortly.

"You had!"

"The crystal forewarned me. Have you forgot?"

"And you had no other knowledge save that? Answer me truthfully."

Whether truthfully or not, Mrs Turner certainly answered volubly and convincingly. How should she know the intentions and movements of the Prince of Wales? My lady did not suppose that he corresponded with Anne Turner?

My lady acknowledged that she did not. She recalled also his obviously genuine surprise at beholding her. She must, then, accept this as a proof of the power of the crystal and of the accuracy of the visions it presented. If that applied to the Prince, it must also apply to Robin Carr, and what the crystal had shown concerning him was not calculated to cast down a lady as intent as my Lady Essex to remember that she was a wedded wife. Yet so downcast and dispirited did she now show herself, that the little widow grew motherly towards her, and in this spirit of motherliness sought her confidence.

The girl gave it as freely as those must whose hearts are surcharged. The sum of it was expressed in the question with which she closed the chapter of self-revelation.

"Is it always so in life, Anne? Do we ever seek to elude that which pursues us, whilst as ardently pursuing that which eludes?"

The widow's narrow eyes grew narrower in sly thought. Pensively she stroked her long upper lip. Towards Sir Arthur she had done her part, and the attitude which Lady Essex disclosed towards the Prince appeared to put an end to that adventure, and so to all chance of profit either for the widow or her lover. The other was a vastly different affair. Mrs Turner looked down a long avenue of possibilities.

After a pause she sighed, and answered very softly and slowly: "There are ways of arresting and overtaking the elusive. There are even ways to compel it to go about and become a pursuer in its turn."

"Ways there may be. But I seem to lack the art of them."

"It is an art that is known to very few. Yet it can be practised, and it rarely fails."

My lady stared at her, struck by the hint of mystery in her tone.

"To what art do you refer? What do you mean, Turner?" The widow took her arm familiarly. There was a new intimacy in her manner, which seemed suddenly to sweep away what was left of the barriers rank had placed between them. Yet oddly enough the Countess of Essex, reared in such proud consciousness of her lofty station, did not now resent it, so urgent was her need. She suffered herself to be conducted to one of the seats embayed in that parapet, and sat there, the widow's hand still within the crook of her arm.

"You shall hear something, child, that I have never told anyone, that I would not tell anyone but you. When you spoke just now it seemed to me that I was hearing my own tale of some years since, when I loved even as you tell me that you love, one who was as unconscious and indifferent as this gallant who has caught your maiden fancy. I speak, my dear, of Sir Arthur Mainwaring. You see, I make no secret with you. I was in despair. I was come so low that I began to think wicked thoughts of taking my own life, since he who was so necessary to me was so completely beyond my reach. That was in the year after Dr Turner died, and when I had set up my shop in Paternoster Row. Sir Arthur used to come there with his sister – she who afterwards married Lord Garston – and I loved him from the moment that I first beheld him."

Lady Essex reflected that love at first sight had been her own case, too, and her thoughts went back to that day in the tilt-yard at Whitehall, three years ago. Her ready sympathy flowed out to this sister-sufferer from the same cruel pangs.

"In my despair I had recourse to the crystal," Mrs Turner resumed. "The blessed gift of scrying has been mine almost from childhood. I first discovered it... But that's nothing to the matter. In the crystal I was shown a man advanced in years, a master of medicine, astrology and alchemy."

She broke off to demand assurances before disclosing more. "What I tell you, child, is secret and sacred between us, not to be shared with any, whoever it may be."

Instantly and fervently the Countess, now a prey to curiosity, interest and hope, gave the solemn undertakings required, whereupon the widow resumed.

"His name and abode were revealed to me together with the assurance that he would supply my needs. I sought him out that night, and told him all. He could give me my heart's desire. Although the price was heavy, had it taken my last angel I must have paid it.

"I came away with a little phial; no more than that, and instructions how to use it. When next Sir Arthur and his sister came to Paternoster Row, I offered them a metheglin which I distilled according to a wonderful recipe. It is the metheglin I gave you this afternoon. They tasted it that day, and in it Sir Arthur drank the contents of the phial, which I had poured into his cup."

She ceased, and sat a moment in silence, bemused, pensively smiling. The Countess shook her by the arm. "Yes, yes? Well? And then?"

The widow continued, the passive smile still hovering about her ups.

"It was in the depth of winter, a foul night of wind and sleet. At dead midnight I was roused by a furious beating on my door. From my window I asked who knocked, and my heart stood still to hear the voice of Sir Arthur imploring me to open. He was drenched to the skin, and splashed from head to foot with mud. He had ridden twenty miles through the storm in obedience, he swore, to an irresistible impulse to come and fling himself at my feet and declare his passion. And until that day he had scarcely been conscious of my existence."

My Lady Essex audibly drew breath. Softly the widow closed her tale.

"There is not in all England, I'll swear, a devouter lover than Sir Arthur has been to me since that night three years ago. Each time I pour for him a cup of metheglin I think of the potion which I mixed in that first cup he had from me, and I bless the name of Simon Forman."

"Who is he?"

"The alchemist who wrought the miracle. There! I've let slip his name. Forget it, my lady."

Her ladyship shook her golden head. Her eyes were preternaturally bright.

"On the contrary," said she. "I must remember it."

Chapter 11

Magic

July was almost out. The weather was insufferably hot, and Whitehall grown stuffy beyond enduring. The King, having dissolved some months ago in a spirit of finality a Parliament too stubborn and recalcitrant to serve his purposes, was determined henceforth to govern Britain without the cavillings and interferences of that vexatious body. Meanwhile he had gone off to indulge his increasing indolence in the comparative cool of Royston, where he hunted and hawked for the benefit of his health. Thence almost daily he wrote fond letters imploring his dear lad Robin to join him.

My Lord of Rochester, pleading urgency of State affairs and yet discharging none of them, lingered on at Whitehall, thereby puzzling Sir Thomas Overbury, who so competently relieved him of the burden of those same affairs which were the pretext of his lingering.

In that workroom of theirs Sir Thomas was at his labours, whilst his lordship, a dazzling figure in claret and silver, with violet hose and violet, silver-edged rosettes to his high-heeled shoes, lounged in his favourite place on the window-seat by the open casement. His listless fingers held a couple of unfolded letters; his pensive eyes stared into vacancy.

Sir Thomas glanced at him furtively so frequently that it is to be doubted if the secretary's interest was really in the documents upon which he laboured. Presently he threw down his pen and leaned back in his chair.

"The King has written to you again, I see," he said, his glance upon the sheets in his lordship's hand.

My lord looked at him almost coldly. His mood was peevish. "You see too much, Tom."

"I need as many eyes as Argus in your service. Be thankful that I have them." He paused as if waiting. Then finding the pause in vain, he resumed: "Does the King's letter to you touch upon this business of the Paris Embassy?"

"No." His lordship showed scant interest. Nevertheless, he condescended to ask: "What business is that?"

"His majesty is considering the recall of Digby. I can perceive no reason for the step. Digby is able and punctual, and he has served us well. Also he is well liked at the French court. His removal would be a blunder, and as a blunder should be avoided."

His lordship nodded almost vacantly. But this was not enough for Sir Thomas.

"Do you agree, Robin?" he asked him, and roused him by the sharpness of his tone.

"Agree? Oh! Ah! You'll have good reasons for what you say. You're better informed in the matter than I am. Of course I agree."

"Then I'll draft a letter to his majesty in that sense."

Again his lordship languidly nodded. "Ay. Do so. But – " He checked on a thought. "Does his majesty give no reason for considering the change."

Overbury's lips tightened in the least suggestion of a smile. "No direct reason. But possibly an indirect one in that he names the man whom he desires should replace Digby."

"Well? Whom does he name?"

"Myself," said Sir Thomas.

"Yourself?" It took his lordship a moment to understand. "D'ye mean you are offered the French Embassy by the King?"

"No less. It's a dazzling offer that would carry my ambitions as far as ever they've soared in dreams."

His lordship's face was blank with astonishment. "By God! The King has grown to love you singularly on a sudden!"

"Is that how you read it? Oh, Robin, Robin! The King but shows how he detests me and desires to be rid of me. And there you have the reason for the recall of Digby clear enough, although not expressed. He desires you at Royston with him, and to all that he already holds against me he now adds the blame of keeping you here at Whitehall. I am a thorn in the flesh of majesty to be plucked out one way or another."

"If that is so, why should you not profit by it, Tom?"

"And leave you where you now stand? That were a poor fulfilment of the word I pledged you when I took service with you. No, no, Robin. You and I stand together. Because you resist the King when he would kick me out of Whitehall, he now tries to lure me away with bribes which he hopes may outweigh my love for you. Let be. All that's to consider is that, after all, the King's letter to me amounts to a royal command, and that to disobey it is akin to treason. It is not, therefore, for me to refuse the office, but for you to put forward the sound reasons, first why it would be impolitic to remove Digby, and secondly, why you cannot possibly dispense with a secretary so skilled as I am in foreign matters. Shall I draft the letter for you?"

"In God's name," said his lordship fervently.

"I'll do it today. Meanwhile it will help if you do as the King bids you, and join him at Royston."

"At Royston?" His lordship's look showed how distasteful was the suggestion.

"In Heaven's name, why do you linger here? What do you find to hold you?"

"Ah!" ejaculated his lordship, and to Overbury's annoyance fell again to musing.

After a moment Sir Thomas returned to the attack: "You neglect your interests and your health in lingering. It is well perhaps to make yourself desired. But within limits. For desire of any kind can languish and perish if starved long enough. And your health would fare better at Royston, than in the hot reek of Whitehall."

"My health is well enough."

Sir Thomas looked him in the face. "I find you, like Hamlet, 'sicklied o'er with the pale cast of thought.' You look distempered for all your finery. Odd's my life, man, why so gorgeous? Your clothes would keep a bishop for a twelvemonth."

"Peace!" It was an irritable growl. His lordship rose. "I am to dine with my Lord Privy Seal."

"Is that the explanation? By the achievement of your tailor, I should judge you to be the guest of the Pope at least." Then on another note he added: "You grow friendlier than may be wise with my Lord Northampton. Nay, now, patience, Robin! For, as your mentor, this concerns me. This suggestion of a Spanish marriage for the Prince of Wales has made two parties in the State where there were three before. The Queen and Pembroke and the Prince himself are on one side to oppose it, whilst the Howards, as Catholics and in the pay of Spain, uphold it. The King in the role of Solomon holds the scales. Either party may prevail with him in the end. Each party knows that it would take a long stride towards prevailing if it could win you to its side. That keeps both civil. Keep them so until the events shall show where the best interest lies. I cannot think that it will lie with Spain; therefore I counsel that you do not grow too close with that fox Northampton."

Lord Rochester considered, fingering his little beard. "He's very amiable and friendly," said he slowly.

"From the teeth outwards. That's Henry Howard's way. The most delusive flatterer in the world, and as false as he's sweet. No man knows what he carries in his heart."

His lordship nodded. "Rest you, I'll practise the like by him." He stood in thought a moment by the table. Then taking one of the two sheets he held, he placed it before Sir Thomas. "Can you resolve this riddle for me, Tom?"

Overbury's attention was at once caught by the fantastic writing. The characters were Gothic, and their elegant form suggested a practised and scholarly penman, who chose this means of dissembling his hand. It was intriguing. More intriguing still was the matter it contained.

Chance has revealed to me the secret of a lady's heart, which my regard and love for your lordship drives me to make known to you. Of this lady I dare no more than indicate that your lordship is already well acquainted with her, that she is sprung from one of the first families in the land, that a prince pays court to her, and that she might not remain insensible to his insistence if she had not already bestowed her virgin heart upon your lordship, of which your lordship is not yet aware.

It bore by way of signature the legend, "One who wishes well to your lordship." Sir Thomas looked up at the magnificent figure beside him. Humour struggled with gravity on his long pale face.

"It is concise and elegantly couched. Writ by a scholar, that is plain. So much it tells me. The rest you should be in better case to infer than I. That is, as to who should be concerned to inform you that the Lady Essex sighs for you."

"Ah! So you, too, think that the Lady Essex is meant?"

"Think? It's plain. What is less plain is why anyone should be concerned anonymously to disclose it to you. Is it a trap, by chance?"

"A trap?" His lordship was startled. Then he brushed the suggestion aside. "Pshaw!"

"I am," said Overbury, "by nature suspicious of all things I do not understand. It is a prudent instinct, common to all animals, including man."

"But to what end a trap?"

"Many things are possible. It might be to increase the discord between yourself and the Prince, who courts her openly; to embroil you with him. Or it might be to make an enemy for you of her husband."

"Her husband is no husband." There was a sudden heat in his lordship's tone. "Besides, he is absent abroad."

"He'll return one day, perhaps before long."

"What then?" The pride and arrogance which his great position at court were engendering in Rochester flashed out in his reply. "To oppose me were but to shatter himself against me."

Sir Thomas raised his brows. "So you've considered it already? You're gulping the bait of this letter?"

His lordship turned away in silence, and sauntered to the window. He spoke presently with his back to Sir Thomas, his eyes upon the Privy Garden below.

"It needed not this letter," he confessed, "to turn my thoughts to her."

Sir Thomas frowned at his lordship's back, and for a moment was very thoughtful.

"You are telling me that this revelation is welcome to you."

"So that if it be a gin, it is one into which I must have walked before long without any beckoning."

"But being beckoned, you'll run instead."

"That is the only difference. And now you know why I am glad to dine at Northampton House. Politics have no part in this. My Lord Privy Seal is not the attraction. I'll keep my head where he is concerned."

"By losing it to his niece. Yet the one may lead to the other."

Lord Rochester wheeled sharply. "It is not in your mind that Northampton may have writ that letter?"

Sir Thomas laughed outright. "I was fool enough to think it for a moment. But on reflection I perceive the thought to be an idiocy. The Essex alliance is too valuable to the worldly Howards that they should jeopardise it to make the daughter of their house your mistress. Besides, they have their pride. No, no. It was no Howard who composed this lure." He sighed and frowned. "If I bid you ignore it, you'll ignore the advice. But in God's name walk warily. You've much to lose, Robin."

"I am not by nature rash."

"By nature, no. But by love the most prudent lose their caution. I trust you'll dine with a good appetite."

His lordship departed to his barge, which waited at the Privy Steps. He was rowed to Northampton House in a state of eagerness such as no previous visit to my Lord Privy Seal's had aroused in him. The letter, as he had confessed, came but to add a spur to inclinations and longings which had been faintly astir in him since last he had walked and talked in the same garden with her ladyship.

Lady Essex was with her uncle when he arrived. Her reception of him was graciously friendly and no more. Sir David Wood was also of the party, and they were moderately gay at dinner, saving that her ladyship fell so far short of her usual norm of vivacity that presently her old uncle rallied her upon the fact.

He found her pale, he declared; asked her on whom she had bestowed the delicate roses that usually blossomed in her cheeks, and marvelled that she did not join the court at Royston and seek the enjoyment of the country air. She replied that she was going tomorrow with her mother. Hitherto affairs had kept her father fast at Whitehall, but it was now decided they should leave him there. And all the while she was nervously fingering a slender phial in her waistband, containing some drops of a precious and very costly elixir which she had purchased from Simon Forman, the alchemist, and asking herself how she could convey it into Lord Rochester's cup of wine. As he sat facing her across the board, circumstances offered her no opportunity. Consequently her spirits sank, and the vivacity upon whose diminishing her uncle had commented became utterly extinct.

Disappointment was not hers alone. As the time for departure approached, Lord Rochester, to whom the letter he had received was as a spark to tinder, began to think that he had his pains for nothing in dining thus privately with my Lord Privy Seal. But a sudden uplifting awaited him at the very last moment. As he was taking his leave, her ladyship announced her own return to Whitehall, and begged a place in his barge for the journey.

He dissembled his joy as he handed her into the carved and gilded cabin in the stern, whose curtains he loosed, to shelter her from the ardour of the sun, and also from the eyes of the watermen in their blue and silver liveries and other wayfarers upon the river.

As the barge was pushed off, he took his seat beside her on the red velvet cushions, bareheaded and tongue-tied. Fortunately she came provided with matter for discourse.

"My lord, I have a favour to beg of you," she announced.

"My lady, you make me happy," said he, with such sudden sincerity and fervour that her gentle eyes fled startled from his glance and a tumult started in her breast.

She repressed her agitation, however, to make her request, and in making it produced a folded paper. It was a petition from Sir David Wood for certain dues, for services rendered.

Sir David, trading upon such interest as his avowal of affection might have awakened, had not scrupled to use her for the purpose of conveying this petition directly to the very fount of patronage, rather than entrust it to the ordinary channels. And she, out of the gentle meekness of her nature, had very readily consented, whilst warning him that her influence with my Lord Rochester was slight indeed.

She went on now to speak of Sir David's worth, his ability and the esteem in which her uncle held him, and was still dwelling upon these matters when his lordship interrupted her.

"What signifies, madam, is that you ask it. You may count the petition granted." He thrust the paper into the bosom of his claret and silver doublet. "Have you no other commands for me? My happiness lies in serving you."

She could look the Prince of Wales steadily between the eyes and chop wit with him when he spoke so. But Robert Carr's comparatively restrained profession of service left her confused and tongue-tied.

"You are very gracious to me, sir," she answered him mechanically.

His right arm was flung along the cushions and the shallow rail behind her. He bowed his head to peer under the brim of her dark beaver hat with its sweeping ostrich plume of green, and his glance was at once ardent and suppliant.

"Could any man whom you honoured with your commands be less?"

She looked up into his face. For an instant their eyes met and held each other, and in that instant all seemed said and all changed between them. Then her glance fled in a panic of shyness, and the next moment he was speaking.

"Frances!"

That was the only word he uttered. But the tone of his voice said all that was ever packed into the most eloquent declaration. It caressed, it avowed, it claimed.

A pause followed. Then he leaned nearer. His right arm was resting, though very lightly and timidly, against her shoulders, his left hand reached across and closed upon both hers where they lay in her lap. She made no attempt to release them. She sat very still, scarcely seeming to breathe.

"Frances!" he said again, and now, in addition to the rest, there was an insistence of entreaty in his voice.

Responding to it, she half turned to him. His right arm closed about her, and his left went round to meet it. She was in his arms, against his breast, her eyes veiled behind lowered lids, the half-gloom of the curtained cabin befriending them.

He bent his head and kissed her lips. Thus for a long moment they clung, and almost swooned in the ecstasy of that first communion. Then they fell apart, to stare, half scared, half laughing each at the other, whereafter she buried her face in sudden burning shyness upon his breast, and in her turn uttered his name, almost upon a sob.

"Robin! Robin!"

The oars slackened, to warn these two, to whom the world about them was just then forgotten, that they were at the Privy Steps.

As he handed her from the barge, something slipped from her left hand and dropped with a tiny splash into the water. It was the phial procured from Simon Forman. The magic of its contents was no longer needed.

Chapter 12

Scandal

The affairs of England represented by those heaped documents which made ramparts about Sir Thomas Overbury's writing table were suffering neglect. Sir Thomas in shirt and breeches sat writing verses. You will not find them in any edition of his *Collected Works*, for these were verses written not in his own name but in that of another. They were being conceived to serve the purpose of an amatory epistle.

As he paused in his labours, he smiled. It was not merely that he took a poet's complacent satisfaction in his conceits, his rhythms and jingles. It amused him that having lent his wits to Carr to build him up into the simulacrum of a statesman and help him win a king, he should now be lending them to provide him with the garment of the complete and perfect lover and so help him win a mistress.

And the thought of this mistress, also, afforded matter for grim amusement and satisfaction to that saturnine gentleman. There should be a pretty scandal presently to the profound vexation of the stiff-necked, worldly Howards, and it should effectively put an end to any danger of alliance between them and Rochester, such as Overbury dreaded on every ground. Therefore he addressed himself with zest to his task on that summer morning, the morrow of the day on which Lord Rochester had dined with my Lord Privy Seal and brought the Lady Essex back to Whitehall in his barge.

121

His lordship had escorted the lady to her lodging in the palace, and thence had come to Overbury hot-foot and aglow with his success.

"I mind me you said once – on that day in the tennis court – speaking of my Lady Essex, that you could write sonnets to her if any would buy them against his needs. Do you remember?"

"I remember well; though I did not say if any would buy them, but if the Prince of Wales would buy them."

"The Prince of Wales or another, what odds, man?" There was a touch of impatience in his lordship's tone. "What skills is the capacity. I want you to exercise it now for me. And this at once. For tomorrow I go to Royston, following your advice."

"What else do you follow in going there? I hear that the Lord Chamberlain's lady is bound thither, and no doubt her daughter will be going with her. But that's no matter. You shall have the sonnet. Tell me where you stand that I may know how to fashion it as if it were your own."

My lord told him, and Sir Thomas was relieved to infer that the letter in Gothic characters, if still mysterious, was, at least, no trap.

The sonnet was now written, and he was adding final touches to it, lovingly polishing it, as a lapidary polishes a gem, when Rochester swept in, a very different Rochester from the one who had lounged there on the window-seat twenty-four hours ago. The gloomy, pensive man of yesterday was transfigured into a being brisk and radiant. He came to fling an arm about the shoulders of his mentor and secretary, his guide, philosopher and friend in the fullest sense of the terms.

"Well, Tom? Well? And is it done? Is it done?"

"It is that," said Overbury, catching as by infection something of the other's Scottish diction. "Look, and content you. I have laboured on it these four hours and more. The Italian manner is plaguily cramping. But not Ben Jonson himself could have served you better."

My lord took up the proffered sheet, and read the first line aloud: "O Lady, all of Fire and Snow compounded... "

There he broke off in sheer enthusiasm. "Man! That's a grand conceit! 'O Lady, all of Fire and Snow compounded!' A grand invocation, Tom! And it expresses her finely. A soul of fire, and a chaste purity, cold and spotless as driven snow."

Sir Thomas coughed. "The image was intended to be purely physical. The fire is in her hair, her glowing eyes, her scarlet lips, which no doubt could be fiery upon occasion. The snow is in her white breast and all the rest of her which we may presume to be as white."

"I see. But why not spiritual, too? Why not?"

"Because I would not have her suppose that you wrote either as a fool or a mocker. A woman has no love for either."

"A fool or a mocker?" My lord was frowning. He took his arm from the other's shoulders and stood stiffly upright. "Why must I be either?"

"The talk of the court is that his highness has singed the wings of his puritanical austerity at her shrine. Were you not to substitute yourself as the holocaust, it is possible that in time he might be quite burnt up."

His lordship was annoyed, and showed it.

"It is not possible at all. And you know it. As for the court's lewd talk... Pshaw! There never was a pure and lovely flower in any garden but slugs must be defiling it."

"It's a poetical conceit," Sir Thomas approved.

My lord shrugged ill-humouredly, and moved away to resume the perusal of the sonnet. As he read his ill humour was dissipated; his eyes kindled and his cheeks flushed with pleasure.

"Man, ye've a gift!" he cried at last.

"Several gifts, Robin; several; as is known to all the world, and to none better than myself. Will the verses serve?"

"Serve! Good lack! It is the very key of Heaven. There's magic in it."

"A magic key! Well, well, let it unlock for you the door to the Garden of Delight."

"I'll copy it at once. Lend me a pen."

123

"Here is the very quill that wrote it: from the pinion of neither Pegasus nor turtle-dove as it should have been, but of a common goose. In time you may come to find that appropriate. Men often do."

But my lord never heeded him. He went about the task of copying the verses in his fairest hand; then folded, sealed and superscribed the missive and took his leave. He was departing for Royston, whence he would write. His train of coaches was already waiting; for he travelled, as he did all things nowadays, like a great prince, with a state inferior only to that of the King himself.

At the last moment he remembered a paper in the breast of his doublet, and plucking it forth tossed it down upon the table.

"There's a petition I desire to grant. My Lord Chamberlain will sign and seal what's needed."

He departed in haste, leaving Sir Thomas to unfold and scan the document at his leisure. Sir Thomas frowned over it. He knew little of the career of Sir David Wood, and of that little nothing that should entitle him to a matter of two thousand pounds from the royal treasury. But he did know of him that he was a creature of Northampton's, and this supplied Sir Thomas with an excellent reason why he should cut down the claim.

Upon his own responsibility, then, Sir Thomas made a grant of half the sum petitioned, leaving Sir David, should that not content him, the alternative of suing through the ordinary channels.

Because he could not to a like extent be the arbiter of all other matters in the stream of affairs that flowed daily through his hands, the ensuing fortnight was one of heavy stress for Sir Thomas, who, in addition to ordinary work, found himself under the necessity of sending copious expositions, elucidations and reports to the absent Rochester.

Now the King had given Rochester upon his arrival a cool and sulky reception, had upbraided him with neglect, and had allowed his unreasonable and womanish jealousy of Overbury to transpire in the course of these upbraidings. Robin, his majesty opined, had made of business a pretext. The truth was that he had remained at

Whitehall because he liked better the company he found there than that which his majesty was able to provide at Royston. Majesty was almost in tears that night when he took Robin to task for his indifference. And he refused obstinately to accept any explanation other than that which his petulance placed upon the favourite's absence. But two or three mornings later, when my lord excused himself from hawking with the King on the ground of pressure of affairs, his majesty had cursed like a stable boy, climbed down from the horse which he had already mounted and went off raging to have the matter out with Robin.

Angrily he burst into his lordship's room, and there suddenly checked his imprecations, and stared with rolling eyes.

At a table strewn with papers two secretaries were at work, and Lord Rochester, in bedgown and slippers, a long document in his hand, was pacing to and fro in the act of dictating to one of them. He broke off as the King, all in green, booted to the thighs, a little feather in his conical hat, a heavy hawking glove on his right hand, rolled into the chamber.

They stared at each other for a moment. Then Rochester bowed, astonishment on his countenance.

Where the King had come to storm he contented himself now with a sulky grumble.

"Can ye not leave all this until later? It's a fair morning, Robbie, and the work can keep until after dinner."

"If your majesty so commands. But after dinner I desired your majesty's own word on several pressing matters. A courier from Whitehall came in with these last night." He pointed to the littered table. "Only the more urgent business has been sent on, and it requires early attention."

"To the Deil with it! Let it wait!" The King was peremptory. "Ye're pale. Ye need the air and a gallop to whip the colour to your cheeks." He shambled forward, and pinched them. "Get you dressed. I'll stay for you."

"Your majesty perceives that it is no more than a postponement?"

125

"Ay, I perceive," and he waved the favourite away.

If the royal manner remained surly, the royal heart was uplifted. Here was proof that what his Robin had told him was true. It was affairs that had kept him from the King's side, and not any indifference such as James had feared and too rashly assumed.

As they rode forth together now, the best of friends once more, the King chid him for his zeal. To the devil with affairs. Let him procure more secretaries, let him so dispose that he should not be thus overburdened. The King would not have him kill himself in the service of the State. The State might go hang before any man he loved should kill himself with the labour of looking after it. Where were Cecil and Suffolk and Northampton and the rest? Indulging themselves in idleness while his Robin's excessive conscientiousness made a slave of him. This must not be.

Rochester took order to comply with the royal wishes. He increased the powers and responsibilities of Overbury and gave him the overt decision of practically all home affairs that were put forward directly or indirectly for his majesty's consideration.

But if this left Rochester more time to devote to the King, some of it again was consumed by his attentions to my Lady Essex, which were now so open and constant as to be matter for comment and gossip.

Their relations so tenderly begun upon mutual physical attraction became spiritually enriched during those weeks at Royston by the gifts of soul which each discovered in the other. For Rochester, having once committed the imposture of employing the choice elegancies of Overbury's writings, was forced to continue Overbury in the business of supplying them. Otherwise he must have been driven to explain the cessation of what the lady, herself described in one of her letters to him as "the silver-dropping stream of your lordship's pen."

Sir Thomas, being endowed with a very fertile literary gift and a full sense of subtlety of thought and melody of words, found in the task some measure of that self-expression which is the craving of every man of letters. Where Rochester in his writings would merely have made love, Overbury made literature as well. He wrote, in fact, precisely as he would have written had he been himself the suitor, which at times he almost imagined that he was.

Into the growing amorousness of letters and verses he wove exquisite patterns of tender philosophy and graceful poesy, revealing coruscating beauties of mind that could not fail to dazzle and enchant a sensitive nature.

Rochester, in high delight, observed the daily growing effect of this wizardry of words upon the lady. In their frequent meetings, for which the freedom of Royston gave opportunity, the theme of her discourse would often be derived from those treasured writings. Thus to the erstwhile mere carnal attraction provoked by the splendid beauty of the man came to be added this intellectual spiritual delight in him, transmuting her passion into an ardent worship based on the belief that such graces of body and of soul had never yet been combined in any single person.

So far the love of these two creatures, who had become transcendentally beautiful in each other's eyes, ran a smooth if restricted course, unruffled by the light gossip to which it was giving occasion, but of which it remained unconscious.

Not until the court's return to Whitehall in September did this gossip suddenly assume the proportions of a scandal. It was the fierce jealousy of the Prince of Wales that fired the train. The talk that linked the names of Lady Essex and Rochester had reached the ears of his highness, to wound him both in his heart. and in his pride. It affronted and mortified him deeply to find himself outbidden in the affections of this lady to whom it began to appear to him that he had stooped. Where now was the austere wifely duty which she had pretexted when he had wooed her? And for what, for whom, had she passed him by? For an upstart whom he detested and despised. Accounting this a sign of her unworthiness, his love was transmuted into emotions akin to hatred. These flamed up in him during a ball at Whitehall, as the radiant pair flashed past him and were lost in the courtly throng. By an evil chance her ladyship dropped a glove, and was unconscious of the loss.

Sir Arthur Mainwaring, standing by, pounced upon that slender perfumed simulacrum of her lovely hand, and in all innocence, hoping to deserve well for it, proffered the token to the Prince.

"May it please your highness, the glove of my Lady Essex!"

The Prince stiffened and recoiled, as if shrinking from the touch of something unclean and vile.

"And what have I to do with it?" he asked, in a tone that withered the smirking courtier before him. Then his lip curled terribly, and in a voice that carried far and rang in a score of listening ears: "It has been stretched by another," he added, and swept on.

Those words lighted such a blaze of scandal that my lady's mother, the easygoing and none too scrupulous Countess of Suffolk, awoke to the necessity of taking steps to stifle it at the source. On the one hand, there was the responsibility towards the absent Earl of Essex which urged her to put an end to this growing and perilous intimacy between her daughter and the favourite; on the other, there was the position and power of Lord Rochester which made it dangerous to apply to the matter the measures she would have taken in the case of any other man.

In her distraction she took counsel with her husband, who, reduced to a like perplexity by the alternatives before them, went off to take counsel in his turn with his uncle, Northampton.

Northampton remained unperturbed. "Why so fearful? It might be turned to account. It might serve to bring Rochester over to our side. And if we have Rochester we have the King."

My Lord of Suffolk exploded. "And I am to pay for that with my daughter's harlotry? God's wounds! Here's pretty counsel for a father!" And the swarthy little man stamped about the room in a passion, tugging at his black beard and using stout sailor oaths from his seafaring days.

The old Earl, lounging back in the chair at his library table, derided him and his milksop scruples. They belonged to some long-dead age, he asserted. His nephew had not kept pace with the times. After all, it was worth some little sacrifice to win the King over to their side. And when all was said, such an affair as this with Rochester would not make Fanny any less virtuous than any other lady at the court of King James.

His nephew declined to hear more. In unequivocal terms he pronounced his uncle a ribald old man of sin.

"You're not even shrewd in your lewdness," he concluded. "For the thing would never bring you the fruits you hope. You'll never have Rochester as long as Rochester has Overbury, no matter what you do or what any of us does."

"So that's the source of your sour puritanism," the old Earl mocked him.

"Think so if you choose. I am going. I am going to write to Essex and tell him it's high time he came home and claimed his wife."

The vulture head of Northampton slewed round on its scraggy neck so that his eyes might follow his departing nephew. "You're a fool, Tom, as I've always known."

My Lord Suffolk slammed the door for only answer. Northampton shrugged and sneered. Then he grew thoughtful. Perhaps Tom Howard was not such a fool, after all. Perhaps he was right when he said that as long as Rochester had Overbury no man should have Rochester, no matter what price he chose to pay. The recollection of those words reduced my Lord Privy Seal to gloomy thought. They brought him to suspect that but for Overbury he would long since have made Rochester his puppet, and, through Rochester, the King. Never had there been such a chance of accomplishing this as now, when Rochester might so easily be lured into the Howard influence by Frances. But in despite even of that, Suffolk was right. Overbury was an insurmountable obstacle. His hold upon Rochester was something as unbreakable as it was incomprehensible to Northampton.

Long he sat there, his chin upon his bony hand, his old head full of evil thoughts from which he could hatch no practical measures, beyond a conviction that if Suffolk were not quite a fool in other matters, he was certainly a fool to bring Essex home at such a moment.

Chapter 13

At Audley End

Alarums and excursions followed now upon the spread of the scandal.

My Lord Suffolk, to remove his daughter from its orbit and from the propinquity of Rochester, decreed that she retire with her mother to the family seat at Audley End.

Frances, in rebellion against a decree which must separate her from her lover, displayed for the first time some of the strength of character and determination which underlay the sweetness of her nature, and offered a firm opposition to parental wishes; and this notwithstanding that my Lord Suffolk's language became more and more that of the rough sea dog he had been, and less and less that of the urbane Lord Chamberlain he was become.

Viscount Rochester went off in dudgeon to take counsel with Overbury upon measures to avenge the deadly insult of Prince Henry's words. Overbury made philosophy.

"You begin to perceive what a disintegrating, explosive and metamorphosing force is contained in love. It can exalt the timid into heroes and spur them on to high endeavour and to glory. It can abase the worthy into clowns and betray them into meannesses and vileness. Prince Henry is suffering from the same distemper as yourself. Its manifestations are different because the course it runs is different. You prosper in it; he does not. Compassionate him. It is humane. It is also prudent. Because, being the King's son, he is beyond the reach of your resentment."

Naturally this did not help his lordship's justifiable anger. He desired, he made it clear, to tear down the sky in his wrath. Sir Thomas sought to pacify him along other lines.

"You may safely leave his highness to the punishment of his own conscience. He is a young man of noble and generous nature who has been false to himself in a moment of jealous fury. So false that he has sought to defile the very thing he worships. It is a common expression of jealousy, and one which he will bitterly regret when the balance of his reason is restored. I doubt if he will ever again be able to look upon Lady Essex without shame. Leave him to the punishment of that. You cannot send the length of your sword to the Prince of Wales. Besides, anything that you may do will only feed the flames of scandal. After all, it is not as if an honest love were in question."

At this Rochester flared up again. In what was his love not honest?

"In that the lady is the wife of another man."

This merely brought down upon Sir Thomas a fruitless exposition of the grotesque nature of a marriage under which the lady had remained a maid. Sir Thomas gently opined that this was a shortcoming which it might be left to the Earl of Essex to repair on his return home, which should be taking place before long.

The scene between them was brought to an end by the arrival of a messenger with a note from Lady Essex. It announced in broken-hearted terms that, succumbing to parental tyranny, she would be leaving the court for Audley End tomorrow. To equip herself with certain necessaries she would be that afternoon at the Golden Distaff in Paternoster Row. Would his lordship come there secretly to meet her, perhaps for the last time?

His lordship went. The lady was already waiting in the parlour, with the eastern carpets, the cut flowers and the gloomy portrait of the late Dr Turner.

Each came to the assignation with a deal to say to the other, all of it plentifully rehearsed in their minds on their way thither. In each other's presence they forgot it all, or most of it, and in each other's arms did little more than sigh and kiss and weep.

What little they did say amounted to vows of eternal fidelity, which no power normal or supernormal should have power to shatter.

"I am yours, Robin, for all the days of my life," she tearfully assured him. "I shall never belong to any other whatever they may say or do to me. Essex may spare himself the pains of seeking me, for I shall never see him. I swear I never shall. I hate him, Robin. Oh, my dear, I wish I were dead!"

He stroked her head. He laid it against his shoulder, and spoke with his lips against her cheek.

"If you were dead, sweet, what would be left in life for me?"

"What is there left in life for us as it is? Shall we live at all if we are doomed to live apart? Will that be life for either of us?"

Thus they talked on, uttering no more than the unpractical rhetoric of love without any attempt to be constructive since, poor things, they were denied the materials for all that they desired so ardently to build. They perceived that they were made for each other; but perceived also the insurmountable obstacles that thrust them apart. They perceived further, and herein lay their only little comfort, that whilst they were thrust apart physically there was no power on earth could sever them spiritually. In soul they were mated irrevocably, whatever might have happened or might happen to their bodies. Passionately they would cling to the thought of this and find in it what strength they could against the dark days ahead.

And so, with repeated final embraces and tear-bedewed kisses they separated at last, and on the morrow Lady Suffolk and her daughter departed for Audley End.

For days thereafter Lord Rochester gloomed about the palace of Whitehall without a smile for anyone, until the King supposed him ill and sent his new French physician Dr Mayerne to minister to him.

But not all the science which Mayerne was credited with having brought from France could heal the desolation in his lordship's heart. Overbury was in better case to serve his needs; Overbury, with his nimble, facile pen and gift of prosody, to express in terms of fitting beauty my lord's anguish in this separation.

And so Sir Thomas, already overburdened with affairs in which his lordship's part grew daily less, spent what little leisure remained him in pouring out another's heart in song, and thus, vicariously, bringing relief to that other heart's surcharge.

From Overbury's point of view this was no better than a waste of time.

His own object had been fully served by the verses he had already written. The scandal had followed and had achieved the desired purpose in putting an end to any possibility of a closer intimacy between Rochester and the Howards.

Therein Sir Thomas was well content. Like the Earl of Northampton, he, too, had come to watch with personal interest the failing health of my Lord Salisbury. But he was less impatient than the old Earl, because, for one thing, he was still young and could afford to wait; and, for another, time was his friend in that it enabled him to consolidate his own position and Rochester's, so that when a successor came to be required to the office of First Secretary of State, his own established experience and ability, backed by Rochester's influence, should abundantly suffice to secure him the coveted and exalted secretaryship. He suspected – indeed, he had evidence of – the same ambition in my Lord Northampton, whose qualifications for the office combined with his rank to make him the only formidable rival. Could Northampton by hook or by crook win Rochester's friendship, he might prove a real danger to Sir Thomas Overbury, frustrating his aims and leaving him to continue as Rochester's ghost with more labour than had ever been shouldered by a Secretary of State and none of the honours and emoluments that should accompany it.

This danger Sir Thomas now accounted set aside. However cynical he might suppose Northampton, he could not suppose him so lost to dignity and self-respect as to fawn for personal gain upon the hand that had cast this mud upon the Howard escutcheon.

So much being achieved, he accounted all further amorous versifying on Rochester's behalf as a tedious piece of supererogation. He was relieved therefore by a letter from the Embassy in Paris, which arrived one dull November morning, and he almost betrayed his relief in the cheerful tone in which he conveyed its contents to Lord Rochester when his lordship paid him his customary forenoon visit to inform himself of the day's news.

Overbury spoke first of some discontent aroused in connection with a certain monopoly recently granted. He expounded the situation at length until his lordship, wearied and bewildered by details which he followed with difficulty, interrupted.

"Yes, yes. Settle it as you deem fitting. You know more of the affair than I do. Prepare what documents are necessary for signature. Is there anything else of importance?"

Sir Thomas fingered the papers before him, considering. "Nothing connected with affairs. But there's something in a letter from Digby that may interest you. When he wrote, the Earl of Essex had been some days in Paris and was on the point of leaving for England."

His lordship threw up his head; his figure stiffened and slowly his colour changed. For a long moment he stood staring vacantly before him; then with an oath he swung on his heel and stalked away to the window.

Sir Thomas pensively studied the back of that tall, athletic young figure so bravely arrayed in grey and gold, and he smiled a little wistfully under cover of his beard. Then he went to fling an arm about his shoulders, and stood there with him looking through the closed window upon the Privy Garden, so melancholy now in its winter habit, wreathed in a vague mist and sodden by the recent rains.

"Take heart, Robin, and accept the inevitable. To struggle against it is to beat your head against a wall. Courage, child. I'll distil your anguish into one last sonnet with which you shall write Finis to this bitter-sweet chapter of your young life."

"Oh, God!" groaned Rochester.

"Ay, ay, it hurts. But it is inevitable as death. And who faces death bravely kills half its terror. Accept what you are impotent to refuse. Stab yourself once for all with that acceptance, and then leave time to heal the wound you'll make."

"Time!" Rochester was scornful. "How could time ever heal such a wound as that?"

"There is no wound of which human soul is capable which time cannot heal, given courage at the outset. If that were not so, life could not be lived. Time buries all that time has brought. Some things it may not bury as deeply as others. But at least it puts them out of constant sight, and so brings surcease of painful recollection. It will be so with you."

"Ah, never! Never!"

"Others have exclaimed as much and as passionately whilst looking upon the corpse of love before time had had a chance to use his shovel. Yet have they survived to love again. It is one of the laws of life. Take comfort in the assurances it brings."

"It brings me none. I do not accept it. Why must I bow? Why submit to the consequences of an infamy perpetrated by self-seeking ambitious fools when they made this marriage between those children? Frances knew not what she did. She was a child of twelve when they bound her, when they defiled the sacrament of marriage out of greed. Is that defilement to stand? Is she to suffer the horror of this stranger's embraces because of a bond in the making of which she had no part?"

"Ay, ay. For indignation there is every ground. But it is the idle indignation over a wrong that is done and cannot be repaired. The bond was made, and cannot be unmade."

"Can it not? She can be widowed." Rochester's eyes were wild.

"Lord save us! These are the days of King James I, not of Saxon Harold. We are a law-abiding people; not savages. If you kill Essex, in what case shall you find yourself? What grievance even have you against the man? He is as much a victim of this bond as you or Frances; as impotent to untie it if he would."

"Is that so certain? If he were as reluctant as Frances to fulfil its obligations, something might yet be done."

"Something that not the whole bench of bishops could accomplish." Sir Thomas shook his head. "You must bow, Robin, before the inevitable, or you'll head for madness and destruction."

To Robin this must have seemed preferable to the imminent finality of the severance; for, yielding to the madness against which Sir Thomas warned him, he went off that day to Audley End, where his abrupt and wild appearance terrified Lady Suffolk.

For the indiscretion of this visit she upbraided him as roundly as she dared upbraid so great a nobleman, whose power with the King was such that if exerted to the full it might suffice to break her husband and her entire family. She protested that what he did was ill done. Harm enough had his indiscreet wooing already brought upon her misguided daughter. He would add to it immeasurably if he pursued it now when Lord Essex was on the point of arriving home to claim his bride. Almost with tears she besought him to be generous, to take pity upon them, and to depart at once.

His lordship, splashed from riding, a little dishevelled and wild-eyed, looked into that broad, crafty, pock-marked countenance that once had been comely, and felt himself shamed and baffled by her reproaches and her prayers.

She was a large woman of a loose untidy shape which no dressmaker and not even the Catherine-wheel farthingale – of antiquated proportions – could dissemble, and in her present distress she waddled in unlovely manner up and down the hall, where she had received him. A bright sea-coal fire burned on the wide hearth and dispelled some of the shadows in that gloomy place, from whose walls dead Howards and others stared down out of their portraits.

Weary in body from his long ride, and weary in soul from the sustained agony of longings unfulfilled, his lordship's courage left him. He felt himself defeated and constrained to accept defeat. But to depart without sight of his beloved Frances from under a roof that sheltered her was more, he felt, than anyone had any right to ask of him.

"It grieves me to distress your ladyship," he acknowledged almost humbly. "It grieves me to have been the cause of so much past distress. Let your ladyship bear with me out of some thought for my own suffering."

It was a welcome speech to her. It showed her how she might dismiss this importunate gentleman and yet retain his precious favour.

She approached him with an air of motherliness, and set a motherly hand upon his shoulder.

"Dear my lord, I do bear with you for that. My heart is raw for you; for you and that poor child of mine. But, my lord, you know that no sacrifice of mine could avail against what is done. I can only beg you, as I beg her, to be brave, and to accept what Fate has decreed."

He looked into the broad face, whose crafty eyes were now veiled in tears, and considered that not Fate, but she and her husband in their greed had decreed the immolation of their child on the cruel altar of loveless ambition.

"Madam," he begged her, "I cast myself upon your mercy, and implore you to let me see Frances before I go."

The woman's hard mouth tightened visibly.

"To let me see her," he added in accents of utter intercession, "for the last time."

"For the last time? " She scanned his countenance. Its beauty and dejection moved her to belief. If that was all he sought, or was now content to seek, there could be little harm in granting his request. Indeed, much good might follow. Once a definite farewell was spoken between the lovers, the road of resignation should be less difficult to tread.

"You are sincere?" she asked him sharply.

"Madam!" He placed his hand on his heart to stress the assurance which in his tone was blent with reproach for the implied doubt.

Satisfied, she herself conducted him to her daughter's bower, and, with a promise to seek him again presently, she left him there alone with Frances for that last farewell.

But in her satisfaction my Lady Suffolk reckoned entirely without her daughter.

My lord found Frances seated in the bay of a window where she sought to profit by the last of the daylight for the piece of embroidery upon which she was mechanically engaged, an art this in which her skill was very great.

She rose at sight of him, and stood for a dozen heartbeats staring at him as if he had been a ghost. And in that little spell he had leisure to consider her, and was stricken to the heart by her appearance. The roses had all faded from her cheeks; there were dark shadows, stains of suffering and sleeplessness and weeping under her brows and all about those gentle wistful eyes, which he had always known so lively and sparkling. Very slight and frail she looked as she stood there sharply outlined against the leaded casement and the fading daylight.

Then he swept across the room to her.

"Robin! "she whispered, and she was in his arms, laughing and crying at once. "Robin! My Robin!"

Awhile he held her mute against him, kissing her eyes, her hair, her lips. Then, at last, she stayed him with a question: "How have you wrought this miracle?"

It brought him to himself. Brought him from the ecstasy of contact with her to the apprehension of things and factors external to themselves.

"By the charity of your mother," he announced miserably, "I am suffered this occasion of bidding you farewell; of seeing you for the last time alone."

"The last time!" Gone was her suddenly risen exaltation. Dismay had thrust it out. "No, no! Not that! Never that!"

He led her gently towards the hearth, his arm about her. He set her in a tall-backed chair, and went down on his knees beside her, his hands clasping hers which lay limp and cold in her lap. There he, who hitherto had listened to no reason, talked reason to her, the reason which others had talked to him. This out of a sense of duty to the word he had pledged her mother. But, as Overbury would have said, he talked reason from the teeth outwards. In his heart there was no such reason as he uttered. He was the miserable captive of a pledge to utterances against which all his nature and his passion were in rebellion, Nevertheless, he was faithful to the bond, and dwelt upon nothing but the hopelessness of their position, the cruel necessity for final severance.

"Your wedded husband comes to claim you, Frances. He is on his way."

On that he closed. But where he closed she opened.

"My wedded husband? I have no husband. I deny him. I repudiate the act that made me his wife at an age when I knew not what I did. I repudiate it. I belong to you, Robin. You may have me when you will, all that is me. All. For I vow to you, to you and to God here in your presence, that I shall never belong to any other man."

He sought to stop her mouth with his hand. "Dear heart! Sh! That oath!"

"It is sworn, Robin, and I'll never be foresworn. Whether you come to claim me for your own or not, yours I am; for you I'll keep myself while I have life. And unless you come to claim me in the end I pray God that I may not have life long."

Her wild firmness – for there was a wildness in the look and gesture that accompanied her assertion – served only to increase his own despair. He had hoped perhaps that by resignation she would help him to the strength which he was told, and which his own senses told him, he must in honour command. Her more direct and simple view was devastating. She loved and she would possess where she loved or she would die unpossessed and unpossessing.

Resentment against the fate imposed upon her swept her with passion, brought her to her feet and away from his where he still knelt, now empty-handed.

"I am waiting for my Lord Essex, to tell him what I have just told you. I owe him nothing, for in my own self I pledged him nothing. The pledge wrung from a little child was not the pledge of the grown woman. It was a child he married. Let him find the child and take her for his own. I am not she. If when I have explained this to him, he would see reason, if he is a man at all – and God knows I do not even know what he is like to look at, into what he may have grown – if he is a man at all, he will consent to petition the King with me to have our marriage annulled."

His lordship got to his feet with alacrity. Hope new-born lent an elasticity to his weary limbs. Here was something all had overlooked, something which this shrewd lovely girl had been the first to see. Of course, it must be so. What man of honour, or of feeling, would deny a woman who met him with such a plaint and such a demand as those which Lady Essex had announced?

Jettisoned then was his pledge to Lady Suffolk. The circumstances were all changed. If Essex consented – as consent he must – to petition the King jointly with her ladyship for the annulment of a marriage which never having been consummated remained no marriage in fact, whatever it might be at law, then Rochester himself would be at hand to add his own intercessions to a King who could refuse him nothing. The horizon so dark before was on a sudden dazzlingly alight with a hope that was almost clear certainty.

In his sudden exaltation, as he turned upon her a countenance now radiant, and held her from him at arms' length by the shoulders, he grew almost lyrical, and soaring in his new-born confidence over every obstacle ended by employing the ill-omened phrase he had used to Overbury. "Let him know at need that if he insists upon your being his wife, it can only lead to your becoming his widow."

Chapter 14

The Earl of Essex

Robert Devereux, Earl of Essex, arrived in England a couple of days after Lord Rochester's excursion to Audley End, and dutifully presented himself at Whitehall.

His first visit was to his father-in-law, whose letters had accelerated his return.

Any hopes which Lord Suffolk might have founded upon the personality of Essex to accomplish the conquest of Frances and efface from her mind all thought of the brilliant fellow with whose name her own had been so scandalously coupled were extinguished by the first sight of his now adolescent son-in-law. The awkward boy of thirteen to whom the Lord Chamberlain had married his daughter was grown into an awkward, dull young man of twenty, incapable of exerting charm or inspiring interest. He was short in stature, stockily built, and clumsy in his movements. He was of a sallow complexion, with lank black hair and heavy black eyebrows over long-shaped eyes set in very shallow sockets. Poor of brow, he was heavy of nose and jowl, yet the heaviness was of flesh, for the chin was softly rounded and of small bone structure. His mouth was thick, obstinate and stupid. His dress was sombre, of an almost puritanical rigour.

Lord Suffolk's keen dark eyes looked him over sharply, and it was with difficulty that his lordship dissembled his disappointment at time's work upon this object of all his present hopes. They exchanged compliments, and with a view to discovering graces of mind where graces of body were so singularly lacking, his lordship led his son-in-law to speak of his travels. After half an hour of it, he came to the conclusion that for all that the fellow had learnt in his foreign wanderings, undertaken for purposes of education, be might as well have stayed at home.

Then Essex spoke of Frances. He hoped that she was well; deplored her absence from Whitehall, since he had counted upon seeing her that very day; touched awkwardly upon the eagerness with which he looked forward to joining her; and announced his intention of carrying her off with the least possible delay to his place at Chartley.

"I hope your lordship agrees with me that the country is the best place for a young wife… Court life with its idleness, luxury and frivolity is unsettling. Myself I have little inclination for it."

Lord Suffolk added to his other unflattering conclusions about his son-in-law the conclusion that he was pompous and a prig, and he began to be really sorry for his daughter. In his reply, however, be affected lightness.

"Faith, that is a matter that you and Frances must decide between you."

Lord Essex did not answer him in words, but the sudden dull set of his face and the contraction of his brows informed his father-in-law of the young man's deprecation of the idea that Frances should have any part in a decision of that character.

The Lord Chamberlain carried him off to pay his duty to his King.

In the crowded audience-chamber Lord Essex found himself an object of interest. The true reason for this not being apparent, his lordship was not slow to assume it due to his own prepossessions, rank and consequence, and possibly to the fact that he was the son of so very well-remembered a man as his brilliant father, who had been so great an ornament of the Court of Queen Elizabeth. In this last surmise he was accurate enough. Men stared at him, marvelling at the disparity between himself and his sire, almost as much as they stared at him for his wife's sake and because of the scandal about her that was so fresh at Court.

The Prince of Wales made his way across the wide room to greet this old playmate of his boyhood.

"A welcome to you, Robert! You are well-advised to return. A man should stand beside his wife. Lady Essex is too lovely a blossom to be left to languish unguarded in the air of courts."

Thus his highness expressed his content that a husband should place Lady Essex beyond Rochester's reach, just as Rochester had placed her beyond his own. It was very human.

His lordship agreed heartily, thereby provoking among those about them some amusement which he could not understand, and he spoke again of his early removal with her ladyship to Chartley, where he looked forward to living simply with her and farming his estate.

"Estates, like wives," said he sententiously, "need closely husbanding."

Since men laughed outright at this, his lordship supposed that he had been witty.

The King, moving leisurely down the room, was approaching them. His majesty leaned heavily upon the shoulder of the handsomest man that Lord Essex had ever seen, a man tall and beautifully made and magnificently tailored in sulphur-coloured velvet. His doublet was peaked to a tapering waist; his mantle was carelessly worn over one shoulder; his dazzlingly white ruff was edged with little points of gold, and above this ruff a noble golden head was nobly carried.

By contrast with so much splendour of person and apparel, the ageing monarch looked mean, boorish, and almost shabby.

The Lord Chamberlain presented his son-in-law, and visibly startled the King by the presentation.

His majesty grunted: "Huh! Huh!" and his eyes rolled significantly as he slewed round his head to bestow a glance on the magnificent favourite beside him. Fragments had reached him of the gossip attributing to Rochester a suitor's ardent pursuit of Lady Essex.

Then he gave his attention to the stocky young Earl and welcomed him in those terms of fatherly kindliness of which he could be prodigal. Lord Rochester, meanwhile, looked down from his fine height with hard, unfriendly, astonished eyes upon the husband of the woman he loved. Was this dull-faced, lumpish lout the mate they had bestowed in marriage upon his peerless Frances? It was fantastic and horrible. Would such an oaf as this have the courage and presumption to claim to wear the loveliest jewel of the English Court?

Lord Essex spoke, answering some questions of the King's on the subject of the French Court and the conditions of it under the regency of the Queen Mother, and his delivery prepossessed men as little as his appearance. There was about him a certain ludicrous self-sufficiency; ludicrous because assumed to cover his dullness, the meagreness of his observations, the colourless paucity of his expressions. By self-assertiveness of manner he sought to dissemble the unimpressiveness of his matter; desire to convey the notion that he was a travelled, cultured man of the world, capable of ruffling it with the best, succeeded only in exposing his rawness.

The King lost interest in him and passed on, whispering of him presently in Rochester's ear: "A feckless, empty dullard."

Overbury, who had looked on from the background, felt his anxieties allayed. If he was any judge of men, such an obstinate aggressive fellow as this would never forgo his rights, never be persuaded to a joint petition with his Countess for the annulment of the marriage. It followed, therefore, that there must be a speedy end to Rochester's entanglement.

Suddenly Sir Thomas found himself face to face with the splendid Pembroke, the scholarly accomplished brother of Philip Herbert, and the virtual head of the strong party which opposed the Spanish marriage. Pembroke was observing Sir Thomas as keenly as Sir Thomas had been observing my Lord Essex. He addressed him; a rare event, for my Lord Pembroke made no secret of his hostility to Rochester and those who stood by him.

"Your master, sir, will need now to walk circumspectly." There was the suspicion of a sneer upon the handsome lofty countenance.

Sir Thomas smiled pensively. "Your lordship appears to suffer from the same necessity."

"I?" The Earl looked him over from top to toe.

"An innuendo based upon court gossip is hardly of the first circumspection," Sir Thomas explained himself.

"You permit yourself odd liberties." His lordship flushed, for he had been stabbed in a vital place. A mirror of the elegancies, an arbiter of manners, it was his claim to contemn the vulgarities of scandal. Yet Sir Thomas had proved him guilty of the offence.

Sir Thomas' smile became one of utmost amiability. He could excel in the art of subtly wounding.

"Si libuerit rispondere, dicam quod mihi in buccam venerit, meaning that if I choose to reply I must be suffered to say whatever occurs to me. Nothing else were reasonable, or worthy of your wit, my lord."

Thus he stabbed Pembroke again, and this time it was a twofold stab. His parade of glib scholarliness towards one who accounted himself something of a scholar, and who based his disdain of Rochester partly upon the latter's ignorance, was in itself a bitterness to the Earl. It deprived him of the luxury of disdaining Overbury for the same reason; reminded him of the fact that as a scholar Overbury's reputation stood well above his own, and was founded upon solid achievement. He was, therefore, the more acrid in his answer.

"I hope, sir, you will adhere always to the admirable principle of frankness you expound so readily. I had not perceived it to be a part of your equipment. In the exercise of it will you, I wonder, indulge my curiosity? My Lord Northampton, yonder, does he join forces with your master?"

"Ah! Now you probe too deep in emptiness, my lord. What should I know of my Lord Northampton's designs? I occupy so small a place, a very rutae folium, the wrinkle of a leaf, as Martial picturesquely has it."

145

The great gentleman smiled disdainfully. "In that case I must content myself with guessing."

"And you would guess, my lord...?"

The venom bubbled out of his lordship. "That though at times my Lord Northampton may have lapsed from wisdom, he will hardly lapse so far as to lean upon a rotten staff."

"It's picturesque," said glib Sir Thomas. "Almost as picturesque as Martial. But it lacks his accuracy of observation. For the staff is very far from rotten. And as for leaning on it... " He paused to nod in the direction of the King, who with his arm about Rochester's shoulders was passing from the audience chamber. "Where the King leans so heavily, there any lesser man may also lean with confidence."

It was true enough, as Pembroke well knew. Robert Carr had never stood so high or so firmly planted; and it was for Overbury who had set him where he stood to maintain him there by every possible means, nor suffer him to weaken his position by any act of folly. Pembroke, he reflected, was but one of many powerful ones who would be ready enough to take advantage of the least gap they could perceive in his armour. Perhaps, Sir Thomas ruminated, Pembroke fancied that he detected one now as a result of this Essex business, and was already sharpening his weapons in anticipation. But Pembroke was deluded by his hopes. The personality of Lord Essex gave security for that.

Rochester that night had much to say to his friend and guide on the score of Essex, expressive of his disgust at the creature. "To think of Frances as the wife of such a man!" That was the burden of his lamentation. But he made it clear that he had not drawn the same inferences as Sir Thomas of the young Earl's character; for his confidence in the divorce not only remained unshaken, but had been strengthened by acquaintance with the husband.

Sir Thomas said little. The time for words of comfort would follow. In that confidence Sir Thomas rested. That it was well justified the sequel was not long in proving.

The Lord Chamberlain took his son-in-law down to Audley End upon the morrow. A courier had gone ahead to announce their approach, and thus had given the young Countess time to school herself into a certain calm in receiving this husband whom she had last seen as an awkward lad of thirteen.

The lad had meant little to her. The man was a horror to her from the moment that she beheld him. Whether his short thick frame, his heavy jowl and foolish eyes, would have revolted her if she had not beheld at his side the graceful ghost of her lover is matter for speculation.

Her effect upon him was, from her point of view, the most disastrous that could have been feared. He had come with a certain curious eagerness to see how time had fashioned the woman out of the child he had married, and he had found this woman desirable beyond any dream he might have entertained during his years of absence. He was in love with her, furiously and passionately, from the moment that his dark slow-moving eyes came to rest upon her white slim beauty.

The calm cold dignity with which she received him served to add fuel to the fire. How finely this cold pride became her. How much it made her appear the great lady, most worthy to be Countess of Essex and reign at Chartley. She suffered him to kiss her hand, and even her cheek; and if he found both cold to the touch of his lips he blamed for that only the raw November weather.

During supper, at which he was placed beside her, little passed between them. The Earl and Countess of Suffolk watched them meanwhile, and particularly their daughter, with anxious eyes. Thereafter, hoping for the best, her parents withdrew early, leaving husband and wife alone together in the library.

Awhile they sat there in silence on either side of the wide hearth, eyeing each other furtively ever and anon, in obvious embarrassment, though the source of it was very different in each.

Presently her ladyship observed in her husband's eyes the kindling of a light of intelligence more hateful to her than their former dullness. He rose, and crossed the hearth to come and stand beside her chair. Then he stooped to put an arm about her, murmuring something which if articulate escaped her comprehension. To elude that embrace she started up and forward, and then wheeled to confront him, standing with one shoulder to the overmantel.

The glow from the fire was reflected on the shimmering white satin of her gown – for by her mother's contriving she was appropriately dressed in bridal white. There was a glow too upon her cheekbones as if to mark the deathly pallor of the lower part of her face. Pearls had been entwined in her bright hair. Pearls hung upon the pearly skin of her ripening breast, of which her modish corsage gave an ample revelation. Slim and straight, her chin high, her eyes well above the level of her lord's, she looked to him the most ravishingly delectable woman that he had ever seen. And she was his to possess and to enjoy, rendered so by sacred bonds which no human power could shatter. He exulted in the thought as he watched her now, discovering a fresh witchery in the swift shy movement by which she had eluded his embrace. He must be patient, he told himself. He must not startle this gentle timid creature. She was delicate and fragile as a flower, and to be handled as tenderly. He must play the lover, and as a lover, woo her to surrender to the husband.

He began to speak, a note of subdued pleading in his voice, the note proper to the humble suppliant: "Sweet Frances… "

He was checked by her suddenly uplifted hand. A jewel gleamed on it, a blood-red ruby of great price, the gift of Carr. Her voice, that voice of which even this dullard had caught the liquid quality, the musical cadence, came hard as flint, forbidding.

"My lord, we must talk, you and I."

"Why so, we must, sweetheart. But thank God we have all our lives before us… "

Again he was interrupted. "Will you sit, my lord?" She waved him to the chair from which she had just risen. Her gesture, like her tone, was imperious. It cowed him. He obeyed. If he was dismayed it was not yet seriously. Women, as his little experience had shown him, were curious creatures, to be humoured at first by him who desires empire over them. He would be patient.

"This marriage of ours, my lord, into which we both entered without any natural desire of it, at an age when neither of us understood its meaning, without knowledge of what we did, without any of the love that alone can sanctify a union, how do you view it now that we have met again?"

That question was easily answered, especially as he perceived how eagerly she seemed to hang upon his answer. "How should I view it, dear child, but as the most fortunate event of all my life?"

"That is merely a gallantry of speech, my lord. I do not ask for gallantries. I am serious. I want the truth from you. Take time to consider if you will, my lord."

"Not an instant!" he cried. "It needs not. And what I said is no gallantry. I have no skill in gallantry. It is the sober, honest truth. I am in rapture..."

"Leave rapture yet awhile, my lord. We are not come to it, nor ever shall."

"What's that?"

"That you saw me at the altar some seven years ago we may leave out of account at present. As man and woman we have met today for the first time. You have known me now for some few hours, too few to permit you to learn anything of me. How, sir, can you welcome to wife a woman whom you do not know?"

"Dear child, I have seen you." His tone was one of expostulation. "To see you is to love you. Has no one told you how beautiful you are? Are you of such a modesty that you will not accept the message of your mirror?"

He saw her lovely mouth fall into lines of scorn, saw the soft eyes grow hard as they looked straightly, disconcertingly into his own.

"You are telling me, my lord, that you desire me as a woman..."

"But why not, since you are..."

"A man may desire a woman as a woman whom he would not desire as a wife. There is a difference, I think. You need not shame me by ignoring it."

Like most dullards, my Lord of Essex was not patient. Again, like most dullards, when he did not readily understand a thing he did not perceive that the fault lay in his understanding, but assumed that the thing was incomprehensible and, therefore, to be brushed aside. He sprang up.

"Faith, if there's a difference, I do not know it, and I do not care."

"But it is necessary that you should do both."

"Wherein lies the necessity? You are my wife. What more is there to say?"

"My lord, you go too fast. I am not yet your wife."

"Not... ?" His jaw fell, his eyes stared at her from their shallow sockets under that shallow brow.

"Will you please to sit, my lord?"

He shrugged impatiently; but he obeyed her and resumed his seat. A man, after all, must practise patience on his wedding night. Later on it would be different. He meant to be her lord in something more than name, and she should be brought to an early perception of that cornerstone of domesticity. But for tonight she might have her head a little longer.

She smiled faintly at his slight gesture of annoyance.

"You begin to know me, my lord. You begin to perceive that I am less smooth than you supposed, that I can be irritating, and move you to impatiences."

He laughed in his confidence that presently he would amend all that. She continued.

"Perhaps if you were to wait until you knew me better, you might come to the conclusion which I have already reached: that a marriage made as ours was made cannot be accounted a marriage until at a riper age it is confirmed by mutual consent."

Blank disappointment showed upon his heavy face.

"Do you mean that I must wait?"

"Not even so much as that, my lord; for this question must be settled here tonight between us."

"Question? What question?"

She was under the necessity of seeking words a moment. "You agree – do you not? – that a marriage such as ours needs the confirmation I have said?"

Again he shrugged. He held out a short stumpy hand in a meaningless gesture. She looked at the hand, and shivered. It was, as most hands are, an epitome of its owner. She would kill herself, she vowed, before ever she would be pawed by such a hand as that.

"If you will," he agreed tolerantly. "But are we not here, together, at last to confirm it?"

"But the confirmation must be mutual. I have asked you, my lord, if now that you see me grown, it is your wish to confirm the thing that was done before either of us was of an age to give intelligent consent."

"And on my soul, I've answered you, I think. But if you will have it again, I say again I do."

"And is that all you say? Have you no thought for me? No thought to show me a like consideration. To ask me the same question in your turn?"

His impatience increased. A dull flush overspread his countenance. "Plague take me if I understand you!"

"Why, then, my lord, I must supply both question and answer." She made a momentary pause. Then, very white, and even trembling a little, but keeping her eyes steadily upon him, she delivered herself of that which was to make all clear. "Whatever your own wishes in the matter, I find myself unable to confirm that act of marriage, to give my consent to it now that I have come to the age of consent."

He stared at her a long while, yet found it necessary to shift his eyes from her clear gaze before he answered her grumblingly. "By Heaven, madam, here's fine talk! Here's a fine welcome for me!" He got to his feet again. "Whether you confirm the bond or not, you'll fulfil its obligations. You will remember that you are my wife…"

"I have told you, sir, that I am not your wife. That thing done seven years ago, that atrocious wrong upon a couple of innocent ignorant children, cannot bind us in the sight of God."

"Let be! Let be! It binds us fast enough in the sight of man. As for the rest, we can wait until we get to Heaven!"

He laughed at his profane jest with the laughter that invites laughter. But her face remained set and stony. A shadow of fear had entered her eyes. She had depended so confidently upon the chivalry, the generosity of the man. She had thought it would all be so easy; that once she explained the situation, this husband of hers would bow to her wishes. She had not reckoned that the Earl of Essex would have the soul of a boor.

"Come, child, come," he was coaxing her, softening his voice again. "What's done cannot be undone, and… "

"It can! It can!"

A ray of hope suddenly illumined her despair. That was the maggot in his mind. This thing, he thought was irrevocable. Once she showed him how the deed could be cancelled, he must consent to do her will; no man short of a lunatic would compel an unwilling woman into wifehood.

"A marriage the…the…obligations of which are unfulfilled, could be annulled by mutual petition. If we were to go together before the King, protesting against what was done to us as children, telling him that we have no intention of living together as man and wife, his majesty would not be hard upon us. He has a kindly nature. He would not doom us to be each other's unwilling gaolers all our lives." She approached him by a step, holding out her hands. "Do you see now?"

His countenance slew her hopes. It was set, and almost grim, the dark brows drawn together by a frown. Long he stared at her with eyes whose glance grew almost malevolent.

This inestimable pearl of womanhood was his. So ran his thoughts. In the hours that were sped since he had come to Audley End that day he had been accounting himself the happiest, the most fortunate of men in the possession of a wife for which all men must envy him. And now this! He was asked to relinquish her, no less. To repress the growing hunger which the sight of her had brought him. To the reasonableness of her plea he gave no thought. To the feelings which he might have aroused in her no more. She had no right to feelings that ran counter to the sacrament which had made them one. She was his wife, and if at first she did not like it, she must come to like it or it would be the worse for her. For he most certainly did not mean to forgo a husband's rights.

He was angry, wounded, almost vindictive. His pride was lacerated, his vanity torn to shreds. Yet such little prudence as he commanded urged him for his own sake yet to be patient.

The embraces of such a woman to be savoured must not be compelled. Dull-witted he might be; but not so dull-witted that he could not perceive so elementary an article in the craft of love. She must be won, for she was worth the winning. So he stamped his anger and his impatience underfoot. He turned, and walked away, out of the island of golden light from the great candlebranch upon the table into the shadows at the room's far end, where rows of books were dimly visible upon their shelves. He came back, and stood once more in silence beside her, leaning his arm upon the overmantel, his brow upon his arm, mastering himself, considering.

Thus in silence they stood there for some time. A log fell with a sizzle to the hearth and a spurt of flame momentarily increased the illumination and the heat. It seemed to rouse him. He turned to her, and spoke gently.

"We will make no decision now. It were unfair perhaps to both of us. You do not know me yet. If you will wait… "

"I warn you that it can serve no purpose. A woman knows her heart, my lord. I know mine. It will not change."

He caught her hand in his. "Say no more tonight!" he implored her. "I can be very patient, Frances. Say no more."

Wearily she passed her left hand across her brow. The ordeal had been more severe for her then he could guess. So severe that even a postponement was now welcome. So she suffered him to kiss her fingers, then summoned a lackey to light him to his chamber.

He went, poor dullard, to stifle as best he could his disappointment on a lonely couch.

Chapter 15

Ultimatum

On the morrow Lady Essex wrote at length to Viscount Rochester giving him the substance of that first and unloverlike interview with her bridegroom.

"No man of honour or of feeling," she wrote, "could deny a woman in such a matter," and upon this she based her abiding confidence that Lord Essex would not deny her in the end. She closed with an appeal to her sweet Robin to love her as stedfastly as she loved him, who was constantly in her thoughts, and with a vow of fidelity to be kept even at the cost of life in the unlikely event that Lord Essex should prove deaf to the dictates of decency and reason.

That letter lifted some of the gloom which in these last days had been settling heavily upon his lordship, and there was about him something of the old buoyancy when he went to lay it before his counsellor and guide.

Sir Thomas perused it carefully. He had seen Essex, and he had read him. He accounted her ladyship over-sanguine.

"Lady Essex is young," he said. "In youth we believe what we hope; in maturity what we fear."

His lordship, checked in his satisfaction, would have argued. Sir Thomas spared him the trouble.

"It was a comment intended only to warn you to wait upon events."

154

"I'll wait. I'll wait." His lordship's tone was confident. "Meanwhile, do you write."

Then Overbury understood fully why he was shown the letter. The situation was such as to require a further flow of "the silver-dropping stream of his lordship's pen and of that Sir Thomas was the source. These impassioned, high-flown vows demanded vows as impassioned and high-flown in answer.

Sir Thomas shrugged, and wrote, counting upon his reading of Lord Essex to render his poetical labours sterile.

His trust was not misplaced. For a week young Essex remained at Audley End, making daily onslaughts upon the ramparts of what he accounted her ladyship's unreason, and daily manifesting how incapable he was of the patience he had promised. He carried the war of aggression against her father and her mother, constraining them into alliance with him to defeat his wife's obstinacy.

But in vain did her mother plead, her father storm in quarterdeck terms, and her husband sullenly interject in support of the arguments employed by one and the other. Lady Essex stood firm as a rock before combined as before separate assaults, letting them perceive, to their despair, that the stoutest spirit may reside in the frailest body.

"If you talk until the crack of doom," she informed them, "you shall not turn me from my present resolve that I will never be Lord Essex's wife."

"You are that already," growled her husband, thus apparently closing this line of argument.

"I am not. I was married without my consent being asked. And only a monster would desire to constrain a woman into fulfilment of such a bond. Your very insistence, my lord, but serves to make you hateful."

He stamped away to one of the tall windows of the hall in which they were met, and stared out at the elms of the park about which the rooks were circling noisily in the fading November daylight.

Lady Suffolk, meanwhile, was answering her daughter, between plaintiveness and irritation.

"This is perverse and stupid. The bond is made. Whatever the wrong of that, it is idle now to speak of it. It is done and cannot be undone, and it is folly and wickedness to beat your head in rebellion against that which is accomplished."

"What's done can be undone," was the steady answer. "It needs but his lordship's consent."

His lordship did not choose to hear because he could not trust himself to answer without violence. He was weary of these reiterations, and but for the restraining presence of her parents he might have taken a short way with her.

And then Lord Suffolk, heaving himself out of his chair by the fire, broke in to swear by God's wounds that what was done could not be undone and should not so be if he was of any account. Thus the war of words dragged inconclusively on.

At the end of a weary week which had reduced them all to despair, the Earl of Suffolk suggested to his son-in-law that he should leave them for a while.

"In the pass to which things are come your case can better be argued in your absence. Come soon again. By then I trust we shall have brought the little idiot to some sanity."

Reluctantly Essex followed the advice, and went off to occupy his house in London, the gloomy mansion in the Strand, towards Temple Bar, where his father had hatched the treason which had cost him his head, the house which later, in derision of him, when he took service with the Parliamentary forces, came to be known to Cavaliers as Cuckold's Hall. There, pretending to busy himself with putting the house in order, he moped and sulked for a fortnight, finally going back to Audley End, to find things exactly as he had left them. The only difference lay in that Suffolk, in his exasperation with his daughter, no longer offered counsels of patience or of prudence.

"She's your wife, Robert," he said, to sum up all, "and it's for you to make her aware of it. I've told her that you come this time to carry her off to Chartley. Once there, if you can't make her docile, faith, you don't deserve her." He set a hand on the young man's broad shoulder. "Take a short way with her. She's yours. Let her know it."

Thus paternally encouraged, his lordship went about taking the short way.

He invaded her bower, booted and splashed as he was from his fifty-mile ride over weather-fouled roads, and ordered out her woman Catharine who was with her. The maid had been sewing, whilst her ladyship was writing one of her almost daily letters to her lover at Whitehall. Looking over her shoulder to see who entered, she thrust the sheets into a drawer and rose to meet him, her face suddenly white, more from anger than from fear.

"You are come again so soon, my lord!" she exclaimed.

He waited until they were alone. "I am come, madam, to announce to you that the time of delays is overpast." He was very stern, but he nowise dismayed her by it.

"How very like a lover! With what delicate arts you go to work to win a woman's heart!"

"You had not found me lacking in delicacy if you had shown me any kindness," he defended himself sullenly.

"Like enough! But since of myself I do not choose to be kind, you are to make me so by being brutal. You march in here, booted and spurred, as if into a citadel which you summon to surrender. This citadel, my lord, does not surrender to manners of that kind."

He curbed his rising temper. "To what kind of manners do you surrender, madam? Inform me, so that I may provide them."

"To none of your providing, sir. I thought you understood."

"You think too much, madam. It is a labour which in the future you shall be spared. Henceforth it will be for me to think and for you to act upon my thoughts."

She looked at him for a long moment, and her lip curled a little in her scorn of him.

"You improve with every hour of our acquaintance. You have your whip, I see. From your tone I almost suppose it a part of your equipment to woo me?"

He flung the whip from him with an oath, and sent his hat after it. "You have resolved to exasperate me," he declared.

"That is my thought of you, my lord."

He considered her dully, a flush upon his sallow face, and considering her, stroked his heavy jowl with that ineffable hand of his. She possessed certain advantage of mind over him of which she made him aware. Resentment of these advantages but served to harden the obstinacy natural to him.

"You are wilfully perverse, my lady," he told her. "But it shall not serve you. Tomorrow you set out with me for Chartley. I have been patient long enough. You are a wife, madam, and you shall behave as one."

He saw the pallor deepen in her face, and in her limpid eyes he caught for the first time the glint of fear where hitherto he had encountered only defiance.

"Even if I were a wife, sir, which I do not acknowledge, I am not to be ordered as a slave."

"You shall be ordered as you deserve," he told her. "If you will be wifely, you shall find me kind and loving. If you are rebellious you shall find me otherwise. But in either case you shall find me your husband and your master. Since you are given to thinking, madam, you had best think of that."

"Oh, God!" she cried out, and then lashed him with her tongue. "You oaf! You boor! You beast!"

Because he had a suspicion that his behaviour justified these titles he was the more infuriated. Because he knew that his behaviour had been provoked by hers, his fury gathered strength. He advanced upon her and took her forcibly by the shoulders, terrorising her by his powerful grip.

"Madam, if I am these things, it is because you make me so."

He had laid hands upon her with intent to shake her, to render her aware of his physical strength. The mute fear in which she suffered his touch stirred compassion to restrain him. Then that physical contact undertaken in anger wrought upon him as he paused. She was so lovely, so desirable, standing so tall and straight in his grasp, that her eyes were above the level of his own. Obeying his instincts he drew her gently towards him, and softened his voice to a pleading murmur.

"Be kind, Frances, and as God's my life you shall find me true and tender in my love."

The words aroused her from the momentary lethargy in which she had been suffering his embrace. She thrust against him violently and suddenly with both hands, and so, taking him unawares, broke loose from him.

"My lord," she said, "I want one thing only from you."

He scowled his anger, embittered now by that frustration. He snarled, then turned on his heel abruptly, and went to pick up his hat and his whip. He stalked to the door, and there turned.

"No more now." His voice was harsh. "Tomorrow we go to Chartley. It is settled. And you go if I have to carry you there bound hand and foot. So best resign yourself with a good grace. You'll find it easier and pleasanter." He went out, slamming the door after him.

Her ladyship, trembling from head to foot, sat down to think. She was at law the chattel of this oafish nobleman who had now clearly shown her that no consideration of kindness or generosity would make him a party to the evasion of that law. Almost she cursed the beauty that rendered her desirable in his eyes. But there were other things to do. Practical things. The facts must be faced, and met somehow.

That night she kept her chamber. They suffered it, humouring her for the last time, since tomorrow her lord and master would bear her off to Chartley.

But on the morrow, when they came to rouse her, they found an empty nest, and her disappearance gave them some moments of panic until they discovered that two horses and a groom had also vanished. Even then their terrors were very far from allayed, and husband, father and mother met in council to concert a plan of action for the recovery of that wayward girl.

The girl meanwhile had startled the old Earl of Northampton by presenting herself at his house in the Strand in the early hours of that chill December morning and claiming sanctuary there.

His lordship, newly risen and wrapped in a bedgown, received her in his bedchamber. Seated on the edge of his bed, he listened not without sympathy to her indignant tale of this horror which they thrust upon her. To him as to her it seemed a monstrous thing that any woman should be flung into the embrace of a man who was as abhorrent to her as was Essex to her ladyship. But going beyond that he sought the source of this abhorrence, and, as it were, led her with him whilst he tracked it down.

He pointed out to her that her attitude rested upon certain unfortunate preconceptions, which themselves resulted from a tenderness which had sprung up between herself and Robert Carr.

"And what if that be so?" she asked him. "Is not a maid to give her love as her instincts bid her?"

"A maid, aye!" he agreed, nodding his old bald head. "But a wife… "

"If I am a wife, I am also a maid; and a maid I'll be as long as I am wife to Essex."

The old man was distressed. He had never known any good to come from struggling against the inevitable. Heartbreak was commonly the only consequence. If Essex had been willing to petition jointly with her, the marriage might have been annulled. But it could not be annulled upon the petition of one party only. No law would sanction it, since to do her right must mean to do Essex wrong. Let her well consider that. Also let her consider the point of view of Essex. Like her he had been bound by a contract before he was of an age to give intelligent consent. But he had no thought to repudiate it because he had found her all that he could have hoped, and more. Who could in reason blame him? Then there were worldly advantages to consider. As Countess of Essex she would enjoy a great position, that of one of the first ladies in the land. Was she to allow a love affair which could never come to any honourable fruition to wreck her life and prospects at the very outset?

Northampton talked at length upon love, from the impersonal point of view of a bachelor who had never taken the passion seriously. It was a singular devastating force which swept men and women off their feet and committed them to unutterable extravagances and follies. But it was a force that spent itself either by abstinence or indulgence, and often more speedily by indulgence than by abstinence. If she would take for that the word of one who was three times her age and who had observed a hundred fine flaming passions fall to ashes, all might yet be well.

Her ladyship would not take his word for it. To her ladyship his views seemed sordidly blasphemous. She perceived with distress that whilst he was reasonable and well disposed, and willing to assist her in the minor details of her present trouble, she could not look to this worldly cynical old man for the heroic support that his affection for her had seemed to promise.

Meanwhile she was afforded the shelter of his house, and the assurance that when her father and her husband came to seek her he would do what he could to postpone the evil moment of her going to Chartley, and even make the attempt to bend the Earl of Essex to her ways by argument. He clearly saw, although he did not mention it, that if the Earl would consent to the annulment, leaving Frances free to marry Rochester – and always provided it could be first ascertained that Rochester were as willing to become her husband as he had been ready to become her lover – nothing would be lost in worldly advantages, and much would have been gained, especially for Northampton himself.

It was clear, however, to her ladyship, that for real and immediate help she must turn elsewhere, and that same morning saw her at the Golden Distaff in Paternoster Row, startling Anne Turner by her sudden appearance there and her feverish manner.

Weston was instantly dispatched to Whitehall to fetch Lord Rochester with all possible speed. Whilst she awaited him, her ladyship made known her plight in fullest detail to the sympathetic little widow. The widow, perceiving how desperate was the case, counselled enlisting the services of Simon Forman.

"How could Forman help?"

The widow spread her hands and raised her shoulders. "I do not know how. But I am certain that if he would he could. He has great power."

There was no decision taken on that matter when his lordship arrived. He came breathless from haste and eagerness.

"Fanny!" he cried, opening wide his splendid arms.

In a moment she was enfolded in them, sobbing against his breast, and the discreet Turner had effaced herself and closed the door upon them.

But after transports of mingled joy and grief came the consideration of action to be taken, and this proved far less easy than kissing.

She laid the whole situation trustingly before him. Confidently she waited for the advice that should redeem them both.

It did not come. He disappointed her. Whilst vowing with all fervency eternal love and eternal fidelity he could be and continued to be glib enough; but when it came to the consideration of practical steps he was halting and nonplussed.

Almost he began to talk as old Northampton had talked. They were face to face with the inevitable. All his hopes had been centred so surely upon Essex doing that which honour and manhood imposed upon him. But since Essex refused to behave so accommodatingly, Rochester knew not where he stood or what to propose.

Only the death of Essex would bring a proper solution to the difficulty. And then from this leapt another thought. He could force a quarrel upon Essex, and attempt his life in a duel. But at this panic seized her. Rochester might himself be killed, and then what should she do? Essex was reputed skilled in arms. She had gleaned so much. It was his only accomplishment. Never would she consent to any such course as that.

But it needed no great insistence on her part to turn Rochester from such a project. A moment's reflection showed him the folly of it. The duel was to King James the unpardonable offence, and even if Rochester were to prevail both in the combat and the King's subsequent indignation, he would face a situation in which his marriage with Frances would have been rendered impossible by the very act that set her free.

The long-drawn-out inconclusive interview came to an end, leaving her a despair almost more utter than that in which she had come to it. Her disappointment distorted her judgment a little, magnified her fears where her Robin was concerned. The difficulties appalled him so much that he seemed ready to relinquish her. Could it be that his love fainted at the sight of the obstacles ahead of it? Could it be that it was diminishing already under the fret of all these influences? She recalled the cynical words of old Northampton on the evanescence of human passions, and to her already overwhelming fears a fresh and terrible one was added now.

Turner was her last hope. If Turner failed, death alone remained.

In that spirit she summoned the little widow.

Chapter 16

Necromancy

Mrs Turner did not fail.

The daughter of the opulent house of Howard could pay for such services as were now required: prodigious, inestimable services, fraught with great peril for those who rendered them, and, consequently, to be rewarded commensurately.

And so on a dark winter's night two cloaked and hooded women, accompanied by a man bearing a lantern and a staff, made their way down the narrow tortuous streets to Paul's Wharf, and there were handed by the lantern-bearer into a waiting boat. The watermen bent to their oars, and the tide serving they made up and across towards Lambeth. By a footpath across fields Weston diligently lighted them with his lantern to a tall lonely house standing in a tangled and neglected garden.

Cautiously admitted by an elderly woman after certain words exchanged with Mrs Turner, they were conducted to a large bare room dimly lighted by two candles in candlesticks of brass some five feet tall that stood upon the bare floor. Between these, on a tripod, there was a copper chafing-dish over a small blue flame, from which a thin wisp of smoke ascended to lose itself in the darkness overhead. The faint perfume of the sweet herbs that were being consumed in it suffused the chamber.

Her ladyship, whose nervousness in this unusual adventure had been increasing ever since she had left the house in Paternoster Row stood hesitating until her companion silently tugging at her cloak, led her across to a carved oak settle that was placed against the farther wall. The sound of their footsteps rang loud and hollow in that silent place, and filled her with a fear akin to that experienced by him who treads unlawfully in another's house and dreads that the sound may betray his presence.

In an eerie silence they sat waiting for some moments. Then suddenly, with a stifled cry, the Countess shrank against her companion. Blue lights, like stars, flickered momentarily here and there in the gloom above them. Mrs Turner gripped her gloved hand to steady her, and the Countess was grateful for that warm human grip in this place of supernatural mystery.

Suddenly at the room's far end a pair of luminous hands appeared at a height of some six feet from the ground. They seemed raised to command. They moved vaguely to and fro for a moment, so that they, too, appeared to flicker, with alternate glowings and vanishings. Then they became fixed and steady, and a great voice boomed upon the silence.

"On your knees! Be humble and attentive! The Master approaches."

Obedient to the command and to the tug she received from Mrs Turner, the trembling Countess knelt beside the widow.

There was a long moment's pause, and then her ladyship caught her nether lip in her teeth to repress a scream. Where the hands had been appeared now a human head and face, dimly revealed at the far end of the room, where the faint candlelight was insufficient to dispel the shadows. Its appearance was so abrupt as to leave no conclusion possible other than that it had materialised there under their watching eyes. It was a majestic, venerable countenance, with a high-bridged nose and a long white beard. The eyes were undiscernible under the overhanging brow. A deep melodious voice addressed them.

165

"Have no fear, my daughters. As you come in peace, so do I give you welcome."

The head advanced, revealing that there was a body attached to it, a tall body in a straight gown of black velvet with a girdle of green stones and with cabbalistic emblems embroidered upon its hem. The head was covered by a tall conical hat similarly adorned.

The man moving with such slow stateliness that he seemed to glide over the ground, the progress of his feet dissembled by his robe, came to stand before them. He held out his hand, and with it raised first Mrs Turner and then her ladyship, who by now found herself able to stand only with difficulty, so treacherously did her limbs tremble under her. His next question, by the knowledge it revealed, added to her terrors.

"What do you seek of me, Frances?" He paused, but as no answer came from her parted lips he added: "Dismiss your fears, and give me your hand. Since your tongue refuses its office, your touch shall tell me all it imports that I know."

Timidly she put forth her hand. He took it and held it long in a clasp so cold and clammy that the chill of it travelled through all her body.

And then at last he began to speak; in a level, monotonous and colourless voice that seemed scarcely human, she heard her own story: her marriage to Robert Devereux, her horror of this bond, her love for Robert Carr, and her ardent desire for happiness in this bond.

At last he loosed her hand.

"So much your touch has told me. What you desire of me, you must tell me with your own lips, my daughter."

She found her voice at last to whisper: "Your help to resolve these troubles."

And now Mrs Turner came to her assistance. Standing with folded hands and lowered head, almost in an attitude of prayer, and addressing this awe-inspiring man as Father, she told him that she had brought her ladyship in the hope that just as his dread skill had power to kindle love so it might have power to stifle it, and that he would of his infinite compassion and benevolence exercise that skill on her unfortunate sister's behalf.

Doctor Simon Forman heard her out in silence, and in silence turned away when she had done. Whatever else may have been spurious about him, his doctor's title at least was genuine. He was a graduate of Jesus College, Cambridge – having taken his degree late in life and after many harsh vicissitudes including a prosecution by the College of Physicians. He possessed great skill as a bone-setter and was endowed with that other curious gift of healing the King's sickness by touch alone. This gift and a certain epileptic exaltation of fancy which included the faculty of self-deception, besides the great profits to be derived from occult practices, may have been responsible for leading him to become a warlock.

Turning from the women now, he proceeded to draw with chalk on the floor a wide circle which had for centre the tripod with its flanking candlesticks. Within this circle he drew a second one, and, in the belt between the two he sketched with incredible rapidity a number of symbols which were meaningless then to the awed eyes of the Countess, but which Mrs Turner was later to inform her represented the twelve Zodiacal signs.

When this was accomplished, he passed with that solemn leisurely step of his to a low writing-pulpit of carved oak, which, with the stool set before it, completed the furnishing of that place of mystery. On this desk stood an immense volume bound in black velvet and closed by ponderous brass clasps, an antique brass lamp of Roman pattern, an hourglass, a human skull and a metal bowl. This bowl Doctor Forman now took up, and he came back with it to stand immediately before the tripod, across which he faced the women. Solemnly he beckoned them.

"Come ye within the circle, my daughters, before my invocation begins. Within its sheltering span you will be safe from all foes among the spirits I am about to summon."

Obediently, the Countess suffered herself to be drawn within that belt of chalk.

"Beware lest you step outside that circle," he admonished them. "Beyond it I have no power to curb the forces that will presently be here, and I cannot answer for your lives."

With a shiver of fear her ladyship drew closer to her companion. Had that which she sought been obtainable by any other than these terrible means, she must by now be regretting that she had come.

Taking a handful of some substance from the bowl, the necromancer flung it into the chafing-dish. Explosively a great blue flame leapt up and vanished, to be followed by a pillar of black smoke which spread so that in a moment all was utter darkness. The candle flames gradually shrank and were finally extinguished.

Cold with increasing fear, her ladyship sought warmth by still closer contact with her companion.

Then from out of the darkness came the doctor's voice, muttering rapidly and presumably in some foreign tongue, for no word of what he said was intelligible to his listeners.

Again a blue flame leapt from the chafing-dish to reveal the room as in a lightning flash and the doctor standing erect with one arm raised in a gesture of command. As darkness fell again, his voice rang loud and imperious in a call which he thrice repeated. Yet a third time was the darkness split by that same flame, and as it vanished the doctor's cry resounded again upon that same commanding note.

Followed a moment's utter silence, and then a faint noise which grew rapidly in volume until it resembled the rush of a mighty wind or the beating upon the air of a multitude of wings. After that, silence again, a silence such as it seemed to the Countess that she had never yet experienced, the utter stillness of the void.

Gradually then in the darkness before her she beheld a vague human face, aglow and flickering as if it were a face of fire. It seemed as she watched it to resolve itself into definite form, and she recognised – and was relieved to recognise – the features of the doctor. An instant later she perceived that the weird apparitional effect was produced by a faint reddish glow arising from the chafing-dish. He appeared to be gazing down into the heart of it, wherein some substance smouldered, and his lips moved the while with a soft sibilant whispering in that same strange tongue that he had used before. Thus awhile, then the lips were still, the eyes intent. Slowly the face thus seen grew dim and at long last vanished with the extinction of those smouldering substances. The darkness was now complete again. Out of it the doctor's voice rang loud and firm.

"Enough! Begone! Avaunt! In your dread Master's name I charge you to depart."

Again the air vibrated with that rushing sound, like the gust of some terrific hurricane, which sent the Countess cowering once more against her companion. Gradually the sound receded and died down, until the silence was restored, and then to set a climax to these marvels the candles were alight again of their own accord. Once more their surroundings were dimly visible and the doctor was to be seen standing beyond the tripod.

"All is now well," he said. "You may move in safety and without fear. Also, my daughter, I may give you hope. The spirits have pointed the way. Study will resolve the rest. By tomorrow I shall have sure news for you."

He came round to the women, moving ever with his stately deliberate step.

"Depart in peace, my daughters," he bade them, and held out his long bony hand with a regal gesture. A green stone glowed from its third finger. Mrs Turner, to set the example, took the extended hand, and going down on one knee, humbly pressed her lips to the magic ring. As he continued, thereafter, to proffer the hand, the high-born daughter of the Howards, nudged by her guide, abased herself in like manner before the warlock.

He folded his hands within the capacious sleeves of his black gown, inclined his head to them, and walked majestically away into the shadows, among which finally he vanished as he had appeared – vanished as if he had walked unfalteringly into the wall.

The door behind them opened abruptly with a clang and apparently without human agency. The Countess jumped in terror at the sound. Mrs Turner took her firmly by the arm.

"Come," she whispered in an awed voice. "There is no more to do tonight."

When presently her ladyship found herself once more following the swinging lantern borne by Weston along the field path towards the faintly gleaming water, breathing once more the pure cold air of the winter's night, all that she had gone through seemed to her a fantastic dream. By comparison with the terrors aroused by that eerie experience, she felt fearless now in the midnight loneliness of the fields. But as physical fear receded, so the misgivings of her spirit returned, and they abode with her until the following noon, when the result of the doctor's studies, guided by the indications of the spirits, was made known.

She had returned to Paternoster Row with Anne Turner, who from being her dressmaker had gradually become her friend, then her confidante, and was now her accomplice. She had spent there what remained of the night and she was but newly risen when the doctor's messenger arrived with a letter, which filled the widow with joy on behalf of Lady Essex.

Guided by the conjured spirits, Doctor Forman had discovered the formula for a powder which could effectively still the yearnings of love, and counteract attraction in such a degree as to transmute it into repulsion. The preparation of the powder was simple, and could be speedily effected if the ingredients were supplied. The chief of these was a sublimation of pearls, which were first to be melted down and distilled. To this were to be added some simpler elements, including some drops of her ladyship's blood.

It was left for Mrs Turner, who was constantly revealing her great lore in these matters, to explain the efficacy of this preparation. The oyster being the least amorous of all animated species, that quintessence of oysterness, which is the pearl, must infallibly, when prepared in accordance with the doctor's magic recipe, produce an oysterlike coldness in any person to whom it should be administered.

Her ladyship, who in ordinary matters was anything but foolish, was, through the very logical quality of her mind, completely convinced by an argument so logical. A large quantity of pearls was required, since it was only the skin or outer film that survived solution and supplied the necessary sublimate. Being without actual pearls on her person, it became necessary to procure them at once, for she was naturally in haste to set to work. The doctor promised definitely that if the materials were in his hands by sunset he would have the powder ready by midnight.

Lady Essex came well equipped with money for whatever might betide; but it was far from sufficient for the present need. She was wearing, however, by a fortunate chance, a carcanet of jewels equal in value to many a gentleman's estate. Without a moment's hesitation she unclasped it and gave it into the hands of the widow, so that she might convert it into gold, purchase the pearls, and send them by a safe hand to the doctor with the least possible delay.

All this was faithfully and expeditiously accomplished, and late that night the Countess repaired once more to Doctor Forman's lonely house at Lambeth, there to witness further and more elaborate marvels.

First there was the powder, the preparation of which the doctor had completed with scrupulous exactitude. He delivered it to her in a little box with a green seal, instructing her to scatter it over her lord's meat, or mix it in his drink, and, desirably, to administer it in three approximately equal doses. He explained to her that in addition to the virtue inherent in the powder itself from the nature of its component parts, it possessed a quite special force due to the cabbalistic manner in which it had been prepared, and to the spirits invoked to preside over the sublimation of which it was the result.

Then he passed to the other matter in which she required his help: the assurance to her of the love of Robert Carr in despite of all difficulties and obstacles. For this, he assured her, no medicine was now necessary. The Viscount's constancy could be maintained and even fortified by spells upon the preparation of which the wonder-working doctor had already been at work.

He produced from a small leaden coffer two little human images modelled in wax, some six or seven inches high. They were joined by a fine silver needle, upon which they were impaled transversely, in such a manner that both were pierced by it in the region of the heart. He explained to her that these images represented one herself and the other Carr; that the needle transfixing them was enchanted, and that the transfixion had taken place under certain all powerful astrological influences fortunately present just then, with Venus in the ascendant. Other propitious starry combinations were to be sought, and he would prepare other similar images for further similar magical operations under their auspices.

"You may rest content, my daughter. Your lord's love for you shall not be suffered to diminish, but shall daily increase and grow under the influence of these spells."

Lady Essex standing with bent head before him was thankful that the light in that weird room was so feeble that he might not see too much of her shrinking glance and shamed flush reflecting her tortured pudicity. It seemed to her that she had stripped herself naked to the soul under the eyes of this warlock, and in her desperate need she had admitted him to such knowledge as a woman never gives to any and rarely recognises in herself. In making free with that knowledge for her service, as was shown by the images and the rest, this stranger and master of repulsive practices overwhelmed her with such shame and confusion that she doubted whether she would have faced the ordeal had she known all that it must entail.

This tall, white-bearded man with the large knuckly hands and the assumed majesty of bearing became suddenly repugnant and obscene, and the very air of the place foul and mephitic. She was pervaded by a burning horror infinitely more intolerable than the superstitious dread which had previously shaken her in those surroundings.

Tears of shame coursed down her cheeks as with Mrs Turner she hurried through the night in Weston's wake towards the waiting boat. The little widow comforted her. Nothing worth achieving was to be had in this world without sacrifice, and, when all was said, all confidences were as sacred to the master as to a father confessor. She was not to regard him merely as a man. He was one to whom all secrets of the human heart and of Nature had been revealed, and she need have no fear that any human soul would ever know what had passed between her and him.

Chapter 17

Constraint

Lady Essex, taking what comfort she could from Mrs Turner's assurances that her shame and humiliation would remain buried from the eyes of the world, returned on the morrow to Northampton House.

By her reappearance there she allayed in part the consternation of her parents, who with her husband had come to the Lord Privy Seal in search of her.

The King had yesterday removed himself to Theobalds, and since Rochester had been among those who accompanied him, it was secretly feared by Lord and Lady Suffolk that their daughter, too, might have gone thither, a step which must have been attended, now that Lord Essex was returned, by the most scandalous consequences. Without betraying this apprehension to her husband, they had dispatched her eldest brother to Theobalds in quest of her, with orders to prevail upon her, if there, to return immediately to London.

It was some relief to them to perceive that this fear, at least, had been unfounded, and however much they might reprove an intimacy so little befitting her station as that which had led her to spend two days and nights at the house of Mrs Turner, they recognised this for a comparatively unimportant evil, and were disposed to make light of it now that she was returned.

In their relief they even found it in their hearts to be lenient in other ways, and to submit to her insistence that she should return for the present to Audley End with them, postponing yet a little while longer her submission to her husband. Since she now spoke of postponement, where before she had announced an irrevocable determination, it was considered wise to indulge her, and Lord Essex was persuaded, with the assurance that Frances at last showed signs of melting, to exercise yet a little patience.

When at the end of a week at Audley End it was announced to her that Lord Essex was about to visit her once more, she further reassured them by refraining from offering any opposition whatsoever. They were not to guess that she had a very definite reason for desiring his presence.

Meanwhile she wrote with great frankness to her lover, at Theobalds, informing him of the magical aid which she had procured and upon which now she counted. It was imprudent, but it was natural that she should desire her beloved Rochester to have these glad tidings, to revive his hopes and buttress any weakening of intention.

The letter produced in Rochester just the effect she hoped, and in buoyant mood he showed it to Overbury, who, less credulous than his lordship, viewed it with secret contempt, offered little comment upon it, and was quite ready to draft the answer to it in the burning poetical terms his lordship required.

By the time that answer reached Audley End, Lord Essex had departed again, and had taken some comfort with him. If her ladyship had continued to hold aloof, this had been less markedly so than formerly. Indeed, having administered Doctor Forman's powder to him in accordance with directions, she placed such trust in its efficacy that she thought it best to await now the manifestations of aversion which it must produce.

Be it as a result of that sublimate which he had unconsciously swallowed with his food, be it from other causes, his lordship was taken violently ill on his return to Town. He was put to bed in his mansion in the Strand, and, the sickness continuing, there came a time when his physician expressed a doubt of whether he could save his life. In this doubt the young Earl lay for some weeks, whilst at Audley End his wife, in despite of herself, recognising the wickedness of the hope, yet entertaining it as the one sure way of determining all her difficulties and loosening the dreadful bonds in which she was a captive, looked daily for news of his death, perhaps even prayed for it.

Death, after all, was a surer agent than Doctor Forman. Death would resolve all her troubles with a clean finality. If she was wicked in this thought, it was a wickedness born of the wickedness of others in so fettering her that she could look to little else for her relief. Thus she wrote to her lover and even to Mrs Turner, and this without any such suspicion as that which instantly crossed the mind of Sir Thomas Overbury that the magician she had employed in promising to render Lord Essex cold may well have had the coldness of death in view, and had probably supplied her with one of those slow-working poisons of whose existence rumour never ceased to mutter.

News of Lord Essex's desperate condition reaching the Court, which had now returned from Theobalds, the King sent his own physician, Sir Theodore Mayerne, to visit him.

This Mayerne was looked upon askance by the College of Physicians, who might have taken pains to curtail his growing favour if he had not been secure in the protection of King James. He was a Swiss of good Protestant family, who had been physician to Henri IV of France, and who, perhaps because of his Protestantism, felt none too comfortable at the French Court under the regency of Marie de' Medici, which followed upon his master's assassination. The English ambassador in Paris, aware of his ability and the confidence he had enjoyed at the hands of Henri IV, had recommended him to King James, with whom he had completely established himself by his skill in dealing with those intestinal troubles which resulted from his majesty's imprudent gluttonies. Moreover, the doctor had other qualities that commended themselves to his majesty. He was plump and jolly of countenance and of a healthy rotundity of figure. He was mirthful of disposition, and quite early in his new office of King's Physician he gave evidence of a discreetness and closeness above praise. Moreover, he pronounced Latin in the Roman manner. This was a man implicitly to be trusted, and if English doctors – resenting that a foreigner should have usurped such a position – spoke of him as a charlatan, they did so in secret and among themselves.

Sir Theodore, rosy and mercurial, appeared at the bedside of Lord Essex, investigated his condition, discovered a state of gastric inflammation which his colleagues appeared entirely to have overlooked, prescribed for him, and reported to his majesty later that he would have his lordship out of bed in a week.

When his bold prognosis was accurately realised, the shrewd doctor merely justified once again the complete trust which King James reposed in his ability.

But in dragging the Earl of Essex from the jaws of death Doctor Mayerne doomed the Countess, as she herself wrote both to Lord Rochester and to Anne Turner, to something infinitely worse than death. For according to Forman, the intervention of pharmaceutical agencies at so critical a stage had undoubtedly had the result of destroying the action of the powders which he had been at such pains to provide and supply.

And now Lady Essex was urged by her parents to return to London, so that she might be near her lord, as was natural for a wife. If they had not consented that she should be the guest of her Uncle Northampton, and if she had been less anxious to see her lover, constraint would have been necessary to move her from Audley End.

Often, however, during the three weeks of his lordship's convalescence, she would disappear from Northampton House upon affairs of her own, connected with Mrs Turner. Lady Suffolk might rail as she pleased against her daughter's intimacy with a woman of Mrs Turner's station. Lady Essex persisted in the intimacy, which was now a cloak for stolen meetings with Lord Rochester. Almost daily, either at Paternoster Row or at Hammersmith, the lovers met, to renew their vows, express their misery, and find what consolation they could in these stolen communions.

She perceived in these meetings, as she believed, the fruits of Doctor Forman's magical operations. Her Robin was hesitant no longer; no longer talked of resignation and of bowing to the inevitable; but showed himself a bold rebel against Fate, determined to oppose it to the last breath. His hopes fed hers, just as her fortitude and her insistent vows that she would be torn limb from limb before she should go to the arms of any other man sustained his own determination. Still confident of the power of Doctor Forman's powders, whose effect on this occasion had been fortuitously destroyed by Mayerne's medicines, she but awaited the occasion to administer to her lord another dose of them with which at great cost she had already equipped herself. For in her despair she had so far conquered her feelings as to visit the necromancer again; and with a martyrdom of her dignity and pride which but gave evidence of the strength and depth of her feelings for Rochester, she had submitted to participation in dreadful necromantic rites in that lonely house in Lambeth.

His lordship's complete recovery came at last to put an end to the lovers' secret meetings. Together with his illness Lord Essex appeared to have shed the last vestige of the patience which he had hitherto commanded. His first visit when he left his house in the Strand was to my Lord Privy Seal, a visit undertaken with very definite intentions.

It was a bitter day of January. The ground of the garden of Northampton House was hard as iron in the grip of a black frost, the river a solid sheet of ice from shore to shore. In the Lord Privy Seal's fine library at the end of the gallery above-stairs the Howards were assembled in force, not to defend but to compel the surrender of the mutinous daughter of their house.

Lady Suffolk, broad and untidy, sprawled glooming in an armchair by the hearth. The Earl of Suffolk persistently tramped the length of the room as if it had been a quarterdeck of his younger days. Old Northampton, pinched by the cold and more vulturine than ever in consequence, stood holding his lean bony claws to the blaze of the heaped fire. Lady Essex, looking very frail, her young face pinched and white, sat a little apart, with lips compressed and eyes that stared out vacantly upon the cheerless icy prospect. Her brother watched her in silence, as sulky as his parents.

Lord Essex arrived. He was pale of face and a little reduced in bulk by his late illness. But his glance was hard, and his mouth obstinate. The Suffolks gave him welcome gravely, Northampton more cheerily, bidding him to the fire to thaw his limbs, Frances not at all, until he had stood staring at her in dull anger for a long minute.

"I suppose," he said at last, bitter resentment in his tone, "that you are sorry to see me on my legs again?"

She looked at him coldly. She hated him, and accounted that there was righteousness in her hatred. In her eyes he was an ogre, a tyrant, a bully and coward to take advantage of the rights conferred upon him by a law that had been unlawfully employed. Her hatred spoke frankly in her reply.

"Has anything in our past conversation given your lordship cause to suppose otherwise?"

Suffolk exploded into oaths. Northampton chuckled as he continued to warm his hands. The old sinner had as much affection for Frances as he was capable of experiencing for any human being, and he accounted the answer a neat one. Also the notion had grown in his mind that alliance with Rochester, if it could be brought about, would be of advantage to his house and particularly to himself. And he found Lord Essex entirely detestable.

"You are frank, madam." The young man spoke bitterly.

"It is a virtue, I believe."

His bitterness became ironical. "I must study to practise it, so that I may not lag behind you. And we'll begin now. Frankness for frankness, then, there has been enough of temporising. I am for Chartley tomorrow, and I beg your ladyship to be ready to accompany me."

"You beg?" said she softly.

179

He raised his voice. "I command, if you prefer it. Or, to be even more precise, I merely announce it as my will."

"You mean that you are not concerned to study mine?"

"It has been studied long enough. Too long. A wife, madam, has no will that is not her husband's."

"I am glad, sir, that my parents hear these amiable views."

Suffolk stormed in. "Enough pertness, my lady ! Your parents not only hear them, but share them. You go to Chartley tomorrow with your lord."

She studied her hands, which lay folded in her lap, so that they should not see her eyes.

"I go under constraint, protesting against this…barbarity. You'll remember that!"

"You go in any way you please. But you go," Suffolk assured her grimly.

Lord Essex bowed to him. Northampton made a noise in his throat. She caught the note of sympathy in that and swung to him.

"You hear them, my lord!"

He set his back to the fire, and clasped his hands behind him, his old head with its bony brow and beak of a nose thrust forward. "I hear them. They are your husband and your father, to whom the law constrains a woman to be submissive. You begin to realise, Fanny, that a woman is not an independent being, but the chattel of some man or other. I give thanks to God that I am not a woman. It's an indignity."

"What the devil do you mean?" Suffolk challenged him.

"The devil knows," said Northampton, and turned his back upon them again.

Lady Suffolk essayed soothing words. "Surely, my lord, we should stand united in this. After all, my Lord of Essex is in the right."

"Who questions it?" barked Northampton.

"I do," said Frances. "I more than question it. I denounce it."

"Denounce and be damned!" said her father. "And that ends it. You go nevertheless."

"Of course. But my lord should ask himself in his own interest if it is worth his while. I perceive that he is not concerned for my happiness. But it is possible that he may be concerned for his own. And I ask him: What happiness does he look to draw from this?"

"The happiness will follow upon the satisfaction of taming you," her father assured them, and Lord Essex quietly smiled his confidence in his powers. He took his leave upon that, since he could perceive no profit or pleasure in remaining, and announced that he would return betimes on the morrow to fetch his bride and carry her off to Staffordshire. He was assured by Lord Suffolk that she would be waiting.

Waiting he found her, when his train of three coaches and a half-dozen mounted grooms drew up in the courtyard of the great red house in the Strand. My Lord of Essex travelled in becoming state with his secretary, chaplain, chamberlain, valet and cook. He had counted upon making the journey partly in the leading coach with her ladyship and partly in the saddle. He may even have flattered himself that during those hours alone with her in the close seclusion of that great machine of wood and leather he might make some progress in his wooing. In this, however, he was frustrated at the outset. Her ladyship came supported by two tiring-women of her own, who were to accompany her.

He perceived at once – although he had not thought of it before – that this attendance was the least that was fitting to a woman of her station, and vexed though he might be, he knew of no good objection that he could make. He did, however, go so far as to suggest that the women should travel with the valet and the cook. But even Lady Suffolk was outraged by the suggestion. So he swallowed his chagrin, climbed into the saddle, and set out on horseback to ride beside the coach containing his lady and her women.

His chamberlain, who saw to such matters and had dispatched a courier ahead, realising that there might be delays in setting out, had decreed that they should proceed no farther than Watford on that first day. When they reached it in the early twilight of the winter afternoon, all was prepared at the best inn for their reception.

My lord, coming chilled from the saddle, found his spirits rise at sight of the bright fire in the best room above-stairs, and the table laid in promise of supper, with a sack posset steaming in a bowl for his immediate refreshment. Her ladyship, entering the room ahead of him, loosened her cloak and went straight for this, whilst he strode to the fire to thaw his booted legs. With her own hands, her back being fully turned to him, she brimmed a cup of the steaming mixture of eggs and milk and Canary, and brought it to him where he stood.

He was almost startled by the graciousness of the act in one hitherto so aloof. But taking it as the first sign of melting on her part he smiled and thanked her. If he was a little exaggerated in the thanks, a little excessive in his bow of acknowledgment, it was because he could not stifle the clumsy ironies of the dullard, and lacked the wit to perceive that playfulness was the least likely means to his ends in the present circumstances.

"You will be cold, my lord," she said in level tones, as if to explain her action.

"Faith, yes! But your kindness warms me more than even the sack itself."

She threw off her cloak, and took a seat by the hearth without answering him.

Anon at table, his own chamberlain and valet in attendance, as well as the cook to carve and to add what seasonings lacked to make the dishes fit for my lord's consumption, he essayed conversation with her ladyship, to be answered only in monosyllables. Himself not a talkative man and with really nothing to say that called for many words in the saying, the talk between them after a few splutterings as of damp powder was completely extinguished. Thereafter his lordship ate copiously, as was his habit, and in silence.

It may have been as a consequence of this that he was troubled in the night with cramps in his stomach and required the attendance of his physician to afford him relief.

Her ladyship behind a bolted door, and with her woman Catherine occupying a truckle-bed at her feet, slept tranquilly through the disturbance.

In the morning his lordship was sufficiently recovered to have forgotten the matter and to be intent only upon setting out early. It was a bright frosty day, and they made good progress over the hard roads as far as Buckingham, where they lay the night, and where again his lordship's slumbers were broken by intestinal trouble. His physician dosed him and remonstrated with him upon indulging his appetite to excess, an offence which his lordship protested he had not committed.

On the third night, which they spent at Coventry, his lordship fell a prey to spasms more acute than those of either of the previous nights, so that he looked grey and sickly in the morning when he came to face the last stage of the journey. Her ladyship had given him the residue of the anti-amorous powder of Doctor Forman, and the dose may thus have amounted to more than either of the previous ones. Craven, his physician, had protested against his lordship's rising in the morning. He was, the doctor swore, in no case to leave his bed, certainly in no case to expose himself to the fatigue of a ride of some five and twenty miles. But his lordship paid no heed. Dead or alive the obstinate man vowed that he would lie that night at Chartley.

He had to be packed into the coach with the women for the last ten miles of the journey, by when he was too weak to protest or to care what happened to him so that he could lie still.

At Chartley, which they reached in the late afternoon, the tenants, forewarned of the coming of their lord and his lady, were assembled to welcome them at the gates, which had been lavishly festooned with evergreens so as to convert the gateway into a triumphal arch. But his lordship was scarcely conscious of this, or of the cap-wavings and hurrahs that greeted him as he drove through the gateway to the long avenue which led to the great gloomy lonely mansion in the very heart of that vast park.

They lifted him from the carriage limp and helpless, and her ladyship following forgot to be thankful for the respite which his condition afforded her, in the fearful thought that Doctor Forman's sublimation of pearls might be responsible for a condition akin to that which had followed an earlier administration of it.

Chapter 18

The Comedy at Chartley

In the person of the young Earl of Essex there was repeated now at Chartley the unpleasant experience that lately he had undergone in London, and this time without the aid of the skilful Doctor Mayerne to help him through it.

Thus the respite to her ladyship endured for some weeks: wretched, lonely, anxious weeks of yearnings holy and unholy, and at moments almost of despair. If the illness of my Lord of Essex once more sustained her hopes of redemption, at the same time these hopes were now shot with a certain horror that if he died it would be as a result of the powders she had given him, although in giving them she had no cause to suppose that they would slay anything more than his obnoxious love.

Nevertheless, in a measure as he improved under the ministrations of Craven, her despair increased.

This is reflected in letters which she wrote at the time – letters which survive – to Anne Turner and also to Doctor Forman.

In these she expounds the situation. She has not seen her lord since his sickness, but is apprehensive of what may happen when he recovers. Those apprehensions, we must suppose, would be founded upon the fear that Craven's physic, like Mayerne's, would interfere with the action of the warlock's powders. She begs Forman to supply her with galls in case of need, and implores him to ensure her the continuance of Rochester's love. "Keep the lord still to me!" is her cry.

You perceive the double fear by which the unfortunate girl was haunted in those days at Chartley: of being possessed by a man whom she detested, and of losing the man whom she so passionately loved.

By March, when the first buds were beginning to appear on the trees in Chartley Park as a result of winter's final dismissal in a week of sunshine and premature warmth, my Lord of Essex was well again and lusty; and then came for her ladyship the great trial of strength which she had been dreading. She had spent a fortune in powders, spells and incantations to avert the evil moment. Nevertheless it overtook her, and found her armed only with her own weak strength of body, her strong will, her wit and the iron determination which she gathered from her love for Rochester.

One sunny morning as she sat in the room over the porch which she had made her bower, his lordship entered unannounced, and drove her women out by the expression of a wish to be alone with her.

He was a little haggard, and again he had lost some weight. But he was still ponderous enough in body as in manner, and he heightened the effect of it by the rigidly fashioned sombre garments in which he arrayed himself like the puritan he was at heart.

He came in a wooing mood, having resolved upon winning her by gentleness, bearing in mind the fable of the Sun, the Wind and the Traveller, which his tutor, perceiving the fundamental obstinacy of his nature, had never wearied of reciting to him, as if to impress it upon him as a philosophy of life.

She had risen to receive him, and remained standing, a little breathless and pale, until he begged her to sit again, and himself drew up a chair and sat down opposite to her. His full dark eyes admired the lissom girlish grace of her in a simple robe of the brown of autumn leaves enlivened by gold lacings. She shrank a little under his glance as if her modesty were violated by it.

"I trust, madam," he said, "that you take satisfaction in my recovery?"

Once before he had said something similar, and her reply today did not greatly vary from her reply on that other occasion. "That, my lord, must depend upon what it means for me."

It was an answer that not only chilled but angered him. Like all egotists, my Lord of Essex desired to impress himself upon the world around him, and like all egotists who lack the intelligence to do so effectively, the desire expressed itself in a natural aggressiveness. There was more than a hint of it in his manner now.

"What it means to you, Frances, will depend upon your own wishes."

The words might have sounded hopeful but for his tone and the short ungainly gesture that accompanied them. How she wished the man would not gesticulate. His movements betrayed the clumsiness of his nature so completely and detestably.

"My own wishes, my lord, have undergone no change since last I announced them to you."

He frowned. "Yet the circumstances have changed; and our moods commonly change with circumstances."

"When you speak of circumstances, sir, you mean environment. You may change environment a hundred times without changing circumstances once."

His resentment grew more sullen. The impertinent chit was presuming to correct him, almost to school him. But still he curbed himself.

"We will not quibble over words. Circumstances or environment, it is all one. You are now in your own house of Chartley, and I look to you to behave as becomes the mistress of the house."

"Has your lordship found my behaviour unbecoming?"

"Plague on it, madam! I am serious."

She smiled a little wistfully. "Does your lordship find me playful?"

"No, madam. I find you exasperating."

There was an end to repression. He got up, seized his chair by its back, lifted it and banged it down again. Thus he worked off some of his ill-humoured need for action.

She answered him quietly. "Can I be expected meekly to conform with the wishes of those who brought me here against my will? If so, something is expected of me which is not within the compass of human nature."

To this he had no immediate answer. He set himself to pace the room, a man ruffled because rendered aware of the impotence of his wit against what he accounted a wall of obstinacy. At last he adopted a fresh line of attack.

"Will you tell me, madam, how long you intend to play this comedy?"

But she met the onslaught in the same way, by taking him up upon a word, and leaving the sense of what he said unanswered.

"Comedy! You think this is a comedy, and that I am playing?"

"What else, madam? What else?"

"To me, it is nearer akin to tragedy – a tragedy which has for aim to slay my soul." She spoke quietly with lowered eyes, and she ended on something suspiciously like a sob. Then she gathered passion, and looked up at him, raising her voice. "Why will you seek to constrain an unwilling woman, who desires of you only her release?"

He paused before her, squarely planted on his short powerful legs. He made another of his absurd gestures, with both hands this time. "It is too late now for that, madam." His tone was one of ironical regret. "It might have been possible before you came to dwell under my roof. You have been here some weeks now. Can you suppose after this that his majesty would still listen to a petition?"

"That was your reason for bringing me here!"

He raised his shoulders. His irony deepened.

"Can you blame me for taking what steps were possible to make sure of the woman I love?"

"Love!" He saw the indignation in the scarlet flame upon her cheeks. "Is this love?" She laughed in his face. "Is a man's love concerned only with gaining its own ends at any cost? That is what you have been supposing all your life, no doubt. But love places the happiness of its object above all else. Your own egregious self-love expresses itself in that you think of nothing but your own desires." Then with an infinite scorn she added: "Do not degrade the name of love by applying it to anything between us. You do not even know the meaning of the word, you oaf!"

Oaf! She had called him oaf! And he was Robert Devereux, Earl of Essex.

Galled beyond endurance, he caught her suddenly by the wrist with one of his powerful paws, and wrenched her to her feet so that she stood confronting him, her face close to his own, which was dark with anger, her breast touching his breast for the first time. But this only for an instant. Immediately she recoiled, notwithstanding that his grip so tightened that she felt as if the bones of her wrist were being crushed.

"Madam, there is a measure of respect due from a wife to a husband."

"I am not your wife. You are not my husband. This is a mockery, an infamy from which... "

His open left hand descending hard upon her face struck her into silence and brought physical fear to her for perhaps the first time in her young life.

"There's to brand you," he mocked her furiously. "You'll bear the mark of my hand upon you awhile to remind you to whom you belong."

"My father shall know of this; my father and my brothers, and my brothers shall kill you for it."

"Ah! Bah! 'Od rot your father and your brothers, and 'od rot you!" He flung her from him in his passion. She hurtled against her chair, and went over with it to lie bruised and breathless upon the floor.

He stood staring down at her, smiling a little out of his livid, anger-distorted face.

"Madam, I've had enough of tantrums! You'll be submissive, or it'll be the worse for you. You shall find me kind or cruel at your pleasure. You shall receive just that which you desire of me."

Painfully she gathered herself up, white and breathless, to answer him. "Since you give me to choose, sir, you leave me something for which to thank you. I shall prefer you cruel, if you please."

Something of her dignity and courage daunted him. In that moment the dull, passionate man could with satisfaction have taken her frail body in his hands and broken it to pieces.

He curbed himself, however, and with a last inarticulate growl where he could think of no words suitable, he strode out of the room slamming the door after him.

Bruised and shaken in soul as in body, her ladyship sat down to write a passionate letter to the Earl of Suffolk, in which she described the brutality of which she had been a victim. She wrote also to the warlock in Lambeth, addressing him as her "Sweet Father," begging his aid by every means human and superhuman to rescue her from her terrible situation. By the help of her woman Catherine these letters were smuggled away and dispatched.

That done, she withdrew to her own room, locked the door, drew the curtains and put herself to bed with her misery. There she remained for a fortnight, seen by nobody but her women, and refusing to present herself at table. His lordship, himself sulking over his wrongs, left her to her own devices. At the end of that time, wearied by a state of affairs which imposed a gloom upon the mansion, so that even his servants moved noiselessly and in apprehension, he went to visit her. He was denied admittance, and departed raging. He came again and yet again, and finally in a fit of temper he beat down the door and forced himself into her presence, to announce to her that he would be master in his own house and to afford practical experience of his mastery.

She was not to imagine he warned her, that she could prevail against him by childish methods such as these; nor was she to suppose that his patience was inexhaustible. If he had consented to humour her so far, the time had come when she must humour him or take the consequences. She announced herself quite prepared for the consequences, and commanded him to leave her. Instead, he laid hands upon her. A pitched battle followed. She defended herself with all the strength of her lithe, supple young body, using tooth and claw and tongue and every missile that came under her eager hands.

It was an indecent battle, the noise of which reverberated through the great house and set servants listening in terror that murder would be the outcome. At the end of it, she flung herself bruised and battered upon the bed, and lay there prone, shaking and sobbing as if her heart would break, whilst his lordship stalked out with a sense of utter defeat, his face bleeding where her nails had torn it.

He bore away with him, to increase his fury, the consciousness that he had been driven to behave like a gutter-blood. But he nursed his resentment aloof from her, and so she had some days of peace in which to recover from that evil morning's shocks. Nor was the scene ever repeated. Her ladyship continued to keep her room; the blinds continued to be drawn; but realising the futility of a locked door as a barrier against this violent man – as she accounted him – she gave him admission when at last he came to seek her. On this and subsequent occasions their encounters did not go beyond words: words which increased in bitterness on either side.

Then he adopted fresh tactics. He would wear her down by inaction. She should grow weary to death of her solitude and be driven to a despairing surrender by sheer loneliness. So he left her now to her own inert devices. He filled his house with neighbouring gentlemen, as a bachelor might have done, so that her presence at table should not be required nor her absence need excuse. Abandoning his puritanical habits, this dour young nobleman took to carousing lustily, so that echoes of these carousals reached her ladyship in her retreat as if to mock her into an increase of bitterness.

Thus the spring came and went, and summer followed, and the armed truce between these hostile forces was maintained with a deepening of exasperation on the one side and a deepening of despair on the other, since Doctor Forman, too crafty to supply evidence that would run his neck into a noose, had left her letters unanswered.

At last, one July morning, his lordship strode into my lady's chamber, and demanded that the curtains should be drawn. As neither of her women present showed alacrity in obeying him, he drew them himself with an ill-humour evident in the vigour he employed. Then he commanded the women to withdraw. Perforce, however, reluctantly, they went.

Her ladyship, still abed, sat up wrapped in a bedgown, her golden hair in disorder, ravishingly beautiful despite the apprehension that paled her cheeks and stared from her dilated eyes. Yet there was little occasion for it today. The beauty which he had found so maddeningly desirable was suddenly grown odious to him. Here was a fruit which however fair to the sight must be sour to the taste. He had hungered for it so long and so vainly that at last it had ceased to provoke his appetite. This is what he was come to announce to her. The situation into which her obstinacy had forced him was become intolerable. He was neither married nor single.

He stood at the foot of her bed, the bust of him framed by the rail and posts, and glowered upon her thence.

"I have come, madam," he announced in words which had been carefully rehearsed, "to summon you for the last time to a surrender to the circumstances in which we find ourselves."

The speech sounded ominous in her ears. But she dissembled her increasing panic, and maintained a steadiness of tone in answering him. "My answer, my lord, is still the same as on the first occasion."

"You obstinately refuse to fulfil the obligations of your marriage?"

"I refuse, not obstinately, to fulfil the obligations of a marriage which I do not recognise."

"The law and your family recognise it."

"Must we go over all this again?" Her tone was almost weary, and she passed a delicate hand over her brow as she spoke, thrusting back the tumbled hair. "We move in a circle of argument, my lord, until we are dizzy. And dizziness does not help us to see things clearly."

As usual, he found himself baffled by her wit, and, being baffled, grew incensed. Yet, remembering the resolve in which he came, he practised patience a little longer.

"If you chose to see things clearly, madam, there would be no need for argument."

"Assume, then, that I do not choose. What follows?"

"You admit the obstinacy in you?"

"Oh, I admit anything you please. Let us come to the matter."

"Very well, madam." He took a deep breath to steady himself. "Very well. The matter is this: I am tired of you, sick of your tantrums, sick of your presence in this house. You are free to depart when you choose. You may go to your father or to the devil without fear that I shall follow to bring you back. I curse the day I first saw you, and I pray to God that I may never set eyes on you again." His voice had soared with his passion as he reached the end of his tirade. He dropped it again, to add with an affection of sardonic calm: "That, madam, I think is all." He bowed between the bedposts. "I have the honour to wish you a very good day." And he went out rolling a little in his gait to display his dignity.

In silence she had heard him, and in silence she suffered him to depart. Almost she feared that this unexpected move concealed some trap. It was so miraculous a solution of all her trouble and her dread. Then she bethought her of Doctor Forman. Although he had sent her no more powders, who could doubt but that he had continued his magical operations on her behalf, and that these had resulted at last in transmuting into hatred Lord Essex's unwelcome love?

She bounded from the bed, summoned her women, issued her orders brisk and excitedly, and went instantly about her packing.

On the following Sunday, as the Earl of Northampton was sitting down to dine in the company only of Sir David Wood, his steward startled him by announcing Lady Essex.

Chapter 19

Capitulation

The moment was one of crisis in other lives than that of Lady Essex.

Robert Cecil was dead. He had breathed his last at Marlborough some weeks ago, as he was homing from Bath, whither Doctor Mayerne had sent him to take the waters in a last endeavour to prolong his life.

His death and the chances which it must bring them had been watched by many, but by none so closely as the Earl of Northampton on the one hand and Sir Thomas Overbury on the other, both of whom aspired to snatch the seals as they fell from his dead hand.

Each waited now, alert and ready to seize opportunity the moment it should appear.

But the King made no decision. Temporarily Rochester – by now to be regarded as the King's alter ego – held the seals, whilst in conjunction with the King himself he conducted the affairs of the exalted office of First Minister of State. The duties of that office whilst thus governed were divided between two shrewd and able gentlemen, Sir Ralph Winwood and Sir Thomas Lake, an arrangement regarded by both Northampton and Overbury as merely temporary.

Whilst he watched and waited, the old Earl sighed over what he considered the daily increasing slenderness of his chances of realising the great ambition of his life, and cursed the obstacles in his path: Rochester whom he despised for an upstart and a fribble, and Overbury whom he feared as a man of parts rendered dangerous by his ability and the hold which he already had upon power.

Thus his niece found him on that Sunday morning when she walked in upon him as he was sitting down to dine. Her advent and the news she bore were oil to the fading lamp of his hopes. If Essex were indeed willing to seek the annulment of the marriage, and, if the marriage being annulled, she were free to make a match with Rochester, the powerful favourite would be brought into alliance with the House of Howard. If he himself were to play the godfather to these lovers such should be Rochester's gratitude that in return Northampton might surely count upon his suffrages with the King.

Very early in that first interview with her uncle her ladyship expressed the desire nearest to her heart, her eagerness to see Lord Rochester at the earliest moment.

The old man frowned as he thoughtfully pulled the tuft of grey hair on his chin. He had been sympathetic with his niece as became an affectionate uncle; he had pinched her cheek and held her chin whilst murmuring soothing words; but at the same time he had spoken only of difficulties in her path.

"If that numskull Essex had but reached this conclusion before dragging you down to Chartley, as well he might have done, all would have been well for both of you. But after keeping you for months under his roof, it seems idle to plead that neither of you desires the fulfilment of the contract."

"Yet it is true. I am no more his wife today than I was the day he took me thither."

"Maybe not. Maybe not. But what rested on evidence before rests now upon assumption."

"The servants at Chartley can bear witness… "

"Ay, ay, up to a point. But only up to a point. Servants are not always watchful. They sleep like other folk. Still, take heart, my dear. Something may be possible. I will write to Essex."

There was no betrayal in any of this of his own eagerness to serve her to the fullest extent of his craft and his power. Similarly now when she expressed her wish to see Lord Rochester, whilst it was what he himself desired, he gave no sign of it; but rather of the opposite. His countenance darkened with thought which might be supposed by an observer to be hostile.

"Were it not better to be off with the old love... "

She interrupted him hotly. "There is no old love. There has never been any love in my life but Robin. I belong to him. I belonged to him long before my lord came back from his travels."

He wagged a lean forefinger in her face, and spoke severely. "You'd be wise, my girl, not to announce that fact too loudly, or indeed at all. The gossip that there was of your relations with your Robin might even now prove an obstacle to delivering you. You cannot want to add to it by such imprudent reminders of something that were best forgotten. If you are wise you will not see Lord Rochester at all, nor communicate with him, until our way to the annulment of the marriage is made clear."

She looked startled at first. Then she smiled wistfully. "Sometimes it is so hard to be wise."

"Generally," he agreed with her, and shrugged. "I have said what I think. For the rest, until you take some order for yourself, this house is yours, and you may use it as your own. I will have rooms prepared for you. You may receive whom you please. But... "

She leapt at him and stopped his mouth with a kiss.

No more was said. But on the following morning, coming unexpectedly into the library, he surprised her in her lover's arms.

He played the astonished and troubled guardian with the histrionic skill of which he was master. He stood dismayed under the lintel for a long spell, whilst the handsome gentleman and the lovely lady disengaged themselves from their embrace.

He put his niece from him when she sought with feminine arts of cajolery to melt the severity in which he advanced into the room.

"If you please, Fanny, I will have a word alone with my Lord Rochester."

My Lord Rochester, scenting trouble from that frosty tone, stiffened visibly before bowing. "As many as you please, my lord."

"You'll not be angry with him? The fault is mine. I sent for him, and... "

"Quiet you. I am not angry with anybody. I desire the best for you. For both of you. That is why his lordship and I must talk."

He thrust her from the room, waved her lover to a chair, and seating himself opposite displayed no more than a grudging friendliness at first. He spoke of the state of things between his niece and Essex; of the difficulties that stood in the way of her divorcement, and pointed out that such visits with such an object as that of which his eyes had beheld the evidence could only increase those difficulties.

Then he melted a little. "I would assure your lordship that in all the world there is no man more conscious of your worth than I am, and therefore more entirely your servant and – if you will concede me the honour of the title – your friend. But my love for my niece must be in this dark hour of her sweet young life my first consideration."

"I must honour you for that, my lord."

"You will therefore bear with me in that I urge prudence upon you, so that nothing that you now do may increase the difficulties confronting her." He paused. "You would not, I am sure, my lord, wish to jeopardise the peace of her future life by some...transient satisfaction."

Lord Rochester coloured. "You misapprehend me, my lord."

The Earl's brows went up interrogatively.

"Or else," Rochester continued, "I do not understand your lordship. Circumstances may not permit me to proclaim it broadcast, which is what I should desire. But here to you at least I may say frankly and freely that I love Lady Essex, and that I yield to no man in anxiety to see this divorcement accomplished so that I may make her my wife."

It was what Northampton desired to hear in explicit terms. His old eyes owlishly pondered the young man.

"You say it to me. That is safe. But a whisper of it elsewhere may grow to a tumult. So set a guard upon your tongue as upon your actions where Frances is concerned."

For that day it was enough. By displaying his willingness to become Lord Rochester's ally in the realisation of his hopes of Lady Essex, the old Earl forged the first stout link of the chain by which he counted upon attaching the favourite to himself.

Lord Rochester went his ways observing the prudence which the Lord Privy Seal had enjoined. He spoke neither of the Essex affair nor of his own hopes therein to any soul but Overbury. Overbury would have been dismayed had he not accounted the obstacles to the divorce insuperable. The only result of these futile struggles would be a still greater scandal, which must widen the breach between the Howards and Rochester, and destroy the bridge which Northampton had so craftily thrown across it. He expressed himself freely as was his habit.

"Since Northampton is too astute to deceive himself with any such hopes, it follows that he deliberately aims at deluding you."

"To what end?" Rochester was impatient of the suggestion.

"You will know that when he seeks your patronage or your favour. Bear it meanwhile in mind. Take all that his lordship may have to offer, but commit yourself to nothing in return until the prize is well within your grasp."

In his confidence that this would never happen, and that Rochester, however much he might make a show of resenting the warning, would, nevertheless, act upon it, Sir Thomas went serenely about his affairs.

He underestimated the pertinacity, resource and ruthlessness of Northampton, qualities which were to be very fully displayed before all was done.

The old Earl began upon Lord Essex so soon as that young gentleman came to Town, which was some weeks later. The dullard showed that he could be violent, and stormed at the Lord Privy Seal on the subject of his niece and of his own passionate desire to make an end of the ridiculous situation in which be found himself.

The old man took a sub-acid tone with him. "One-tenth part of this zeal to do as her ladyship desired of you before you went to Chartley would have availed you more than one hundred times the amount of it, vigorous as it is, that you display at present."

The young man, who was not usually addicted to profanity, had recourse to swearing.

"I would to God..." he was beginning, when Northampton crisply interrupted him.

"Let us leave God out of it. The King is our more immediate concern. And let me implore your lordship to bring more calm to the consideration of your difficulties."

"They are your niece's difficulties no less; and she created them."

"You created them between you. But that is not now important. What matters is to discover how this very imperfect creation may be effaced."

"I am prepared to petition jointly with her ladyship for the annulment."

"You already know the difficulties resulting from your obstinacy in dragging an unwilling woman down to Chartley. I do not remind you of this to annoy you, but so that you may see how it has changed the face of matters."

Essex had suspected as much. Nevertheless, to hear it calmly stated by one who knew the law and spoke with authority was cold water to the heat of his indignation.

"Are we then to remain, bound thus, neither wedded nor single, until one of us dies?"

"At first I thought so. But I have since considered. There is a way." The old serpent spoke very slowly. He moved away now so that he had his back to the young nobleman, who sprawled carelessly in a chair. He went to stare through the window at the boats on the bright river and the green meadows of the Surrey bank across the water. "The wedding still remains no wedding after all these months. Your lordship lays the blame for that upon my Lady Essex. Her reluctance in the matter would hardly be accounted a proper ground even if it were believed. To accept such a state of things would be to establish a dangerous precedent. But if – and the course would certainly be a more chivalrous one in your lordship – you were to take the blame upon yourself, the issue would be rendered infinitely more easy."

Lord Essex considered, his brow rumpled with perplexity. The old man continued to present his back to him. At last he confessed himself baffled.

"I do not perceive the difference," said he.

"Yet it is plain enough." His lordship slowly turned, and explained that which to a mind less dull should have required no explanation.

Essex bounded from his chair. "Never!" he swore. "Shall I make myself a laughing-stock for the whole lewd world?"

"You will be that in any case. You cannot now escape ridicule whichever way you turn."

"But I turn not that way." He was very determined.

Northampton slowly raised his shoulders and spread his hands. "In that case, my lord, you must resign yourself to spending the remainder of your days in the impossible situation in which you now find yourself. I am sorry for you, and sorry for my niece."

They got no further that day, nor for many days thereafter. Weeks passed before the heat of indignation engendered in my Lord Essex had simmered down to the extent of enabling him to renew the discussion with Northampton.

They were weeks in which the lovers were driven almost to frenzy as they observed the apparent wilting of hopes which had seemed on the point of blossoming. They saw each other constantly, and since Northampton discouraged these meetings, they met sometimes at Hounslow, where her ladyship had taken up her residence at a house purchased from Sir Roger Aston, sometimes at Turner's house at Hammersmith, sometimes at the Golden Distaff in Paternoster Row, and more rarely at Northampton House.

His assiduity in these stolen meetings caused Rochester to neglect his duties at court and about the person of the King, and but for the remonstrances of Overbury, who looked on with some apprehension, this neglect might have been carried to unpardonable lengths.

At last, in the early days of September, after some four or five weeks of fruitless brooding, Lord Essex once more sought the Earl of Northampton. He came to announce again that he would take any way but the way which Northampton suggested. But he was less vehement in announcing it. And by the time they parted Northampton had at least succeeded in bringing him to perceive that whether he went that way or not it was the only way open to him, and that until he resolved himself to treat it, further discussions between them were but a waste of time. At parting, however, Northampton softened the harshness of this by a little worldly advice.

"After all, my lord, what is this price of a little ridicule that you need boggle to pay it, considering that with it you purchase liberty from your present bonds? For liberty men have been glad enough to put their very lives in pawn. You avoid the ridicule at the cost of wasting your life. Is that worth a sane man's while?"

Lord Essex departed to think it over, and decided that it was not; he came yet again, to capitulate; to announce at last that he would do whatever Northampton desired of him, so that the result should be the cancellation of his marriage.

Northampton commended the wisdom of the decision, and went to work. Himself he drew up the petition that was to be laid before the King, having secretly taken counsel upon it with Rochester, whom he had kept informed step by step of what was happening. Thus the intimacy between the Earl and the Viscount grew rapidly in those days in which they might be said to be accomplices.

Northampton chuckled as he conned the document which Rochester was to lay before his Majesty. If he knew the King at all, this would afford him such a chance to play Solomon and Pontiff in one, to display the depths of his erudition in law and in theology, as he could scarcely ever have hoped to grasp. He imagined how James would slobber and gurgle in delight over the pedantic periods which he would pen on the subject and the learned discourses he would hold to guide bishops and lawyers in reaching a decision.

Chapter 20

The Alarm

My Lord Northampton did not over-rate the King's delight at the prospect opened out before him by the Essex petition.

His majesty sent for his Robin, and, closeted with him alone, showed him the document the preparation of which his lordship had witnessed, and entertained him at great length with the theological, legal and, physiological intricacies which its contents aroused. His majesty was almost tearful on the subject of the poor Howard lassie, and the harshness of Fate to have sent so dour a visitation to that innocent little lamb.

If the petition was founded upon the truth – and his majesty could not conceive that human wickedness could invent a falsehood which if present must in the sequel be rendered apparent – there could be little doubt of how the bishops would decide; and if when he came to weigh it carefully he concluded that it was true – for if false he depended upon the sagacity which had fathomed at a glance the nature of the Gunpowder Plot – he would proceed at the earliest moment to appoint a Commission to try the matter.

Then he bethought him that once upon a time the gossips had linked Rochester's name with the lady's, and questioned Robin thereupon. Rochester came prepared for this, and was frank enough in his reply.

"It is true, sire, that I entertained, and still entertain, the deepest sentiments of affection for her ladyship."

"The deepest? And how deep may that be? Deep enough for marriage if she were free?" The great eyes so full of wondering sadness considered the fair face of the young favourite. Rochester smiled a little. "Deep enough for that, may it please your majesty."

"Tush! Tush!" His majesty was fretful. "Why can ye not be frank with me? D'ye want the lass?"

Rochester was frank. "As I want salvation, sire."

"Huh!" The intensity of his lordship's tone almost startled the monarch. He fidgeted a moment nervously. Then took a sip of the thick sweet Malaga wine from the goblet at his elbow, wiped his sandy moustachios with a handkerchief, and at last delivered himself. "If ye want the lass, ye must have her." He stretched up his hand to pinch his lordship's cheek. "Rogue!" he said, and gurgled his satisfaction at being able to gratify so signally his beloved Robbie. "There'll be the less delay in appointing the Commission." Then the law-giving and theological sovereign rising above the good-natured, fatherly fellow in him, he made haste to add: "Ye must have her, that is, if the Commission favours the petition."

Rochester reported the King's words to Overbury. And Overbury experienced his first real pang of apprehension; he began to ask himself whether he had not held his hand too long, deluded by his confidence that no acceptable petition could be framed. He learned now for the first time its basis, and almost sneered as he asked Rochester how this was to be established. Rochester shrugged the question aside as unimportant, and went to bear his good tidings to Northampton, and later to her ladyship at Hounslow.

Frances wept when she heard them. Her lover, as uplifted as she was, after having suffered scarcely less, kissed her tears away whilst swearing to her that he would make it his life's object to see that the future held no weeping for her.

Things did not move, however, as rapidly as these impatient ones desired. The King, and his court with him, were concerned at the time with the coming of the Palsgrave, who was to marry the

Princess Elizabeth, and in the bustle of preparation for so momentous an occasion, other affairs underwent postponement.

But although the King had as yet taken no steps towards the appointment of the Commission, rumour was soon at work bringing in its train an unfortunate revival of the old scandal touching the rivalry of Prince Henry and my Lord Rochester for the affections of Lady Essex. It infuriated Rochester, who perceived here matter to daunt the bishops in their task when they came to it, or at least to render them unpleasantly inquisitive.

Prince Henry, whose feelings towards Rochester had not been improved by the ever increasing intimacy between the King and the favourite, was moved to fury by the news. The Queen, the Earl of Pembroke, and all those nobles who made up the great party hostile to Rochester, now joined the Prince in a deeper rancour against this insolent favourite who rode roughshod over the rights of his betters and who apparently was become so powerful with the King that he could ride equally roughshod over the laws of God. They stood united in the intention of using every measure to thwart the petition when it came to judgment. They would use their influence with the bishops to be appointed to the end that these might refuse the divorcement.

Sir Thomas Overbury, who in those days employed a little army of spies to keep him informed of what was passing, was presently able to dismay Lord Rochester by a full exposition of this state of affairs. He followed up the unwelcome news by advice that was still more unwelcome.

"Do you see, Robin, amid what gins you are walking? Do you see how a false step may ruin you?"

"Plague take you, Tom, I'm not so easily ruined." Straight, tall and handsome, magnificent as ever in his raiment, he looked indeed a man to hold his own against the world; for in these last two years he had ripened richly in the benign and constant sunshine of royal favour.

Sir Thomas fetched a sigh. "It is such overweening confidence as yours which has deluded many a tall fellow to walk with his nose in the air until a pitfall brought him down."

Rochester questioned him by a frown.

"These Howards, now," said Sir Thomas. "I've warned you against them since the outset, since long before this woman came to bewitch you."

"What's that to the matter?"

"In their toils you will be a lost man, and I see you walking into those toils whilst your eyes behold nothing but this girl's beauty. For God's sake, Robin, rouse yourself before it is too late."

"Too late for what?"

"Before that happens which will topple you from your precarious eminence."

"I do not perceive its precariousness."

"All eminences that depend upon royal favour alone are precarious. The caprice that raised you may cast you down again."

"Oh 'Sdeath! Do I depend upon caprice alone, do you say?"

"No. You have something more. You have me," said Sir Thomas steadily. "But not even I can hold you where you stand unless you heed me."

Rochester moved about the room ill-humouredly. Sir Thomas used, he thought, an unnecessary and indelicate frankness. And he exaggerated. He was not so valuable a prop to my lord's greatness as he supposed. His lordship said so with some petulance. Sir Thomas showed no resentment. He answered with patient calm.

"You and I make one between us. That was the compact from the start. You supply the brawn, the beauty and the personal grace which have captured the fancy of the King. I supply the intelligence, the knowledge of affairs and the industry which have made you, and preserve you something more than the minion to display a tailor's tricks and gauds to the sneers of a court."

"By God, you're frank with me!"

"By God, I mean to be." Sir Thomas banged the writing-table with his clenched hand. "Each of us is nothing without the other."

"I cry you thanks for that, at least. I'm glad you own that without me you would be nothing."

"Just as you are nothing without me. United, we have this England under our hand. In all the world there's not another man to serve you as I have served you, just as in all the world there is no other to serve me as you have done. If I claim much, I acknowledge much. Break up this partnership, Robin, and you break us both. I shall sink back to the Temple whence I sprang, to pick up a living in the practice of the law. You will sink back to the minionship and fribbledom in which you fretted when I found you. When it is seen that your hand no longer grasps the tiller of the ship of State, your influence will depart from you, the homage will cease, the King himself will begin to regard you differently, and will cease to regard you at all the moment another fresher younger minion attracts an eye in which you, as a mere minion, will have grown stale."

"By Heaven, man, d'ye mean to quarrel with me?" Lord Rochester was furious by now.

"I mean to avoid it," said Sir Thomas, cold as ice.

His lordship stared angrily into that narrow, finely featured, sensitive face.

"On my soul, then, you take an odd way to your ends."

"That is only because you do not yet perceive my ends."

"I perceive that you have said things which I would brook from no other living man."

"There is no other living man entitled to say them. There are not two other men in all the world who stand to each other as you and I. We are between us body and soul. Understand it once for all before that happens which by parting us may ruin us both. Remember the oath we swore to each other when we entered upon this partnership of ours."

"I do remember it." Rochester was at the height of exasperation. "No need to remind me of that. But perdition catch my soul if I understand you. Who is like to part us?"

"You are."

"I! You're mad, Tom."

"Oh, not wittingly, nor with your eyes open to the fact. But stupidly and blindly by persevering in your present courses. This Essex business is a pitfall for you and a dangerous one. The scandal that there was is as nothing to the scandal that there'll be if you persist in your determination to marry her ladyship. Have you considered how the Commission may find if your name continues to be coupled with hers, whilst your enemies – Pembroke, the Queen, the Prince and the rest of them – are at work to pull you down by any means in their power? Do you not yet perceive what an opportunity you are affording them to ruin you? Do you not see that even the King himself will scorn to protect you if certain things should become known."

"What things?" Rochester demanded out of a sudden intimidation.

"The real depth of your relations with her ladyship before her husband came home from abroad. Court gossip is naught, we know. A court is a place of scandalmongers. But if the scandal can be shown to have a foundation of truth?"

"And who's to show that?"

"Who? Can you be sure that no one knows? What of Anne Turner? What of her servants? That fellow Weston and others? What of that warlock over in Lambeth?"

"He died some weeks ago."

"But his wife survives, and might be brought to show that Lady Essex practised against her lord's life."

"That she never did!" thundered Rochester.

"I only say that Forman's widow might be brought to show that she did. Letters may have survived into which such meanings could be read. Her ladyship was none too prudent. And such an accusation would gather confirmation from the fact that my Lord Essex was twice sick to the point of death whilst in the company of her ladyship. Where should you stand if all that were brought to light?"

His lordship's blank countenance showed the dismay that had gathered in his heart. He sat down heavily, staring at the ever calm Sir Thomas. "My God!" he groaned, and again: "My God!"

"You begin to understand," said Overbury.

His lordship made some recovery. "You seek to affright me with peasebogles," he complained. "You state what might happen. But there's no such likelihood. You present the worst to me."

"A prudent man keeps ever before him the worst that may befall; and this however much he may hope for the best."

"So be it. You indicate the danger. How is it to be averted?"

"In one way only. It may cost you a bitter wrench. But the alternative may mean the loss of all. Put this marriage definitely from your mind. Renounce it, and announce the renunciation."

"Not while I live!" Rochester bounded from his chair. "I'll take my chance of ruin before I do that."

Sir Thomas shrugged. "To that you would have the right if you stood alone. But I stand with you. Our partnership is a deal older than this love affair. And if you ruin yourself, you ruin me."

"And I'll ruin us both before ever I contemplate this step you advise. Have you no heart, Tom? Are you just a cold, calculating brain?"

"I hope I do not lack a heart. But certainly I have brain enough to know how transient a thing is the love of a woman. This love of yours will fade the more quickly if you sacrifice your great position to it. Who knows, indeed, if you hold to your present course and ruin overtakes you, whether the marriage for which you risk so much will ever come to pass?"

"If I were beggared Frances would still cleave to me. I love her with a love beyond the understanding of such men as you."

Sir Thomas smiled a crooked smile. "Yet I should understand it, seeing that it was I expressed it. Do you forget my letters and my sonnets with which I won her for you?"

"You won her for me? You?"

"Did I not? Have you forgot?"

Leaning towards him across the writing-table, Rochester was within an ace of striking him, and might indeed have struck him, but for Sir Thomas' next words.

"Robin! Robin! Are we to quarrel, you and I, after all that we have weathered side by side? Is a woman to come between us, and drive us asunder?"

His lordship straightened himself. "It is not the woman that will come between us, Tom, but your lack of regard for her, which, loving her as I do, I must resent. No more of this, or we quarrel mortally, and there is but one human being with whom I should be more loth to quarrel than with you. Let me hear no more of it. The dangers may exist. But they're none so imminent as your timidity supposes." He strode to the door. "I'll face them, and you must face them with me. There's no help for it. And that's my last word." He put an end to the discussion by going out abruptly.

Sir Thomas leaned back in his chair, his fingers toying idly with a quill, his countenance calm. He was checked, but very far yet from being checkmated. There were several moves he perceived by which to avert a marriage which would turn Rochester into a puppet for old Northampton. And for Rochester's sake as well as for his own he accounted it his duty to make those moves in season.

Chapter 21

Sir David Wood

Across the serenity of those blissful days for Lady Essex, days in which she sunned herself in the high hopes of the future and the fulfilment of the love that was her life, there fell, to chill her, the shadow of Sir Thomas Overbury.

Rochester in his trouble of mind exposed to her the perils to which Sir Thomas had drawn his attention. It was weak of him to afflict her with fears which might never be realised; but he justified himself by the reflection that these perils threatened her as closely as they threatened him, and that he had no right to leave her in ignorance of them.

They stood in the lofty, pillared hall of her somewhat Italianate house at Hounslow on the October morning after his last interview with Overbury, and there he urged the matters that oppressed him.

She was not at first perturbed. From the cushioned oak settle, at right angles to the hearth with its tall, carved overmantel, she looked up at his clouded countenance, and smiling, shook her head.

"Turner is true as steel, nor dare be otherwise. Is she to tell the world the part she played in helping me? It would go hard with her if she did. As for Weston, he is silenced by the same gag. The rest is naught. Gossip is never to be stifled, and is not deeply regarded by any person of worth. The only other who knows is Sir Thomas Overbury. How comes he to know these matters, Robin?"

Robin shrugged. Her words had put a fresh complexion on the matter, presented points which he had missed, and thus had instantly restored his equanimity. He had started at shadows. He answered her question, but not truthfully, because he dared not tell her of the graces of mind he had borrowed from Overbury to help him in his wooing.

"It was an indiscretion, perhaps," he confessed. "But Tom and I have had no secrets from each other."

She frowned a little in thought. "Yet this was not your secret only. It was mine as well. More mine than yours."

"I confess it," he said contritely. "But don't blame me. Like you, I was troubled in soul and eager for advice. There was no one else whom I could trust, and no one of so acute a mind as his."

"If he is fully worthy of your trust, if he is staunch and loyal, you have done no harm. Can you be sure of that?"

"As sure as of myself."

"Why then you may dismiss your every fear." She rose, and came to put her arms about his neck with a melting tenderness. "There are no obstacles ahead, Robin. At least none that are not presently to be surmounted. The road to happiness lies before us, my dear. We shall look back upon our little pangs, our anxieties and momentary despairs, and count them a little price to have paid for the glory that is ours."

"My heart!" he cried, and caught her to him, swearing that he would pay more than that at need; that to find a haven in her arms he would give all he had and was.

And so trusting that Turner and Weston would be silent because they must, and Overbury because be was loyal and true to her Robin, she went in happy confidence of the finding of the Commission which the King was appointing, with Abbot the Archbishop of Canterbury at its head. Thus until the shadow fell.

It happened at Northampton House. Sir Thomas Overbury was not the only one to employ spies. The Lord Privy Seal found them necessary both to a proper discharge of the duties of his office and to the shaping of his own personal concerns. And these spies brought him word that the rumours afloat concerning the real and illicit object of the Commission – illicit since it had for object to break up an existing marriage so as to give Lady Essex to the favourite who had formerly been her lover – were being disseminated in Paul's and at the ordinaries by Sir Thomas Overbury himself. If on the one hand Northampton was aghast at the discovery, on the other he perceived a certain capital to be extracted from it. Its disclosure to Rochester should suffice for the breaking of Overbury.

Northampton sent for Rochester and laid before him the information of his spies.

Rochester refused to believe the tale. It was unthinkable.

Northampton swore that unless the damned scab – as he now called Overbury – were checked, he would ruin all.

Rochester, still trusting to the loyalty of his friend, taxed Overbury with the matter, and suffered the source of his information to be drawn from him. Then Sir Thomas laughed.

"Northampton, eh! The pestilent, noisome old fool! A secret recusant that should long since have been Star Chambered! Haven't I warned you against him and all that hell-brood of Howards? Do you not perceive the fellow's aim? It is to embroil us, to part us, so that he may have you under his hand to obtain him whatever he covets. I'll hear no more of this. But I warn you again that if you keep to your course you'll be forced in the end to choose between the Howards and me, which means that you'll be forced to choose whether you'll be served by me or live to serve the Howards."

His lordship was bewildered, and knew not what to hold by. His friendship with Overbury in one way and another was being marred. What would follow if it were ended? In the depths of him he feared that it might be no less than Sir Thomas foretold. Therefore he persisted in believing what he hoped, which was that Northampton's spies had been at fault.

Lady Essex, however, took a different view. Northampton saw to this, hoping that she might prevail with Rochester where he could not. The old Earl perceived quite clearly the motives actuating Sir Thomas; understood perfectly that Sir Thomas was not at all concerned with the rights or wrongs of the marriage, but merely with his hold upon the favourite which the marriage threatened. It became a secret duel between Northampton and Overbury for the possession of Rochester, a duel in which neither dared to clearly show his hand.

Meanwhile, Lady Essex, driven to distraction, took affairs into her own hands, with that firm direct independence of spirit which she had ever displayed.

Again, as of old, there hovered about her frequently in those days at Northampton House the slim, elegant person of Sir David Wood, who once had paid court to her and announced himself for evermore her servant. As if in confirmation of this he still bore himself with a certain gallantry towards her, although fully informed of what was to follow upon the dissolution of her marriage. She determined to put his sincerity to the test. She had heard of him that he had a certain reputation as a swordsman, and that he plied a very nimble rapier. She broached the matter to him at last, taking him up on one of his ever-recurring protestations that his life had no purpose but her service.

"These are smooth words, Sir David, and easily uttered." She shook her sunny head and smiled. "What if I were one day to take you at your word?"

"I should count myself the happiest of men," said he promptly.

She laughed outright. "Why, if it will bring you happiness, I forgo my last scruple." She became serious. "I have a very dangerous enemy hereabouts. A snake of a man who may do me mortal hurt. It happens that you have already suffered at his hands, which in a way makes in this a bond between us."

Sir John lowered his hand to his sword hilt, and thrust up the blade behind. "His name, my lady?" said he, at once converted into your truculent fire-eater for her admiration.

"His name is Overbury."

He sucked in his breath. "That dog! What affront does he dare offer you?"

"He defiles my name in public with scandalous stories."

He looked ineffable things, but said nothing until she pressed him. Then he displayed a certain hesitancy. "The knave stands high. He is well protected. Lord Rochester now..."

She interrupted him. She had no wish to discuss Lord Rochester's part in this. Instead she offered a further stimulus.

"What was your loss at his hands, Sir David?"

"A matter of a thousand pounds at least."

"Well, here's to pay the debt and to recover the money at the same time, Sir David. When you have settled your own score with him as a gentleman should, you shall have the thousand pounds from me in satisfaction of the service you will have rendered me at the same time."

Sir David bowed. She flicked him sharply with her reminder of what became a gentleman in his position, and being needy she had tempted him beyond his powers of resistance with the glitter of that thousand pounds.

"His friends may order his winding-sheet," he said in your fire-eater's best manner, and went about the business.

That evening found him in King Street just as Sir Thomas was returning to the handsome house which he now maintained there in the neighbourhood of the palace. By an odd coincidence he reached the door almost at the same moment as Sir Thomas, so that they were within an ace of colliding with each other. Each drew aside to give the other passage.

"I go no farther," said Sir Thomas. "This is my house."

"Your house? Odso! Then you'll be Overbury?"

His tone drew Overbury's eyes more sharply, and Sir Thomas recognised him for Northampton's creature and got the scent of mischief breast high at once.

"I have long desired to meet you, sir," said Sir David.

"The desire was easy of fulfilment. I am not difficult to find. You are, I think, Sir David Wood, a friend of my Lord Privy Seal?"

"I am honoured by your memory. But perhaps you have occasion for it?"

"Occasion? I call none to mind."

"Yet there was one in which your intervention was of a cost to me of a thousand pounds."

Sir Thomas looked him over with that glance of his which he could render so frosty and distant. "Was it on this that you desired to meet me?"

Sir David nodded. "On this."

The door was opened at that moment by Overbury's man Davies, a brisk, well-set-up lad of a little more than twenty, with a comely brown head, pleasant-faced and neatly attired, who was entirely in his master's confidence.

Overbury waved his hand in invitation. "Let us in, then."

Sir David hesitated a moment, then, bowing slightly, crossed the threshold. From the narrow passage he was ushered by Sir Thomas into a long low room that was almost bare of furniture. A little oval table of oak stood in the window, and four tall chairs were ranged against the wall. On a rack above the overmantel were hung a half-dozen rapiers, whose padded points announced them for practice swords. As many targets with daggers attached to them were ranged on either side of this rack.

The long space of floor was bare, and in the middle of it was boldly drawn a square of chalk whose sides were some seven feet in length. Within the square, touching its sides at a tangent, there was a circle, and within the circle a network of lines curious and mysterious to the staring eyes of Sir David Wood.

Sir Thomas smiled a little under cover of his moustache as for a moment or two he watched the other's puzzled inquiring glance. Then he uttered a little laugh, scarcely more than a chuckle.

"You admire my magic circle, Sir David?"

Sir David started; almost he changed colour.

"Magic!" he echoed. "Do you practise necromancy?"

Sir Thomas laughed, more freely this time. He divined the thoughts that raced through Sir David's mind and left the flitting shadows of their passage on his swarthy countenance where men might read them. Since Overbury was not only a warlock but had the impudence to proclaim it, there should be a short way to deal with him. King James's witchfinders should do his business.

"Necromancy?" Sir Thomas was echoing through his laughter. "That is divination by the dead. Oh, hardly that. The sorcery of this is of a different order. This is the Circle of Thibault. You're a travelled man, Sir David. You'll have heard of Thibault of Antwerp."

Sir David shook his head, his face forbidding. "I do not meddle in such matters. Thank God!" And he added: "Ye're singularly rash and bold, Sir Thomas."

"Bold, aye. But rash! On the contrary, I am prudent. We are at cross purposes, I think. When a man has so many enemies among the envious, the dishonest and the greedy, it is well that he should make use of some magic to protect himself in extreme cases. So I have taken up the magic of the sword. Telomancy, it might be called. Thibault is the greatest living master of the sword. Upon the schools of Capoferro and Paternostier he has built a system of his own. That circle with its lines is necessary for the perfecting of his methods." He turned about to Davies, who stood grinning in the doorway, relishing his master's jest at the expense of this stranger. "Come hither, Lawrie. Strip off your doublet, and we'll show Sir David the mysteries of Thibault. That is," he added quickly to his guest, "if the display will afford you interest, sir."

Sir David, crestfallen a little by the explanation which destroyed almost as soon as they had sprouted those hopes of seeing Sir Thomas burnt at the stake, was nevertheless still profoundly intrigued.

"It would interest me deeply," said he.

Sir Thomas offered him a chair, and only after he had taken it did it occur to him that Overbury, having divined the purpose of his visit, did this to mock and intimidate him at the same time. No mean swordsman himself, however, he was assured that he would not easily be scared by any display of foreign tricks, and that when these displays were over the laugh should be with him.

Meanwhile Sir Thomas rid himself of his cape-cloak, untrussed his points, threw off his doublet, and stood forth tall and active as a cat, the lithe proportions of him now fully displayed as he came on guard in shirt and breeches, armed with sword alone, whilst the slightly shorter Davies faced him with sword and dagger.

He explained the reason to Sir David. "Nature, as you perceive, has endowed me with a more than ordinary length of reach, which in itself gives me advantages over most opponents. To render the contest with this lad more equal, I discard the dagger. I desire you carefully to observe my feet. It is in their movements that the magic lies, and it is to guide them that these lines are drawn."

Davies led the attack. As Sir Thomas side-stepped, parried and riposted, he explained the movements, and Sir David was swordsman enough to perceive before long the magic of it. Presently it was Sir Thomas who attacked, and as Davies fell back before him, he feinted suddenly, and overtook him by a lunge under his guard of crossed sword and dagger which hit him fairly in the stomach.

The lunge as yet was little understood among swordsmen, and Sir David opened his eyes a little wider as he looked on. A moment later Sir Thomas hit his opponent again by simple imbrocade achieved on a sudden straightening of his arm after deflecting a thrust. Later still, when Davies lunged vigorously, Sir Thomas stepped aside to withdraw his body from the line of that hard-driven blade, and at the same moment presented his point at the other's face over his guard.

"Enough," he cried, and stood at ease. "That will suffice to show Sir David the peculiar magic of my circle. Away with you, Lawrie. If Sir David requires a closer acquaintance with Thibault, he may take your place."

But Sir David did not. As the door closed upon the departing lad, he rose to take his leave. He had seen enough to show him that he would never earn his thousand pounds that way. But Overbury did not intend that he should go as easily as he had come. There was a strain of sardonic humour in Sir Thomas, as his writings abundantly show, which he now proposed to indulge.

"And now, Sir David, to business." He was fastening his doublet as he spoke. "You had something to say to me, I think?" And lest Sir David should now be reluctant to say it, Sir Thomas' next words barred and bolted his every exit. "You had some satisfaction to demand of me, I think. Some accusation that I had been the means of losing you a thousand pounds. I well remember the occasion. You sought to make use of patronage to obtain something to which you had no honest title. You did not first take the precaution to inform yourself that my Lord Rochester has never made any awards that should be against the interests of the Crown, just as unlike most founts of patronage he has never accepted a bribe from any suitor. This being my Lord Rochester's policy – of which at this time of day every man is I think aware – and I being my Lord Rochester's vehicle, it is foolish in you to have expected or to resent any other issue. That, sir, I think, is all."

And Sir Thomas smiled pleasantly into the other's angry face.

"All? By God! It is by no means all. You spoke of honesty, I think?"

"Does that word puzzle you? Have you no knowledge of its meaning?"

"Od's wounds! You are insolent!" stormed Sir David.

"Unusually frank, perhaps. The matter is some two years old. Why have your remonstrances waited until now? Is it that they are being used as a cloak for some design you come to execute as the lackey of my Lord Northampton?"

The swarthy face of Sir David Wood was livid. With difficulty he curbed his fury so that he might answer coherently. "You make it very plain that your purpose is to affront me."

"Am I not amiable? Is not that the purpose with which you sought me? I am meeting you halfway." He smiled ever with that deadly, infuriating mockery. "You cannot in reason require me to go farther."

"Indeed, no," said Sir David. "You have gone quite far enough." Sir David was committed. Whatever his reluctance to engage this man since the exhibition he had witnessed, honour did not now permit him to withdraw. "When will you cross to France with me?"

Sir Thomas shook his head. "I have no thought of it. Affairs demand my presence here in London. If you desire satisfaction of me, you must obtain it here."

"Here! With the edicts? The King would break the survivor."

"Need that trouble you?"

"By God, sir, you're insufferable!"

"You are not required to suffer me. I shall await your friends."

Either Sir David was reduced to frenzy or he made pretence of it. It is difficult to avoid a suspicion that he welcomed the way out which the other's attitude afforded him.

"You count on your protection by your powerful friends at Court. But in what case am I? Who will protect me? Sir Thomas, you presume upon your position. Again I invite you as a man of honour to cross to France with me."

"And as a man of honour I decline the invitation."

Sir David gave a long stare, and finally shrugged. "There is no more to be said at present, then." And he moved towards the door.

Sir Thomas made haste to open it for him. "Should you change your mind and decide to meet me here, I shall be prompt to oblige you."

Sir David disdained to answer. In the passage the waiting Davies gave him exit to the street.

He went off to report his failure to her ladyship. His tale was that the cowardly Sir Thomas refused to meet him anywhere but in London, well knowing that no man of sense could agree to a step that must bring down upon him the stern displeasure of the King. In his eagerness to parade his valiance he went too far. Sir Thomas Overbury, he asserted violently, counted upon sheltering himself from the consequences behind my Lord of Rochester.

"And if," said her ladyship slowly, "I were to promise you his lordship's protection against what may come after?"

Sir David felt like one who has stepped foolishly into a trap. "If your ladyship will bring me two lines in that sense above his lordship's signature... "

"You ask too much," she interrupted him. "How could his lordship afford you that? It could be used to proclaim him a hirer of bully swordsmen."

Sir David was downcast. "Yet short of that, my lady, I hardly dare to venture."

"That's it! That's it!" said she. "You hardly dare to venture."

"Madam!" Indignation swept through him at the taunt, "You do me a deep injustice."

"How can that be, Sir David! I use no more than the words in which you have passed judgment on yourself?" She smiled a little, pensively wistful. "I mind me of the day on which you protested that your life was mine in any need of it to serve me. Yet when the moment comes – and to serve not only me but also your own self – you are soon daunted."

"Daunted!"

"It is clear that Sir Thomas was not daunted, and Sir Thomas has no romantic object to allure him. You spoke of his cowardice, I think, Sir David. Are you so sure that that fault lies in him?"

"You mean that it lies in me?"

"He is ready, at least, to do that which you confess you dare not do."

Sir David rode back to London with a black rage in his heart. To the mortification he had suffered at the hands of Sir Thomas Overbury, my Lady Essex had added immeasurably by telling him what he knew to be the truth. There is in the human heart no hatred more bitter than that which is aroused by discovery of mean verities concerning him which a man seeks to dissemble from his own self. The fact that Sir David had undoubtedly been stirred to love for Lady Essex but served to deepen the complexion of his present rancour.

It was a rancour that was later to bear fruit.

Chapter 22

The Quarrel

The great party hostile to Rochester received in November of that year 1612 a shattering blow in the comparatively sudden death of its most powerful, influential and active member, the Prince of Wales.

On the fifth of the month, whilst bonfires blazed and fireworks crackled and exploded in London streets to commemorate – as commanded by the King – his majesty's miraculous preservation from the gunpowder barrels of Guy Fawkes and his associates, Prince Henry lay dying in St James's Palace. Never had the engaging and able young Prince been more firmly established as the popular idol; never had the gulf between himself and his father been wider. Out of this grew dreadful rumours at the time, which received colour from the fact that Mayerne, the King's foreign physician, had been sent to attend the Prince in his last illness, and was known to have quarrelled violently with Hammond, the Prince's doctor, on the subject of the measures to be taken. There was a deal of talk of the enmity between the Prince and my Lord Rochester and of the excessive love of the King for his favourite, and from all this conclusions were drawn very useful for the enemies of Lord Rochester, and some which even dared to go beyond him in pointing the accusing finger.

But not all the rumours afloat or to be invented could diminish my Lord Rochester, who, never more secure in the royal favour, never exerting a greater influence over the doting King, was now at the meridian of his power, a fixed and glowing star of unrivalled magnitude in the firmament of the English court, deriving an added lustre from the partial eclipse of that group which in the past had striven under the aegis of Prince Henry to curb his growth. One who sought him at Royston in the course of the new year has left it on record that there was no need to ask direction to his lodgings there, since the great crowds that flocked about it fully advertised its whereabouts.

The only flaw in his present happiness was that provided by Overbury's hostility to his relations with my Lady Essex, a hostility spurred now by the sense of personal peril aroused in him by the affair with Sir David Wood. The matter reached a sort of climax late one night during the following April.

They were gay in the King's apartments at Whitehall in the course of a protracted carousal over which his majesty presided. But Rochester was not of the party. Indeed, of late, in the pursuit of his love affair and presuming upon his favour with the King, he had been a little negligent of his duties at his majesty's side. If the King was aggrieved, he displayed it as a woman displays her anxieties over a lover's negligences, by increased attempts to please him.

Rochester came back from Hounslow a full hour after midnight, and going straight to his quarters was surprised to find Overbury there with his secretary, Harry Payton, in attendance.

The consciousness that Overbury knew why he was so belated, and that he disapproved of the matter which was the occasion of it, acted as an irritant upon Rochester. He had almost a boy's sense of having been discovered in something that must bring him a reproof.

Staring from the threshold upon his friend who sat at the writing-table, his head resting on his hand, Rochester challenged him sharply. "How now? Are you still up?"

Slowly Sir Thomas raised his head. His eyes swept over that brilliant figure from the diamond buckle in his plumed hat to the rosettes on his high-heeled shoes, and a sneer curled his thin lips.

"And what do you returning at this time of night? I have urgent papers here that wait your signature."

Lord Rochester came forward slowly, a scowl on his brow. Sir Thomas waved Payton away; bade him go wait in the gallery outside.

"What are those papers?" quoth Rochester.

Sir Thomas rose, thrusting back his chair, and proffering it by a gesture to his lordship. The documents were spread upon the table. "Sit," he said, almost curtly, "and see for yourself."

His lordship looked at him, and might have observed that his narrow face was very pale and that his eyes burned as if he had the fever. He sat down ill-humouredly, and reached for a pen. He dashed his signature at the foot of the first document almost without glancing at it, and put it aside to take the next one. In a few minutes all was done, and he flung down the pen. "Could they have not kept until morning?" he asked.

"They could not." Overbury's tone was cold. He had remained standing by the table. "They are of the utmost urgency. A courier waits below to ride to Dover. These papers are for France, and they should have gone long since. But to be sure the whole progress of the State must stand still while you seek the company of your woman."

"Woman?" cried Rochester, coming sharply to his feet "Woman, did you say?"

But Overbury, with the thought of Sir David Wood to deepen his bitterness, did not mince his answer.

"Aye! And base! Like all her lewd brood, from her bawd of a mother."

He stood straight and tense, and by the quality of the anger in him seemed a man at once of fire and ice, so that at one and the same time he chilled and scorched his lordship with his person and words. Some curious magnetic quality of dominance he possessed to restrain Rochester from striking him in that moment. "Will you deny it? Can you? Cast your mind back upon all that there has been: her relations with you whilst her husband was abroad; her commerce since with that bawd Turner and with filthy necromancers, practising the devil knows what evil rites to gain her ends with you and Essex."

"Be silent, man! In God's name!" Rochester was livid. The door to the gallery stood ajar and Overbury's voice was vibrant and far-reaching. "Be silent, or I'll strike you dead."

"And like the bee slay your own self in killing," sneered Overbury. "For without me, I tell you again, you are naught. I have borne you up on my shoulders, and from these have you climbed to the eminence you hold. Yet now all my pains and all my patient labours are to be turned to naught by the ruin of your honour and yourself, which is what will follow for you upon this marriage. You go not forward in the matter by my consent. I warn you now that if you do, you had best look to stand on your own legs."

But now his lordship met sneer with sneer. "Why, here's a threat! You may leave me when you please, and the devil go with you. My own legs are straight enough to bear me up, I warrant you."

"You may find it otherwise; for your tailor and I have made a man of you between us."

They glared at each other, these two who had been as Damon and Pythias, and hatred was in the eyes of each. Each curbed himself by an effort from giving it the expression of physical violence. It was Rochester who spoke at last, in a dull concentrated tone.

"You have said things, sir, which may be neither forgotten nor forgiven. Things for which, as God's my life, I will be even with you yet."

"So be it," said Overbury with ominous quiet, the volcano of his passion smothered to outward view. "I desire that tomorrow we part. Let me have that portion which is due to me, and I will leave you free to yourself."

"So that you leave me free of you, it is what I most desire," he was answered, and upon that Lord Rochester flung out of the room in a passion.

Overbury stood there for a spell after he had gone, immobile, thoughtful. Then mechanically he folded the documents into a package, tied and sealed it, and summoning Payton, handed it to him for delivery to the waiting courier. That done he departed the palace, and walking like a man in a dream, he went home to his house in King Street. But not yet to bed. The April dawn was near when at last Sir Thomas sought his couch. Nor did he sleep even then. The turmoil of his thoughts kept sleep afar. Here was the end of all his soaring hopes and proud ambitions. His years of patient toil were wasted. Tomorrow he would be naught again, he who had wielded an almost kingly power, whose smile had been courted, whose nod obeyed. The bond into which he had entered with Robert Carr when first he had come five years ago, to lift him by the power of his genius to the dizzy eminence on which he stood, was broken now. The breach, as he had said, meant ruin to them both. And all this for a woman, a golden-headed, blue-eyed enchantress, whose beauty, which would stale with custom, blinded the fool to everything else within his purview.

In these bitter reflections was the night consumed – it was in bitterness that he went next day to that workroom of theirs in Whitehall, there to await Rochester, so that they might come to their final accounts and close this partnership which had been so portentous to them both.

By dinner time he had not yet seen his lordship. The day wore on, and still his lordship did not come. He sent to seek him more than once. But each time his messenger brought word that my Lord Rochester was nowhere in the palace.

Unopened dispatches lay upon his table awaiting attention. To clerks and secretaries who came to him for orders upon this matter or upon that Sir Thomas vacantly returned the answer that they had best await the coming of his lordship. He accounted himself already a dismissed servant, presently to depart almost as empty-handed as he had come. For just as Rochester had through all his time of power remained incorruptible, so had Overbury. Looking back now, he dubbed himself a fool for his honesty. Another, foreseeing the possibility at least of such an end as this, would have taken advantage of his position to enrich himself. He pondered these things now in his bitterness, as he sat there, waiting, dejected of countenance and blear-eyed from lack of sleep.

Lord Rochester, meanwhile, was spending most of that critical day closeted with my Lord Privy Seal. By last night's action Sir Thomas had finally accomplished the very thing he sought to avoid, and the dread of which had been at the heart of his rage. He had definitely thrown Rochester into the ready arms of the Earl of Northampton.

Northampton, between elation and alarm, had heard him out, his grey predatory old countenance expressionless as a mask.

"We must seal the mouth of this damned scab without delay and before he can do more mischief."

"As to that," said Rochester, "there's an end to him. It was agreed last night between us. We part at once, and he shifts for himself hereafter."

There was a faint note of contempt in the voice that answered him.

"That's not the end of him by any means. He knows too much; far, far too much. You have been so free in your commerce with him that he may even hold evidence of what he knows; and even without evidence he could deliver and maintain by his infernal wits a tale so formidable that he would entirely wreck the chances of the nullity when the Commission shortly comes to sit."

"God help us!" cried Rochester in such dismay that Northampton laughed outright if none too pleasantly.

"It's a timely prayer," said Northampton in derision. "The ground of our petition is about as firm as quicksand. Only Essex's despair made such a document possible. As it is, the Archbishop has already expressed his hostility, and it will need the utmost care in the appointments to ensure a Commission which will give a majority in our favour. Leave Overbury free to talk – perhaps even to come forward as a sworn witness to the things that are actually within his knowledge – and there's an end to all our hopes."

The truth sent a chill through Rochester. "What then?" he asked helplessly.

They were in the library. Northampton was sitting at his writing-table, his profile clear-cut against the window on his left. He leaned his head on his hand, and his low-lidded eyes were hidden from the younger man. His voice came soft and sibilant, pregnant with terrible significance.

"His silence must be absolutely ensured."

Rochester seemed to crumple in his chair. There was no mistaking the meaning of that terrible old man, and Robin, whose nature was warm, generous and kindly, was aghast at the practical ruthlessness of this veteran in intrigue. He recalled a March twilight in a firelit room at Whitehall, when he had passionately cried out against the splendours which were but evidences of his shame in being no better than a fribble despised by all men of worth. He remembered how Overbury had offered himself, the glowing promises he had made of what should come of their association. He could see him again, tall, straight and slender, his sombre garments redly illumined by the leaping firelight, putting forth his hand to the clasp which was as the seal upon the unwritten bond between them. And he heard his own voice saying: "Stand by me, Tom, to make common fortune with me, as I with you," to which he was to add a moment later: "It is a bond in which I'll never fail of my part." Swiftly his mind surveyed that long, and at times, arduous road which in the last five years they had travelled together. How loyally in all things Overbury had kept to the bond, how generously and utterly he had given the service which he promised.

And now on this April day he sat here in this fine room with all its evidences of wealth and culture about him, and listened to its owner, this old man who, whatever else he had learnt in more than seventy years of life, had never yet learnt pity, proposing coldly and emotionlessly that Overbury should be blotted out lest his tongue should threaten the aims of that same old man's ambition. For Rochester was under no delusion on the subject of this ambition. Overbury had made that clear, and the conviction of Overbury's accuracy came to his lordship now with the perception of Northampton's ruthlessness.

Suddenly he broke the silence, to cry out, shuddering: "Never that! Never!" And he rose as he spoke, urged forward by his emotion.

The pallid eyelids of the old Earl were suddenly raised. They seemed to roll back like the membrane from some reptilian eye, and two bright steely points stabbed sharply at the young man.

"Never what?" quoth he in his passionless voice. "I have made no proposals. You answer your own thoughts, sir, rather than my words."

Rochester moistened his lips as he stared back to meet that burning gaze.

"What…what, then, is in your lordship's mind?" he asked, his tongue stumbling over the question.

Faintly Northampton smiled. "Why, nothing yet, beyond the fact I have stated. Overbury's silence must be assured. How to do it is yet to be considered. Could he be bought, do you suppose?"

Mechanically Rochester shook his head. He could not yet free himself from the conviction of Northampton's earlier meaning. "No gold would buy him."

"Preferment, then?"

Rochester turned away, and walked the length of the room in thought, his chin sunk to his breast. Slowly he came back. An idea had dawned in his mind.

"I might secure him an embassy abroad."

Northampton considered. "It might serve, provided he were sent far enough away."

"We need at this moment an envoy in Muscovy. The appointment is being considered now."

"That should be far enough. Will he accept it, do you think?"

"I cannot answer for that. But in the pass to which things have come, it is very probable."

"If he refused it…" Northampton checked on the thought. There was a sudden gleam from his steely eyes. "Od's life! I have it. I see a way to seal him up until you're safely married and his blabbing can do no harm." And Northampton expounded a plan in which he displayed so much craft and guile that Rochester was awe-stricken by the glimpse it afforded into the old man's mind.

But the plan was ample for their present needs; and that hardly less would serve, Rochester was quick to perceive, and when at last he departed to Whitehall he bore with him the resolve to act upon it.

He found Sir Thomas waiting for him in that room of their close and intimate association, that room in which their joint fortunes had been so gradually and laboriously consolidated. Rochester advanced briskly and held out his hand. Pale and stern, Sir Thomas rose, looked at the hand and then into his lordship's handsome face.

"How now?" he asked, almost mistrustfully.

"For the sake of all that's gone between us, Tom, if part we must, at least let us not part enemies. Something I may yet do for you, even though henceforth we go separate ways."

A moment yet Overbury hesitated before taking the proffered hand, and when at last he took it there was no warmth in his grip. Rochester set his other hand on his friend's shoulder.

"We were distempered with each other last night. We uttered words which should never have passed between you and me."

"Whose was the fault?"

"Leave that. We have unfortunately come to a pass in which we can no longer stand together. You disapprove the course I take. You are determined to oppose it, and I am determined to pursue it. We cannot agree. So that's the end of that. But it need not be the end of all between us."

"I do not see what's left."

"What is to come to you, Tom? What shift will you make for yourself?"

And now Overbury laughed, but with an undercurrent of bitterness. "Why, in your own words last night, my own legs are straight enough to bear me up. I'll tread my ways upon them, never fear."

"I might help to make those ways pleasant, profitable, of consequence. How if I brought the King to offer you the Paris Embassy, sending Digby to Muscovy instead?"

"So that's the aim. To send me packing."

"But at least not empty-handed, Tom. At least with an honourable office which may lead you in time to the fulfilment of your every ambition."

Sir Thomas thought of the Treasurership which he had accounted so nearly within his grasp, and by comparison with which an embassy was but a paltry affair. Still, it was honourable, as his lordship said. Certainly better than going back to seek a precarious livelihood in the Inns of Court, and with his talents it might conceivably lead him in time to better things.

So, like the philosopher he was at heart, he thrust down his bitterness, and made his peace with Rochester upon those terms.

It was agreed that what had passed between them should be forgotten; that Overbury on his side should cease all active opposition to the divorcement of Lady Essex, and should not either by word or deed throw any obstacle in the way of its accomplishment. Until his future was settled he would continue here to discharge the functions of his secretaryship.

His gloom and dejection scarcely mitigated, Sir Thomas sat down again to open the dispatches which had lain all day untouched upon his table.

Chapter 23

The Trap

The Lord Privy Seal was closeted with the King.

His majesty had supped in his bedchamber, as was often his habit, alone save for the three gentlemen who had waited upon him. He had washed his fingers, and wiped them on the napkin Haddington had proffered him. Then my Lord of Northampton had been admitted, the gentlemen in attendance had been dismissed to the antechamber, and the Earl and the King were alone together.

His majesty, who was now approaching fifty, had aged considerably since that day in the tilt-yard, seven years ago, when first he had taken notice of Robert Carr. Persistent gluttony and excessive drinking of sweet sugary wines had combined with indolence to dispose him towards obesity of body above limbs which remained shrunken. His florid face was growing wrinkled, his eyes more lachrymose than ever.

He lolled in an armchair, untidily, his quilted doublet half unbuttoned, and his sandy head was covered by a hat, a black velvet cone with a jewelled buckle to secure the band. On the table before him stood a beaker and a goblet. He had filled the latter with dark syrupy Frontignac which he loved to sip very gradually as he talked.

The Earl having announced that the matter which brought him was of a certain gravity, was invited by the King to speak with complete frankness. Yet he hesitated a little, standing there beyond the table, his chin in his lean claw, his beady eyes fixed and thoughtful.

"There is," he said at last, "a certain scab who is uttering rumours, dark hints and other false lewdnesses which may come to embarrass the Nullity Commission."

"What's that?" The sudden change of the royal countenance warmed Northampton with the assurance that he touched his majesty in a tender place.

For days King James had toiled with pedantic infatuation upon the matter. He had pored over Scripture, the Fathers of the Church and the Laws of England.

He had resolved deep problems of civil and canon law on the subject of divorcement, and he had particularly considered the knotty question of whether a petition for divorcement could, in any case, be made on behalf of a woman; and he had spent long hours in cogitation and in setting down the fruits of all this labour before reaching the decision to appoint a Commission. When that decision was reached it was merely so that an authoritative body of lawyers and divines should pronounce the judgment which his majesty had already reached.

Not his *Counterblast to Tobacco*, not the infinitely more learned and profound work of Daemonology, not even the *Basilicon Doron*, nor any other of his pedantic outbursts had ever brought him such rich delight in his own erudition as this treatise upon the case of Lady Essex, a treatise which ransacked all history, divinity and law, and must, if published, leave the world aghast at the stupendous compass of his learning: a treatise which, if he had been the meanest clerk instead of King of Britain, must still have made his name immortal.

And now he was told that some kennel rat by the use of scandal was at work to nibble at the foundations of this mighty edifice. He could not have heard aright. Therefore he demanded that his lordship should repeat to him this incredible thing. His lordship repeated it, and added to it a little.

"This scab dares in his effrontery to criticise the policy of your majesty in appointing the Commission."

" 'Ud's death!" James almost choked on the oath. "My policy? My policy! Who's this ye speak of?"

"His name is Overbury. Sir Thomas Overbury."

The anger that now arose in King James was a different thing from the erstwhile indignation of his offended vanity. It turned him pale by its addition to the score against a man whom already he hated so implacably. His goggle eyes stared at the Earl. His jewelled fingers shook so that they were forced to abandon the mechanical attempt to take up the cup before him.

It was some time before his majesty spoke. When he did so his voice was strainedly calm.

"And he talks, you say, of this policy of mine?"

"So much, your majesty, that it is high time he were silenced."

"It is what I'm thinking."

Northampton had never seen the King so grim. Never had he beheld so completely in eclipse that quality in James which had led Overbury to speak of him once in private to a crony as a faux bonhomme. He sat a while huddled there, his jewelled fingers toying with the buttons of his doublet. "If after this, Robin should still stand between that rat and me… " The sentence closed in an inaudible mumble.

Presently his lordship ventured a comment on a sigh. "Lord Rochester has a great kindness for the rogue."

"Too great a kindness," growled the King. "Had it not been for Robin I'ld have laid him by the heels long since. And even now Robin will come storming to me and cluttering my wits with his clavering in defence of this rogue. But, by God's death, I'll not be moved to weakness this time."

Yet even as he took the oath he seemed shaken by a doubt of his power to keep it if it ran counter to the wishes of his pampered favourite, and by rage to think that his darling Rochester should waste such love on that worthless rogue. Misgivings, jealousies and choler brought him almost to the point of tears. He slobbered

233

fearfully. "Some years since," he complained, "I'ld ha' sent him ambassador to France, paying even that price to be rid of him from about the Court, so that my sight should not be troubled by that eye-sorrow. But Robin would not have it. Robin must keep him here beside him, never heeding my heart-scald. Ud's death!"

"If your majesty were to offer him the same again – some foreign embassy – my Lord Rochester might not now oppose it. He has some knowledge of Overbury's loose talk, and would, I think, be as glad as any of us to have him away, at least for the present time."

"Ay, ay! But would he go? Would he go, the insolent, swaggering carle?"

Northampton raised his shoulders. "If he did not... " And there abruptly he checked, so abruptly that the King stared up at him with his pale, bulging, watery eyes.

"What's in your thoughts, man?"

"If he did not go," said Northampton slowly and very quietly, "there would be the Tower." He paused to add in the same quiet tone the explanation: "For disobedience to a royal command; for an affront to majesty."

They remained looking into each other's eyes, and the craft in Northampton's was slowly mirrored in the King's.

"We'll be hoping," said the King slowly, "that he disobeys. He'ld be safer a deal in the Tower than in Muscovy, and he deserves it better."

Northampton's eyes narrowed. "It might be contrived, sire, by the exercise of a little adroitness, that he should refuse the embassy."

"And who's to exercise it? The adroitness?"

"If your majesty will trust me in this."

"You'll prove yourself trustworthy, indeed, aye, and adroit indeed, if you can bring about so desirable a consummation."

"I shall hope to deserve your majesty's approval."

When presently he was dismissed, it was in the assurance that by the interview he was a gainer in two senses: the result should enhance his credit with the King and rid the Court of the plaguily inconvenient Sir Thomas Overbury.

Interviews followed between Northampton and Rochester in which the utmost frankness was employed, and between Rochester and the King, which was less ingenuous. It was Rochester who broached the matter to his majesty upon the morrow, in the course of their daily discussion of affairs.

"The embassy at Muscovy awaits the appointment of an envoy."

"Ay, ay," said the King. "Have ye any names to lay before the Privy Council?"

Rochester paused a moment. "Sir Thomas Overbury is about to quit my service."

"Is he so? Ah well! I'll not pretend that I'm not glad of it. I never loved the cullion, nor ever knew why you should love him. But what has he to do with Muscovy?"

"He is better qualified for that or any other embassy than any man I know. Your majesty held some such opinion of him once when you offered him the embassy in Paris."

"Did I so? Belike it was to be rid of him, Rabbie. Ah well, lad, Muscovy'll be better for him than Paris. Russia is a country in which he may cool his superabundant heats. And it'll take him farther from me, though hardly far enough for my pleasure. Ye see I'm frank about the carle. If you ask it for him he shall have the office."

And so it fell out that two days later Sir Thomas Overbury received a visit from the Lord Chancellor Ellesmere, who came formally in the King's name to offer him the embassy to Russia.

Sir Thomas was taken aback. Muscovy was not Paris. In Paris with his fluent French and his close intimacy with French affairs he could rapidly impress himself as a man of weight. But Muscovy was altogether different. He had no Russian, knew little of Muscovite ways and less of its politics. Moreover, it was almost as far as the Antipodes. Had Rochester, he asked himself, but played a game with him?

Of all this, however, he allowed no glimpse to escape him. Soberly he received the proposal, and soberly answered it that he would take time to consider, an answer which caused the old Chancellor to raise his brows. For a man of Overbury's apparent position at Court an embassage was a great honour, the acceptance of which should require no reflection. Moreover, the offer was in the nature of a royal command. Lord Ellesmere, however, did not stay to argue with him, but left him to the consideration for which Sir Thomas demanded time.

All the time he required was to lay the matter before Rochester, who heard him out with a serene countenance.

"The King," he was answered by the favourite, "is loth to displace Digby, who has served him well in Paris. But your reasons are just enough, and if you refuse the offer of Muscovy I nothing doubt that France or the Low Countries with which you are so well acquainted will presently be opened out to you."

Sir Thomas was relieved by this assurance, and trusting to it, desired Lord Rochester to inform the King that respectfully he declined an appointment for which he did not feel himself equipped.

Two days thereafter, late in the afternoon, there came for Sir Thomas a summons to appear before the Privy Council. He went without hesitation or any apprehension of what awaited him.

With his brisk step he passed between the two scarlet yeomen of the guard who kept the portal, and confidently entered the council chamber.

It was a room of moderate proportions, hung with Flemish tapestries, and lighted by a high window at the farther end, between whose mullions the leaded panes were aglow in the evening sunlight. A long table covered by a Persian carpet occupied the middle of the room, and the lords of the council were ranged in their seats on either side of it. At a lesser table apart sat the clerk with his scribes.

Sir Thomas, tall and elegant in his rich dark suit and delicately starched ruff, came to take his stand at the vacant end of the council table. Facing him, the King's great gilded chair stood empty, and as his keen eyes raked the two lines of councillors, gliding over the Lords Northampton, Pembroke, Nottingham, Southampton and the rest, he observed on his right another empty chair. Lord Rochester, too, was absent from his place.

All eyes were turned upon him, and he knew that not a single pair could he count as friendly. Not a lord present who was not secretly his enemy, however much the greater part of them might in the past have expressed a spurious friendliness which did not deceive him, whilst some, like Pembroke and Shrewsbury, had ever been avowedly hostile.

Although he had ruffled it for years on equal terms with them, yet he was not one of them, and they made him conscious of it now, allowed him to perceive in their bearing their contempt of him.

His fine sensitiveness was quick to apprehend all this. And yet it scarcely galled him. What they were, they were by right of birth, a right by which the most worthless may parade the honours carved him by a forebear. What he was, he was by right of his own worth, his talents and his industry. They were but descendants. He was of the stuff of which ancestors are made.

In that consciousness he stood calm and firm, if a little puzzled, under the volley of their glances.

The Lord Chancellor rose in his place to give him formal welcome, and formally to repeat the offer of the Russian embassy.

Calmly Overbury announced his well-considered reasons for declining an appointment to which he did not feel himself competent to do credit. To answer the haughty stare with which his refusal was received, Sir Thomas added to the reasons already expressed to Rochester in private certain excuses on the grounds of health. The climate of Russia was of a rigour which he did not feel himself physically able to confront.

But before he had come to the end of this Lord Pembroke had interrupted him.

"Sir Thomas, I'll make so bold as to remind you that the King intends this gracious offer for your good and preferment, and I'll beg you to weigh well your answer."

Overbury looked round the board, and everywhere met hostile eyes and sneering lips. Did they venture not only to browbeat him, but to do it with contempt? He felt singularly alone in that moment, like the hart when it turns to face the hounds that race to pull it down. But like the hart at bay, he fronted them boldly, and answered them out of the anger which their enmity was kindling in him, and also out of his trust in Rochester.

"I have weighed it, may it please your lordships. It is not my desire to leave my country for any preferment in the world. But since the King commands I will submit to go, provided that I am sent to some place where I can serve with advantage to England and honour to myself. Russia, my lords, is not of these for the reasons I have given."

The Lord Chancellor compressed his lips and inclined his head. Less to Overbury than to their lordships he announced that he must take the King's pleasure in the matter, and upon that went out, leaving Overbury where he stood.

Their lordships took no further heed of him, but broke into murmured talk among themselves. Conscious that he was being deliberately ignored, he continued to stand there, keeping his head high and his glance steady for all that every moment that passed added to the calculated indignity of his position.

They were bitter moments for Sir Thomas, the more bitter since in the pass to which things were come the future was likely to offer little opportunity of paying off the score with these gentlemen who now so calculatedly insulted him by their disregard. But for my Lady of Essex how different would all this have been. But for the schemes of that scaly-headed Northampton yonder, who peered at him now and again from under his reptilian eyelids, these gentlemen, whatever the hostility in their hearts, would be fawning upon him cap in hand, as they had fawned aforetime, knowing him for the man who ruled the favourite who ruled the King.

The moments passed leaden-footed, and there were many of them to pass before, at long last, the Lord Chancellor, moving gravely in his fur-edged robes, re-entered. He was followed by an officer and two yeomen of the guard, whose appearance made some stir among the gentlemen about the council table.

Overbury, too proud to yield to curiosity and turn his head, did not yet see them, and certainly did not suspect their presence, or else he might have had some indication of what was coming.

Lord Ellesmere advanced to the council table. "His majesty, may it please your lordships, is rightly indignant at that, in his own words, he cannot obtain so much of a gentleman, and one of his own servants, as to accept an honourable employment from him. Rightly he accounts this insolence of Sir Thomas Overbury's a matter of high contempt, and he commands us to commit him for it."

He made a sign to the clerk of the council, who thereupon grew busy upon a parchment, whilst Sir Thomas, recovering from his momentary stupefaction, broke forth into protest.

"My Lord Chancellor, will you give me the law of that?" He was white, and his dark eyes smouldered wrathfully.

"The law of it?" The Lord Chancellor raised his grey eyebrows. Someone at the table laughed.

"Aye, the law of it," insisted Overbury. "I am myself more than something of a lawyer, my lord, and before you lend yourself to this I demand to know by what law of England the King can compel a subject to leave the country."

"You shall have law enough to comfort you ere all is done," he was assured, and then the clerk approached him with the document he had been preparing.

Those preparations had been suspiciously brief, as Overbury was presently to remember. Meanwhile he was still protesting and demanding, no one heeding him, and he was still at it when the warrant signed by the Lord Chancellor and countersigned by Pembroke was handed to the waiting officer.

Only then, as they ranged themselves on either side of him, did Overbury become aware of the two yeomen of the guard. He looked from one to the other with dilating eyes. Then commanding himself, and sweeping their lordships once more with his haughty glance, he took his leave of them.

"Well, well, my lords! It seems we must argue this another day."

They led him out, and marched him swiftly along the gallery, and so by way of the Privy Gardens to Whitehall Stairs. Not until he stood there and beheld the waiting barge of the Lieutenant of the Tower did he perceive how complete were the preparations and understand the trap that had been laid for him. But as he stepped aboard the barge there was more scorn in his heart than dismay. They were fools indeed if they thought him a man so easily to be repressed, and whatever followed he would see to it that Robin should repent this perfidy. Thus, neither his courage nor his confidence deserted him. Better for him had it been otherwise.

Chapter 24

Temptation

The arrest of Sir Thomas Overbury set Town and Court agog with rumours. The most prevalent of them was that it was no more than a prelude to the fall of Lord Rochester himself.

This was also the most foolish of them, since there can be little doubt that his majesty already had in view the further aggrandisement of his beloved Robin on the occasion of his marriage to which the Nullity Commission should clear the way. And to ensure that the Nullity Commission should not fail in this, his majesty continued to give his exalted attention to the suit.

He went out of town, carrying Rochester with him; but whether at Theobalds, Newmarket, Royston, or elsewhere, and whatever else was at hand for his entertainment – be it hunting, hawking, or cock-fighting – the enthusiasm of his majesty's labours knew no abatement. He still pondered and wrote for the enlightenment of the divines and lawyers who were to deal with the suit, and was so transported by his own learning and casuistry that he almost lost sight of the object to be served in his delight over the manner of serving it. Had the desire to please his darling Robin by setting free for him the lady of his choice been entirely absent, had the parties concerned in this divorcement been utter strangers to him, he still must have delighted in so extraordinary an occasion to parade talents whose compass, now that he came to employ them, astounded even himself.

In this stage stood matters some three weeks after Overbury's consignment to the Tower, by when the Commission headed by the honest, God-fearing Archbishop Abbot came to sit, and the fruits of its first sittings were laid before the King at Theobalds.

In the course of his closely reasoned opposition to the suit the Archbishop desired to know by what text of Scripture of either the Old or the New Testament a man might have warrant, on the grounds set forth by the petition, to make a nullity of â marriage solemnly celebrated; or what ancient Fathers, Greek or Latin, or ancient Council, General or Provincial, so interpreted any text. And he proceeded to quote Melancthon, Pezelius, Hemingius, and several others.

Abbot's gravely couched exposition threw the King into a slobbering rage. Was the Archbishop a knave or a fool that he so utterly ignored the masterly notes the King had sent him for his guidance, and still dared to ask questions which the King did not hesitate in his reply to stigmatise as "preposterous."

From that moment Viscount Rochester was for nothing in the matter. His majesty fought now not to please his favourite, but to vindicate his own views and his own authority. It became a duel between the King affronted in his vanity, and the Archbishop entrenched in his honesty. Fiercely the King went to work again upon a lengthy dissertation to confound the Archbishop's arguments.

Abbot nevertheless stood firm, and by his firmness so far swayed the doctors and divines who sat with him that by July it came to be generally known that the Commission was divided in its findings. Let the King rage as he might, a deadlock had been reached, from which the only issue appeared to be through the appointment of a fresh Commission.

The delay was vexatious to the lovers; but infinitely more vexatious were certain rumours which showed that not even his confinement in the Tower could suffice to muzzle Overbury. He had been receiving visitors, and he had been writing letters, and the tone of his utterances grew daily more minatory in a measure as the continuation of his imprisonment increased his indignation at the perfidy of Rochester.

To his first upbraidings Rochester had replied in mild and friendly terms, assuring Sir Thomas that if he would exercise a little patience all should presently be well with him, and upon his enlargement would follow some honourable office to compensate him.

In this there is no cause to doubt that his lordship was sincere. All he desired was that Sir Thomas should be kept close until the nullity were pronounced and he could do no further mischief.

When Overbury complained in June that he was ill as a result of his confinement, Rochester in a letter of solicitude for his health sent him a medicinal powder, and upon the heels of that his own physician Craig to minister to him.

Northampton, however, was inspired by no such gentleness. His relations with Rochester had now become of the closest. As a result of this, when the King and his favourite went out of town, Northampton stepped into the position of First Secretary of State. He directed the courses of Winwood and Lake, who nominally held the Treasurership between them, and he was virtually head of the realm.

He took steps at once to increase the rigours of Overbury's confinement. He sent orders to the Tower that Sir Thomas was no longer to be allowed the exercise of walking in the grounds, that he was to be denied all visitors, and that his man Davies, who had hitherto attended him, should be dismissed.

The faithful lad wept when he received the order to go, offered in vain to be shut up with Sir Thomas in his prison if they would allow him to continue to serve him.

Next, and as a warning to other visitors of Overbury's who might be disposed to talk, Northampton ordered the arrest of a gentleman named Sir Robert Killigrew, who was known to have repeated Overbury's assertion that he was in possession of knowledge which when divulged would bring the Essex nullity suit to naught.

Nor did his measures end there. Sir William Wade, the Lieutenant of the Tower, was already under a cloud over the matter of the escape of Seymour – the Lady Arabella's lover – from prison. Detested by Northampton for his remorseless persecution of Catholics, the Earl lent a ready ear to the accusations against him of dishonesty in the matter of some jewels belonging to the Lady Arabella, and, using this as his pretext, avenged himself of the knight's laxity concerning Overbury by depriving him of his position.

In his place, and on the recommendation of Sir William Monson, the Master of the Armoury, Northampton appointed a staid, dull and elderly Lincolnshire gentleman, Sir Gervase Elwes, to the office.

These measures sufficed to reassure the Lord Privy Seal; but they were inadequate to allay the alarm of his niece.

The dreadful rumours, which were already affording matter for the ballad-mongers in Paul's Walk, came to renew the dismay in which she wrote to her lover, absent in the King's train, and to fill her with shame and indignation to find her name a subject for rhymed ribaldries. She wearied her father, her mother, her brothers, and even old Northampton, with her bitter plaints. And they accounted her unreasonable in that she would not be quieted by the Lord Privy Seal's measures to tighten the bonds of the prisoner in the Tower. Only Anne Turner listened to her with the sympathy and feeling which it seemed to her that her case deserved.

They were on the Italianate terrace of the house at Hounslow, occupying a stone seat on which a carpet and some cushions had been spread. It was a hot and breathless day of July, and in the garden below the shrubs hung motionless and listless under the bright sunshine.

Her ladyship leaned forward, one elbow on her knee, her little pointed chin cupped in the palm of her hand, and she looked straight before her as she spoke.

"There is not one amongst them all who serves me for myself, or ever has done. Not my Lord Northampton, nor my father, nor my mother. They married me to improve their own fortunes. Now they are lending a hand to my divorcement because they perceive how it may be to the family advantage. Well might my Lord Northampton say one day that he thanked God he was not a woman. That to be a woman is an indignity. I have been made to savour that, God knows! I am savouring it now. What dignity have they left me? To what indignities have they not driven me? None knows better than yourself, Turner. In my despair I sought the assistance of your warlock Forman, and lent myself to abominations at the memory of which I burn with shame. Then there were the indignities of Chartley; that long-drawn contest; the insult of being wooed by a man by whom I was repelled; the physical fear in which I went of him, justified by his manhandling of me. And with all this, as if it were not enough torture for any woman, the agony of my yearnings for Robin, the distracting thought that we two, who love each other as sincerely as man and woman ever loved, were held apart by the infamous detestable bond of my unholy marriage."

The little widow sought to soothe her. She set an arm about her shoulders.

"Why dwell on all this now? It is to harass you for no good purpose. All that is over and done with at last, and the future is to make amends for what you have suffered."

"Is it, Turner? Is it? Who will assure me of that? What peace of mind is there for me while that fellow Overbury has it in his power to ruin all even now? Think of it, Turner! After all that I have endured, to find this villain threatening to lay everything waste again, and this merely for ends of his own, merely out of vindictiveness to find his own ambition thwarted. What have I ever done to the wretch that he should bring this evil upon me? Is it my fault that he has been sent to the Tower and that he has lost all that he possessed and his hopes of more? What need had he to meddle between my lord and me? Why could he not have had some thought for my wretchedness? Why should he deny me the little peace I have bought by years of suffering? Why? In God's name, Turner, why?"

Her stony impassivity was gone. She was in tears now, a panting, desperate, broken creature.

"Quiet, child! Quiet!" the widow crooned, tightening her grip of the heaving shoulders. "All that is now safely overpast. Let him lie and rot where he is. He can do no further harm."

"Can he not? How do I know that? Remember that foul ballad you brought me in which my name is held to the lewd mockery of lewd men. If he is not himself the author of it, at least it could have had no author but for the wickednesses he has uttered against me. A little more of this and it will suffice to make an end of the nullity. Already those words of his spoken in the Tower are ringing through London, to encourage my Lord Archbishop in his obstinate courses, as I hear."

"Peace, child! Peace! It is not so bad as your fears make it appear."

"Peace?" She laughed fiercely in her grief and bitterness. "There is no peace for me while that man lives. Himself he has said it, Turner."

"Then kill him." The widow heard herself pronounce the words before she was even aware that the thought was in her mind.

The Countess echoed them. "Kill him!" She spoke musingly, ever on that note of dreary bitterness. Then she sat up and uttered a short, hard laugh. "Should I hesitate, can you think, if it lay in my power? He is as a snake in my path, threatening my existence with his poison. Could any blame me if I put my heel upon his head?"

The fair little widow sucked in her breath. Her long eyes had narrowed in thought. Instinctively she looked about her in the pause that followed. They were quite alone, and all was silent on that terrace save for the hum of the bees that were foraging in the wallflowers along the foot of the stone balustrade.

"Do you mean it?" she asked softly.

"Mean it?" The delicate golden head was turned, the dark blue-violet eyes looked solemnly upon Mrs Turner out of that tear-stained face. "Mean what?"

"Why, what you've said. That you want him dead."

"What if I did?"

The widow pursed her lips. Her voice sank lower. "These things can be contrived."

Lady Essex shuddered. "O God! No, no! What's in your mind? More necromancy? But Forman is dead, thank God!"

"There are others still alive. I know of more than one who is able to do all that ever the doctor could do."

"No, no!" The musical young voice rang sharp and firm. "Not to save my soul, Turner! There has been enough of that. I can thank God that Forman's dead because the memory of my shameful dealings is buried with him. I'll never soil myself in that way again."

"There is no need why you should do anything at all."

Her ladyship's eyes questioned the widow, and the widow answered. "I know of one who, if less skilled in magic than was Doctor Forman, by much excels him in the use of medicines. He boasts a water that can slowly kill a man and leave no trace."

Her ladyship disengaged herself sharply from the other's sheltering arm. "What is it you suggest to me, Turner?"

"Dear child, I seek ways to help you. Did you not say you want him dead?"

"I did not! I did not say it!" Her ladyship's voice shrilled up a little in her vehemence, as if behind that vehemence of denial there was something that appalled her.

"You said that there is no peace for you while this man lives."

Lady Essex leaned forward again, both elbows on her knees. "There is a difference between wishing a man dead and setting out to slay him. And yet..." She broke off. "I am a hypocrite, Turner. Just now you made me shudder; you made me afraid of you; you awoke my horror. Yet you but pointed down a road that I have already desired to tread. Yes, even to that has desperation driven me." She paused a moment before adding the full explanation. "There was a man, a gentleman who vowed he loved me, announced himself my servant in all things, made big talk of being glad to die for me. It happened also that he, too, had been wronged by this fellow Overbury. He is reputed a deadly swordsman. I charged him to pick a quarrel with this man. He failed me. But that's no matter. I am nice, you see, in my discriminations. I start in horror when you propose in one way what already I have sought to accomplish in another." She rose abruptly. "God help me, Turner! They'll drive me mad, I think, before all's done." She pressed her hands to her brow. "My uncle Northampton is right. It's an indignity to be a woman."

The widow sat very still, and waited. There would be great profit in thus serving Lady Essex. The deadly water would be fully as costly as Forman's sublimate of pearls. But not on that account would she press the matter, or display any eagerness. She prospered in her various trades by knowledge of the human heart. She knew what a fruitful soil it can become under despair. She had planted her seed. Now let it germinate.

"I but sought to help you, child," she repeated presently. "It breaks my heart to see you so distraught. There is nothing I would not do to serve you, dear my lady."

The tenderness of her voice produced its effect. Her ladyship turned, swift grace in every line of her. "I know, sweet Turner; I know. Forgive me if I was harsh. I am curst as a shrew these days. Let us leave that now."

No more was said either in the matter of Sir Thomas Overbury or her ladyship's troubles. But in the week that followed the widow's words were too often in her ladyship's mind for its peace.

At the end of that time, fretted by lack of news of how things were going in London, she took coach and repaired to Northampton House. The King was at Newmarket, and Rochester was with him. But her uncle was able to inform her that not on that account was the matter of the nullity being neglected.

"I have letters from Rochester that his majesty is solving the difficulty of the deadlock, by appointing two further commissioners upon whom he can depend: the Bishops of Rochester and Winchester. But the whole matter is now put off until the end of September."

The delay was in itself a blow to her hopes. She knew how readily dangers are increased by delay. She sat down wearily, and looked at him in silence. He observed her face to be pale and peaked, and commented upon it whilst coming to pinch some colour into her cheeks with his lean old fingers.

"Fie ! Fie! What will Robin say to his lady if he finds the roses all withered in her countenance?"

"Will he marvel, do you suppose, considering the sleepless nights he must guess me to have spent? I am stretched by suspense as by a rack, and now you tell me that this must drag on, and that perhaps I must go again before the Commission to answer all their dreadful questionings."

"Scarcely that. But what then, provided all come right in the end? And right it will come, unless that scab Overbury works a miracle."

She caught her breath at the mention of that detested name. "Unless, do you say?"

He hunched his shoulders, standing before her with hands folded behind his back, his long black robe hanging loose about his lean shanks. "It is the only thing I fear. Elwes, the new Lieutenant, has his orders. But it's a world of fools and traitors, and I hear this devil Overbury is loud and confident in his daily swearing that while he lives no nullity shall be pronounced."

He fell to brooding, his chin upon his breast. Then after a while he laughed, with a display of yellow fangs, and patted her cheeks, and bid her down to dine with him.

But his doubts and misgivings had made her heart too sick. She could not eat. It was a dreadful thing that her fate, her whole future destiny, should hang in the balance thus; an intolerable thing that at any moment the balance might be brought down against her by the intervention of one who cared not what havoc he made of her life so that his own ends were served. Sir Thomas used her, as it seemed to her, to constrain her lover and her friends. It was as if he held the point of a sword at her breast and said to them: "Yield me my requirements or I slay her."

Was she to stand passive under that menace to herself and to them when by a single gesture, a single word, she could put an end to it?

Her smooth brow was furrowed, her sweet and gentle countenance darkly overcast by her soul's travail to find the answer to that question.

Chapter 25

The Bishop's Move

Sir Thomas Overbury was ill in body and in mind, and it may well be that his bodily sickness derived from his mental distemper. Denied exercise or visitors or communication of any kind with the outside world – saving only my Lord Rochester – he was treated, as he violently complained to the new Lieutenant, with as much rigour as if he had conspired against the State or plotted against the life of the King.

Sir Gervase Elwes, that grave, dull man, gave a stolidly courteous attention to his plaints, but denied responsibility in the matter or power to ameliorate the conditions. Sir Gervase merely acted upon his instructions. In one particular only did he mitigate the severity of the prisoner's condition. The servant for whom Sir Thomas clamoured as a necessity to him since the removal of his man Davies, a removal which he dubbed with the rest as a deliberate inhumanity, was presently supplied him in the person of a lean, elderly man with a forbidding countenance and a slight cast in one of his eyes, who answered to the name of Weston. Sir Thomas, however, yielding to his bitter humour, renamed him Cassius, from, as he said, his lean and hungry look. A memory, this, of one of Mr Shakespeare's plays which he had seen performed some time ago on Bankside. The fellow inspired him with hope.

He looked so utterly a scoundrel that Sir Thomas concluded he would prove corruptible.

Assured by now that Rochester was playing him false, Sir Thomas had reached that point where he would pass from threats to action. He recked nothing now of what might follow to himself – accounting that in any case his ruin was assured – provided that he could punish the perfidy of the man whom he had served so stoutly. One certain way there was to accomplish it. From his brother-in-law Lidcote and the others who had visited him he had learnt the honest attitude taken up by Archbishop Abbot in the matter of the nullity. If Sir Thomas could contrive to be brought before the Commission to give evidence, he knew that he would not only wreck the nullity, but stir up such a scandal that the King, to save his own face, would be constrained to sacrifice Rochester to the popular indignation. From his knowledge of King James's ways, he had no doubt whatever that in such a difficulty his majesty would never hesitate. There were elements of comedy in the situation that moved him to laughter as he considered them.

The resolve to communicate with the Archbishop was now formed. The vehicle, he thought, had been found in this new servant who had been sent to wait upon him in his wretched quarters in the Garden Tower, which for so many in the past had been but the antechamber of death. He knew the corrupting chemistry of gold upon most men's loyalties, and studying his lean and hungry Cassius, he concluded that here was a rogue who would pawn his soul for a handful of money.

He went to work with art. He sought to stir the sympathies of the fellow with the unnecessary rigour of his treatment considering the littleness of his offence. There were things he needed: linen, books and the like. Yet he must forgo them because he was not allowed to write to those who could supply them. If Weston would smuggle a letter to Sir John Lidcote, Sir Thomas would add a postscriptum to that letter instructing Sir John to give the bearer five pounds.

He saw the covetous gleam in those shifty eyes which never seemed to meet his own, and his hopes were encouraged.

Weston demurred. If it were discovered, it would go ill with him. Said Sir Thomas, who cared nothing what might happen to the rogue, that he would so provide that there should be no risk of discovery. Weston yielded, and left Sir Thomas to write his letter. Now it is not by precipitancy of action that such men as Sir Thomas Overbury win to eminence.

Sir Thomas wrote his letter. But it was just such a letter as he had pretended to Weston that he desired to write. A letter informing Lidcote of his health, of his hopes of delivery shortly by the favour of my Lord Rochester, and requesting his brother-in-law to send him some shirts and some books, which he enumerated. He added the instruction that the bearer was to have five pounds.

Weston did what Sir Thomas feared he might do. He carried the letter straight to Sir Gervase Elwes. Sir Gervase examined it, and although finding it no more than was pretended, acted strictly upon the instructions he had received from my Lord Northampton, which were that no letters, excepting only such as might be written to my Lord Rochester, should be allowed to pass. Sir Gervase sent the letter to the Lord Privy Seal.

Days passed, and neither shirts nor books came for Sir Thomas. He took Weston plaintively to task, and at the same time called him a fool for having lost this opportunity of earning five pounds without any harm done to anyone. Weston had by now reached the same conclusion independently. He made a frank confession, adding to it that if Sir Thomas would write again, he would this time contrive the delivery of the letter.

But still Sir Thomas practised caution. He wrote again, precisely as before, merely adding a complaint that Sir John Lidcote should not have heeded his previous request, and an injunction that this time he should send the articles not as if in answer to a request for them, but as the result of his own assumptions that Sir Thomas would be needing them.

Three days later came a parcel to the Tower, which after close inspection by the Lieutenant was handed to Sir Thomas. It contained the shirts and other things, and so brought Sir Thomas the assurance that his letter had been delivered, and that henceforth he would have no difficulty with Weston.

But before he could take further action he fell violently ill, as a consequence, it seemed to him, of something that he had eaten or drunk, and for days he lay tortured by pain and fever in that sparsely furnished stone chamber. It gave him a pretext for writing to Lidcote again. His condition brought about fresh requirements, and again he tempted Weston to convey a letter for him. Weston showed reluctance, whereupon Sir Thomas raised the price to ten pounds, and Weston succumbed on the condition that he should read the letter before it was sealed.

Sir Thomas allowed him to read it, and thereafter turned to the table to fold and seal it. For an instant only was his back to Weston, but in that instant he did all that was required. Into the letter he slipped another note, already folded and held in readiness within the palm of his left hand. It was an operation he had previously rehearsed. Weston was at his side as he tied and sealed the missive, and had no cause to suspect the juggling.

The man earned his ten pounds, and Sir John Lidcote found himself in possession of a note for the Archbishop of Canterbury, which he was to deliver either upon receiving from Sir Thomas a request for peaches, or at the end of three weeks if in that time he should not have received any communication at all from the prisoner.

It was then that Sir Thomas wrote his fiercest, frankest denunciation to Rochester and his renewed threat that unless he were shortly restored to liberty he would take such steps as should effectively make an end of all his lordship's hopes of a nullity.

After that Sir Thomas, still weak and shaken from his last illness, fell sick again, much as he had been sick before, and did not hesitate to assert to the Lieutenant who came to see him that he was being poisoned.

"But you may warn my Lord Rochester," he said between gasps, "that if I die, his nature shall never die, for I have taken such steps to publish it as will make him the most odious man alive. If you have any love for his lordship, or you desire to serve him, you would do well to warn him to have a care for my health, since nothing more terrible could happen to him than that I should die."

If Sir Gervase conveyed the warning, Rochester made no sign. Overbury must abide where he was until the nullity should have been pronounced. But Sir Gervase took measures to have the cell better ventilated, and left instructions that the rushes on the stone floor, which he found foul and noisome, should daily be renewed.

Thereafter the prisoner's condition improved; but his weakness abode in him. His vigour was sapped, and at the end of five months' imprisonment he was the ghost of the man who had come there on that April day in the Lieutenant's barge.

And meanwhile the three weeks were sped, and Lidcote, true to his instructions, and taking steps to conceal only the channel through which the letter was conveyed, forwarded Overbury's communication to Archbishop Abbot.

The middle of September had been reached, and the Nullity Commission was about to sit again, strengthened now from the point of view of Rochester by the two bishops who would vote as they were desired.

The Archbishop was in the depths of wretchedness. He perceived that he was being made the tool of worldliness, yet lacked the means to establish this so that he could combat it as his conscience bade him. When the letter from Sir Thomas Overbury reached his hands he regarded it as an intervention from on high to enable him to establish that which in his heart he already knew to be the truth.

Sir Thomas wrote that the nullity suit was based on falsehoods and concealments which it lay in his power completely to unmask, since no man apart from those interested in the proceedings was better informed than he of what actually had occurred. And he demanded in the interests of truth and of justice, human and divine, to be summoned before the Commission to give the evidence that was in him.

The King was at Whitehall again, and without loss of more time than was required to harness horses, the Archbishop got into his coach at Croydon and rolled up to the palace to voice Sir Thomas Overbury's demand.

My Lord of Canterbury reached Whitehall in the forenoon, and as the King came through the audience gallery he observed the sturdy figure and solemn overcast countenance of Abbot standing prominently on the edge of the crowd of courtiers. His majesty was attended by Rochester and Haddington, and his face darkened at sight of the divine who was so obstinately opposing his royal expositions upon divinity.

Nevertheless, he advanced towards him, and gave him his hand to kiss, whilst Rochester stood stiff and haughty in his splendour, looking down upon the portly, short-necked prelate whom he must regard as his enemy. Haddington, on the King's other side, betrayed a faint mischievous amusement at this meeting.

The King disengaged his arm from Rochester's and laid a hand upon the shoulder of the Archbishop. He looked into that grave countenance, with its kindly eyes and broad spade beard, and asked his lordship bluntly how the great cause went forward.

"I am here to speak to your majesty upon it," Abbot answered. "If your majesty would graciously hear a word in private... "

"In private?" mouthed the King. "Huh!" He paused, hesitating, then abruptly consenting, he almost propelled the Archbishop forward by the pressure of that hand upon his shoulder, and so leaning upon him, thrust him across the gallery into the recess of a window, where they were quite alone. "What is your private word, my lord?"

The Archbishop did not falter. He looked the King squarely in the face as he replied.

"Your majesty already knows that I have no liking for this suit."

"What's that to the matter?" wondered the King discouragingly. "I do not perceive the necessity in a judge for liking any matter whereupon he is called to pronounce."

"It matters if he should be rebuked for doing no more than his duty according to his conscience. It is naught to me that the Lady

Frances remain wife to the Earl of Essex or be married to another man. But I may not give a sentence where I see no proof."

His majesty frowned at this. But the prelate held to his course.

"I have lived fifty-one years almost, and had my conscience uncorrupted. I know not how soon I may be called before God, and I am loath against that time to give a wound to my soul. All my grief is that your majesty's hand is in this. For now there comes one who promises such evidence that will make plain the injustice of this suit."

"How now? And who may this be?" The bulging eyes looked startled.

For answer the Archbishop unfolded and proffered the note he had received. The King took it in his plump jewelled fingers and glanced at the signature. He uttered a grunt. "Huh! My old friend Overbury! Huh!" He strove to keep his mobile countenance inscrutable, studied to shut out of it the dark anger that welled up in him as he read.

A foolish fellow in many things, in others this James Stuart was of an almost diabolical acuteness, and never so acute as where effects upon himself were concerned. At a glance he perceived all the mischief Overbury might make, and all the scandal that might recoil upon his own head, rendering ridiculous in the eyes of the commissioners those masterly arguments of civil and canon law by which he sought to coerce them, and himself contemptible in the eyes of the world for endeavouring to juggle with justice and corrupt it for the profit and pleasure of those he favoured.

Underneath that fatherly benignity which he affected there was all the ruthless cruelty of the weak man, just as under that air of simplicity amounting at times to foolishness there was a depth of guile and craft which may not even now be plumbed. Never was a man better epitomised than he in the mot of Sully which pronounced him the wisest fool in Christendom.

Under the searching, almost stern eyes of the Archbishop he was now all benign fatherliness and simplicity. In the depths of him passion boiled unsuspected, his craft was being swiftly exercised.

Too long had this insolent fellow Overbury been a thorn in his flesh and a source of friction between himself and his darling Robbie. And not even now that he had flung him in the Tower did the fellow cease from gaffing him; indeed, he threatened things which in their ruthless, reckless sweep were a menace to majesty itself.

The King tugged at his beard whilst he read the note a second time and pondered it. He lifted his plumed hat and scratched the back of his fulvid head whilst he read it yet a third time, and all the while he was considering. At last his countenance reflected a decision taken, a benign decision, the Archbishop was relieved to see.

"Aye, aye! If the man can say aught that signifies, he must be heard. But what can he say of his own knowledge? He can but retail scandals and gossip and suchlike. Still..." The King paused and sighed. "Far be it from me to give grounds for a reproach that I lightly stopped the mouth of any man. You must have him before their lordships, and hear the evidence he pretends to have. If it prove naught but vindictiveness without any solid foundation of fact, we'll deal with him afterwards. I see the fellow says he's sick and infirm. But no doubt he'll be well enough to come before your lordships. I'll take order about it."

The Archbishop, who had feared a raging refusal to the reopening of evidence, was moved to thank his majesty almost with tears in his honest eyes.

The King patted his shoulder, murmuring some empty words in commendation of his lordship's honesty of which he assured the Archbishop that he had never held a doubt, or else he would not have placed him where he stood. Then, with Abbot beside him, he shambled back across the gallery towards a group of watchful Howards – Northampton, Suffolk, and some others of the family, with whom now was Rochester.

At the moment his majesty said nothing of the matter to any of them. But after dinner, when he was withdrawing for his afternoon rest, he beckoned Rochester away with him, and in the privacy of his bedchamber, having driven out the valet Gibb, who waited, he not only showed his lordship the Archbishop's note, but informed him of the Archbishop's natural insistence that this witness should be heard.

"Obstinacy, I've aye observed," said the King, "to be a strong characteristic of Churchmen. They care not a rushlight what havoc may be wrought so that they keep rigidly to the line of conduct which their doctrine-ridden sense of duty points to them. So that they may sleep tranquil in the sense of duty done, they care not if half the world goes sleepless."

His lordship was not listening. With dismay on his fair, handsome face he stood there, lost to everything but the cardinal point in this business.

"You'll never consent, sire!" he exclaimed at last.

"Consent? D'ye perceive what it means? The clattering of this man's venomous tongue has already brought my policy in the matter of the nullity under criticism. Will I now consent that these criticisms be made to appear justified, and have my judgment held up to the opprobrium of the vulgar and the ignorant? Will I consent to that? Well may ye assume that I will not. But his lordship of Canterbury insists that I do, and if I oppose that plaguey insistence the consequences to myself may be even worse. D'ye perceive in what a cleft stick we're held by this sweet friend of yours whom in an evil hour you brought to be your secretary? Ud's death! He aims at destroying your happiness and my honour at one and the same blow!"

The royal countenance was flushed. It had lost the last trace of its usual foolishly benevolent expression, and the bulging eyes were bodeful.

Yet even in that moment Rochester must pause to defend the friend whom his conscience told him that he had already used with excessive harshness, and that it was this harshness and the fear, perhaps, of worse to follow that drove Overbury to use in self-defence the only weapon remaining him. Something of the kind he said, fetching a sigh as he said it, and thereby increased his majesty's anger by a revival of his jealousy.

"Can ye defend him even now?" he bawled. "Can ye defend him when he's threatening your prospects as well as the findings of my wisdom? In God's name, Rabbie, what is the love that lies betwixt ye?"

"It's an old friendship," said his lordship. "And I hope I shall ever be loyal to my friends."

"Your friends! He's your friend, this scum of mankind?" There was froth on the royal lips. Then he changed to a tone of bitter sarcasm. "I am, then, to allow him to go before the Commission lest your loyalty to him shall be affronted?"

"No, no! In God's name, no!"

"I'm glad we're of a mind at least in one particular concerning him. Will ye tell me, then, how it's to be prevented? How am I to avoid keeping my word to the Archbishop, which was that Overbury should be heard."

"Your majesty has already promised that?"

"A pox on your dull wits, Rabbie! How could I not without betraying bad faith? It was imperative that the promise be given. It's just as imperative that it should not be kept. Will ye tell me how I am to accomplish this?"

At a time of less mental trouble and confusion it must have been perceived by his lordship that the King was pressing him to some definite course, demanding of him a clear expression of something already in the royal mind. As it was, Rochester heard only the words, and entirely missed their accent.

With rumpled brow and his glance on the ground, he answered thoughtfully: "It's to be considered."

The King's glance was dulled by disappointment. "Very true," said he dryly. "Very true. It's to be considered. And if I am to preserve my dignity and you are to marry Frances Howard, the answer must be found." He rose and shambled towards the day-bed which Gibb had prepared for him. "Go, leave me now," he said in another tone, and yawned almost as he spoke.

Rochester bowed himself out a very troubled man.

Chapter 26

The King's Move

My Lord Rochester was still troubled on the morrow, when in attendance upon his majesty he went to Windsor, whither the King chose to retire until the Nullity Commission sitting in Lambeth Palace should have done its work.

It occurred to his lordship presently that before leaving town it would have been prudent to yield to the impulse to visit Sir Thomas in the Tower. He might have succeeded in dissuading him by pleading with him, in the name of their old friendship and by sincere promises of good to follow, to abandon the vindictive course he was bent upon pursuing. As it was, even if Overbury's uncorroborated evidence did not suffice to wreck the nullity, it would raise such a scandal as must make impossible Rochester's subsequent marriage with Lady Essex.

It is little wonder that his lordship was moody and thoughtful during the first three days at Windsor. He moved in dread of a further discussion of the matter with the King. Yet, oddly enough, his majesty never again alluded to it, nor seemed unduly troubled, hunting daily in a spirit which almost suggested that he had no care for anything else in the world.

And then, on the third day came news which completely and finally disposed of the whole matter.

Sir Thomas Overbury was dead.

He had succumbed suddenly in the Tower to the disease which it was now divulged had been consuming him for months.

Thus wrote my Lord Privy Seal to his majesty.

For Lord Rochester there was a brief note from Northampton to inform him that all had been done for Sir Thomas which the necessary rigours of his confinement permitted, and that as lately as Tuesday he had been visited by the King's physician, Sir Theodore Mayerne. Sir John Lidcote had viewed the body, the coroner had held his inquest, and burial had immediately followed.

His majesty sent for Rochester, and made no secret of his elation. The fellow had died most opportunely, a bare twenty-four hours before he must have appeared before the Commission to give evidence. The nullity was now assured.

Rochester, however, did not share the elation. No consideration could lift him above the gloom resulting from Sir Thomas Overbury's death in the circumstances in which it had taken place. He remained oddly conscience-stricken, obsessed now by the memory of the bond that had been between them, of the high hopes in which they had mutually entered upon it, of the generous manner in which Sir Thomas had fulfilled his part until lately, and of the pitiful manner in which it was now determined.

In some sense he felt as if he were the murderer of Overbury, for it was by the duplicity he had practised towards him that Overbury had been placed in circumstances whose rigours had destroyed him. It did not greatly help him to consider that Sir Thomas had brought this upon himself by his own intransigence. On a generous mind the ills that are suffered compare very lightly with the ills that are wrought, and Robert Carr, whatever his failings and shortcomings, was generous to the point of weakness.

The King's leer and his half-chuckle as he announced to Robin that Nature had intervened most opportunely filled his lordship with horror and remorse.

Opportunely was the word that re-echoed through his mind. On the eve of being brought before the Commission, Sir Thomas' death was opportune indeed. Singularly opportune. Suspiciously opportune. Rochester, closeted with his majesty, was appalled by the sudden twist of his thoughts. They raced down a fresh avenue gathering confirmation at every step.

The King, looking up at him from the chair in which he lolled with a bedgown loosely pulled about him – for the dispatch from London had reached him while he was still abed – was startled by his aspect.

"Why, what ails you, Rabbie? Are ye sick, man?"

And Rochester looking down upon him with stern, accusing eyes, answered slowly:

"Ay! Sick!"

"Man What's sickened ye?" The royal uneasiness was manifest in his goggling eyes.

"The opportuneness, as your majesty has said, of Tom Overbury's death. Was it truly Nature that intervened so seasonably?"

"Nature, surely, since disease is but a weapon of Nature's; and the fellow had been far gone these weeks they tell me."

"Yet your majesty hoped he might recover?"

"Nay, now, nay!" James almost smiled at this. "Ye cannot impute quite so deep a charity to me as that, and I'll not be a hypocrite to assume it."

"The facts impute it. That, or something else. So solicitous was your majesty on the matter of Tom's health that you sent your own physician to wait upon him."

James' loose mouth fell open in astonishment and dismay.

"I have it in a letter from my Lord Privy Seal," Rochester informed him. "Sir Theodore Mayerne visited Tom on Tuesday. And on Wednesday he died. On Thursday he would have given evidence before the Commission. These facts make up a singular procession."

"Ud's death, man! What d'ye imply?" The King displayed an anger that was not entirely histrionic.

His lordship, livid of countenance, shrugged disrespectfully and sneered into the face of majesty. "Why did you send Mayerne to visit him? Was it that Mayerne might cure a man whose death would be, in your majesty's own words, so very opportune? A man for whose recovery it were, again in your majesty's own words, too deep a charity to impute to you that you should hope."

"Stop!" The King heaved himself up out of his chair. He was trembling, and well may it have been with anger at the contemptuous tone in which he was addressed by this favourite to whom he had given many liberties. "You forget to whom you are speaking." He pulled the loose gown about him, and strove to bring an appearance of majesty into his untidy person. "Sometimes, my lord, you appear to forget that I am the King."

"Sometimes," he was boldly answered, "your majesty forgets it."

They stood eyeing each other like men who are about to draw and engage. The King's usually florid countenance was ashen. He shook with wrath.

"I'll not forget this, Robin," he mumbled indistinctly. "I'll be even with you for this."

"My God!" It was a cry of horror from Rochester. He covered his face with his hands. "Those were the very words I spoke to Overbury, as he has since written to remind me. And dying he'd think it was my hand that struck him down."

The pain in his voice moved the King oddly. His queer affection for this bonny lad whelmed forth in pity to drown his wrath. He made a noise of clearing his throat, and shambled forward to Rochester's side. With one hand he held his bedgown about him, with the other he patted Rochester's shoulder.

"He'll know better now, lad," were the extraordinary words with which he sought to soothe him. "He'll know better now. He'll know ye're not to blame; that ye had no hand in it; and he'll know that he brought it entirely upon himself. Why, what's to greet over, when all's said?"

Rochester lowered his hands from a face that was ghastly.

"Come, Rabbie, come! Here's weakness. If the rogue had lived he would have wrecked your every hope of happiness, and not only yours, but hers, which, if ye're a lover worth the name, should be of more account to you than your own. Hasn't the poor lass suffered enough for love of you that she should have been left to suffer more by this fellow's malice? And what of me, Rabbie? Do I count for naught? Is your love for Overbury far above your every other feeling that in your sorrow for his death ye can take no thought for the sorrows his life would have brought those who love ye? Away with you to London, lad, to see her ladyship, and bid her be of good cheer; tell her from me that the nullity is as good as pronounced and that the wedding bells will soon be ringing now. Away with ye, until ye can think more kindly of your old dad and gossip James, and realise that ye've no better friend in all the world."

Rochester bowed and stumbled out with no word answered, leaving his majesty very thoughtful.

But it was two days later before he returned to town, keeping until then to his own lodgings in the castle. In that time, having recovered from the shock of the news, he came to take a less compromising view. There was, after all, much in what the King had said. Overbury had become a menace not only to himself, but to King James and to Frances. On their behalf, if not on his own, let him now put all resentment from him. What King James had done he had a perfect right to do in self-defence and in the exercise of kingcraft against one who openly avowed his aims to bring the King into contempt. And since further he must suppose that King James had also been actuated in part at least by solicitude for himself, he could not in justice bear him rancour.

Nevertheless it was with a sad heart that he rode to town with his little troop of lackeys, and sought the Lord Privy Seal at Northampton House.

In the library there he found his lordship steeped in all those affairs which but a few months ago had been in the charge of Overbury acting on behalf of Rochester himself. He could not repress a pang to observe in how short a time his lordship had gathered into his own hands all those threads of policy and power, and how completely by almost imperceptible degrees he himself had been elbowed aside, until today he knew of affairs no more than others chose to report to him.

My Lord Northampton came to meet him with a fond welcome. Like the King, he pronounced most opportune the decease of Overbury. Like the King, he perceived in the event only grounds for thankfulness on my Lord Rochester's behalf. The thing, he confessed, was making some stir. His agents reported that Paul's and the ordinaries were full of rumours. The idle and the malicious must ever be talking to the detraction of their betters. There was a tale abroad that Overbury had been poisoned, and it was being said that the hand that had administered the dose was the same that had struck down Prince Henry.

"But let them talk," the old Earl added with a contemptuous shrug. "They will the sooner weary. What matters is that the fellow's death has put a term to all our troubles and misgivings."

"Yet I would that end might have been achieved without his death," said Rochester heavily.

The keen, crafty old eyes surveyed him. The Earl sighed. "So would we all, to be sure. And there's none to blame. All that could be done for him was done. The King's own physician ministered to him, as I told you, yet could do nothing to save him."

Rochester looked sharply at the Earl, wondering did he know, or did he suspect. But the old rogue's inscrutable countenance told him nothing.

He muttered empty platitudes, and went in quest of Frances when Northampton told him that she was in the house.

With his arms presently about her, he found at last the balm his wounded soul was needing. She was pale and fretful with dark shadows under her lovely eyes heightening to feverishness their lustre. He realised without being told that these were the signs of all the anxieties she had been made to suffer by the activities of Overbury, which threatened to thrust her back into the hell from which at last she was to win respite. Realising this, and realising as he held her how intolerable to him must have been the irreparable loss of her, he came at last to think with the King and with Northampton that Overbury's death in all the circumstances had been most opportune.

Chapter 27

Marriage

After a jury of matrons had been empanelled, and its evidence heard, the packed Commission delivered its sentence of nullity, transforming the Countess of Essex back again into the Lady Frances Howard, within a week of Sir Thomas Overbury's death.

The seven commissioners who voted in favour of it earned thereby the lasting approval of the King; the five who opposed it deserved his unuttered rancour. Nor did it soften this to discover that among the great majority of his subjects, noble and simple, the opposite view was taken of the respective merits and demerits of his commissioners.

Six weeks later his majesty gave fresh proof of his love for Rochester by creating him Earl of Somerset and bestowing upon him the Barony of Brancepeth with its broad acres to add to his already vast possessions, who seven years ago had been a simple esquire owning little more than the suit of clothes in which he stood.

And now all the talk of Court and Town was of the forthcoming marriage. To provide for it on a sumptuous scale at a time when the Treasury was empty, the prodigal King was driven to a sale of crown lands, and every penny proceeding from this source was recklessly squandered in gifts and in junketings that lasted for a week from December 26th, the day on which the marriage was celebrated.

The Lady Frances, all in virginal white and with hair unbound, was led to the altar by the Duke of Saxony, then on a visit to the English Court, and her great-uncle Northampton, who counted confidently upon achieving through her the gratification of his every ambition.

Always of a supple slightness, her ladyship was now seen to have grown slighter still in the last few months, and on her countenance there was an etherealising pallor and in her eyes a look almost of fear. This was compassionately assigned to all that she had borne in the course of her unhappy marriage to Lord Essex.

After the banquet at Whitehall, the masque especially written by Campion for the occasion, and the dancing that had followed this, Robin carried her off to the village of Kensington and the house which he had rented there from Sir Baptist Hicks.

Wearied to exhaustion by the strain of the day and the revelry of the night, she reclined in an armchair, whilst her bridegroom knelt to her in all his own bridal finery of shimmering white satin laced with silver. Thus reverently kneeling, he took her slim, shapely hand in his, and swore so to use her as to make amends for all that she had suffered and all that for love of him she had so bravely fronted.

That oath of his appeared to galvanise her into fresh energy.

"It was! It was!" she declared with a vehemence odd in one who a moment earlier had seemed so lethargic. "All, all was for love of you, Robin. To make me yours without let or hindrance. Always remember it, Robin mine. Always remember it."

"Should I forget it ever, child? Could I?"

Her fingers made play absently with his golden curls, which were on a level with her breast. "Let it forgive all! Let it condone all."

"Forgive? Condone?" He laughed at her earnestness and slipped an arm about her waist. "Child, you're overstrained."

"I am." The caress of his voice drew tears from her. "Oh, Robin, Robin!" She looked down upon him, smiling wistfully. "We have bought and paid in advance – aye, and paid heavily – for happiness. See to it that nothing cheats us now."

"Why, what should cheat us sweetheart?"

"I... I don't know. I am full of fears."

He rose and drew her up with him, and held her close against his breast, tenderly stroking her wet cheek. "Rest you, dear wife, and put all fear behind you. We've done with fear and with evil of every kind. Rest you, sweetheart." He kissed her fondly, gently. "I'll call your women."

But there was no enduring rest just yet, for body or for mind. The wedding festivities were no more than begun. They were to continue for a week and on a scale such as no wedding at Whitehall had ever witnessed.

Gifts of unparalleled munificence even in that prodigal reign were showered upon the happy pair. The King alone bestowed jewels on the bride to the value of ten thousand pounds. Masques were performed nightly for a week, Ben Jonson writing one of them, Campion another, and Sir Francis Bacon yet another, which he mounted entirely at his own charges and with that reckless extravagance which was already distinguishing him and giving grounds for conjecture. The Lord Mayor entertained the new Earl and his Countess at a great banquet in the Merchant Taylors' Hall, and in the very tilt-yard in which Mr Robert Carr had first tumbled into the lap of fortune a tourney was held in which no colours were seen but his own and his lady's. Moreover, the occasion appeared to be one which had reconciled all parties. Even the Queen had been induced to put aside her hostility to Carr, and she appeared so far to forget the opposition she had encouraged to the nullity as to lend her countenance to these festivities to the signal extent of presenting the marriage bed to the bride. And the noble Pembroke, the chief and most avowed of all Carr's enemies in the past, actually rode in the tilting-match wearing the Earl of Somerset's colours of green and gold.

This, however, was to prove no real alliance, but merely a truce in hostilities which the events were abundantly to nourish.

The marriage so ardently desired and reached by such arduous labour, and over obstacles apparently insurmountable, had the effect of placing Somerset entirely in the power of Northampton and the

Howards. With at least a dozen members of the family in prominent offices at Court, they made up a formidable party, immeasurably strengthened now by the inclusion of the royal favourite.

Very soon this had the effect of creating an opposing faction. The Herberts, the Seymours, the Russells and others bitterly resented this monopoly of Court favours by a single family, and a family, moreover, of secret recusants.

Somerset perceived all this, and was far from easy or happy in his position. He cast about him for means to secure himself, and in that hour missed Overbury as he had never missed him yet. He needed Overbury's sound judgment and shrewd counsel to guide him. He perceived already that he was on the wrong side. He saw the forces of the anti-Howard faction daily swelling, until it included almost every man of any worth and weight, and he had a presentiment that sooner or later a storm would break in which the Howards would be swept away, and he with them. He remembered now all Overbury's warnings against alliance with the Howards and with that old scoundrel Northampton in particular.

In his unguided casting about him for security, he took perhaps the most disastrous step of his career. The appointment of Secretary of State was still to make, and as the desperate emptiness of the Treasury made the assembling of Parliament at last a necessity, that appointment could no longer be delayed. Sir Thomas Lake and Sir Ralph Winwood continued to discharge the duties of the office, whilst hoping for ultimate appointment. In addition one of the Nevilles was another candidate.

His lordship considered, and made choice of Sir Ralph Winwood. A big, bulky, swarthy man this, with a plain, fleshly face, blackbearded, and with calm, shallow-set eyes. He was unprepossessing and sombre of demeanour and puritanically sombre of dress. But he had diligently sued Lord Somerset's favour, and he had come to the wedding laden with munificent gifts in token of his service. He was, too, a man of parts, shrewd and able, and Somerset fancied from his staid unpretentious carriage that in him he might find another

Overbury, diligently to discharge the duties of the office whilst leaving its honours to his patron.

The King, yielding as usual to his favourite's wishes, bestowed the exalted office as required upon the least likely of the three candidates. Neville was put off with some minor perquisites and retired in sulky resignation. Not so Sir Thomas Lake. His claim had been far the weightiest, based upon years of faithful service and ripe experience in affairs acquired under Elizabeth. He took his exclusion as a personal affront from Somerset, accounted himself injured and insulted at one and the same time, and he went over to the camp of the favourite's enemies, to become the bitterest and most vindictive of them all, a man vigilantly waiting for an opportunity to pay off the score.

A full year went round before that opportunity came, and in that year a great deal happened.

The Earl of Northampton died in June, performing that last act of his life with a pomp and circumstance which sorted well with his ambitions. It was an irony that he should have held for no more than a few brief months some portion of the power for which he had waited, schemed and striven down the years.

The Privy Seal went to Somerset. Upon Suffolk, at last, was bestowed the Treasurership which Northampton had coveted, and Suffolk's vacated office of Lord Chamberlain was also filled by Somerset to the exasperation of the stately Pembroke, who had stout claims to the office and was supported by the Queen in suing for it. It seemed as if the King's infatuation and Somerset's greed knew no bounds.

All these fresh hostilities sprouting about him, quarrels with Lennox and Hay over the question of a Spanish alliance, and the tangle which appeared in foreign affairs under Somerset's unguided control, began to exacerbate him.

In the Low Countries Spain and Austria had joined forces against the Protestant States. The Elector Palatine was in danger, and was calling upon his father-in-law, King James, to fulfil the treaty obligations by assisting the allies, and the good faith of Somerset came under suspicion in consequence of the pro-Spanish leanings into which the Howards had manoeuvred him.

Bewildered by events which he lacked the skill and judgment to control, he longed for Overbury more passionately than ever. Overbury's wits would have made all clear and would have pointed the safe road, and Overbury's miserable end thus brought remorsefully to his mind helped to increase his moodiness and irritability.

It was said of him in those days that he was hag-ridden. His erstwhile radiance had definitely left him. His easy affability was dissipated, his gaiety and good humour lost. He became gloomy, arrogant and inaccessible, a man whose nerves were frayed and ragged.

In disagreements with the King, which were now of common occurrence, finding himself without the ready arguments which Overbury had formerly supplied, he adopted a bullying tone, and a manner so outrageously overbearing and disrespectful that at last his majesty uttered an indignant warning, which the headstrong Somerset would have done well to heed.

"You'll be wise to remember, Rabbie, that all your being, except your breathing and soul, is from me."

"For which I have given such loyalty as you never had from any, not even though he were of your own blood," was the haughty answer.

The King's watery eyes considered him from under sullen frowning brows.

"Am I to repent having raised a man so high that he shall pierce my ears with such speeches?"

His lordship shrugged contemptuously and turned sulkily aside, which brought the King to his feet in a passion.

"And now y're insolent! By God's death, man, never let me apprehend that you disdain my person or undervalue my qualities, unless you would have my love for you turn to hate. Get you gone! Go study a proper carriage and a humble behaviour before you seek me again, so that you may wash out of my heart your by-past errors. Go!"

Somerset bowed sulkily and went out, and the King, bruised at heart, sat down to weep, like a woman whose lover grows cold.

The only living person towards whom Somerset still maintained the erstwhile gentleness, affability and graciousness which once had enabled him to override the prejudice begotten by his sudden elevation was his Countess.

They had moved from Kensington to Chesterford Park, near Theobalds; and thence in consequence of her ladyship's delicate health to Isleworth, where they were now established. Her condition gave him some concern, and may have increased the tenderness of the fond devoted lover he remained. But if he was never harsh, at least he could not even in her presence put aside the increasing melancholy growing out of the difficulties he was daily encountering: the hostility by which he was surrounded, and his sense of uncertainty in the handling of affairs.

He gave her, as men will when troubled, more of his confidence; told her more of the past than he had ever told her yet, and dwelt particularly on the stout services Overbury had rendered him, unburdening himself, to her infinite and obvious distress, of the remorse that gnawed at his conscience.

Phrases from Overbury's last dreadful letter were seared as with an acid upon his brain:

Your story shall be put down to betray and so quit a friend... All this ill nature showed by the man whose conscience tells him that trusting to him brought me hither... My share to be a prison upon such terms that no man suffered yet... And he that is the author of all and that hath more cause to love me, yea, perish for me rather than see me perish.

Thus from memory he quoted gloomily one day, until her ladyship, deathly white and breathing hard, ran to him where he sat, entwined her arms about his neck, and drew his golden head down upon her breast as if to shelter it there and protect it from this foul legion of memories that harassed and unmanned him.

"Dear love, you see but the fruits and not the cause in this. How could he call you the author of his ills that was the wanton author of his own?"

"Yet by my betrayal of him was he cast into an imprisonment whose rigours resulted in his death."

"It would not have been so rigorous had he not made it so."

"Perhaps not. And yet sometimes I feel myself his murderer. And I loved the man."

She uttered a little moan, and held him closer. "That you were not. You never meant his death. Yet, if you had, who that knew all could blame you? It would have been something done in self-defence, to save the ruin of all your life – of all your life and mine. And mine. Have you forgotten that? Have you forgotten the unforgivable things he said of me on the night you quarrelled? Many a man would have slain him on the spot without pity."

"Better that," he answered. "It would have been cleaner and more honest. But there was that between us…so deep a debt of love and service… A bond into which I entered in my need of him.… "

"Yet had he lived, he would have ruined our hopes. He would have doomed me to a living death as Essex's wife, and you… O, my dear, my dear! You start at shadows. You remember but the half of what is done."

"Because I miss him and need him now more than ever I did. Because I feel myself rudderless without him. There, I've confessed it. I perceive now how I should have acted. I should have heeded his appeals on the score of sickness; I should have explained patiently to him how much the nullity meant to me, how all my happiness was bound up in it. I could have melted him. I surely could. He loved me. And I… I left him to die like a rat in the trap I had sprung for him."

"Robin!" It was a cry of pain. "Of your pity do not torture me with more of this."

"Ah! Forgive me, sweet." He stroked the pale lovely face that looked so strained and anguished.

"Time," she assured him, "will soften all."

"Time?" He stared before him with haunted eyes. "Time can but make me more conscious of my loss. Daily his absence weighs upon me more heavily."

"Leave all this," she whispered to him with a sudden urgency of entreaty. "Leave the cares of office, the duties, the labours, the Court. There is no happiness in ambition. Let us go and live quietly at Rochester or Brancepeth or where you will. We have each other. Is not that enough, my Robin? Once away from all this you will find ease."

Well for him perhaps had he listened. But to the man who has wielded it, power is as a drug without which there is no savour in life.

Chapter 28

Mr Villiers

The opportunity for which the vindictive Sir Thomas Lake waited with vigilant patience presented itself at Cambridge in the following March.

The King, accompanied by Prince Charles, was paying the town a royal visit at once to honour the University and its Chancellor, the Earl of Suffolk. A great concourse of gallants attended the King, but it was to be observed that there were only seven ladies in the party, and all of these either by blood or alliance members of the Howard family. This had resulted from Suffolk's deliberate omission to invite the Queen, an omission deeply resented and calculated further to widen the gap between the Howards and the opposing faction.

Among the various functions offered for his majesty's entertainment was a performance of *Ignoramus*, a burlesque written in Latin by a fellow of Clare's and played by fellows of Clare Hall and Queens' College. Clare Hall, where the performance was held, had been tricked out and festively hung for the occasion, and a little tribune had been erected for his majesty, where he sat enthroned with the Earl and Countess of Somerset and the Earl and Countess of Suffolk in immediate attendance upon him, to be stared at by the academic groundlings.

The King showed great relish of the tedious, pedantic show, and its ponderous humour provoked the royal mirth to frequent outbursts. Clare Hall that evening was, however, to supply his majesty with another object of interest besides this play.

During the first of the interludes, whilst raking the ranks of the audience with his rolling watery eyes, the royal glance came to rest upon a slim, straight youth of perhaps a little over twenty, very gracefully made, arrestingly beautiful of countenance. He wore a suit of black that once may have been modish, but was now rusty and frayed, and what took the attention was that not even so shabby a setting could diminish the innate grace of his movements or detract from the innate nobility of his face in its frame of glossy chestnut hair.

The King favoured the young man with that almost intolerable persistent ogling which he bestowed upon all those who attracted his attention. He even went so far as quite openly to point him out to the Countess of Suffolk. The young man, grown conscious of this, blushed and shifted a little uncomfortably on his feet where he stood within short range of that volley of glances.

Among the observers was Sir Thomas Lake, whose dark eyes suddenly lighted with interest and whose keen face became suddenly keener.

During the next act Sir Thomas edged his way gradually across the hall, and at the ensuing interval the young man found a tall, stately and richly dressed courtier at his elbow, who smiled upon him ingratiatingly, sought his acquaintance, and presently displayed his interest in him by the questions he asked concerning his family and himself. Whilst talking to him Sir Thomas watched the royal tribune out of the corner of his eye, and assured himself that the royal attention had nowise diminished and that the royal ogling continued in increased measure to see one of his gentlemen deeply engaged with his lovely lad.

The young man answered Sir Thomas' questions with ingenuous candour. His name was George Villiers, and he hailed from Leicestershire, where his family had been established for four centuries. His father had been dead some ten years, and had left his family none too prosperous. The young man had been to France to finish his education. He was newly returned, and having been home to embrace his mother was now on his way to London to seek his fortune. The presence of the King and Court and his natural curiosity to behold them had delayed him in Cambridge.

"And so afforded me the happy chance of becoming acquainted with so excellent and accomplished a young gentleman," said the fine courtier further to embarrass him. "My name is Lake. Sir Thomas Lake. Inquire for me at Whitehall when you come to Town. It may be my privilege to serve you."

Now, whatever the ambitions of Mr Villiers, he was very far from imagining the destiny in store for him, nor to guess as he stared in wonder at this magnificent and influential gentleman that the day was not far distant when he was to be as far above him as he now accounted himself below. He summoned his wits to express becoming thanks, and he did so with a grace of phrase and bearing which Sir Thomas, closely noting, accounted of excellent augury for the project which as yet was but an embryo in his fertile mind. It was an embryo destined to a more rapid growth than even Sir Thomas could have hoped. Nor was it to be necessary for Mr Villiers to ask for him at Whitehall. Fate was to contrive that Mr Villiers should travel thither with him.

It was in the third interlude that this began to become apparent.

Sir Thomas suddenly found himself beckoned by the King, and assailed by questions concerning that admirable young man. Sir Thomas ventured to embroider his information. The lad was not only of good family which had fallen upon diminished fortunes, but was the son of a man who had deserved well for his stout loyalty, and yet, as sometimes happened, had been entirely overlooked. Sir Thomas might have been hard put to it to have produced evidence of this; but he shrewdly guessed that if the royal interest were aroused as deeply as he hoped, the King would be glad enough to accept the statement without any confirmation.

The King desired that the lad be presented, and so at the end of the performance you behold the valedictory proceedings suspended while his majesty utters a few benign and fatherly words to handsome young out-at-elbows Mr Villiers, who stands modestly blushing before him, and expresses a desire to see Mr Villiers at Whitehall, there to signify his appreciation of his father's loyalty and make amends to the son for having neglected suitably to reward that loyalty in the father's own lifetime.

It was a bewildered and rather confused Mr Villiers who stood gracefully to hear these surprising words spoken with a smile of such extreme friendliness as to become almost a leer, to receive a friendly fatherly tap upon his smooth cheek from two soft fingers, and to be aware of innumerable eyes focused upon him, and in particular a pair of fine blue eyes, cold as agates, by which a handsome, gorgeous, golden-headed gentleman at the King's side regarded him.

He found words in which to thank his majesty for this gracious condescension, and, still bewildered, suffered himself to be carried off by Sir Thomas Lake, who did not mean to lose sight of him again just yet. For Sir Thomas was now persuaded that in this out-at-elbows young Adonis he had found the necessary lever with which to dislodge the Earl of Somerset from his high place.

Still more bewildered was Mr Villiers, who deemed the incident closed for the present, to find Sir Thomas waiting upon him at his mean inn betimes on the following morning whilst he was still abed. The fastidious, accomplished man of courts seated himself upon the only chair – and this a broken one – which the room boasted, and proceeded to inform Mr Villiers that the King was greatly pleased with him and that he was commanded to attend the performance of a Latin pastoral in Clare Hall that evening. Sir Thomas inquired if Mr Villiers had much Latin, and Mr Villiers told him frankly and bluntly that he had none. The courtier seemed momentarily disappointed.

"No matter," said he, upon reflection. "It was the same in another case. His majesty will no doubt find interest in your instruction."

To Mr Villiers this was a sentence without sense. Nor did Sir Thomas waste breath in explaining it. He urged the young man to be stirring, and when presently Mr Villiers had arrayed himself in his suit of black, which looked rustier and shabbier than ever by daylight, he was carried off by his self-constituted mentor, to spend the time until dinner in ransacking the shops of Cambridge tailors and haberdashers.

There came a moment when Mr Villiers, who saw money being laid out on his behalf with a reckless indifference to its value such as he had never witnessed in his needy young life, demanded an explanation of conduct he was so very far from understanding. A little, too, he resented being swept without a by-your-leave along some course which this masterful courtier appeared to have predetermined.

Sir Thomas smiled tolerantly and adopted frankness, as men must when deception will not serve.

"Have I not said that the King is very pleased with you and desires your better acquaintance? That, sir, is your good fortune. Mine lies in being at hand to see that his majesty is gratified in his wishes. When you have been a little longer at Court, you will understand that this is the surest road to advancement."

The gentleman spoke as if Mr Villiers were already established at Court. It took his breath away. He could only stare. Answering his look, Sir Thomas employed a still greater frankness.

"Count this not merely for generosity in me. Experience has shown me how high a man may climb who has taken the King's eye. If I expedite your rise, I put my trust in your gratitude. When you are up, you shall repay the debt by reaching down a hand to me."

It was not quite the truth, but it sufficed to quiet the remonstrances of Mr Villiers' self-respect, and made him regard this matter of equipment as a transaction between gentlemen to be adjusted later. In this conviction he now submitted with a good grace.

That evening, as my Lord of Somerset sat in Clare Hall immediately behind the King, yawning under cover of his hand over the pompous dullness of the Latin pastoral which was delighting his majesty, he suddenly became aware of a lithe, graceful figure very elegantly attired in a suit of mulberry velvet that was all puffed and slashed, a satin cape-cloak, thrust up behind by a gold-hilted rapier, rosetted, high-heeled shoes, and glossy chestnut hair falling heavily about an oval face of exceptional beauty. At the elbow of this arrestingly elegant figure stood Sir Thomas Lake to supply a clue by which his lordship recognised the youth for the shabby young man from Leicestershire whom the King had held last night in talk.

He asked himself why Sir Thomas had been at such pains to turn the crow into a jay, and guessing the answer sneered at what he accounted so much waste of labour. Nor was he at all discomposed when presently, in the interlude, the King's roving eye discovered the young man, and beckoned him to the tribune so that he might hold him again in talk.

His majesty spoke of the play, repeated a line which he had accounted witty and of whose Latinity he approved, and desired Mr Villiers' opinion upon it. Mr Villiers, who was not such a fool as to affect knowledge which he did not possess, frankly deplored that his ignorance of Latin allowed him to do no more than admire the motions of the players, having previously informed himself of the argument of the play.

The King's expression was saddened by the information. Behind him Somerset softly laughed his scorn, for which presently when Mr Villiers had retired again he suffered the unusual experience of a rebuke from his master.

"Ye're ungenerous, Rabbie, to sneer at an ignorance that was your own until I mended it."

Somerset flushed, and his mouth momentarily tightened. But his answer, an instant later, was suave and level.

"Your majesty mistakes me. I laughed at the notion of a man wasting hours upon a play in a language he does not understand."

"Yet a man may waste hours in one way and gain much in another. It was not to hear the play that Sir Thomas brought him."

"Or busied his tailors with the fellow."

"Aye, aye! But did ye mark how well he wears his clothes? Sir Thomas thought to please me."

"Sir Thomas paid you a poor compliment, sire, if he accounted you pleased so easily."

His majesty winced at the sneer, and said no more. He was learning to hold his tongue when his darling Rabbie adopted that tone; but not on that account did he forgo resentment of it, and this resentment, from being stifled, grew of an increasing bitterness.

It may or it may not have been due to this that at the end of the performance the King kept the company waiting whilst once more he engaged in talk with Mr Villiers. At the end of it he commanded the young man's company at a banquet to be given at Trinity on the following evening with a dance to follow.

It was in this dance that Mr Villiers at last earned a general meed of admiration, for the grace with which he carried himself and his proficiency in an art which he had learnt in France. He was the recipient of so many compliments afterwards that he was almost as elated as was Sir Thomas Lake. Somerset, whose splendour of dress, ease of deportment, beauty of person and haughty assurance of manner filled Mr Villiers with awe, looked on languidly with that curl of the lip which was becoming almost habitual with him. As he watched the King's ogling of the lad and his foolish slobbering as he talked to him, contempt for a man whose delight was so easily aroused and whose displays of it were so wanting in dignity began to stir in him.

Sir Thomas Lake went swiftly to work to build upon those foundations which he had laid so cunningly at Cambridge. Having brought his protégé safely to Whitehall, he had sought the Earl of Pembroke, whose rancour at the loss of the office of Lord Chamberlain was altogether beyond allaying; he had sought Abbot, the Archbishop, whose righteous indignation at the nullity he had been forced to pronounce for Somerset's ends was never likely to diminish; and he had sought the Queen whose momentary favouring of a man she had always detested was extinguished now by the insult of her exclusion from the Cambridge junketings, for which, although perhaps unreasonably, she chose to blame Somerset as well as his father-in-law Suffolk.

To each of them he pointed out the man he had discovered who should drive out Somerset as one nail drives out another, and each of them was ready enough to enter into league with him, although the Queen was a little of opinion that the ultimate gain would be dubious. These minions were supple enough at the outset; but once firmly established in favour and in power, they had a way of becoming scorpion whips for the shoulders by which they had climbed. Mr Villiers might today be modest and humble and disposed to gratitude. So had Robert Carr once been. And as Robert Carr now was, so might George Villiers become. Still, this was something of which they might take the risk.

Thus came the conspiracy to be formed, and the necessary moneys supplied for the further equipment and maintenance of the new minion, and for the purchase for him of the office of cupbearer to his majesty whereby he would be officially established in the palace.

Somerset went his ways unruffled. Beyond an occasional sneer at the royal manifestations of infatuation, his lordship ignored the young gentleman from Leicestershire. This until a flagrant event warned him of the peril ahead, and revealed to him there was here an organisation that was at work against him.

The Earl of Pembroke entertained some gentlemen to dinner at Baynards Castle. Sir Thomas Lake was of the company, and the chief spokesman when they had dined. Among the others were Herbert, Hertford, and Bedford, and not a man of the dozen or so assembled there was not the sworn enemy of Somerset. They met to concert measures for the further preferment of George Villiers at the favourite's expense and to his ultimate discomfiture and downfall. The immediate necessary step, it was decided, should be to procure Mr Villiers' advancement to a knighthood and to the position of one of the Gentlemen of the Bedchamber. The Queen, Sir Thomas assured them, was in the business, and would be their ally in this, and a particularly valuable ally considering the pretences of uxoriousness which King James maintained.

The company returned to Westminster in a spirit of merry turbulence, and in an elation resulting as much from the decision taken as from the wine consumed, espied in Fleet Street outside a painter's shop a portrait of the Earl of Somerset exposed for sale.

They drew rein to consider it, to jeer and flout a portrait whose original was still too high for direct insult. Finally, to indulge his personal hostility of that original, one of the gentlemen commanded his servant to bespatter the canvas with mud.

The deed accomplished, and with many a gibe for the outraged painter who rushed from his shop belatedly to protect his wares from damage, the company rode on in delight and pride of the puerile achievement.

The painter, in deep resentment, went off to Whitehall, to bear his plaint to my Lord of Somerset.

His lordship heard the story, and if he changed colour a little, he yet commanded himself sufficiently to assume contemptuously that it was an act of drunken folly which was beneath the dignity of his serious consideration. Nevertheless, he inquired the names of the gentlemen in question. Having obtained them, he compensated the painter, and pondered his course of action.

These gentlemen were without exception not merely enemies of his own and of the Howards, but they were those who had most signally manifested their friendship for Mr Villiers. He concluded that the best retort would be to deal with their pet as they had dealt with his lordship's portrait.

And so it fell out that some days later a cousin and namesake of his own whom he had made a Gentleman of the Household, and who happened on that day to be one of the servers at the royal table, upset as if by accident a dish of soup over the brave satin suit of Mr Villiers.

Mr Villiers, whilst gay and friendly and easy-going, was not yet old enough to have learned to curb impetuosity. Annoyed by the ruin of his finery and enraged by the instant suspicion that it was due to no accident, he leapt to his feet so abruptly that his chair crashed over behind him. With a foul word he caught the offending Scot a buffet on the side of the head that made him reel.

There was a general outcry, a belated attempt by immediate neighbours to restrain him, and then silence and utter stillness.

283

Mr Villiers, immediately conscious of the enormity of his offence, though hardly yet of the penalty imposed by statute, stood abashed and foolish, making no attempt to wipe the dripping mess from his doublet. Young Carr, recovering his balance, earned admiration by his self-command. Swinging half round to face the King, he brought his heels together, and bowed as if in expression of a respect for majesty too utter to admit of his attempting reprisals.

The King, open-mouthed, his tongue protruding, presented a picture of foolish dismay.

Somerset, on the King's right, looked on with a faintly cruel smile about his lips and eyes that were bright and hard as steel.

The remainder of the company at the long table, numbering fully a score, and the half-dozen gentlemen servers in the background against the tapestries of the banqueting hall, awaited the sequel in consternation.

Presently Somerset spoke, after a pause calculated to heighten the suspense. His voice cut cold and incisively into the silence. His words were those which in the circumstances his office of Lord Chamberlain required of him.

"The guard," he said shortly, and his cousin sprang to obey, and went swiftly to the door.

A shadow crossed the King's face. But he said nothing. Respect for the forms struggled within him with his own personal inclinations.

Came the officer of the guard, a vivid figure in a coat of dull red velvet, carrying his plumed hat in his right hand, his gauntleted left upon the pommel of his sword, his spurs jingling musically as he advanced. He halted, and grave and impassive awaited orders, which again, quite naturally, were given him by the Lord Chamberlain.

"Captain, you will escort Mr Villiers to his quarters and detain him there under guard until his majesty makes known his pleasure."

Mr Villiers in distress made a movement as if to address the King. His majesty motioned him to silence by a wave of the hand.

"Ay, aye!" he said thickly. "You'd best go."

Prudently the young man commanded himself, bowed, and went out with the officer, the King's staring, almost vacant, eyes watching him to the door.

As he disappeared the stillness was broken at last by a rustling stir. Lord Somerset sighed audibly, and spoke lightly.

"Mr Villiers is over young in temper and in knowledge for a court."

"That," said the King's mumbling voice "may excuse him."

His lordship raised his eyebrows. "There's no such provision in the statute."

"The statute!" His majesty was startled. He glanced at Somerset and away. "Huh!"

Somerset signed to the servers to resume their duties. But the King suddenly got to his feet. That mention of the statute had agitated him. Shortly he commanded Somerset to attend him, and went out.

Not until they were in his own closet and he had flung himself irritably into a padded chair did the King speak again. "What's this blather of a statute?" His eyes avoided Somerset's.

The favourite, standing easily and gracefully by the table on which his majesty's elbow rested, explained that which required no explaining.

"I allude, as your majesty well knows, to the statute of King Henry VIII, which provides quite clearly the penalty for Mr Villiers' offence. For a blow given in the presence of majesty the offending hand shall be struck off at the wrist. It's a statute that concerns my office closely, for it is the Lord Chamberlain's duty to see the forfeit made, and to be in attendance to sear the stump."

The King shuddered at the mental picture evoked. His glance grew scared.

"Na! Na! Ye're not supposing that I'll be governed by any such statute of that old lecher?"

"Lecher or not, he was King of England, and a king of some weight in his day, and his statutes are good law."

"To the devil with good law; aye, and with you, Rabbie! Ye're never thinking I'll suffer the mutilation of that bonnie lad? It's blasphemy to think of it."

"It would have the advantage of making a repetition of the offence impossible."

"Why, ye heartless loon! I'll not have it, I tell ye!" He slapped the table with his open hand.

Somerset bowed composedly. He even smiled. "I do not urge it, sire."

"I thought ye did. And it's well for you ye don't."

"It should suffice to send him packing. His manners will suit Leicestershire – or is it Lincolnshire? – better than Whitehall."

"That's for me to settle."

"Less would scarcely become your kingly dignity."

"Ye may leave me to guard my kingly dignity."

"Yet in some sort it is within the duties of your Lord Chamberlain."

"Hold your clavering tongue! Will you be manifesting your spite of this braw lad? Ye'll make me believe that ye'd be glad to see his hand struck off, Rabbie. Hah!"

"I'll be content to see him go."

"He's not going."

"Not?" My lord was supercilious. "I await your majesty's commands concerning him."

The King glowered at him, resenting his manner.

"Send him to me here. I'll read him a lesson on courtly behaviour. That shall suffice."

"Your majesty is indeed clement!"

"You make me aware of it. If I were not I'd never tolerate your sneers. I'm finding you over-graceless these days. The higher I place you, the more intolerable you grow. It's an ill requital for the liberties I grant you to be wanting in respect to me."

"Is it lack of respect to your majesty to desire some punishment for one who has been flagrantly lacking in it?"

"Ye ken well that's not the point. Your lack of respect lies in the tone and manner you adopt with me, and I tell you I'll not brook it from any man."

"Yet you brook worse when you suffer a blow to be struck in your presence".

"It was an act of impetuosity. The lad was annoyed, and with some justification, by your kinsman's clumsiness."

"So that now my kinsman becomes the offender! Faith, your majesty finds every excuse for Mr Villiers." Somerset was bitter now. "Some days since mud was flung on a portrait of mine in Fleet Street by this young upstart's friends. Yet your majesty forbade me to take action against them, although that was no accident."

"Was this?" The King fired the question abruptly, and his eyes narrowed.

Somerset gaped and then laughed.

"You'll excuse him now on the grounds that the thing was deliberate."

"It's what I'm suspecting. The lout who spilled the broth was your kinsman. Did ye suppose I'ld not observed it? There's little I don't observe, Rabbie, as you should know by now."

Somerset became really angry. He hectored it roundly, breaking into unmeasured upbraidings. It was always so, he declared. The King would listen to any man before himself, prefer any man's word to his own. He was insulted on every hand, and debarred by the King's will from all redress, whilst his majesty listened to every tale that was carried to him. He ranted on, unreasonably and petulantly piling up imaginary grievances as vehicles for his spleen until the King checked him in a passion.

"Will ye rail at me like a carted street-walker?" He rose trembling. "Now as God's my judge, I'll have no more of this. Do you persuade me that you mean not so much to hold me by love as by awe, and that you have me so far in your reverence that I dare not offend you or resist your wishes? Which of us is King? Have you forgot? And have you forgot that you are my creature and hold all by my favour, and that as I set you up so I can put you down? Have you forgot that? Away with you now, and remember it in future."

Somerset departed, but did not remember. There ensued a succession of unworthy and undignified wrangles between King and favourite on the subject of Mr Villiers, soon indeed now to become Sir George Villiers and a Gentleman of the Bedchamber.

His knighthood came to him by the Queen's help and favour in the following April. It was on St George's Day that her majesty begged her royal husband to bestow the accolade upon young Villiers in honour of St George, whose name he bore.

The Earl of Somerset had made objections, especially to the young man's advancement to be a Gentleman of the Bedchamber, and he had again hectored the King in the matter. Nevertheless, his majesty conquered his awe of the favourite, and took refuge in the mock-uxoriousness which he loved to practise.

"It's the Queen, herself, who asks it, Rabbie! Would ye have me refuse our dear wife the Queen?"

To this his lordship could make no answer. He was driven into sullen retreat.

Buxom Anne of Denmark personally led the comely young Villiers into the King's presence, and ordered him to kneel, whilst with her own hands she proffered James the naked sword for the accolade.

Somerset looked on ill-humouredly, whilst the King, shuddering as he ever did at the sight of naked steel, took the sword, and averting his eyes from the flash of it almost poked Mr Villiers in the face in the act of dubbing him knight.

From that moment Sir George Villiers may be considered as fully launched upon the ocean of Court life. His new duties brought him into constant contact with the King; and those responsible for this watched with satisfaction the good use which the comely, intelligent young gentleman from Leicestershire made of his opportunities. They observed with equal satisfaction the growth of the King's favour, beheld the King, himself, taking in hand the lad's tuition and providing him with tutors for some of the arts necessary in a courtier.

Soon Sir George was appointed Master of the Horse, by which time his fame had spread and his name was on every tongue, and already he had his court within the Court and no lack of suitors for his favour and patronage.

Somerset, looking on with ever increasing ill temper, beheld here repeated the early steps of his own career, grew conscious at last that a formidable rival had arisen and that there was ample ground for his jealous apprehension of ultimate supersession. With this added fear to plague him, he increased daily in sullenness and irritability.

One last attempt the King made to soften him and to allay the jealousy which he perceived to lie at the root of it, but which he was mistaken in supposing to be its only source. He desired Sir George Villiers to seek the Earl's favour. Thus he thought to conciliate Somerset by permitting him to suppose that no advancement was possible to any man without his countenance.

Sir George presented himself modestly before the great favourite, and delivered himself of a speech in which he had been well schooled.

"My lord, I desire to be your servant and creature, and to take my Court preferment under your favour, assuring your lordship that you shall find me as faithful a servant as ever did serve you."

Somerset remained seated and covered, his handsome face obscured by the shadow of his hat. His answer was of an uncompromising harshness.

"I desire none of your service, and I have no favour for you. I will, if I can, break your neck. Of that be confident."

The younger man, bristling with anger, drew himself up to reply, when Sir Humphrey May, who had conducted him, restrained him by a hand upon his arm. Thus checked, Sir George bowed distantly and departed.

Somerset's contemptuous laugh followed to inflame him.

Chapter 29

Gathering Clouds

My Lord Somerset's dismissal of Sir George was duly reported to his majesty, and lost nothing in the process. His majesty was deeply incensed at this affront to his darling Steenie, as he now called Villiers, from his imagined resemblance to a lovely faced picture of St Stephen that hung in the banqueting hall at Whitehall. Yet, despite his loud assertions that he would not be ruled by awe, the King dared not take Somerset to task for his gross treatment of the young knight.

No resentment can be deadlier than that which must be carried secretly. Driven inwards it rarely fails to transmute love into hate. And so now, as the sequel serves to show, the King, whilst still continuing for the sake of peace to make a show of cherishing his Rabbie, was in his heart beginning to detest him.

Thus far by his petulance and peevishness had that unfortunate hag-ridden man unwittingly conspired with those who sought his overthrow.

The two most active agents of his downfall were, oddly enough, those two candidates for the office of Secretary of State: Sir Thomas Lake, to whom Somerset had denied it, and Sir Ralph Winwood, upon whom he had bestowed it. The motives of the first are plain enough, and they have been seen at work. They are humanly straightforward if not to be admired.

The motives of Sir Ralph, however, are far less obvious. He owed his appointment to my Lord of Somerset's favour; therefore it would seem that he should be grateful, and grateful no doubt he would have been if he had found in the office that which he was entitled to expect.

But Somerset, in appointing that grim, dour man, had thought to provide himself with another Overbury: one who would be content to remain in the background, discharging the onerous duties of the secretaryship, whilst placing at his lordship's disposal the fruits of his experience and knowledge of affairs so as to enable his lordship to continue to enjoy the power and glory of guiding the country's destinies.

Sir Ralph, however, had not proved at all willing so to be used. Since he was confined to drudgery, to drudgery he would confine himself. He gave no counsel, offered no advice, did not even trouble to keep his patron fully supplied with information. Annoyed by the limitations imposed upon him, he sulked strictly within them, and left my Lord of Somerset to blunder as he chose. But he resented his position, and studied to improve it, to render it in fact what it was in name. Perceiving that as long as Somerset reigned no improvement would be possible, he was quite ready to exert himself to curtail that reign. Like Sir Thomas Lake before him, he watchfully awaited opportunity to complete what Sir Thomas had so admirably begun.

He observed the growing favour of Sir George Villiers, and whilst in his dour puritanical heart he despised Sir George for a minion, yet he knew from experience that minions sometimes grow into great ministers of State, and since they have the King's ear they must be regarded as specially supplied by Providence for the advancement of better men. To George Villiers, properly handled, belonged the future, and that future should be realised with a speed proportionate to Somerset's relegation to the past towards which he was already striding.

Sir Ralph did two things. He began sedulously to cultivate the favour of Sir George Villiers, in which he but followed the fashion of the Court, and he watched diligently for an opportunity of accelerating the descent of my Lord of Somerset to the limbo of things that have been, in which he was also not entirely out of fashion.

And then quite unexpectedly something happened whose ultimate issue Sir Ralph was very far from foreseeing. In his capacity as Secretary of State, a letter reached him from the King's agent in Brussels, which he did not choose to disclose to his master the Earl of Somerset, or, indeed, to anyone. The agent, Mr Thoumbal, wrote that he had a secret of importance to communicate touching the death of Sir Thomas Overbury. He would not write of it further, but would come over in person to acquaint Sir Ralph with it if a licence for his return to England could be obtained.

The dour Sir Ralph considered. He remembered old rumours of foul play that had been circulated at the time of Overbury's death. Assuming now that Overbury had been done to death, Sir Ralph propounded to himself that sound old initial question in such inquiries: Cui bono fuerit? Much that had happened subsequently might conceivably be assumed to point to the Earl of Somerset as the person to whom the elimination of Sir Thomas Overbury had been desirable.

It was a thought that acted as a spur upon the resentful Secretary.

So Mr Thoumbal was quietly brought over from Brussels, and Sir Ralph listened to a startling demonstration of the old adage that murder will out.

An English lad, an apothecary's assistant named William Reeve, lying sick at Flushing and being taken with the fear of death, had confessed that Sir Thomas Overbury had been poisoned in the Tower by an injection of corrosive sublimate, administered by Reeve himself acting upon the orders of his master the apothecary, Paul de Loubel, who had attended Sir Thomas on the day before his death. Because of what he knew, the lad had been given money by his master and sent abroad immediately afterwards, which is how he came to be in Flushing.

Sir Ralph, his dark swarthy face inscrutable, made careful note of what Thoumbal told him, procured the agent's signature to those notes, and dismissed him back to his post at Brussels.

After that Sir Ralph informed himself cautiously of Dr Paul de Loubel's whereabouts – no difficult matter, since the apothecary was well known – and he descended upon him on a sultry day of August at his house set in the reek of Lime Street near the Tower.

Doctor Loubel was a little startled by the sudden appearance in his modest dwelling of this bulky, black-bearded, black-attired gentleman of forbidding countenance, who announced himself as the Secretary of State and requested a word with him in private. He ushered him into his dingy parlour on the ground floor, and invited him to sit. The Secretary remained standing, his back to the window, in such a way that, to confront him, the doctor must present his face to the light.

"I desire," he said in his deep booming voice, "a word with you on the subject of an apprentice of yours named William Reeve."

"William Reeve? Ah, yes!" The doctor appeared a little nervous, a little flustered, which, after all, considering the rank and consequence of his visitor, was not surprising. It had never before happened to him to have a Secretary of State stand questioning him in his parlour. "William Reeve. Yes. I remember him."

Sir Ralph said nothing for a long moment, during which his solemn dark eyes pondered the slight, neat, nervous figure before him. Loubel was something over fifty, lean and pale of face, with lively intelligent eyes and a tight mouth. His hair was thin and grey. His speech and gesture proclaimed his French origin.

He waited respectfully now for the Secretary to make known his wishes, one hand folded over the other at the level of his breast, his eyes attentive.

"You sent this lad abroad, I understand, some two years since?"

"Send him? Ah no. Not send. He desire to go."

The Secretary's black brows came sternly in a frown. "You are not to prevaricate with me, Doctor Loubel. I warn you that my information is very full."

The doctor looked distressed, even bewildered. "I prevaricate? I? But to what end? Worshipful sir" – and he became emphatic – "the lad chose to go, desired to go. That is no prevarication."

"You gave him money to go," said the heavy voice.

"Money? Ah yes, I give him money. There was somet'ing I owe' him, somet'ing I keep and save for him. He was two years here with me. To that I added a little present. He was a good lad. He want to see the world. I admire ambition. I help him a little. But all told the moneys I give him were no great amount."

"What was the amount?"

"The amount?" Loubel reflected, forefinger laid against his nose a moment. Then he shrugged and flung out his hands. "But how shall I remember the amount? It is two years since, as your worship has said. I have forgot the amount."

There was a moment's silence in which Sir Ralph pondered him with those solemn owlish eyes. Then the Secretary changed his line of attack.

"This lad Reeve was with you when you visited Sir Thomas Overbury in the Tower?"

Something crossed the Frenchman's face and was gone. It was as if a shadow had flitted over it, too elusive for interpretation by the watchful eyes of the Secretary. The eyelids too had flickered over those quick keen eyes at the mention of Overbury's name. But these signs, gone in a flash, left that countenance as it had been, alertly nervous, but otherwise composed.

"It is possible," he said. "It is probable. My assistant commonly accompanies me. Oh, undoubtedly, yes."

In his mind Sir Ralph wrote him down for a baffling fellow, with his short jerky sentences which answered questions with the greatest possible economy of words, and yet contrived at the same time to colour the answers. Sir Ralph liked voluble men. They invariably betrayed themselves sooner or later by saying too much. This fellow by his terseness was forcing Sir Ralph into the open; and however much he might deplore it, into the open he must go.

"The lad at the point of death has made a confession," he announced.

Now at last be had succeeded in startling the little apothecary. The man's eyes dilated. His pale face seemed to grow paler. But a moment later, his words explained all this away. It was not the fact of the confession that had scared him. Or at least so his words made it appear.

"At the point of death? Oh! He is dead, then, that poor William? Dead! Oh!" He let his arms fall limply to his side, the palms turned outwards.

Sir Ralph damned him for a play-actor. "Whether he's dead or not, I don't know. He thought he was dying, and confessed. That's all that matters."

"To you. Yes. Maybe, worshipful sir. But to me… Oh, the poor William!"

Thus the man clung to grief over the lad's death, and ignored the matter of his confession, as if it were of no account. Willy-nilly, Sir Ralph must come still further out.

"Leave that!" he said sharply. "It is his confession that signifies."

"His confession?" The keen eyes, laden with inquiry, looked up into that great pear-shaped countenance, broader at the base than at the summit. "But what, then, did he confess?"

"His share in the business of which Sir Thomas Overbury died."

Loubel stared and stared at him, his countenance expressing only bewilderment. At last he flung out his hands in that expressive gesture of his. "I do not understand," he said flatly. "I do not understand. Your worship has some purpose to come here. You do not come just for the honour of my house. No? If your worship will ask frankly what you desire to know, I will answer frankly if I can."

It was almost a rebuke, and the ponderous Sir Ralph was angered by it. He was angered, too, by the fact that he was making no headway. He laid all his cards on the table, abruptly.

"This boy confessed that Sir Thomas Overbury was murdered in the Tower. He was murdered by a poisoned injection – an injection of corrosive sublimate. This was prepared by you, Monsieur Loubel, and administered by him under your directions."

Blank stupefaction was spread for a long moment upon the lean white face of the apothecary. Then he burst into laughter loud and prolonged, in the course of which he more than once smacked his thigh with his open palm.

Sir Ralph stood stiff and resentful, waiting until these spasms of indecent mirth should abate.

"Oh, but that is most comic! Most droll!" Loubel wiped a tear from his eye. "Be'old! I wish to poison Sir Thomas Overbury with corrosive sublimate; therefore I do not fail to tell my assistant what I am doing, so that I can be sure that he shall betray me! Oh, the clever way to poison, so that nobody shall ever know about it!" And he went off into his explosive laughter again, holding his sides.

"Silence, buffoon!" roared the elephantine Sir Ralph.

But Loubel was no respecter of persons. He suppressed no more of his laughter than was necessary to permit of his replying. "It is not me who is the buffoon in this, Sir Ralph! Not me. And it is the best buffoonery I ever hear in all my life as an apothecary."

"What do you mean, sirrah?"

Loubel returned to gravity. But it was a gravity behind which he showed that mirth still lurked. "Oh, but ask yourself, Sir Ralph. Consider the tale that is to tell. I am to poison a gentleman in the Tower. He is nothing to me, this gentleman. I do not know him. But I am to poison him. Very well. We admit that first preposterous part. I choose to do so with corrosive sublimate, and by injection. All very clumsy. But we admit that too. I do not give the injection myself. Oh no. That would be too secret, and when we poison anybody we never desire to be secret. So I take my assistant, and give him the clyster so that he makes the injection for me. And at the same time I say to him: Observe, William, this clyster contains corrosive sublimate. I tell you this so that you may know that I am poisoning Sir Thomas Overbury, and so that you may go afterwards and tell Sir Ralph Winwood, the great Secretary of State, and get me hanged for doing it.

"This is the tale, is it not, Sir Ralph? And you do not understand why I laugh? You think I laugh because I am buffoon?"

Under the lash of the apothecary's sarcasm Sir Ralph stood foolish and with empurpling countenance. But there was yet a little more to follow.

"And you forget, Sir Ralph, that I act as apothecary to my brother-in-law, Sir Theodore Mayerne, his majesty's physician. I give Sir Thomas only such things as Sir Theodore prescribe. And if I give him corrosive sublimate it must have been upon the prescription of Sir Theodore. I have his prescriptions; all of them. Would your worship wish to see them?"

His worship would not. In a minatory tone his worship announced that others might follow who might desire to see them, and he charged Loubel to keep them secure as he valued his own neck when he came to be examined by others. He also ventured a sarcastic hope that when this happened Monsieur Loubel would be as ready to laugh as he was today. On that Sir Ralph took his departure with a sense of discomfiture rendered the more utter by his conviction that it had been encompassed by the clever wits of a rogue who had known how to make the truth wear a preposterous appearance.

Others should deal with Monsieur Loubel. But before taking steps towards that end he had better lay the matter as it stood before the King. He had forgotten until Loubel reminded him – if, indeed, he had ever known – that Overbury had been attended at the end by the King's physician. Even a King's physician need not be incorruptible, especially a foreigner. The narrow, puritanical Sir Ralph was one of those Englishmen with an innate mistrust of all foreigners. Mayerne might easily have been within reach of my Lord of Somerset's bribes. Thus regarded, it looked more than ever as if Somerset might be in the business. But this his majesty should determine.

And so you behold Sir Ralph Winwood posting out of London in quest of the royal Solomon. His majesty was on a progress at the time, and Sir Ralph came up with him at Beaulieu in Hampshire at the house of my Lord Southampton.

Admitted late at night to private audience with the King, who had guzzled himself into a crapulous condition, Sir Ralph made known what he had learnt from Thoumbal.

It was remarkable to Sir Ralph how sobering an effect the scent of business had upon his majesty. At the disclosure of the confession made by Loubel's assistant, the vinous flush departed from his majesty's countenance, leaving it pale, the glitter of his eyes changed from one of intoxication to one of alertness. The whole expression of his face was altered and sobered. When Sir Ralph spoke of his visit to Loubel, he was interrupted by reproof.

"God's death, man! Why this, before ye had seen me?"

Sir Ralph's great bulk was doubled in a bow. "I accounted it my duty, sire."

"Your duty, sir, is to do my bidding; and ye had no bidding from me in this. Well, well? A God's name!" His majesty was testy. He thumped the table with a fist that trembled. "Well? What said this man Loubel?"

"He laughed at me, sire," Sir Ralph exploded, and repeated the sarcasms with which the apothecary had met him.

The King eyed him contemptuously. "D'ye not find it matter for laughter yourself?" he asked. "D'ye not perceive the absurdity of it which this fellow Loubel has made so clear, that ye must come troubling me with such a cock-and-bull affair?"

Sir Ralph was disconcerted for a moment. Then, recovering, "I might," he said, "if it were not for the fact that this apothecary's lad was given money and sent packing abroad."

"And what said Loubel to that?"

Sir Ralph told him. The King shrugged. "In all the circumstances it's a sufficient answer. There's no proof or shadow of proof of any other motive." And on that he dismissed the Secretary with an admonition not to waste time in future on mare's nests.

Smarting under something akin to a rebuke, Sir Ralph withdrew in dudgeon, very far from satisfied that the royal acumen had not here been at fault, and therefore all the more determined to get to the bottom of this mystery at the first opportunity. Apothecaries' boys are not given sums of money and sent abroad by their masters out of sheer generosity. No one would persuade Sir Ralph of that.

The opportunity for which he watched came in the following week. Sir Ralph was dining with the Earl of Shrewsbury at his Town house in Broad Street. The Countess of Shrewsbury was at the time a prisoner in the Tower as a result of the part she had played in the attempted escape of the Lady Arabella. To procure her what comforts he could, the Earl was paying court to Sir Gervase Elwes, the Lieutenant of the Tower. Sir Gervase was of the party, and with a view to advancing his fortunes was by the Earl presented to the Secretary of State. The presentation was accompanied by a request to Sir Ralph that he should take the Lieutenant into his favour.

Sir Ralph received him courteously. During dinner he was very thoughtful, like the dour, uncommunicative man he was reputed. He was considering what advantage he might derive from this meeting with the Lieutenant.

When dinner was done, he drew Sir Gervase away from the company, and invited him to take a turn in the open. Sir Gervase, willing enough, and accounting this a sign that Sir Ralph was disposed to give attention to my Lord of Shrewsbury's recommendation, went with him into the sunlit garden. As side by side they paced its alleys, the dry, elderly, trim Lieutenant in red and the dark bulky Secretary in black, Sir Ralph startled his companion by his opening remark.

"I should be glad enough to take you into my friendship, Sir Gervase, and to serve you in any way that it lies within my power; but I must first desire that you might clear yourself of a heavy imputation the world generally places upon you touching the death of Sir Thomas Overbury whilst in your charge."

The Lieutenant checked in his stride. Sir Ralph, checking with him, observed that he had lost colour, that his grey eyes were very round and solemn.

"You know, sir, what was done?" Sir Gervase asked, making it plain that he had no thought of dissimulation.

Sir Ralph slowly nodded his big dark head. "Oh yes. But not how it was done, nor your own part in it, with which I must now be more immediately concerned."

"My part in it? Faith, my part was to do what I could to save the wretched man in so far as this was possible without hurt to my own self. For my Lord Privy Seal was in the business."

"My Lord Privy Seal!" Sir Ralph's heart missed a beat in his excitement. "D'ye mean my Lord of Somerset?"

"No, no. The Lord Privy Seal that was then. My Lord Northampton. The Lady Frances Howard, that is now Countess of Somerset, was in it too; and I know not who else might be behind them. So that in moving to thwart their ends I ran some risk, Sir Ralph; yet for my conscience's sake I never hesitated. But in the end, as I believe, they prevailed in spite of all that I could do. And that, Sir Ralph, is all the part I had in the matter of that unfortunate gentleman. I take God to witness."

Sir Ralph nodded slowly, and they moved on between the privet hedges. They went some little way in silence, the Secretary's chin upon his breast, his eyes thoughtful.

Here was a pretty tale to tell the King. Would his majesty still agree that Sir Ralph busied himself with a mare's nest when he found it odd that an apothecary's boy should be given money and sent abroad by his master? And the Countess of Somerset was in it, and my Lord of Northampton, who at the time had been Lord Somerset's closest friend. Was it to be doubted that the Earl of Somerset was in it too, and that here was a weapon with which finally to destroy the upstart favourite?

Sir Ralph spoke slowly at last: "Sir, you must convince me of this a little more: that your own part was what you say it was. What were the measures that you took to guard your prisoner when you discovered that his life was being attempted, and how came you to make the discovery?"

The Lieutenant answered without any hesitation. "As to the last, it seemed to me at the time the result of Divine Providence. There came to the Tower to be servant to Sir Thomas a fellow named

Weston, recommended by the Master of the Armoury. He replaced Sir Thomas' own servant, who could not be trusted not to carry messages. When Weston had been there a week, I met him one evening as he was carrying up the prisoner's soup. He held up a small phial, and asked me: 'Shall I give it to him now?'

" 'Give him what?' said I.

" 'Why, this,' and he added in a whisper: 'The rosalgar.'

" 'Rosalgar?' I said. 'Are ye mad? What is't ye mean, fellow?'

"He fell into great confusion at that. 'Surely, sir, you know what's to be done!' he cried.

" 'To be done, sirrah?' I answered him, and I took him by the collar of his coat, demanding a plain tale with a threat to have him flogged if he lied to me, with perhaps worse to follow. In his terror the man shielded himself behind those that had set him on. He was acting, he swore, upon orders of Mrs Turner, who was employed by persons in high places, and since there was no reason in the world why so mean a fellow should have ends of his own to serve against Sir Thomas, it was not difficult to believe him.

"I took the phial from him and flung away the poison. I realised that I was swimming in dangerous waters, nevertheless I adjured him by God and his conscience to be no party to anything so foul as murder, and that if the offences of Sir Thomas Overbury were such as to merit death it must be death in lawful manner and after trial.

"After that there were some delicacies sent to the prisoner from my Lady Frances, by a woman named Turner. They came from time to time: tarts and jellies, and once a partridge, all of which I intercepted, and had others prepared in their stead, keeping my own counsel in the matter, lest I provoke against me the resentment of those who were at work. But in the end they had their way in despite of all my vigilance, and it was, as I believe, and as Weston hath since confessed to me, by a rascally apothecary's servant who was corrupted. His master was an approved honest man, as I thought and still do, acting upon the directions of Doctor Mayerne, who was sent from Court to minister to Sir Thomas when he was sick."

Such was the Lieutenant's tale, and to Sir Ralph it was a triumph to find himself justified of the suspicions which the King had treated with such contempt. Moreover, it afforded him at last the thing he sought. It should make an end not only of Somerset, but of the Howards and all the Spanish party.

"This man Weston?" he inquired. "Where is he now?"

"He has remained with me in the Tower."

Sir Ralph nodded slowly. "Let him continue there awhile." He turned fully to face the Lieutenant. "You have been frank and honest with me, Sir Gervase, and I must esteem you for it, however much I may wish you had taken an earlier opportunity of disclosing your full knowledge of this dark affair. Let us now return." He took him by the arm in friendly fashion and led him back to the house. "You shall hear from me soon again," he promised him, and this with a smile which entirely reassured the unfortunate Sir Gervase.

Chapter 30

The Avalanche

Once again Sir Ralph sought the King, this time at Windsor, and being private with him, once more announced that it was touching the death of Sir Thomas Overbury that he desired to be heard.

The King startled him by the vehemency of the passion into which he was flung.

"God's death, man! Am I never to hear the end of that knave?"

"There are matters touching his end," said the grim Secretary, "with which it imports that your majesty should become acquainted." And he proceeded calmly to repeat what he had extracted from Sir Gervase Elwes. The royal irritation gave place to blank stupefaction.

"Tell me this again," he begged, when Sir Ralph's tale was done. "Let me have it all from the beginning."

He was very attentive during that repetition. Sitting very still, with his hat pulled over his eyes, whilst his fingers toyed absently with the diamond buttons on his green velvet doublet. Long after Sir Ralph had done he sat on in silence, blinking solemnly what time he turned the matter this way and that in his mind.

"Look you, friend Winwood," he said at last, "command me this fellow Elwes to set down in writing what he has told you. Let me have it under his own hand, that I may consider it."

Winwood departed, and was absent on the business for three days. On his return he brought a letter from Sir Gervase Elwes which set forth all that the Lieutenant had already orally disclosed. It was the letter of a man who had nothing to conceal, and who was glad, as in the course of it he asserted, to ease himself of a heavy burden.

The King read and reread the document, and announced at last the opinion that the matter was one for the Lord Chief Justice.

"You had best send that letter to Coke, and bid him act upon it."

Sir Ralph opined that a beginning should be made by the arrest of Loubel, and by this opinion provoked the King's wrathful contempt.

"Loubel will laugh in the face of Coke as he laughed in yours. Loubel's answer is plain. If he had prepared an injection of corrosive sublimate he'ld never have confided the fact to his assistant. That much is clear. And if we begin by provoking ridicule, how shall justice ever be done?"

Sir Ralph ventured to point out Sir Gervase's assertion that the apothecary's servant had been corrupted; that Weston had said that the lad had had twenty pounds for his work.

"Aye, aye," the King agreed. "The apothecary's apprentice may well have been corrupted; but not by the apothecary who had no need to do it. Elwes says himself that he's an approved honest man; and ye'll remember that he was acting for Mayerne, his brother-in-law, whom I myself sent to minister to Overbury. There are grounds for arresting the lad. But ye tell me he's dead, or dying, abroad. So we'll begin at the other end. Let Weston be examined first. Bid Coke attend to it."

Sir Ralph accounted the King unreasonable and the procedure wantonly irregular. But the royal command was definite, and Sir Ralph dared not trifle with it. He returned to London, and conveyed those commands exactly to Sir Edward Coke.

The Lord Chief Justice got promptly to work, and an avalanche followed.

Weston was arrested, examined and re-examined, cluttered out of his senses by the bullyings of Coke until he confessed all that was required of him and probably a great deal more than was true. The phial with which Sir Gervase had surprised him had been given to him by one Franklin, an alchemist and necromancer, who dwelt behind the Exchange; on another occasion he had received through his son from Lady Essex another phial of yellowish water for the prisoner, which again he had taken to Sir Gervase, who had broken it and thrown away the contents; and there had been pots of jellies and tarts and other delicacies supplied by Mrs Turner, by whom he had been formerly employed.

Thus the affair began, and out of Weston's examinations followed promptly the arrests of Mrs Turner and Franklin, whom he had incriminated. Next Sir Gervase Elwes was placed under arrest as an accessory, and when he informed Coke that Weston had been employed by him as a result of the recommendation of Sir Thomas Monson, Sir Thomas also was arrested. From him was elicited the fact that he had recommended Weston at the request of Lady Essex and my Lord Northampton.

Next the Lord Chief Justice summoned before him for examination Paul de Loubel, Overbury's servant, Lawrence Davies, and his secretary, Payton.

Loubel stoutly maintained that Sir Thomas had not been poisoned at all, but had died, in his opinion, of consumption, and that anyway, for his own part, he had given Sir Thomas no physic save such as was prescribed for him by Doctor Mayerne, whose prescriptions he put forward. Since this was not at all the evidence Coke desired, Loubel was troubled no further.

Davies and Payton between them cast suspicion upon the Earl of Somerset: the first by asserting that he had carried letters from the Earl to Sir Thomas in one of which there was a powder; the second by telling of the violent quarrel he had overheard between Overbury and the Earl one night at Whitehall some days before Overbury's arrest – a revelation which seemed to supply a motive for the crime.

Forman, betrayed also by Weston, was dead, and could no longer be brought to answer for his dark practices. But, unfortunately, some letters to him from Lady Essex survived which were capable of a terrible construction, and certain puppets in wax and lead which obviously had been employed for purposes of incantation and witchcraft.

And now, seeing that great names were being named, the Lord Chief Justice petitioned the King that others of greater rank be joined with him to form a Commission of investigation, and his majesty, acceding, appointed the old Chancellor Ellesmere, Lennox and Zouch.

Echoes of the proceedings reverberated through the country, magnified by rumour in their progress. They came to startle the Court, which in those days of early October was at Royston, and no member of it more than the Earl of Somerset, for all that he did not yet begin to guess the extent to which his own name and that of his lady were being tossed about.

His relations with the King had been going from bad to worse ever since the brutal rebuff which he had administered to young Villiers. As if to compensate the latest favourite for what he had suffered at the hands of my Lord of Somerset, the King had shown him an increasing tenderness, and this had but served further to nourish his lordship's rancorous jealousy. It was in vain that the King sought to reason with him and to assure him that none should ever stand higher in the royal esteem than himself. Somerset preferred the evidence of his senses to assurances, and dreaded whither the favour shown to Villiers might ultimately lead. Possibly with Overbury behind him to steer him in matters of statesmanship and clearly to point the way he might have kept his head, content that the King should fondle and toy with his darling Steenie so long as power remained in his own hands. But groping his way more or less blindly now through matters of statecraft, conscious that he was little more than a tool in the hands of the Howards for their own ends, which might well be dangerous ones, his confidence deserted him and he was in no case to suffer any rivals.

Hence those unseemly outbursts of jealousy which at once infuriated and distressed the King. Once, indeed, just before coming to Royston, his majesty had threatened him that if he persevered in his arrogance he would be deprived of his offices and dismissed the

Court, which had merely served to goad Somerset into an exasperatingly unreasonable retort.

"Ha! So the murder's out! That is what you desire. To be rid of me. After all the fond, faithful service I have given, I am to be discarded for the first pretty fribble that takes your majesty's eye. That is your aim; and to make it easy you find fault with me, and provoke me into giving you justification."

The King, infuriated by the calculated perversity of this interpretation of the facts, which it seemed idle to attempt to combat by reason, gibbered and stormed and threatened, and finally wept.

After that Somerset kept out of the King's way, sulking. He accompanied the Court to Royston, dragging at his heels a veritable court of his own made up of his gentlemen and attendants, and at Royston he continued to sulk in his lodgings until the King sent for him. That was on the morning on which the Commission of Inquiry had been appointed to assist the Lord Chief Justice in the matter of investigating the death of Sir Thomas Overbury.

As Somerset stepped into the chamber where the King awaited him alone, James, despite his half-formed resolve to make an end of relations that were become impossible, could not help rolling his eyes over the man in sheer admiration of his grace and beauty. He was dressed in blue velvet slashed in the sleeves and the ballooning trunks to show a satin lining of paler blue. His stockings, drawn creaselessly tight and rolled at the knee, were gartered with broad ribbons fringed with gold. He was partly swathed in a blue satin cloak, and, emerging from its folds, a fine hand, almost as white as the lace cuff of his sleeve, rested on the gold hilt of his sword. Erect and broad of shoulder, whence he tapered gracefully, he carried his golden head proudly upon his fine cambric ruff. His hair and beard were carefully dressed. His splendid eyes, once gently liquid and appealing, were now proud and compelling in their level glance.

The King combed his beard, feasting his eyes upon him in silence for some moments. There was a virility in the man, a beauty that was entirely male, such as his majesty delighted to behold. At last he shifted in his chair, and fetched a sigh, perhaps at the thought that so fine a fellow should by his own wilfulness have doomed himself to be broken.

"I've sent for you, Robin, to show you a note I had from Coke this morning. The matter concerns you something closely."

His lordship advanced, flung hat and gloves upon a chair, loosed his cloak and took the paper which his majesty proffered. He moved aside to the window to read it, for the October morning was dull, the light indifferent, and the Lord Chief Justice's hand a crabbed one.

The King watched him furtively the while from under his sandy brows, his slightly protruded tongue moving slowly upon his nether lip. His majesty was seated at his work-table, whose surface was a marvel of untidiness. Books large and small were heaped upon it, documents of every character littered it, and some that were important were buried there almost beyond recovery; and mingling with all this dusty array of scholarship and statesmanship lay varvels, jesses, feathered hawk lures, a dog whip, a hunting horn and other odds and ends belonging to the chase or to the stables. His majesty himself was wrapped in a sad-coloured dressing-gown, a blue velvet nightcap pulled tightly down upon his brows. Thus he lolled there watching Somerset as he read, observing the man's violent start, and the gradual draining of colour from his face. For what the Lord Chief Justice had written was that there was vehement suspicion against the Earl of Somerset as accessory to the poisoning of Sir Thomas Overbury before the fact done.

He faced the King again, and laughed harshly and without mirth, his eyes a flash with anger in his white face.

"Here's midsummer frenzy from Coke!" he exclaimed. "God's death, was the man drunk when he wrote this?"

The King looked scared as he met the fury of that glance and tone. But he commanded himself, and even achieved an assumption of dignity and of judicial calm.

"Ye'll observe that he speaks of no more than suspicion."

"Aye! Suspicion. Vehement suspicion. A plague on his soul for his impudence, the fool! As I live, he shall be taught a proper respect for his betters. He shall learn what it means to meddle with me."

"Tush! Tush! Coke is Lord Chief Justice. In suchlike matters he has no betters in this realm; and he must proceed to them by such courses as seem proper to him."

"However improper in themselves?"

"On my soul there's naught improper here. If in such evidence as he already possesses Coke finds grounds for suspecting what he says is suspicious, am I to blame him?"

His lordship flung himself without ceremony or invitation into a chair. He was trembling with anger. To steady himself he leaned forward, elbows on knees, facing the King.

"Who started this hare?" he demanded. "This hare of Overbury's being poisoned?"

"Sir Ralph Winwood was set upon the trail by the Lieutenant of the Tower."

"And this trail leads to me, does it?"

The King showed no resentment of the courtier's disrespectful vehemence. He maintained his quiet, half-cowed manner.

"At present Coke appears to think so."

"And if he follows it, he must find that it leads to me only in passing; that it leads beyond me. That it leads upwards to heights along which Coke may hesitate to pursue it."

The King raised his eyebrows, opened wide his pale, watery eyes in a fine display of astonishment. "Why, Robin! Then ye do know something of this matter?"

"Know something?" Somerset was leaning farther forward, scowling at him now. "Know something?" he repeated on a rising inflexion. Then he laughed in anger and scorn. "I know what your majesty knows."

Still the King showed no resentment. Amazement seemed his only emotion.

"What I know? What I know? And what do I know, Robin?"

Somerset got up abruptly. "What no man in England knows better. How Sir Thomas Overbury died."

There was a silence in which they eyed each other, Somerset taut as a bowstring, his air fierce, the King sagging together in his chair, his face entirely vacuous. At last his majesty moistened his lips with his tongue, and spoke, quietly and slowly.

"God knows what ye're implying, Robin. God knows what strange maggot's burrowing in your brain. Yet in a sense what ye say is true. In a sense there's no man better informed than myself of what happens in this realm. Of this business I know all that's known up till this present, from the notes Coke has sent me. Ye'd best look at them. It'll help you to understand how the suspicion against yourself has come to be formed. Here, man!" and he held out a little sheaf made up of some four pages.

Dumbfounded, marvelling, intimidated by the royal manner in the unusual calm of which there was something formidable, Somerset took the papers.

They were in Coke's writing, and they presented a summary of the evidence supplied by the persons so far examined: Weston, Monson, Elwes, Davies, Franklin and Payton.

As Somerset read, following the spoor that had been started by Sir Gervase Elwes, and saw how it led through his own wife to himself, his senses reeled. The solid earth of reality seemed to be slipping from under his feet.

He cast his mind back to that interview with the King some few days before Overbury died, when the King's own interest in the man's suppression was revealed, and he passed from that to the interview that had followed Overbury's death when he had all but accused the King of having sent Mayerne to murder him, an accusation which the King had not attempted to deny. Yet here was a circumstantial tale, confirmed and corroborated ad nauseam by a host of independent witnesses, which established something altogether different, which already deeply incriminated his Countess and might end by incriminating himself as deeply.

If his reason was bludgeoned by those notes, yet his instincts rose up violently to reject them.

" 'Tis all false, impossible!" he cried out. "Your majesty knows it to be false!" His arrogance was all gone. He was a man distracted, terrified, a change which the watchful King was not slow to observe.

"How should I know it to be false?"

"Because your majesty knows what really occurred."

"Aye! I know it now, from those notes. They leave little room for doubt, unless all those men are liars and have agreed to tell the same tale. Yet I never knew men to agree to lies that would put the rope round their necks, and there are several there who have admitted that which must bring them to the gallows. Will you still blame Coke for his suspicions?"

Somerset looked blankly at the King. His wits were broken.

"There is something here I do not understand," he said weakly, passing a hand over his brow in a gesture of mental distress. "But this I know, as God's my witness, I had no hand in Tom's death, nor, I'll stake my soul's salvation, had Frances."

"Yet you perceive what feeds the suspicion of Coke. You stood to profit by his death. Both of you stood to profit by it. He might have said that which would have made your marriage impossible."

"Does your majesty believe this?" Somerset was almost fierce again.

"Na, na! It's no question of what I believe, but of what Coke believes, of what these several rogues who have confessed justify him in believing. And you'll have to answer it when he sends for you, as send for you no doubt he must. Ye'll see that I cannot arrest the processes of law; no, not though you were my own son, Robin."

The young Earl's thoughts flew instantly to his Countess. If he must answer, then so must she, against whom the suspicion was even more vehement than against himself.

"My God!" he groaned. "Is Coke to bully Frances? She's in no state of health to bear it."

And then he bethought him that she, after all, might be able to explain how all this came about, point out the flaw in this dreadful chain that had been forged against them. "I'd best go to her," he said. "If your majesty will give me leave, I'll go at once." His tone was humble. He was a beaten man.

The King looked at him almost wistfully. "Aye, aye, Robin. Get you to her. Then come to me again."

Somerset took his leave, gathered up his hat and gloves, and went out in quest of grooms and horses. His majesty sat very still at his littered table after the Earl had departed; the prominent pale eyes were wistful, but there was the least vestige of a smile about the loose-lipped mouth.

Chapter 31

Valediction

By heavy, miry roads, against a chill October wind, and through a country all golden now in its autumn garb, the Earl of Somerset rode recklessly from Royston with no more than two grooms to attend him. He covered the distance almost at a stretch, with only two brief pauses at Hitchin and St Albans, where fresh horses were procured, nor slackened from a gallop until nightfall and darkness made it imperative to go more cautiously.

He came at last towards midnight, a spent man on a spent horse with two spent attendants labouring after him, to the gates of the great house at Henley, where the Countess was then residing.

Haggard and splashed with mud from head to foot, he reeled like a drunkard into the chill hall to which her chamberlain admitted him. He ordered lights to be brought, servants to be roused, and a fire to be kindled in the small room on the right of the hall. And thither, whilst his orders were still being executed, almost as soon as they had dragged the muddy boots from his legs and brought him a hot posset of sack, came her ladyship, alarmed by this midnight arrival, to inquire into its reason.

She came wrapped in a quilted gown and with hair unbound, her bare feet thrust into fur-lined slippers. She was very pale, with dark shadows about her lovely eyes which seemed to increase their size and heighten their brilliance. Her face looked thin and pinched. She was now in the seventh month of her pregnancy, and bethinking him of this as he regarded her, his tenderness welled up, and his distraction increased at the thought of how he came to trouble her.

Very gently he took her in his arms, stroking her hair and soothing the alarm his abrupt appearance had begotten; and she clung to him, protesting that whatever it was that brought him she was glad to have him with her, and hoped that he would remain some days.

This while the half-clad servants still came and went in the room in their ministrations for his comfort. At last, when they were gone and the logs crackled aflame on the hearth, he told her as gently as he could of the dreadful business that brought him.

They were standing before the fire, his lordship leaning upon the overmantel, when he began the tale of Coke's suspicions, and no sooner had he come to the matter of Weston's allegations than with a little moan she sank against him and his arms went round her to save her from falling.

She lay thus against his breast, with closed eyes, and breathing heavily, a pallor as of death upon her face, and for a moment he thought that she had swooned. But she made an instant recovery, and bade him continue, assuring him of her attention.

In increasing trouble of mind, his loyalty battling against the most dreadful fears, he resumed his tale, and as he talked on she gradually and by an effort recovered herself from the shock the first intimation of the business had dealt her.

When he had done there was a long silence. His trouble of mind increased with every moment of it, until at last, unable to endure it longer, he begged her to say something, to show him the flaw in this chain of evidence that had been wrought against them. He knew, he protested, that these were but the assertions of evil-minded men who, be it to protect themselves or so as to hurt him, were deliberately lying. But liars seldom were consistent. At some part of every falsehood the proof of it was revealed. So must it be now. Let them consider this thing together; let them see at what point the pieces did not fit. Her own knowledge of her relations with Mrs Turner, whose

servant Weston had been, must help her there. He implored her to
speak, and to set his fears at rest.

She squatted down before the fire, sitting on her heels, mechanically
holding a white hand to the blaze. Her unbound hair hung like a
golden mantle about her white-clad shoulders. Standing beside and
above her, leaning again upon the overmantel, he could not see her
face, and it was some moments before he heard her voice, its tone
dull and level.

"Be patient with me, Robin. Be merciful."

"Merciful?" Something seemed to grip his heart and tighten upon
it. "Merciful?"

"Aye, merciful. Was it not Montaigne who said, as Christ might
well have said, that to understand all is to forgive all?"

A silence followed. He leaned on, looking down upon that
huddled, pathetic heap of womanhood all white and gold at his feet.
A chill crept up through his body, so that he felt his skin contracting
and roughening. From the park outside came the call of an owl,
harsh upon the stillness. Within there was no sound save the hissing
of the logs, and, as it seemed to him, the thudding of his heart.

"Forgive all?" he echoed at last, in a hushed voice of horror.
"Forgive all? Frances, is it forgiveness that you need ? Is it true, then,
this foulness?"

She seemed to crouch lower, as they crouch who fear a blow. "I
loved you, Robin, as I love you now, and shall always love you, come
what may. This man would have denied that love its full fruition. I
had suffered so much through my love for you. I had been brave.
Dear God, how brave I had been! And when at last the reward was
within reach, that knave would have interposed himself between
you and me. Remember that, Robin. Think only of that when you
judge me."

"Oh God!" he groaned. He folded his arms upon the overmantel
and laid his head against them. "You confess to being a murderess!
You, Frances!"

She did not answer him. She sat on, huddled there, rocking a little, feeling as if she would swoon in her agony, yet making no sound.

"God!" he said again, in a thick voice of passion. "By your deed you justified him of his attitude towards you."

It was crueller than a blow. Yet it did not numb her wits.

"His attitude towards me justified my deed," she answered him. "Do not reverse the order of these happenings. I had reached the limit of endurance. This man, for the sake of his own ambition or else out of the evil of his heart, would have imposed upon me a suffering greater than any I had yet borne. I had to choose. I had to choose between him and myself. What mercy did he deserve at my hands who showed me none? Be just, Robin! In God's name be just!"

"Just!" he echoed, and then he laughed. "You may reserve these pleas for Coke."

"Coke!" She threw back her head and looked up at him. He beheld the leaden pallor of her face, the sudden terror which abruptly had effaced its beauty.

"Ah! That frightens you!" he sneered.

She rose to her knees. "Aye, it frightens me, but not for myself. If this knowledge should destroy your love, I care not what becomes of me. But there is the child to think of, Robin."

He strode away from the hearth, and set himself to pace the room, a man distracted by the sudden and utter collapse of all his world about him, a man incapable in that dreadful hour of marshalling his thoughts in a coherent sequence. One fact stood out. He was faced with ruin. Ruin complete and irreparable. At a single thrust he was toppled from the great eminence to which he had climbed. And he remembered then that he had climbed to it with Overbury's help. Overbury alone could have hoisted him to it, Overbury alone maintained him permanently there. And she had murdered Overbury; and now the inevitable consequences of Overbury's fall were overtaking him. He was to be dragged down after him, even as

Overbury had foretold, and to be dragged down in ignominy, in infamy.

She rose labouredly, and stood watching him, supporting herself against the overmantel even as he had supported himself. Her sensitiveness required no words from him, no spoken upbraidings; she gathered from his silence, his pacing and his distracted mien, all that was passing in his tortured mind, and sensed something of the aversion to herself that was rising in him. Presently she spoke.

"Robin, I need your help, your mercy."

He paused, and his wild eyes glared at her. "And do you hope for it?"

She shook her head. "Not for myself. For myself I would not ask it. I have said that if knowledge kills your love I care little what may befall. But there is a child – your child and mine – quickening in my womb. If I am destroyed, that innocent is destroyed with me."

"Is it not better so?" he asked her grimly. "Is it not better that this child should never live, than that it should bear the brand of infamy? That it should be pointed out as the offspring of assassins, of poisoners? For in this ruin I shall be involved with you. Your conviction inevitably must drag my own at its heels."

Thus he started a fresh terror in her, brought her love for him to over-ride even her maternal instincts. "That it never shall!" she cried fiercely. "I will tell the whole truth; declare that the whole guilt is mine; that you had no part in it. And since you had no part in it, what evidence can there be against you?"

"Evidence?" He laughed shortly. "My enemies will see to that. You have delivered me into their power, doomed me to such a ruin as they could never have hoped to encompass."

She wrung her hands, driven almost to frenzy. Yet by a stupendous effort still commanded herself, so that she might grasp the tiller and steer the frail barque of their lives through these angry seas. "Then for your own sake and for the child's, you must make a fight, Robin. I ask it not for myself. I have played and lost, God knows. I matter nothing now, and you need not weigh me. Think only of yourself, of the child and yourself. You can sway the King. You have influence with him. Show him your peril. Be frank with him. Confess my part in this. He will never abandon you to your enemies, and for the child's sake you must prevail upon him not to abandon me. Afterwards, if it is your will, I will go my ways, and never trouble you again. Oh, Robin, Robin, I would so gladly give my miserable life for you!"

He stood there frowning, white and helpless. Torn this way and that, between anger and pity.

"What can the King do now? The engines of the law have been set in motion. Can the King arrest them? Can he command Coke to desist from bringing these malefactors to justice? Upon what grounds would that be possible? Weston, Franklin and Turner have revealed themselves for foul rats who live by evil, who make a trade of it. Are they to go free? And if they do not, how shall those escape whom they will betray for having employed them? The King can do nothing in this pass." He swung about and resumed his pacing. "I came to you in such confidence that between us we could tear this thing to shreds, and now..."

He fell silent and paced on, his chin sunk to his breast, his eyes on the ground, his countenance distorted. At last he paused to look at her. She was shivering, as she leaned faintly there by the hearth; her teeth were chattering, her lips were blue.

"You are cold," he said dully, mechanically, and added: "Get you to bed. There is no more to be done or said."

She realised the truth of it. That night something had been slain and buried, something which she had laboured so hard and, in desperate need, so ruthlessly, to bring into existence. She bowed her head and moved stiffly across to the door. There she paused and turned.

"What shall you do, Robin?" she asked him piteously.

"So soon as it is dawn I shall set out to return to Royston."

"Shall I see you before you ride?"

He shook his head. "To what end? All has been said, I think."

She opened the door. Yet on the threshold she paused again, and stood a moment hesitating. "Will you kiss me, Robin...for the last time, perhaps? I may never see you again."

At that the man in him broke, and he fell suddenly to sobbing like a child. He ran to her, gathered her to him, and still sobbing, kissed her face and neck, whilst she, dry-eyed, clung to him in thankfulness and anguish.

"All is not yet lost," he vowed in a broken voice. "What man can do I'll do. I'll see the King. I'll cast myself upon his mercy. I'll go on my knees to him. He'll be content to banish us, perhaps. Keep up your heart, my Fanny. All is not yet lost. Trust me. Trust me. Now go. Go rest you, child, and pray."

Thus in that sudden short, sharp gust of pity for her, for himself, and perhaps for the unborn child.

But when, two days later, he was back at Royston – for the weakness of the flesh prevented the return journey being accomplished in a day – it was not in sackcloth and ashes, nor in any mood of humility that he sought the King.

As he rode, there had recurred to him certain aspects of the case which at Henley had been temporarily blotted out by the distraction his wife's revelations had brought him. He remembered again that interview with James which had followed immediately upon Overbury's death, remembered it more particularly now, recalled the very words the King had used. If ever words admitted guilt, the King's had admitted it when he had bidden Somerset be reconciled. There was a dark mystery here which baffled Somerset as he rode, until as a result of much brooding he suddenly perceived the light. It revived his broken courage, mantled him once more in his wonted arrogance, and sent him with firm step and chin held high to seek the King, indifferent to the covert sneers and sly, mocking glances that followed him as he crossed the antechamber.

It was close upon dinner time when he came seeking his majesty, and he took it for a good omen that, notwithstanding this, the King made no attempt to postpone the meeting, but dismissed the gentlemen who were with him in his closet, and sat as before at his work-table to hear the result of my lord's excursion to Henley.

"Ye're well returned, Rabbie," he was greeted, "and in good time, for Coke has sent for you to go to London."

Somerset raised his eyebrows. But he did not appear dismayed. "Already?" he exclaimed.

"It's no matter for delays, man. Coke is a diligent servant. And I hope you'll prove no less."

"Coke can wait," said his lordship composedly, for all that his face was white and jaded, his eyes red from weariness. And he added: "I'm not going."

"Not going? What's that ye're saying? It's a summons of the law. If Coke sent for me I should have to go. There's no avoiding it."

"Your majesty may yet come to a different opinion. You may come to consider sending word to Coke that the matter of these notes of his examinations is just so much rubbish so far as my incrimination or that of my Countess is concerned."

"Rubbish, man? Rubbish?"

"Consider, sire, the sum of the tale these rogues tell, when all is added together. Over a period of five months Weston is in the Tower to administer poisons to Overbury, which he says are procured for him by Mrs Turner and by Franklin. There is rosalgar, arsenic, aquafortis and Heaven knows what else besides; and yet in all this time Sir Thomas does not die."

"Because the Lieutenant of the Tower was watchful, and had moved Weston to play a double game: to accept the bribes of those who had placed him there without carrying out their orders."

"It nowhere says in these notes that Weston ultimately complied with those orders, and gave any of the poisons to Sir Thomas."

"Yet he must have done so, as is clear; or else Sir Thomas would not have died."

"Not unless someone else had stepped in at the last moment: someone who did not hesitate to do that which Weston dared not do since he had been discovered and intimidated by the Lieutenant."

The King's glance shifted uneasily. He stroked his beard, spreading his hand so that the gesture partly concealed his gaping mouth.

"Nay, as to that I know naught. It is a matter for Coke."

"But the notes say something to the matter. Weston, in fact, declares as much. And so does Sir Gervase Elwes. There was an apothecary's boy with Overbury two days before he died."

"The boy is dead," the King snapped, "and cannot now be brought to testify."

"No need for it." His lordship was almost airy. "He is but a tool of no account. He did no more than he was bid. The apothecary himself would be with him; and the apothecary would be of a certainty Doctor Mayerne's man, to do as Doctor Mayerne prescribed. Now Mayerne was sent by your majesty to minister to Overbury who at the time was sick, and it would be – would it not? – preposterous to suppose that Mayerne was guilty of procuring his murder?"

They looked into each other's eyes a moment. There was a certain grimness in his lordship's glance, complete vacuity in the King's.

"Preposterous indeed," said the thick, guttural voice of James.

"Then it becomes clear, I think, that Sir Thomas was never murdered at all."

"The depositions are plain. And these rogues assert that they were acting upon the orders of Lady Somerset and my Lord Northampton."

"To shield themselves it is natural they should name persons of great rank."

"Yet Payton brings you in to show a motive; and Lawrence Davies speaks to a powder you sent Sir Thomas, which made him extremely sick."

"A powder I sent him three months before he died! Can it be pretended that he died of that?"

Again the King stroked his beard. The short reddish hairs upon his hand glinted in a shaft of sunlight that at the same time revealed his ghastly pallor. The Earl observed that the hand shook a little.

"Well, well," said his majesty at length. "These are matters for Coke. Maybe ye'll persuade him by such arguments. I perceive their logic."

"Your majesty still considers that I must go before Coke?"

The very suggestion of disobeying the summons of the Lord Chief Justice seemed to startle the King more deeply than formerly. "Ud's death, man! What else? Have I not said that if Coke sends for me, even I must go?"

"Very well," said his lordship quietly, for all that his countenance grew overcast. "Then I shall see to it that Coke pursues to its end this matter of the apothecary's boy."

The King sucked in his breath. "Ye would be best advised to leave the line of inquiry to Coke himself. That line must follow the trail that's been started by the Lieutenant."

He spoke with the quiet impressiveness of a man who conveys more than the literal meaning of his words. "Any other line must lead to your destruction, Robin, and as God's my life I do not desire that. I love you overwell to desire your hurt." Still more impressive grew the tone. "So be discreet and place your trust in me, and whatever the lawyers make of it, no harm shall come to you or to your lady." He set his hands on the table and heaved himself up, thrusting back his chair.

For a moment the King and the Earl stood facing each other, the latter a little wild of eye. It had been in his mind to interrupt the King with a vehement threat of what he would do, of how he would drag the truth into the light if he were unduly pressed, insisting upon the examination of Mayerne, and by means of it establishing the fact that side by side with the aborted plot which his unfortunate Countess had set on foot had run another, instigated by the King, which had succeeded. In his wrath and resentment at the treachery of James, at his employment of old methods for providing scapegoats for his royal dignity, Somerset had been on the point of threatening a complete exposure which should place the brand of Cain upon the King.

Betimes, however, he had checked. "Whatever the lawyers make of it, no harm shall come to you or to your lady." That was the promise that had given him pause. Could he trust it? Swiftly his mind balanced the question. He thought of Frances and of the unborn child she carried. If he did not accept this compromise those two would be destroyed together with himself.

"Come now, Rabbie." His majesty spoke gently in the old fatherly tone, addressing him by the old intimate diminutive of his name. "Come. You shall dine with me, and afterwards away to Coke in London."

When the King entered the dining-room leaning upon Somerset's stalwart shoulder, fondly as of old, there was consternation almost among the gentlemen who waited there, who for some days now had confidently been pronouncing that his lordship's star had definitely set.

Throughout the meal the King glozed an abiding nervousness with jocularity. He pledged his dear Rabbie, and drank deep, so that even Sir George Villiers grew thoughtful and uneasy.

When dinner was done, and it was announced that my Lord of Somerset's coach was waiting, it was the King himself who escorted him to it, hanging an arm round his neck as he went with him, and slobbering kisses on his cheek.

"For God's sake when shall I see thee again? On my soul I shall neither eat nor sleep until I see thee again. When shall it be, Rabbie?"

His bewildered lordship answered that he counted upon returning on Monday.

"Shall I? Shall I? For God's sake let it be Monday."

Still lolling about his neck, the King went down the stairs with him, and at the stairs' foot detained him again, and again reached up to slobber his neck.

"For God's sake give thy lady this kiss for me!" he cried, and then, lowering his voice so that only Somerset should hear his words: "Set your trust in me, Rabbie, and whatever may seem, be sure no harm shall come to your lady or yourself."

Somerset bent his knee, and kissed the royal hand in leave taking, then went briskly out and stepped into his waiting coach.

The King, following him with his watery eyes, waved to him from where he stood at the stairs' foot. Then, as the coach rolled away, unless the gentleman standing at the royal elbow who overheard him and reported it was a liar, the whole expression of his face was seen to alter, and with narrowing glance he muttered thickly: "Now the devil go with you, for I shall never see your face again."

Chapter 32

Prelude

If, as it seemed to him, policy or the needs of kingcraft drove King James at times into illegal courses, into violations of the law of which he was the custodian, into, in short, acts which must be accounted criminal, yet he usually knew how to cover up his tracks by a further abuse of his kingly powers, and so to dispose that no definite accusation could be sustained against him. More than once in his career he was driven the lengths of providing a scapegoat upon whom he could fasten the imprudence or the crime of which he had himself been guilty, and in such a course, when it became necessary, no scruple appears to have deterred him. For whilst the woman in him shrank from contact with violence or cruelty, yet he would never boggle at the ruthlessness of a deed which he was not called upon to witness.

An instance of this is provided by the affair at Gowrie House, in which young Ruthven and the Earl of Gowrie were coldly butchered, an affair the truth of which will never be known, but which certainly does not lie in the mass of falsehood provided by the King's own account of a conspiracy against his life. Another instance is possibly provided by the murder of the Earl of Murray, which many believed to have been done at the King's instigation, although Huntley, whose actual hands shed the blood, bore the public blame of it and was by James imprisoned for the deed. Yet a third instance is supplied by the case of Lord Balmerino. When an imprudent letter of James Stuart's to the Pope was brought to light in which the Protestant monarch was found to have been coquetting with His Holiness with a view to obtaining papal support for his claims to the crown of England, his majesty took refuge in denouncing the letter for a forgery. He accused his secretary, Elphinstone, who was afterwards Lord Balmerino, of having forged his signature, flung him into prison for the crime, and actually went the length of having him sentenced to death, although afterwards in the exercise of the royal prerogative of clemency he pardoned him.

My Lord of Somerset, who knew as much of these and other similar matters as any man alive, had leisure to reflect upon them as he rolled through Hertfordshire in his clumsy coach, and to perceive quite clearly that in this matter of Sir Thomas Overbury's murder, King James was playing the same game.

It was quite clear from the evidence assembled by Coke that there had been a plot against the life of Sir Thomas. This plot had failed. But, notwithstanding its failure, it could be turned to such account as to provide definitely and conclusively against any accusation ever being levelled at the King. Undoubtedly several persons would be tried, convicted and executed for a murder which they had not committed. But that need not trouble the royal conscience, since those persons were undoubtedly guilty in intent; they had certainly conspired to kill Sir Thomas, and if they had not succeeded, this had been due to an accidental intervention which nowise reduced their guilt. They were scoundrels all, and the world would be well rid of them in any case.

All this was clear to my Lord of Somerset, and because of it, and of the King's parting assurance to him, he rode to London in some confidence that no more than a formal examination awaited him, that his denials would be accepted by Coke and. that he would be back at Royston by Monday as he had promised.

The future, it is true, looked dark. His position hereafter would be increasingly difficult, and the ghost of Overbury must ever stand between himself and Frances. Out of his abiding pity, to which her approaching motherhood may have contributed, he sought to be just; to be more than just; to practise clemency in his judgment. He compelled himself to remember that she had sinned for love of him; that it was as much to ensure his happiness as her own that she had stooped to those abominable practices and enlisted the services of those vile creatures who would now betray her. But his conception of her had changed. His lover's fancy had exalted her into a holy thing to which he had given worship. Now the veils were rent and his goddess stood revealed as basely human. Still, he must do what he could to protect her. He must reveal to her the shield which they possessed in his knowledge of the King's guilt.

When he should have shown her that, however Overbury had died, it had not been as a result of any measures she might have taken against him, she would find strength to deny and to persist in denial.

After all, against her there was nothing but the word of discredited rogues who could not but be proven liars in the course of the examinations. It was true that there were some dreadful letters which she had written Forman. But these had no bearing upon the case of Sir Thomas Overbury nor concerned anything that might have been meditated against him.

His lordship was anxious to reach London and to have done with his business with Coke, so that being free to return he might seek her at once and instruct her in the bearing she must assume in any examination to which she might be subjected.

His confidence reviving thus, he came to London, to have it all shattered again almost in the hour of his arrival. At his sumptuous lodging near the cockpit he found an officer awaiting him, and a letter signed by the four members of the Commission, in which they professed themselves his lordship's very loving friends, but required him in his majesty's name to keep his chamber, without suffering the access of any to him other than his own necessary servants until his majesty's pleasure should be further known.

Somerset having read the letter of his "very loving friends," let it flutter from his nerveless fingers. He sat down heavily and took his head in his hands. His thoughts were with the King who but yesterday had been slobbering his cheeks with kisses and protesting in maudlin accents that he would neither eat nor sleep until Robin should return. And all the while the King knew that Somerset went to arrest, to be detained in isolation from all until "His majesty's pleasure be further known."

He heard again the King's thick, slurring voice: "For God's sake give thy lady this kiss for me."

The kiss of Judas, the kiss of betrayal it had been. James had flung him naked to his enemies to be destroyed. And then, through the bitterness of his resentment, through the fierce resolve that James should yet come to repent this unspeakable falsity, the memory of his own betrayal of Overbury surged before him to turn him ice cold with horror and with the sense that he was but being repaid in the coin which himself he had uttered.

Deceived by those smooth words and Judas' kisses, he had walked into the trap without ever a chance to communicate again with his Countess, to warn her and school her as he had been determining. And now it was certain that no chance would be afforded them of communicating with each other until separately or jointly they were brought before Coke and the others for examination.

Meanwhile, the Countess of Somerset was also virtually under arrest by order of Coke and his fellow commissioners. She had been brought to Town at about the same time that the Earl had come thither, and she was placed in the care of Sir William Smythe in Lord Aubigny's house in the Blackfriars. She had come attended, as befitted her rank, by six women and several men servants; but of these only two of the former were suffered to remain with her and every precaution was taken to prevent her communicating with the outside world.

She bore this with the stoicism which follows upon the cessation of all hope. She had played her desperate game, made her desperate throw for happiness, and she had lost. Of that she was now fully assured. It was not a matter that depended upon the issue of any trial that might lie in store for her. It was not for life that she had played;

but for Robin's love without which life was of little account. And whether she lived or died, Robin's love was irrevocably lost to her. His worship of her had been for that ideal of womanhood which she had incarnated for him. This ideal she had befouled and destroyed in her very endeavours to preserve it for him. Could irony go further?

It was not only that her hands were imbrued with Overbury's blood, but that all her body, her very spirit, was defiled by the necromantic practices to which she had lent herself and by the evil associations which she had made her own. In her husband's eyes she was leprous. She had seen that plainly enough in his face on that dreadful night at Henley, before it had been momentarily effaced by the gust of pity which had shaken him – a pity whose memory, now that it was fully understood, set her shuddering. Better would it have been, she thought, had he reviled and beaten her.

It was finished. The game was played. Love, its greatest forfeit, had been lost. The sooner life followed, the sooner oblivion came, the better now. And in the time of waiting it but remained her to bear herself with such fortitude as she could command and such dignity as she could counterfeit, for of real dignity no rag was left her. She was as one exposed naked to the public gaze.

Meanwhile, the Earl of Somerset wrote passionate letters to the King protesting against his betrayal and full of covert threats of what he must disclose if the betrayal were pushed too far. One letter the King wrote him in answer, a letter obviously composed for publication, wherein his majesty protested that he would do his duty honestly and not tamper with justice.

That justice lost no time in getting to work. On October 19th, at the Guildhall, began the Great Oyer of Poisoning, as Coke described it, with the trial of Richard Weston.

Thus at the very outset the dishonesty of the proceedings is apparent. Weston was an accessory. Both on his own evidence and that of Sir Gervase Elwes, besides the confession of the apothecary's boy in Flushing, Sir Thomas Overbury had died following upon an injection prepared by Loubel. Therefore Loubel was the principal, and only after Loubel's conviction of the murder could the field have been extended to include Weston and the others. But Loubel was tried neither then nor subsequently, a circumstance regarded by many as the most mysterious part of what is known as the Overbury Mystery, whereas, in fact, it is the clue to it. Nor was the evidence of the coroner put in, so that there was no real preliminary formal proof that Overbury had been poisoned at all.

The indictment against Weston alleged four several attempts to poison Sir Thomas. One on the ninth of May, 1613, when rosalgar was said to have been used, another on July 1st by means of white arsenic, and a third on July 19th by mercury sublimate contained in some tarts and jellies sent in to the prisoner. Finally, on the fourteenth of September of that same year, Weston, it was charged, in conjunction with another man, had administered an injection of corrosive sublimate to which Sir Thomas had succumbed.

Coke, acting as judge and prosecuting counsel in one, secured a verdict of guilty from the jury, and the unfortunate Weston was hanged at Tyburn two days after sentence.

In the first week of November Anne Turner was brought to trial. The charge against her was of comforting, aiding and abetting Weston, who was no longer there to answer anything he might in reason have been asked. Terrified, the frail little widow pleaded not guilty.

Coke, from the bench, bespattered her with some ordures of speech by way of shortening the work in hand and helping the jury to an opinion about her. He dubbed her whore and bawd and witch and papist and several other things, thereby reducing the dainty golden-headed creature to an outburst of passionate weeping.

The charge was established by the production of letters which had passed between the Countess of Essex and Simon Forman and some of the puppets in wax and lead which had been prepared for purposes of enchantments. Mrs Turner had obtained possession of these on the death of Forman, but she had neglected to destroy them. The constable had found them in her house, and they effectively set the rope about her pretty delicate neck.

She made her last appearance at Tyburn, dressed with the modish care which had ever distinguished her, and wearing the ruffs and cuffs starched in yellow which she had rendered so fashionable, but which thereafter were never to be seen again.

The next victim on the charge of being an accessory was the unfortunate Sir Gervase Elwes, but for whom no word of all this business might ever have been divulged. He defended himself vigorously, skilfully and manfully, and must by his grave appearance and demeanour have commanded some respect and compassion. But he was foredoomed by the ruthless Coke, and was destroyed upon a lying assertion by Franklin that he was in league with the Countess. Although it must have been clear that if any of what was alleged against him had been true Overbury's poisoning would never have taken five months to accomplish, he was sentenced and hanged. Because he had been Lieutenant of the Tower he was executed on Tower Hill, as being a place less infamous than Tyburn.

After Elwes came Franklin, the doctor and warlock, who in some mad hope to save himself had suggested in his examinations that he could incriminate half the kingdom, and this not only for the poisoning of Sir Thomas Overbury, but for many other mysterious deaths beginning with that of Prince Henry. He lied recklessly and fantastically. He is comparable only with a squid which throws out an inky cloud in the hope of being himself lost in it to the view of his pursuers, and it was in the course of his wildest lies that the Earl was for the first time seriously mentioned as having any direct connection with the fact of poisoning. The falsehood of his depositions was rendered obvious by their own glaring inconsistencies. He delayed his fate by asserting even after sentence that he had still more to reveal, and he would have continued these revelations to the end of his natural life had not even Coke grown weary of his fabrications and cut them short by dismissing him to the gallows.

In the first days of December Sir Thomas Monson was brought to trial. His guilt lay in having procured Sir Gervase Elwes to be Lieutenant of the Tower in place of Sir William Wade. This was assumed to be something done in order to pave the way for the murder. He bore himself arrogantly and contemptuously before the court, and eventually he was put back in order that he might be a witness against the Countess. Nor was he ever brought to trial again.

There ended the prelude to the Grand Oyer of Poisoning. The drama itself was to follow some six months later, sumptuously staged in Westminster Hall. Meanwhile out of all that had gone, and out of the unfortunate wretches who had been hanged, enough material had been squeezed, as evidence was then understood, to serve for the destruction of the Earl and Countess of Somerset by men who were determined to destroy them.

Chapter 33

The Ambassador

In the early days of December of that dreadful year the young Countess in her duress in the house in Blackfriars was joylessly delivered of a daughter.

She had vowed that she would not survive the event; she had even taken steps to destroy herself together with the child before its birth; but in this she had been frustrated by those who watched over her. The King, being informed of her intentions and attempts, had, with a kindness that was almost cruel, sent physicians to take charge of her and nurses to watch over her constantly, so that she might be preserved for all the suffering that awaited her.

She may have spared some of her pity for herself to bestow it upon the infant at her breast. No joybells announced its advent; there was no pompous christening graced by royalty for the offspring of a daughter of the great House of Howard and the wife of one who had been First Minister of State and the greatest man in England.

In March she was conveyed to the Tower, and given the lodging which Sir Walter Raleigh had lately quitted to sail upon the disastrous El Dorado adventure. Her babe was delivered into the care of the Countess of Suffolk and taken to Audley End, where the Lord Treasurer's lady was in residence during those unhappy days.

As for Somerset, he had already preceded his wife to the Tower, where, however, they were still not suffered to communicate with each other.

The Earl now perceived quite clearly that in spite of all his letters to the King it was not only the intention to bring him to trial, to arraign him like a criminal before men who in the past had gone in awe of him, but that the issue of that trial was foregone. Already he had been stripped of his great offices of State. The privy seals had gone to the Earl of Worcester, whilst the Lord Chamberlain's wand of office was grasped at last by the Earl of Pembroke. Soon, he supposed, they would be parcelling out his lands and possessions, and out of them, no doubt, the upstart Villiers would be richly endowed.

He writhed in justifiable anger, and took oath that he would never submit to be so tamely broken. Then he curbed himself, and wrote again to the King. This time, however, he did not rave and threaten wildly. He sent a precise, cold and closely reasoned statement which so fastened the guilt of Overbury's murder upon the King that if it were publicly made it could not be suffered to remain unanswered. And publicly made it should be, Somerset warned his majesty, if he or his Countess were brought to trial for a crime which no one knew better than the King that neither of them had committed, and which Somerset himself had never contemplated.

Nor did he leave the matter there. So that the King should see that he fully intended what he threatened and that means of publication were not lacking, he uttered to Sir George More threats of what he could and would do, knowing full well that Sir George would perform his duty and report these words to the King. Without being explicit to the Lieutenant, he announced the intention of laying an aspersion on his majesty of being an accessory to the murder.

To Sir George the King replied that this was no more than a trick of Somerset's idle brain, by which he hoped to shift the trial. Under that airy answer he dissembled the panic into which the letter had flung him. Somerset had revealed quite clearly how completely he held the King; what dreadful havoc he could make if in open court he were to repeat the statement he had set down, and demand the examination of Mayerne, who had prescribed, and of Loubel, who had administered, the poisoned injection. It was a demand that could not be refused once the accusation were lodged, for to refuse it would be an admission of fear which could have but one interpretation. The evidence upon which Weston had been hanged had already established that it was the injection which, being poisoned, had ended Sir Thomas Overbury's days. This was a blunder of Coke's for which the King in his present rage and terror could cheerfully have strangled the Lord Chief Justice. It was a blunder of which Somerset's exposition took the fullest account. Loubel, being examined, must shelter himself behind Mayerne; and Mayerne, when his turn came, must betray the King to save his own neck.

And what should King James look like in the eyes of the nation if the truth were told at this stage? He would stand revealed not merely as a murderer, but as a murderer on so ruthless and infamous a scale that to screen himself he had already allowed four persons, however venal, to suffer death unjustly for a crime of his own, and was seeking to add two victims more.

He was panic-stricken at the perception of the situation into which Somerset showed that he could thrust him. The chink which he had always known to exist in his armour gaped wider than he had supposed possible, and the wound which Somerset threatened to deal him through it was one which it might be impossible to staunch before his majesty was bled white of credit and reputation.

On the other hand, so much had already been alleged against Somerset by those who were eager to implicate him; Coke had been so liberal in the course of the preliminary trials in assertions of his lordship's guilt, of which he said that the proofs were pregnant against him, that if King James now intervened it would be said that he had hushed up the scandal to save the arch-offender after the lesser ones had suffered.

In this horrible quandary, his majesty finally resolved to send Lord Hay as his plenipotentiary not only to Somerset but to the Countess as well.

The splendid courtier who had so often and so brilliantly represented his Prince at foreign Courts had possibly never undertaken a more delicate embassage or one in whose inmost particulars he was less instructed.

He landed at Tower Wharf on a brilliant morning of May, when the scent of lilac was strong upon the tepid air, and having presented his credentials to the Lieutenant was straightway conducted to her ladyship.

In that lodging which had been Sir Walter Raleigh's, with the furnishings which had served that bright adventurer, and even some of his books and effects about her, she sat pale and listless, a neglected volume of poems in her lap. She had wasted a little during her confinement, and there was something now almost ethereal and unearthly about her delicate beauty. She was dressed with great care, but in black, which threw into greater relief the snowy whiteness of her skin and the bright gold of the heavy clumps of hair protruding on either side of the braided coif with which her head was covered.

She rose at sight of the great courtier disclosed to her by the opening of the heavy oaken door, and her faithful woman Catherine who was at her needlework by the window rose with her.

Lord Hay came quickly forward, scattering the rushes on the floor in his haste to have her resume her seat. Hat in hand, he bowed low over the hand she extended mechanically in greeting, and brushed it with his lips.

The action almost surprised her. It brought tears to her eyes, and a warmth surged in her heart for this gallant gentleman to whom a woman's hand was still a woman's hand even though stained as hers must be accounted stained.

She looked into his bold, handsome face, and as memories arose she wondered whether he who had been Robin's first friend was destined now to be his last. She knew that there had been differences between them; that for a time Lord Hay, entirely devoted to French interests, had been hostile to Robin when he had seemed to favour Spain. It was possible even that there might be resentments of the great eminence to which the royal favour had hoisted one who had first made his appearance before King James as a simple esquire in the train of Sir James Hay, as he then had been. How well she remembered that scene ten years ago in the tilt-yard at Whitehall. And how much had happened in the time that was sped. Lord Hay himself had aged considerably since that day when he himself had been one of the favourites of a King who loved handsome men. Yet because he had never climbed to such vertiginous heights as Robin, he had been able to maintain his foothold in security.

His lordship, with head deferentially inclined, announced himself a messenger from the King and requested to be private with her.

She dismissed her woman to the outer room, and resumed her armchair. To stand immediately before her, his lordship turned his back to the window and the light.

"I bring your ladyship a message of hope," he announced.

"Of hope?" she echoed, and the sadness of her smile cut him more sharply than any tears.

He had been of those who had voiced the spreading execration of this woman stained with such guilt as had been brought to light by the confessions of scoundrels who had already suffered for a crime of which she must be supposed the instigator. But in her presence now, her beauty, her pallor, her wistfulness, the physical frailty of her worn body, brought him to weigh the temptation she had suffered against the sin she had committed, and he cast out every thought but that of pity.

"The hope of royal clemency," he explained.

"The only clemency I crave," she answered him, "is to pass swiftly out from...all this, before I come to the terrible ordeal of my trial."

"That ordeal you may sensibly lessen by your own act, my lady. If you will confess, the trial, instead of being a minute and close examination into your errors, will become little more than a formality. You must submit to sentence; but that sentence will never be carried out. I bring you his majesty's assurance of this, provided that you will confess your guilt."

"Confess?" she echoed.

He thought she questioned the necessity, still clinging to hope that she might defeat her accusers and make it appear that the evidence against her was insufficient. To dispel that imagined hope he briefly recited what had been betrayed by Weston, by Turner, and by Franklin, showing how their evidence was intercorroborated. She displayed little interest until he mentioned Sir David Wood and told her how this gentleman had come forward to bear witness that once she had sought to hire him to kill Overbury. She raised her eyes at this, and looked at him, a smile of scornful pity on her lips.

"Even he!" she exclaimed, and slowly shook her head. "Those other poor wretches I can understand. They hoped to save their lives by putting the blame on me, where indeed it belongs."

This was a generous admission considering that, after all, Turner had been the serpent who had tempted her to her destruction.

"But Sir David! He was my uncle's man and owed him much. At one time he professed to love me, and vowed himself for ever my servant. Behold his service! It can nothing profit him to help to break me, and yet he comes to add what he can to my load of shame. But let be. It little signifies."

"Except, madam, that it serves to complete the ring that has been drawn about you. That is why I urge you in his majesty's name to make a full confession, thereby disarming justice."

She rose abruptly. Some colour kindled in her cheeks. She appeared to be swept by a sudden passion.

"It would not occur to his majesty that this thing which I am urged to do for clemency, I must already have decided to do for love."

"You mean, madam?"

"Mean, my lord? Is not my meaning plain? Must I give tongue to the little virtue that is left me? Must I tell you, after all that has befallen, that my love for Robin has been the lodestar of my life? Evil has come of it, God knows. But do you think that it could beget naught but evil? Do you not see that evil came because evil was made a necessity to its fulfilment? Oh, my lord, in itself my love was neither good nor evil. It was just love. The overwhelming desire to possess and be possessed. It made use of good or evil indiscriminately for its compelling needs. Where evil alone would serve, it used evil perforce, as freely as now it must use good, since through good alone can it continue to manifest itself."

She paused. My Lord Hay was a little bewildered by the passion which lent her clarity and eloquence. Then more quietly she continued.

"You may be wondering, my lord, what is all this to the matter. You may tell his majesty that I shall confess fully and freely; that already I had resolved upon this; but not out of any hope of mercy; not to gain a single day of a life that must henceforth be empty. I shall confess because were I to deny, were I to attempt to combat or disprove any of this that has been alleged against me, I must endanger Robin, who is already suspect upon no better grounds than that he is my husband. Those suspicions my confession shall clear away. It shall be seen that my Robin had no part or share in this, that no impeachment can be made against him. That is why I shall confess, taking all the blame for this upon myself where it rightly belongs. It is all that I can do now. The only amend, alas!"

She sat down again, wearily, folding her hands in her lap. His lordship stood a moment looking at her, as if undecided. Then he bowed from the waist, and in that attitude spoke his farewell.

"Madam, the resolve is as wise as it is deserving. I will communicate it to his majesty. And I pray that you may yet be spared for many years."

"Ah, pray not that! Pray not that! Let it be clear to his majesty that I have made no bargain. That I neither ask nor desire mercy. That all that I can seek is rest when this last duty to Robin shall have been fulfilled."

His lordship departed in a mood blending compassion with complacency. So far he had succeeded, and his royal master should be well pleased with him. If only he could accomplish as much by my Lord Somerset, the royal satisfaction should be complete.

The Lieutenant, who had waited, conducted him by gloomy dank passages, up one flight of stone steps and down another, to the lodging of the Earl.

Somerset was writing busily when Lord Hay was ushered in upon him, and the older man was shocked to perceive the change which a few months had wrought in the prisoner's appearance. His beautiful red gold hair which always had been so scrupulously combed and frizzed was lank and ill kempt, and odd strands of grey had made their appearance in it. His face was thin and pallid. Its bone structures were thrown into prominence, filling with shadow the hollows thus produced. His eyes, once so clear and commanding, were dull, blood-injected and sunken into his head. He was negligently dressed, this man who once had been a mirror of the elegancies. Wrapped in a purple quilted bedgown, his collar open at the throat, his feet were thrust into slippers, and black silk stockings, carelessly gartered, hung in creases about his calves.

As the door opened, he looked up, almost savagely. At sight of Lord Hay he rose, startled, and for a long moment remained staring at the man who once had been his master, subsequently had been a humble suitor for his patronage, more lately one of his enemies, and held now in the royal favour a position rendered the more assured by Somerset's eclipse.

"My lord!" was all that he could ejaculate, a certain bitterness rising in him.

Lord Hay bowed to him as deferentially as if he were still the favourite and First Minister of State. He moved forward. But as Somerset did not stir to meet him or make shift to proffer his hand, the royal messenger contented himself with bowing again.

Sir George More closed the door and effaced himself to wait beyond it.

"I am from the King," Lord Hay announced, and plunged straightway into the business. "I am to tell you, Robin, that his majesty deeply resents the threat in your letter to make him in some sort accessory to your crime."

"My crime!" Somerset's face was convulsed with anger. "My crime!" he repeated. "He's determined then to father it upon me? Well, well! We shall see. His majesty's resentment shall go deeper yet when I make it clear that I am being used by him as a scapegoat for a deed that is his own. Tell him from me, as I shall tell their lordships if I am brought to trial, that I am neither Balmerino nor the Earl of Gowrie. That if he wants my silence he may send Haddington to murder me as he murdered Ruthven. Short of that, if he insists upon dragging me to Westminster Hall, I shall not be silent upon what I know, nor will I consent to wear the mantle of his infamy."

"My lord, my lord!" Hay became formal again in his remonstrance. "These are wild, mad words!"

"The country shall judge their madness if I am brought to trial."

"And mad the country will judge them. If you are guilty of so infamous an attempt to shift the blame, you will seal your own doom irrevocably."

"To shift the blame, does he dare to say? I shall not seek to shift it; but to nail it down where it belongs."

"Where it belongs?" Hay stood stiff and straight and calm as he looked into the wild eyes of Somerset. He frowned a little. "Robin, you delude yourself, indeed, if you dream that such measures can avail you, that they can produce any effect upon your judges or the country, or that you can intimidate his majesty by such threats. The burden of evidence is too heavy against you."

"Evidence! What evidence can there be since I am innocent?" His lordship's fury vibrated in his voice. "I had no hand in the murder of Tom Overbury, as none knows better than the King. All the world shall know where the blame lies before I've done, if either I or my Countess be brought to trial."

Lord Hay nodded grimly. "That is true enough. The world shall know it upon the word of her ladyship herself; indeed, upon her confession that she contrived the deed. Against that, what shall your threats avail, how shall the scandals you will attempt to raise ever touch the King?"

Somerset stood quite still, suddenly calmed. The high colour which indignation had whipped into his cheeks receded, leaving them paler than they had been before. He sat down heavily at the deal-table which was strewn with his papers, quills and inkhorn, the table by which Lord Hay was standing.

"She confesses!" He spoke hoarsely, scarce above a whisper.

Here was a factor he had left out of his calculations; stupidly, as he now perceived. In the light of her confession what indeed could it avail him to speak to the King's guilt? Since there was one who confessed to the crime, what could it avail to seek to fasten it on another? She should have entrenched herself in denial; denounced those wretches who had been bullied and tormented into self-accusation for liars when they sought to implicate her in their guilt. The rest she could have left to him and the tale he could tell which must have made the whole thing look like a base conspiracy against them. So long as she maintained that attitude the King would never dare to bring them to trial, aware of the mischief Somerset could do.

But since she confessed, she destroyed them both. Against that confession there was no battling, as Lord Hay now warned him. Yet still he resisted. "If she confesses, she confesses to something that is not true, although she may believe it true."

"Could any man persuade their lordships of that?" said Hay gently.

Somerset ignored the question. "Yet even though she confess, that confession cannot include me."

"It must, my lord. By implication. Her motive was common to you both. Their lordships will not be slow to perceive that. The Commission, my lord, has perceived it already, and that perception alone sufficed them as a reason for placing you under restraint."

Somerset rose again, grumbling in his throat, and paced away to the barred window, dragging his loose-shod feet. He stood staring out a moment; then swung round and came slowly back.

"And so," he said bitterly, "the King thinks to have my head under his girdle?"

"The King," Lord Hay replied in a tone of reproof, "desires to assure you of his continued affection, and desires you to make it possible to show you mercy."

"Mercy for what?"

"For the crime with which you are charged."

"I thank you, my lord, for not saying the crime which I have committed. And as I have committed no crime I desire no mercy. I desire only that my innocence may appear. I shall defend my honour to my last breath, and in spite of all the traps and snares that may be laid for me. Tell the King that. Tell him, as I said at the beginning, that I am neither Gowrie nor Balmerino."

Lord Hay shook his fine head. "I should not be your friend if I bore that message."

Lord Somerset smote the table with his open palm. "You will not be my friend if you do not." With a touch of his old haughtiness he added: "There is no more to say, my lord."

Lord Hay accepted the dismissal. He gathered his satin cape-cloak about him and resumed his hat. "At the moment, perhaps not, my lord. But you will reflect upon what I have said. You will remember that you hold the key to the gates of royal mercy. It is for you, my lord, to determine whether you will employ it. God light you to a wise decision."

"God cannot wish me to destroy my honour," was the Earl's last word.

They bowed to each other, and Lord Hay went out.

Alone, Somerset sat down again, folded his arms upon the table, and laid his head upon them with a groan. He was tasting, he knew, the bitterness that had been Overbury's when Overbury was trapped in that same prison even as he. Like Overbury, he was fighting for his life and liberty by threats of the havoc he could wreak by his disclosures. He was punished, indeed, poetically for his betrayal of his friend.

Chapter 34

The Mercy of King James

After many delays and postponements, the true cause for which must be sought in the conscience of the King and the fears that sprang from it, the Countess of Somerset was brought to trial on a Friday towards the end of May.

Betimes she was conducted by the Lieutenant from the gloom of her prison into the brilliance of that May morning and the dazzling sunshine which glinted upon the corselets and headpieces of her escort and upon the terrible axe which the headsman carried before her with averted edge.

She had dressed herself with care and thought for the dread part she was to play in the thronged theatre of Westminster Hall. She wore a gown of black tammil, relieved at throat and wrists by cuffs and ruff of cobweb lawn, and on her head a chaperon of cypress crepe. The funereal raiment but served to render her white beauty the more startling.

With Catherine, her faithful woman, following, she embarked in the Lieutenant's barge, and with the tide at half-flow she arrived in less than an hour at Westminster steps, where pikemen kept the curious crowd in check.

Within the vast hall, which since six o'clock that morning had been packed to suffocation by the nobles and gentry who could afford to pay the high prices demanded for so rare a show, a stage had been erected for the peers who were to sit in judgment upon her. They entered in procession, twenty-two of them, in their robes, in the wake of the feeble Lord Chancellor Ellesmere, who filled the post of Lord High Steward, and followed by the Lord Chief Justice and seven judges in scarlet.

The Lord High Steward, moving slowly and preceded by the bearers of his white staff, his patent and his seal, and six sergeants-at-arms shouldering their maces, took his place under the scarlet cloth of estate, bowed to the assembly and sat down. Their lordships, covering themselves, sank with a rustle to their seats on either side of him; more noisily the great crowd settled itself down again in the sweltering heat of that May morning, and on the ensuing stillness beat the droning voice of the Clerk of Arraigns. Then came a fresh stir as the Countess, followed by her woman, was conducted by the Lieutenant of the Tower to the bar. Her pallor was deathlike, but her feet did not falter. With lowered eyes she took her place before their lordships, and spread her fan, so as to conceal the half of her countenance from those cruelly inquisitive probing glances.

The voice of the Clerk of Arraigns rang challengingly, like a trumpet call.

"Frances, Countess of Somerset, hold up thy hand!"

She obeyed, being compelled for this to put aside her fan; and stood so whilst the indictment was read to her, tears flowing down a face which might have been carved of marble so white and rigid did it remain.

At the end of it came the question: "Frances, Countess of Somerset, how sayest thou? Art thou guilty of this felony and murder or not guilty?"

She paused a moment in the deathly stillness all about her, swaying a little before she answered with the single word which surely must deliver her Robin of all peril. Although she spoke that word low and fearfully it was widely heard in the silence.

"Guilty."

It may have occasioned disappointment, for it curtailed the sport which those who had paid so extravagantly for their places might have derived from the contest arising out of a defence.

Sir Francis Bacon, the Attorney-General, sleek and elegant, was instantly on his feet, to charm the audience with his silken voice and well-balanced periods, commending the course she had taken. He had his orders from the King. She was to be dealt with leniently in view of her confession, and no odious or uncivil speeches were to be given.

It was not the supple Bacon's way to be odious or uncivil. Such gifts as his do not need to employ bullyings and browbeatings, nor was there any occasion for them here.

He stressed the fact that she was a spectacle of awe and commiseration. He hinted in plain terms that the royal clemency would follow. Meanwhile, however, he invited their lordships to pass to the discharge of their duty.

"This lady," he said at one point in his graceful oration "meets justice in the way by confession, which is the cornerstone either of mercy or judgment. It is said that mercy and truth be met together. Truth you have in her confession, and that may be a degree to mercy, which we must leave to him in whose power it resides. In the meantime this day must be reserved for judgment."

At the end the Clerk of Arraigns demanded of her formally what she could say why judgment of death should not be pronounced against her.

What she replied was uttered in so low a voice that no more than the sound of it was audible save to those immediately about her. Of these it was Sir Francis Bacon who repeated the words after her to Lord Ellesmere.

"I can much aggravate but nothing extenuate my fault... I desire mercy...and that the lords will intercede for me with the King."

The frail old Chancellor, taking his white staff, delivered judgment. He tempered it by an expression of the belief that, in view of the humility and grief in which she had confessed, the King would be moved to mercy, closing in the words prescribed.

" …That you shall be carried from hence to the Tower of London, and from thence to the place of execution, where you are to be hanged by the neck till you be dead. And the Lord have mercy upon your soul."

She staggered and swayed as if about to fall. To steady herself she clutched at the rail before her, and remained a moment clinging to it, whilst her woman hastened to her at a sign from Sir George More. Then, at another signal from the Lieutenant, the halberdiers advanced, Sir George proffered her his hand, and thus led by him, again preceded by the headsman, this time with the edge of the gleaming axe towards her, she passed out of the hall under the gaze of that great concourse, which included the short sturdy figure of the young Earl of Essex, who watched her with grim sullen eyes.

The crowd surged out into the sunshine to babble of the show and of the greater show that was to follow on the morrow when the Earl of Somerset should come there, not meekly to surrender it was said as her ladyship had done, but fiercely to battle for his life.

Meanwhile, however, my Lord of Somerset was protesting passionately that he would not go at all, and that if they carried him there in his bed by main force he would stand mute and refuse to plead. Such were the fierce assurances he gave Sir George More, when the Lieutenant, on his return from Westminster Hall, went to inform his lordship of how it had fared with the Countess.

Her confession created no fresh consternation in him. It did not move him at all. He had been prepared for it, and he was not to guess that she had been led to make it more for his sake than for her own, induced by the assurance that it would earn leniency for both of them.

He waived it aside, as something done and irretrievable, but something which did not touch him. His concern was now entirely with his own trial upon the morrow, for which he was desired to prepare himself. He would not prepare himself, he announced to Sir George More, because he would not be required to go; because the King dared not bring him to trial.

"These are grave words to use of his majesty, my lord," Sir George reproved him.

"They are. And there are grave facts behind them. I have sent him word already that I am neither Gowrie nor Balmerino. He'll have read my meaning. He will know what to expect. He will understand that I do not mean to provide a holiday for my enemies, to be gloated over in Westminster Hall by those who for years have fawned upon me for my patronage. If he dreams that he can doom me to that and himself escape the punishment of this dastardly betrayal, he's more of a fool than I've ever deemed him. But he dare not do it, sir Lieutenant. He dare not do it."

Sir George withdrew again more troubled than ever; and he was almost relieved when there came to him a command to wait upon the King at Greenwich. Sir George found the King abed, a very scared and shivering monarch, who fearfully desired to know if my Lord of Somerset had decided to confess. When he had heard the Lieutenant's tale, he mouthed and slobbered fearfully, and finally gave way to tears, rocking himself like a distracted fishwife upon his great bed.

"What's to be done with him, Sir George? What's to be done with him?"

Sir George, standing stiff and bewildered before the agitated King, announced himself ready to do whatever his majesty commanded.

"Have ye made it clear to him that it is not my intention he shall suffer any harm to life? That if he will confess this thing, of which Coke says the proof against him is pregnant, he may be sure that my mercy will defeat the sentence?"

"His answer to that, sire, is, that he is neither Balmerino nor Gowrie, whatever that may mean. I was to say so, your majesty."

The royal mouth fell open. The royal cheeks were ashen. The protruding royal eyes rolled fearfully in their sockets. "God's sake!" he gurgled. "God's sake!" His majesty flung back the bedclothes and slewed himself round to face the Lieutenant more squarely, his thin naked legs dangling above the floor. A look of craft came now to harden that loose countenance. In Somerset's love for his lady the King thought he perceived the move that would checkmate him.

"It only remains," he said, "to let him perceive the opposite, and perceive it plainly. Tell him from me that if he dares to utter a single word that may bring me into contempt, he will seal not only his own doom but that of his Countess as well. Tell him that I shall withdraw my mercy from them both, and that, whatever betide himself, his Countess shall hang in accordance with the sentence passed upon her. Tell him that. Away with you now."

And the King peremptorily waved a dismissal, which he checked before Sir George could begin to obey it. "No, no. Stay!" He considered a moment, combing his beard and audibly sucking in his breath. "One other thing, Sir George. At his trial tomorrow let him be attended by two men with cloaks ready to muffle him at the first word he may utter that does not directly bear upon the charge against him. If he should mention me, or if he should attempt to broach any matter connected with Loubel the apothecary, let a cloak be thrown over his head. Let him be carried back to the Tower at once, and the trial proceed in his absence."

Sir George stood aghast. The court would never permit such a violation of its rights over the prisoner. But the King, reading his alarm in his troubled countenance, reassured him.

"The Lord Chancellor shall have a line from me to prepare him in case it should come to this. He will understand that reasons of State require it, and none will interfere with you. Away with you now to the Tower, and warn friend Somerset of what is prepared for him, so that he may perceive the futility of attempting any such treachery as he may have in mind."

The flush of the May dawn was already in the sky when Sir George, back in the Tower, conveyed his majesty's message to Lord Somerset. His lordship set his teeth, and answered nothing. The King had checkmated him. The threat to withhold mercy from himself should he dare to execute his threat he would have laughed to scorn. But the threat to withdraw the promised clemency from the Countess was another matter. The Countess had already confessed, and upon her confession had been sentenced. She therefore lay utterly at the King's mercy, and not all the influence of the Howard family could suffice to rescue her.

Somerset could not deliver her to the hangman; therefore he must, whatever it might cost him in bitterness, abandon the line of retaliatory attack upon which he was depending for his defence. In spite of all that he had boasted, his must be the part of Balmerino; to be silent as to where he knew the real blame to lie.

Of this, however, he said nothing to the Lieutenant. Not yet would he give Sir George the satisfaction of knowing that he was defeated in his intentions. In other matters he did not yet accept defeat. Since he was thus constrained to plead, he would make a stout fight for his life and his honour. At least there should be no weak-kneed confession from him of a crime which he had not committed.

Anon he rose and arrayed himself with all his old scrupulous care in a rich suit of black from which the blue ribbon of his George detached with startling brilliance, for deliberately he donned his George and Garter as if to flaunt it in the faces of those nobles who on a presumption of his guilt would already have had his arms removed from the chapel at Windsor. His servant came to dress his hair and trim his golden dagger beard, and at last at a little before nine, having broken his fast, he descended with the Lieutenant to the waiting barge.

His pride sustaining him, he made his appearance in Westminster Hall with the same outward assurance and arrogant demeanour which he had worn in the Privy Gallery at Whitehall in the old days, when those two-and-twenty peers assembled there to judge and, if possible, convict him of infamy had been wont to bend their backs obsequiously before him.

On either side of him and a little behind him stood unobtrusively those two yeomen of the guard, each with a cloak over his arm, detailed to muffle him at a sign from the vigilant Lieutenant. He paid no heed to them.

Summoned to plead, he pleaded "Not Guilty" in a firm resonant voice.

The Lord High Steward, in charging him to speak boldly in his own defence, gave him the last hint of what was desired of him by the King.

"Remember," the old Chancellor admonished him, "that God is the God of truth. A fault defended is a double crime... Take heed lest your wilfulness cause the gates of mercy to be shut upon you."

Sir Francis Bacon in his opening speech for the Crown promised to carry the lantern of justice, which is evidence, before their eyes, upright. Nevertheless, all the evidence he had to offer was – as he well knew – presumptive, and much of it depended upon the confessions of rogues who had been hanged and were no longer there to be questioned by Somerset. The Attorney-General made much of the quarrel between Somerset and Overbury, arising out of the latter's opposition to the love between Somerset and that unfortunate lady, the Countess of Essex, as she was then. This was urged as the motive for the crime. He revealed the trap in which Overbury was taken and committed to the Tower, and dwelt upon the appointment of Sir Gervase Elwes to the Lieutenancy and the attachment to him of Richard Weston, which it was now implied had been done for his own nefarious ends by my Lord of Somerset. There was an allusion to her ladyship's attempt to bribe Sir David Wood to kill Overbury. Then certain obscure letters which had passed between Somerset and Northampton were put forward and such meanings read into them as suited the purposes of the prosecution.

When this formidable array of emptiness so far as his lordship was concerned had been fully displayed, he was again summoned by Lord Ellesmere to make a frank and full avowal of his guilt.

Curtly and proudly he dismissed that appeal. "My lord, I came hither with a resolution to defend myself."

Thereafter they came to the powder which Somerset had sent Overbury some four months before the latter's death.

"Four separate juries," announced Sergeant Montague, "have found that this powder was poison, and of this poison Sir Thomas Overbury died."

It was a preposterous statement and flagrantly at variance with the indictment, which had it that Sir Thomas had died of an injection of corrosive sublimate.

From all the frivolous and uncorroborated lies with which that scoundrel Franklin had sought to delude the Lord Chief Justice, certain imaginary conversations with Lord Somerset were now cited to convict him.

The whole of the prosecution was taken up with the weaving of those strands of evidence into a web in which to muffle him. It was a cobweb which a single strong breath of truth should have blown to fragments. That breath it was well within his power to supply. But he knew that at the first attempt these two fellows standing just behind him would hoodwink him and carry him away, and that all hope of mercy would be denied his Countess. So in his fight for life and honour he must keep narrowly to the trumpery matters that had been urged, matters which taken severally, as they must be taken, were so vague and impalpable that there was no seizing them.

It was evening before the prosecution closed, and already many of those who had been mere spectators were in a fainting condition, and withdrew, unable to endure more.

Lights were brought, and once again the thin voice of the Lord High Steward summoned his lordship to set a term to the business by pleading guilty.

"Your wife," Ellesmere reminded him, "yesterday confessed the fact, and there is great hope of the King's mercy if you now mar not what is made."

It was, as he well perceived, at once a bribe and a threat. He was meant to understand that unless he also now confessed, mercy might be withheld not only from himself but also from his wife. This was an attempt to narrow down the bargain he had accepted, and was asking of him a price altogether higher than that which had been first concerted, a price which he could not pay.

"I am confident in my cause," he answered, "and I am here to defend it."

To that defence he now addressed himself. He had come to trial without foreknowledge of what evidence was to be preferred against him, and all the assistance he had received had been in a supply of pen and ink and paper so that he might prepare his defence in a measure as the prosecution unfolded the case. Even a skilled counsel might have found such a course beyond his powers. Somerset was without training in such matters; he felt the more helpless because the chief witnesses against him were already dead and could not be brought to be questioned by him on their testimony; therefore he must rest his defence entirely upon argument, and his wits were bewildered and exhausted by that day's long ordeal.

As he stood there, leaning upon the rail, faltering and pondering where he should begin, the thought of Overbury surged in his mind. If only that ready witted fellow were at hand to speak for him now! How he would have torn that tissue of false and fabricated evidence into shreds and flung them into the faces of those who urged it! He perceived the tragic irony of such a thought at such a time and in such a cause. He put it from him, and addressed himself to the task in hand.

He began with matters in which common knowledge must bear witness for him. He vehemently denied that he had been a party to any plot, or, indeed, that any plot had existed, to remove Sir William Wade from the Lieutenancy of the Tower, so as to bring in Sir Gervase Elwes in his stead. Their lordships well knew that Wade was removed from his charge on the grounds of dishonesty towards the Lady Arabella.

He passed on to the evidence of Franklin, the only evidence that definitely linked him with his Countess in the practices she had admitted against Overbury. He denied all knowledge of that perjured knave. He had never seen him in his life, and he challenged them to prove by independent testimony that any relations had ever existed between himself and the man.

Lastly he came to the powder which he had sent Overbury and which it was now alleged had caused Overbury's death. He admitted having sent it, but he denied – as the facts themselves abundantly denied – that it was poison. On the contrary, it was good physic, of which their lordships held evidence. He called for the production of the letter in which Overbury had thanked him for it and had acknowledged the gentle effect it had produced in him.

But he called in vain, and being denied in this he perceived suddenly how hopeless was all his striving. Already weary, he grew now confused and disheartened by this clear perception that no defence could here avail him. This court was determined upon his conviction, since that was the pleasure of the King, to the end that all questions touching the death of Sir Thomas Overbury should finally be set at rest.

He abandoned the futile struggle with a last plea to his peers that they should not take circumstances for evidence and an oath before God that he was neither guilty of nor privy to any wrong that Overbury suffered in this kind.

Thereupon the Lieutenant withdrew him from the bar, and the peers retired for a little while. On their return the Lord High Steward resumed his place under the scarlet canopy, the sergeant-crier called each lord by name; each one answered in turn, and each one in turn pronounced the prisoner guilty.

The Earl of Somerset was once more conducted into court to be asked what he had to say why sentence of death should not be passed upon him.

Calm and pale he stood in the flare of the torches, for by now darkness had closed down upon the scene. His glance swept the ranks of the peers who had pronounced him guilty. He looked at the stately Pembroke, who had ever been his enemy, and who now held the office of Lord Chamberlain from which Somerset had been deposed; he looked at the Earl of Worcester, who now held the Privy Seal of which Somerset had been deprived; onward his glance moved over those nobles who in the past, willingly or unwillingly, had courted him and hung upon his favour. It was a bitterness indeed to have been left thus at their mercy, to be spurned and trampled by them.

If in the shadows to which it had passed the spirit of Overbury was troubled by vindictiveness towards the friend who had betrayed him, that spirit should now be appeased by the magnitude of the punishment which had descended upon him. Deprived of his offices of State, to be stripped of the greater part of the vast possessions which by the King's bounty he had held, branded with infamy, he was now asked what he could say why sentence of death should not be pronounced against him. Why should he say anything? What attraction could life still offer one fallen as he had fallen.

Steady and firm rang his voice with the only answer which in the circumstances he could make.

"I only desire a death according to my degree."

But not even the axe was to dignify the sentence, which was that he should be hanged by the neck until he was dead. Having pronounced it, the Lord High Steward broke his staff and dissolved the court. It was past ten o'clock. The trial had consumed twelve hours.

The Lieutenant reconducted him to the waiting barge, hemmed about by his guard of pikemen, on whose corselets and steel caps the red glare of the torches cast reflections that were like stains of blood.

Through the luminous May night the great barge slipped down the river on the bosom of the ebbing tide, conveying him back to the Tower.

There, the sentence of death remitted by a King who did not desire the blood of a discarded minion, he was to languish together with his Countess for five miserable years, to be ultimately banished with her into rural remoteness from a Court whose chief pride and ornament he once had been. Reduced in circumstances, they were to live out their embittered lives in the ruin which Overbury had foretold him would follow upon his association with the House of Howard.

Perhaps he had some foreknowledge of this as the Lieutenant's barge brought up under the black shadow of Traitor's Gate, trusting to the King's word that just so much merciless mercy would be shown him and his Countess in return for a silence which would have been enforced had he attempted to violate it.

And lower down the river, at that same hour, a King who shivered and sweated by turn in panic awaited news in a fever of anxiety that had endured since morning. To every boat that since noon he had seen landing at the bridge below the palace he had sent a messenger for tidings of the trial; and when each messenger returned empty-handed, his majesty had slobbered curses at him, growing increasingly fearful as the day wore on, unable to find distraction, to eat, or even to sit still. Despite all precautions, the Earl of Somerset might yet have succeeded in betraying him. He might have contrived to point out the connection between Loubel and Mayerne, demanding to know why Loubel should be permitted to go free in view of all the admitted facts, and why Mayerne had not been called for examination; demanding, indeed, that these omissions should now be rectified before judgment was pronounced.

Such questions as these could be asked in a few words flung out before the Lieutenant's men should have time to hoodwink the prisoner. And once asked, those questions, although not answered by the court, would be answered by the people thronging Westminster Hall who had heard them. The hoodwinking and carrying away of the prisoner not only would prevent their being answered, but would guide public opinion in answering them in such a fashion that the royal dignity and honour would be for all time besmirched.

In such fears as these did the King spend the hours of waiting in Greenwich Palace, fears which mounted steadily as the day advanced, until at last they were grown into convictions. That which he dreaded must have come to pass. There could be no other explanation of the protraction of the business. To the end Somerset had said that he was neither Gowrie nor Balmerino. It was proof, thought the maudlin King, that Robin had never truly loved him.

And then, at last, late at night, when he was almost prostrate from panic and exhausted from lack of food, there came a dusty messenger who had ridden hard to bring him news that the headstrong passionate Robin had suffered conviction without any word that should betray his King.

He licked his lips as he heard the news. The colour crept slowly back into that normally florid face. He even contrived a smile as he waved the messenger away. Then he heaved himself up on to his rachitic legs, and beckoned from amongst his surrounding gentlemen the handsome, resplendent Villiers. He flung an arm about the young minion's neck.

"So that's ended, Steenie," he mumbled. He fetched a sigh, and his pale bulging eyes grew watery. "He shall know how clement I can be. For never could it be said of me that I could put entirely from my heart any creature I had truly loved." Then on an altered brisker tone, and pinching the lad's smooth cheek: "For God's sake let's to supper!" he cried.

Rafael Sabatini

Captain Blood

Captain Blood is the much-loved story of a physician and gentleman turned pirate.

Peter Blood, wrongfully accused and sentenced to death, narrowly escapes his fate and finds himself in the company of buccaneers. Embarking on his new life with remarkable skill and bravery, Blood becomes the 'Robin Hood' of the Spanish seas. This is swashbuckling adventure at its best.

The Gates of Doom

'Depend above all on Pauncefort', announced King James; 'his loyalty is dependable as steel. He is with us body and soul and to the last penny of his fortune.' So when Pauncefort does indeed face bankruptcy after the collapse of the South Sea Company, the king's supreme confidence now seems rather foolish. And as Pauncefort's thoughts turn to gambling, moneylenders and even marriage to recover his debts, will he be able to remain true to the end? And what part will his friend and confidante, Captain Gaynor, play in his destiny?

'A clever story, well and amusingly told' – *The Times*

Rafael Sabatini

The Lost King

The Lost King tells the story of Louis XVII – the French royal who officially died at the age of ten but, as legend has it, escaped to foreign lands where he lived to an old age. Sabatini breathes life into these age-old myths, creating a story of passion, revenge and betrayal. He tells of how the young child escaped to Switzerland from where he plotted his triumphant return to claim the throne of France.

'…the hypnotic spell of a novel which for sheer suspense, deserves to be ranked with Sabatini's best' – *New York Times*

Scaramouche

When a young cleric is wrongfully killed, his friend, André-Louis, vows to avenge his death. André's mission takes him to the very heart of the French Revolution where he finds the only way to survive is to assume a new identity. And so is born Scaramouche – a brave and remarkable hero of the finest order and a classic and much-loved tale in the greatest swashbuckling tradition.

'Mr Sabatini's novel of the French Revolution has all the colour and lively incident which we expect in his work' – *Observer*

Rafael Sabatini

The Sea Hawk

Sir Oliver, a typical English gentleman, is accused of murder, kidnapped off the Cornish coast, and dragged into life as a Barbary corsair. However Sir Oliver rises to the challenge and proves a worthy hero for this much-admired novel. Religious conflict, melodrama, romance and intrigue combine to create a masterly and highly successful story, perhaps best-known for its many film adaptations.

The Shame of Motley

The Court of Pesaro has a certain fool – one Lazzaro Biancomonte of Biancomonte. *The Shame of Motley* is Lazzaro's story, presented with all the vivid colour and dramatic characterisation that has become Sabatini's hallmark.

'Mr Sabatini could not be conventional or commonplace if he tried'
– *Standard*

19399055R00196

Made in the USA
Lexington, KY
17 December 2012